CIBOLA BURN

CIBOLA BURN

BOOK FOUR OF THE EXPANSE

JAMES S. A. COREY

orbit

www.orbitbooks.net

Orbit
Hachette Book Group
237 Park Avenue, New York, NY 10017
HachetteBookGroup.com

First Edition: June 2014

Orbit is an imprint of Hachette Book Group, Inc. The Orbit name and logo are trademarks of Little, Brown Book Group Limited.

The Hachette Speakers Bureau provides a wide range of authors for speaking events. To find out more, go to www.hachettespeakersbureau.com or call (866) 376-6591.

The publisher is not responsible for websites (or their content) that are not owned by the publisher.

Library of Congress Cataloging-in-Publication Data
Corey, James S. A.
    Cibola burn / James S. A. Corey. — First edition.
        pages cm — (Book four of the expanse)
    Summary: "The gates have opened the way to thousands of habitable planets, and the land rush has begun. Settlers stream out from humanity's home planets in a vast, poorly controlled flood, landing on a new world. Among them, the Rocinante, haunted by the vast, posthuman network of the protomolecule as they investigate what destroyed the great intergalactic society that built the gates and the protomolecule. But Holden and his crew must also contend with the growing tensions between the settlers and the company which owns the official claim to the planet. Both sides will stop at nothing to defend what's theirs, but soon a terrible disease strikes and only Holden—with help from the ghostly Detective Miller—can find the cure." —Provided by publisher.
    ISBN 978-0-316-21762-0 (hardback) — ISBN 978-0-316-21760-6 (ebook) — ISBN 978-1-4789-0082-5 (audio download)
    I. Title.
PS3601.B677C53 2014
813'.6—dc23
                            2013045273

10 9 8 7 6 5 4 3 2 1

RRD-C

Printed in the United States of America

To Jay Lake and Elmore Leonard.
Gentlemen, it has been a pleasure.

CIBOLA BURN

Prologue: Bobbie Draper

A thousand worlds, Bobbie thought as the tube doors closed. And not just a thousand worlds. A thousand *systems*. Suns. Gas giants. Asteroid belts. Everything that humanity had spread to, a thousand times over. The screen above the seats across from her showed a newsfeed, but the speakers were broken, the man's voice too fuzzed to make out the words. The graphic that zoomed in and out beside him was enough for her to follow. New data had come in from the probes that had gone through the gates. Here was another image of an unfamiliar sun, circles to mark the orbits of new planets. All of them empty. Whatever had built the protomolecule and fired it toward Earth back in the depths of time wasn't answering calls anymore. The bridge builder had opened the way, and no great gods had come streaming through.

It was astounding, Bobbie thought, how quickly humanity could go from *What unimaginable intelligence fashioned these soul-wrenching wonders?* to *Well, since they're not here, can I have their stuff?*

"'Scuse me," a man's phlegmy voice said. "You wouldn't have a little spare change for a veteran, would you?"

She looked away from the screens. The man was thin, gray-faced. His body had the hallmarks of a childhood in low g: long body, large head. He licked his lips and leaned forward.

"Veteran, are you?" she said. "Where'd you serve?"

"Ganymede," the man said, nodding and looking off with an attempt at nobility. "I was there when it all came down. When I got back here, government dropped me on my ass. I'm just trying to save up enough to book passage to Ceres. I've got family there."

Bobbie felt a bubble of rage in her breast, but she tried to keep her voice and expression calm. "You try veteran's outreach? Maybe they could help you."

"I just need something to eat," he said, his voice turning nasty. Bobbie looked up and down the car. Usually there would be a few people in the cars at this time. The neighborhoods under the Aurorae Sinus were all connected by evacuated tube. Part of the great Martian terraforming project that had begun before Bobbie was born and would go on long after she was dead. Just now, there was no one. She considered what she would look like to the beggar. She was a big woman, tall as well as broad, but she was sitting down, and the sweater she'd chosen was a little baggy. He might have been under the misapprehension that her bulk was fat. It wasn't.

"What company did you serve with?" she asked. He blinked. She knew she was supposed to be a little scared of him, and he was uneasy because she wasn't.

"Company?"

"What company did you serve with?"

He licked his lips again. "I don't want to—"

"Because it's a funny thing," she said. "I could have sworn I knew pretty much everyone who was on Ganymede when the fighting started. You know, you go through something like that, and you remember. Because you see a lot of your friends die. What was your rank? I was gunnery sergeant."

The gray face had gone closed and white. The man's mouth pinched. He pushed his hands deeper into his pockets and mumbled something.

"And now?" Bobbie went on, "I work thirty hours a week with veteran's outreach. And I'm just fucking sure we could give a fine upstanding veteran like you a break."

He turned, and her hand went out to his elbow faster than he could pull away. His face twisted with fear and pain. She drew him close. When she spoke, her voice was careful. Each word clear and sharp.

"Find. Another. Story."

"Yes, ma'am," the beggar said. "I will. I'll do that."

The car shifted, decelerating into the first Breach Candy station. She let him go and stood up. His eyes went a little wider when she did. Her genetic line went back to Samoa, and she sometimes had that effect on people who weren't expecting her. Sometimes she felt a little bad about it. Not now.

Her brother lived in a nice middle-class hole in Breach Candy, not far from the lower university. She'd lived with him for a time after she got back home to Mars, and she was still putting the pieces of her life back together. It was a longer process than she'd expected. And part of the aftermath was that she felt like she owed her brother something. Family dinner nights was part of that.

The halls of Breach Candy were sparse. The advertisements on the walls flickered as she came near, face recognition tracking her and offering up the products and services they thought she might want. Dating services, gym memberships, take-out shwarma, the new Mbeki Soon film, psychological counseling. Bobbie tried not to take it personally. Still, she wished there were more people around, a few more faces to add variety to the mix. To let her tell herself the ads were probably meant for someone walking nearby. Not for her.

But Breach Candy wasn't as full as it used to be. There were fewer people in the tube stations and hallways, fewer people coming to the veteran's outreach program. She heard that enrollment at the upper university was down six percent.

Humanity hadn't managed a single viable colony on the new worlds yet, but the probe data was enough. Humanity had its new frontier, and the cities of Mars were feeling the competition.

As soon as she stepped in the door, the rich scent of her sister-in-law's gumbo thickening the air and making her mouth water, she heard her brother and nephew, voices raised. It knotted her gut, but they were family. She loved them. She owed them. Even if they made the idea of take-out shwarma seem awfully tempting.

"—not what I'm saying," her nephew said. He was in upper university now, but when the family started fighting, she could still hear the six-year-old in his voice.

Her brother boomed in reply. Bobbie recognized the percussive tapping of his fingertips against the tabletop as he made his points. Drumming as a rhetorical device. Their father did the same thing.

"Mars is not optional." Tap. "It is not secondary." Tap. "These gates and whatever's on the other side of them isn't our home. The terraforming effort—"

"I'm not arguing against the terraforming," her nephew said as she walked into the room. Her sister-in-law nodded to her from the kitchen wordlessly. Bobbie nodded back. The dining room looked down into a living space where a muted newsfeed was showing long-distance images of unfamiliar planets with a beautiful black man in wire-rimmed glasses speaking earnestly between them. "All I'm saying is that we're going to have a lot of new data. Data. That's all I'm saying."

The two of them were hunched over the table like there was an invisible chessboard between them. A game of concentration and intellect that wrapped them both up until they couldn't see the world around them. In a lot of ways, that was true. She took her chair without either of them acknowledging she'd arrived.

"Mars," her brother said, "is the most studied planet there is. It doesn't matter how many new datasets you get that aren't about Mars. They aren't about Mars! It's like saying that seeing pictures of a thousand other tables will tell you about the one you're already sitting at."

"Knowledge is good," her nephew said. "You're the one who always told me that. I don't know why you're getting so bent about it now."

"How are things for you, Bobbie?" her sister-in-law said sharply, carrying a bowl to the table. Rice and peppers to use as a bed for the gumbo and a reminder to the others that there was a guest. The two men scowled at the interruption.

"Good," Bobbie said. "The contract with the shipyards came through. It should help us place a lot of vets in new jobs."

"Because they're building exploration ships and transports," her nephew said.

"*David.*"

"Sorry, Mom. But they are," David replied, not backing down. Bobbie scooped the rice into her bowl. "All the ships that are easy to retrofit, they're retrofitting, and then they're making more so that people can go to all the new systems."

Her brother took the rice and the serving spoon, chuckling under his breath to make it clear how little he respected his son's opinion. "The first real survey team is just getting to the first of these places—"

"There are already people living on New Terra, Dad! There were a bunch of refugees from Ganymede—" He broke off, shooting a guilty glance at Bobbie. Ganymede wasn't something they talked about over dinner.

"The survey team hasn't landed yet," her brother said. "It's going to be years before we have anything like real colonies out there."

"It's going to be *generations* before anyone walks on the surface here! We don't have a fucking magnetosphere!"

"Language, David!"

Her sister-in-law returned. The gumbo was black and fragrant with a sheen of oil across the top. The smell of it made Bobbie's mouth water. She put it on the slate trivet and handed the serving spoon to Bobbie.

"And how's your new apartment?" she asked.

"It's nice," Bobbie said. "Inexpensive."

"I wish you weren't living in Innis Shallow," her brother said. "It's a terrible neighborhood."

"No one's going to bother Aunt Bobbie," her nephew said. "She'd rip their heads off."

Bobbie grinned. "Naw, I just look at them mean, and they—"

From the living room, there was a sudden glow of red light. The newsfeed had changed. Bright red banners showed at the top and bottom, and on the screen, a jowly Earth woman looked soberly into the camera. The image behind her was of fire and then a stock image of an old colony ship. The words, black against the white of the flames, read TRAGEDY ON NEW TERRA.

"What happened?" Bobbie said. "What just *happened*?"

Chapter One: Basia

Basia Merton had been a gentle man, once. He hadn't been the sort of man who made bombs out of old metal lubricant drums and mining explosives.

He rolled another one out of the little workshop behind his house and toward one of First Landing's electric carts. The little stretch of buildings spread to the north and south, and then ended, the darkness of the plain stretching to the horizon. The flashlight hanging from his belt bounced as he walked, casting strange moving shadows across the dusty ground. Small alien animals hooted at him from outside the circle of light.

Nights on Ilus—he wouldn't call it New Terra—were very dark. The planet had thirteen tiny, low-albedo moons spaced so consistently in the same orbit that everyone assumed they were alien artifacts. Wherever they'd come from, they were more like captured asteroids than real moons to someone who grew up on the planet-sized satellites of Jupiter. And they did nothing to catch and reflect the light of Ilus' sun once it set. The local nighttime wildlife was mostly small birds and lizards. Or what Ilus' new human inhabitants thought of as birds and lizards. They shared only the most superficial external traits and a primarily carbon base with their terrestrial namesakes.

Basia grunted with effort as he lifted the barrel onto the back of the cart, and a second later an answering grunt came from a few meters away. A mimic lizard, curiosity drawing it right up to the edge of the light, its small eyes glittering. It grunted again, its wide, leathery, bullfrog-shaped head bobbing, and the air sac below its neck inflating and deflating with the sound. It waited for a moment, staring at him, and when he didn't respond, it crawled off into the dark.

Basia pulled elastic straps out of a toolbox and began securing the barrels to the bed of the cart. The explosive wouldn't go off just from falling on the ground. Or that was what Coop said, anyhow. Basia didn't feel like testing it.

"Baz," Lucia said. He flushed with embarrassment like a small boy caught stealing candy. Lucia knew what he was doing. He'd never been able to lie to her. But he'd hoped she would stay inside while he worked. Just her presence made him wonder if he was doing the right thing. If it was right, why did it make him so ashamed to have Lucia see him?

"Baz," she said again. Not insisting. Her voice sad, not angry.

"Lucy," he said, turning around. She stood at the edge of his light, a white robe clutched around her thin frame against the chill night air. Her face was a dark blur.

"Felcia's crying," she said, her tone not making it an accusation. "She's afraid for you. Come talk to your daughter."

Basia turned away and pulled the strap tight over the barrels, hiding his face from her. "I can't. They're coming," he said.

"Who? Who's coming?"

"You know what I mean. They're going to take everything we made here if we don't make a stand. We need time. This is how you get time. Without the landing pad, they've got to use the small shuttles. So we take away the landing pad. Make them rebuild it. No one's going to get hurt."

"If it gets bad," she said, "we can leave."

"No," Basia said, surprised to hear the violence in his voice. He turned and took a few steps, putting her face in the light. She was weeping. "No more leaving. We left Ganymede. Left Katoa and ran away and my family lived on a ship for a year while no one would give us a place to land. We're not running again. Not *ever* running again. *They* took all the children from me they get to take."

"I miss Katoa too," Lucia said. "But these people didn't kill him. It was a war."

"It was a business decision. They made a business decision, and then they made a war, and they took my son away." *And I let them*, he didn't say. *I took you and Felcia and Jacek, and I left Katoa behind because I thought he was dead. And he wasn't.* The words were too painful to speak, but Lucia heard them anyway.

"It wasn't your fault."

Yes, it was floated at the back of his mouth, but he swallowed.

"These people don't have any right to Ilus," he said, struggling to make his voice sound reasonable. "We were here first. We staked claim. We'll get the first load of lithium out, get the money in, then we can hire lawyers back home to make a real case. If the corporations already have roots here when that happens, it won't matter. We just need time."

"If you do this," Lucia said, "they'll send you to jail. Don't do that to us. Don't do that to your family."

"I'm doing this *for* my family," he said softly. It was worse than yelling. He hopped up behind the controls and stomped on the accelerator. The cart lurched off with a whine. He didn't look back, couldn't look back and see Lucy.

"*For* my family," he said again.

He drove away from his house and the ramshackle town that they'd started out calling First Landing back when they'd picked the site off the *Barbapiccola*'s sensor maps. No one had bothered to rename it when it had moved from being an idea to being a place. He drove toward the center of town, two rows of prefab buildings, until he hit the wide stretch of flattened dirt that served as the main road and turned toward the original landing site. The refugees who'd colonized Ilus had come down from their ship in small shuttles, so the only landing pad they'd needed was a flat stretch of ground. But the Royal Charter Energy people, the *corporate* people, who had a UN charter giving the world to them, would be coming down with heavy equipment. Heavy lift shuttles needed an actual landing pad. It had been built in the same open fields that the colony had used as their landing site.

That felt obscene to Basia. Invasive. The first landing site had significance. He'd imagined it someday being a park, with a monument at the center commemorating their arrival on this new world. Instead, RCE had built a giant and gleaming metal monstrosity right over the top of their site. Worse, they'd hired the colonists to build it, and enough of them had thought it was a good idea that they'd actually done it.

It felt like being erased from history.

Scotty and Coop were waiting for him at the new landing pad when he arrived. Scotty was sitting on the edge of the metal platform, legs dangling over the side, smoking a pipe and spitting on the ground below his feet. A small electric lamp that sat beside him colored him with an eerie green light. Coop stood a little way off, looking up at the sky with bared teeth. Coop was an old-school Belter, and the agoraphobia treatments had been harder for him than others. The thin-faced man kept staring up at the void, fighting to get used to it like a kid pulling off scabs.

Basia pulled the cart up to the edge of the pad and hopped out to undo the straps holding the barrel bombs down.

"Give me a hand?" he said. Ilus was a large planet, slightly over one gravity. Even after six months of pharma to build his muscles and bones everything still felt too heavy. The thought of lifting the barrels back to the ground made the muscles in his shoulders twitch in anticipated exhaustion.

Scotty slid off the landing pad and dropped a meter and a half to the ground. He pushed his oily black hair out of his eyes and took another long puff on his pipe. Basia caught the pungent, skunky smell of Scotty's bathtub-grown cannabis mixed with freeze-dried tobacco leaves. Coop looked over, his eyes fighting for focus for a moment, and then the thin, cruel smile. The plan had been Coop's from the start.

"Mmm," Coop said. "Pretty."

"Don't get attached," Basia said. "They won't be around long."

Coop made a booming sound and grinned. Together they pulled the four heavy barrels off the cart and stood them in a row next to the pad. By the last one, they were all panting with effort. Basia leaned against the cart for a moment in silence while Scotty smoked off the last of his pipe and Coop set the blasting caps on the barrels. The detonators sat in the back of the cart like sleeping rattlesnakes, the red LEDs dormant for now.

In the darkness, the township sparkled. The houses they'd all built for themselves and one another glittered like stars brought down from the sky. Beyond them, there were the ruins. A long, low alien structure with two massive towers rising up above the landscape like a termite hill writ large. All of it was run through with passageways and chambers that no human had designed. In daylight, the ruins shone with the eerie colors of mother-of-pearl. In the night, they were only a deeper darkness. The mining pits were off past them, invisible as all but the dimmest glow of the work lights on the belly of the clouds. Truth was Basia didn't like the mines. The ruins were strange relics of the empty planet's past, and like anything that was uncanny without posing a threat, they faded from his awareness after the first few months. The mines carried history and expectations. He'd spent half a lifetime in tunnels of ice, and tunnels that ran through alien soil *smelled* wrong.

Coop made a sharp noise and shook his hand, cursing. Nothing blew up, so it couldn't be that bad.

"You think they'll pay us to rebuild it?" Scotty asked.

Basia cursed and spat on the ground.

"We wouldn't have to do this if it wasn't for people wanting to suck on RCE's tit," he said as he rolled the last barrel into place. "They can't land without this. All we had to do was not build it."

Scotty laughed out a cloud of smoke. "They were coming anyway. Might as well take their money. That's what people said."

"People are idiots," Basia said.

Scotty nodded, then smacked a mimic lizard off the passenger seat of the cart with one hand and sat down. He put his feet up on the dash and took another long puff on his pipe. "We gonna have to get gone, if we blow this. That blasting powder makes serious boom."

"Hey, mate," Coop shouted. "We're good. Let's make the place, ah?"

Scotty stood and started walking toward the pad. Basia stopped him, plucked the lit pipe from between his lips, and put it on the hood of the cart.

"Explosives," Basia said. "They explode."

Scotty shrugged, but he also looked chagrined. Coop was already easing the first barrel down onto its side when they reached him. "It's buena work this. Solid."

"Thank you," Basia said.

Coop lay down, back against the ground. Basia lay beside him. Scotty rolled the first bomb gently between them.

Basia climbed under the pad, pulling himself through the tangle of crisscrossed I-beams to each of the four barrels, turning on the remote detonators and syncing them. He heard a growing electric whine and felt a moment of irritation at Scotty for driving off with the cart before he realized the sound was of a cart arriving, not leaving.

"Hey," Peter's familiar voice yelled.

"Que la moog bastard doing here?" Coop muttered, wiping his hand across his forehead.

"You want me to go find out?" Scotty asked.

"Basia," Coop said. "Go see what Peter needs. Scotty hasn't got his back dirty yet."

Basia shifted himself out from under the landing and made room for Scotty and the last of the four bombs. Peter's cart was parked beside his own, and Peter stood between them, shifting from one foot to the other like he needed to piss. Basia's back and arms ached. He wanted this all over and to be back home with Lucia and Felcia and Jacek.

"What?" Basia said.

"They're coming," Pete said, whispering as if there were anyone who could hear them.

"Who's coming?"

"Everyone. The provisional governor. The corporate security team. Science and tech staff. *Everybody*. This is serious. They're landing a whole new government for us."

Basia shrugged. "Old news. They been burning eighteen months. That's why we're out here."

"No," Pete said, prancing nervously and looking up at the stars. "They're coming right now. *Edward Israel* did a braking burn half an hour ago. Got into high orbit."

The copper taste of fear flooded Basia's mouth. He looked up at the darkness. A billion unfamiliar stars, his same Milky Way galaxy, everyone figured, just seen from a different angle. His eyes shifted frantically, and then he caught it. The movement was subtle as the minute hand on an analog clock, but he saw it. The drop ship was dropping. The heavy shuttle was coming for the landing pad.

"I was going to get on the radio, but Coop said they monitor radio spectrum and—" Pete said, but by then Basia was already running back to the landing pad. Scotty and Coop were just pulling themselves out. Coop clapped clouds of dust off his pants and grinned.

"We got a problem," Basia said. "Ship's already dropped. Looks like they're in atmosphere already."

Coop looked up. The brightness from his flashlight threw shadows across his cheeks and into his eyes.

"Huh," he said.

"I thought you were on this, man. I thought you were paying attention to where they were."

Coop shrugged, neither agreeing nor denying.

"We've got to get the bombs back out," Basia said. Scotty started to kneel, but Coop put a restraining hand on his shoulder.

"Why?" he asked.

"They try to land now, they could set it all off," Basia said.

Coop's smile was gentle. "Could," he said. "And what if?"

Basia balled his fists. "They're coming down *now*."

"See that," Coop said. "Doesn't inspire a great sense of obligation. And however you cut it, there ain't time to pull them."

"Can take off the primers and caps," Basia said, hunkering down. He played his flashlight over the pad's superstructure.

"Maybe could, maybe couldn't," Coop said. "Question's should, and it's a limp little question."

"Coop?" Scotty said, his voice thin and uncertain. Coop ignored him.

"Opportunity, looks like to me," Coop said.

"There's people on that thing," Basia said, crawling under the pad. The nearest bomb's electronics were flat against the dirt. He put his aching shoulder against it and pushed.

"Isn't time, mate," Coop called.

"Might be if you got your ass in here," Basia shouted. The blasting cap clung to the barrel's side like a tick. Basia tried to dig his fingers into the sealant goo and pry the cap away.

"Oh shit," Scotty said with something too much like awe in his voice. "Baz, oh *shit*!"

The cap came loose. Basia pushed it in his pocket and started crawling toward the second bomb.

"No time," Coop shouted. "Best we get clear, try and blow it while they can still pull up."

In the distance, he heard one of the carts taking off. Pete, going for distance. And under that, another sound. The bass roar of braking engines. He looked at the three remaining bombs in despair and rolled out from under the pad. The shuttle was massive in the black sky, so close he could make out the individual thrusters.

He wasn't going to make it.

"Run!" he shouted. He and Scotty and Coop sprinted back toward the cart. The roar of the shuttle rose, grew deafening. Basia reached the cart and scooped up the detonator. If he could blow it early, the shuttle could pull out, get away.

"Don't!" Coop shouted. "We're too close!"

Basia slammed his palm on the button.

The ground rose up, hitting him hard, the rough dirt and rocks tearing at his hands and cheek as he came to a stop, but the pain was a distant thing. Some part of him knew he might be hurt very badly, might be in shock, but that seemed distant and easy to ignore too. What struck him most was how quiet everything was. The world of sound stopped at his skull. He could hear his own breath, his heartbeat. Everything past that had the volume turned down to one.

He rolled onto his back and stared up at the star-speckled night sky. The heavy shuttle streaked overhead, half of it trailing fire, the sound of its engines no longer a bass roar but the scream of a wounded animal that he felt in his belly more than heard. The shuttle had been too close, the blast too large, some unlucky debris thrown into just the right path. No way to know. Some part of Basia knew this was very bad, but it was hard to pay much attention to it.

The shuttle disappeared from view, shrieking a death wail across the valley that came to him as a faint high piping sound, then sudden silence. Scotty was sitting beside him on the ground, staring off in the direction the ship had gone. Basia let himself lie back down.

When the bright spots it had left in his vision faded, the stars returned. Basia watched them twinkle, and wondered which one was Sol. So far away. But with the gates, close too. He'd knocked their shuttle down. They'd have to come now. He'd left them no choice.

A sudden spasm of coughing took him. It felt like his lungs were full of fluid, and he coughed it up for several minutes. With the coughing the pain finally came, wracking him from head to foot.

With the pain came the fear.

Chapter Two: Elvi

The shuttle bucked, throwing Elvi Okoye against her restraints hard enough to knock the wind out of her and then pushing her back into the overwhelming embrace of her crash couch. The light flickered, went black, and then came back. She swallowed, her excitement and anticipation turning to animal fear. Beside her, Eric Vanderwert smiled the same half-leering, half-hopeful smile he'd flickered toward her over the past six months. Across from her, Fayez's eyes had gone wide, his skin gray.

It's okay," Elvi said. "It's going to be okay."

Even as she spoke the words, a part of her cringed away from them. She didn't know what was going on. There was no earthly way she could know that anything was going to be okay. And still her first impulse was to assert it, to say it as if saying it made it true. A high whine rippled through the flesh of the shuttle, overtones crashing into each other. She felt her weight lurch to the left, the crash couches all shifting on their gimbals at the same time like choreographed dancers. She lost sight of Fayez.

A tritone chime announced the pilot, and her voice came over the shuttle's public-address system.

"Ladies and gentlemen, it appears there has been a critical malfunction at the landing pad. We will not be able to complete the landing at this time. We will be returning to orbit and docking with the *Edward Israel* until such time as we can assess…"

She went quiet, but the hiss of an open line still ran through the ship. Elvi imagined the pilot distracted by something. The ship lurched and stuttered, and Elvi grabbed her restraints, hugging them to her. Someone nearby was praying loudly.

"Ladies and gentlemen," the pilot said. "I'm afraid the malfunction at the landing pad has done our shuttle some damage. I don't think we're going to make it back upstairs right away. We have a dry lake bed not too far from here. I think we're going to go take a look at that as a secondary landing site."

Elvi felt a moment's relief—*We still have a landing site*—followed at once by a deeper understanding and a deeper fear—*She means we're going to crash.*

"I'm going to ask everyone to remain in their couches," the pilot said. "Don't take off your belts, and please keep your arms and legs inside the couch's shell where it won't bang against the side. The gel's there for a reason. We'll have you all down in just a couple minutes here."

The forced, artificial calmness terrified Elvi more than shrieking and weeping would have. The pilot was doing everything she could to keep them all from panicking. Would anyone do that if they didn't think panic was called for?

Her weight shifted again, pulling to the left, and then back, and then she grew light as the shuttle descended. The fall seemed to last forever. The rattle and whine of the shuttle rose to a screaming pitch. Elvi closed her eyes.

"We're going to be fine," she said to herself. "Everything's okay."

The impact split the shuttle open like lobster tail under a hammer. She had the brief impression of unfamiliar stars in a foreign sky, and her consciousness blinked out like God had turned off a switch.

Centuries before, Europeans had invaded the plague-emptied shell of the Americas, climbing aboard wooden ships with vast canvas sails and trusting the winds and the skill of sailors to take them from the lands they knew to what they called the New World. For as long as six months, religious fanatics and adventurers and the poverty-stricken desperate had consigned themselves to the uncharitable waves of the Atlantic Ocean.

Eighteen months ago, Elvi Okoye left Ceres Station under contract to Royal Charter Energy. The *Edward Israel* was a massive ship. Once, almost three generations before, it had been one of the colony ships that had taken humanity to the Belt and the Jovian system. When the outpouring had ended and the pressure to expand had met its natural limits, the *Israel* had been repurposed as a water hauler. The age of expansion was over, and the romance of freedom gave way to the practicalities of life—air, water, and food, in that order. For decades, the ship had been a workhorse of the solar system, and then the Ring had opened. Everything changed again. Back at the Bush shipyards and Tycho Station a new generation of colony ships was being built, but the retrofit of the *Israel* had been faster.

When she'd stepped inside it the first time, Elvi had felt a sense of wonder and hope and excitement in the hum of the *Israel*'s air recyclers and the angles of her old-fashioned corridors. The age of adventure had come again, and the old warrior had returned, sword newly sharpened and armor shining again after tarnished years. Elvi had known that it was a psychological projection, that it said more about her own state of mind than anything physical about the ship, but that didn't diminish it. The *Edward Israel* was a colony ship once more, her holds filled with prefabbed buildings and high-atmosphere probes, manufacturing labs and even a repeat-scatter femtoscope. They had an exploration and mapping team, a geological survey team, a hydrology team, Elvi's own exozoological workgroup, and more. A university's worth of PhDs and a government lab's load of postdocs. Between crew and colonists, a thousand people.

They were a city in the sky and a boat of pilgrims bound for Plymouth Rock and Darwin's voyage on the *Beagle* all at the same time. It was the grandest and most beautiful adventure humanity had ever been on, and Elvi had earned a place on the exobiology team. In that context, imagining that the steel and ceramic of the ship was imbued with a sense of joy was a permissible illusion.

And all of it was ruled over by Governor Trying.

She'd seen him several times in the months they'd spent burning and braking, then making the slow, eerie transit between rings, and then burning and braking again. It wasn't until just before the drop itself that she'd actually spoken with him.

Trying was a thin man. His mahogany skin and snow-dust hair reminded her of her uncles, and his ready smile reassured and calmed. She had been in the observation deck, pretending that the high-resolution screens looking down on the planet were really windows, that the light of this unfamiliar sun was actually bouncing off the wide, muddy seas and high frosted clouds and passing directly into her eyes even though the deceleration gravity meant they weren't in free orbit yet. It was a strange, beautiful sight. A single, massive ocean scattered with islands. A large continent that sprawled comfortably across half of a hemisphere, widest at the equator and then tapering as it reached north and south. The official name of the world was Bering Survey Four, named for the probe that had first established its existence. In the corridors and cafeteria and gym, they'd all come to call it New Terra. So at least she wasn't the only one swept up by the romance.

"What are you thinking, Doctor Okoye?" Trying's gentle voice asked, and Elvi had jumped. She hadn't heard him come in. Hadn't seen him beside her. She felt like she was supposed to bow or make some sort of formal report. But his expression was so soft, so amused, she let it go.

"I'm wondering what I did to deserve all this," she said. "I'm about to see the first genuinely alien biosphere. I'm about to learn things about evolution that were literally impossible to know until now. I must have been a very, very good person in a past life."

In the screens, New Terra glittered brown and gold and blue. The high atmospheric winds smudged greenish clouds halfway around the planet. Elvi leaned in toward it. The governor chuckled.

"You will be famous," he said.

Elvi blinked and coughed out a laugh.

"I guess I will be, won't I?" she said. "We're doing things humanity's never done before."

"Some things," Trying said. "And some things we have always done. I hope history treats us gently."

She didn't quite know what he'd meant by that, but before she could ask, Adolphus Murtry came in. A thin man with hard blue eyes, Murtry was the head of security and as hard and efficient as Trying was avuncular. The two men had walked off together, leaving Elvi alone with the world that was about to be hers to explore.

The heavy shuttle was as large as some ships Elvi had been on. They'd had to build a landing pad on the surface just to support it. It carried the first fifty structures, basic array laboratories, and—most important—a hard perimeter dome.

She had filed through the close-packed hallway of the shuttle, letting her hand terminal lead her toward her assigned crash couch. When the first colonies had begun on Mars, the perimeter domes had been a question of survival. Something to hold in air and keep out radiation. On New Terra, it was all about limiting contamination. The corporate charter that RCE had taken required that their presence have the smallest possible footprint. She'd heard that there were other people already on the planetary surface, and hopefully they were also being careful not to disturb the sites they were on. If they weren't, the interactions between local organisms and the ones that had been shipped in would be complex. Maybe impossible to tease apart.

"You look troubled."

Fayez Sarkis sat on a crash couch, strapping the wide belts across his chest and waist. He'd grown up on Mars, and had the tall, thin frame and large head of low gravity. He looked at home in a crash couch. Elvi realized her hand terminal was telling her that she'd found her own place. She sat, the gel forming itself around her thighs and lower back. She always wanted to sit up in a crash couch, like a kid in a wading pool. Letting herself sink into it felt too much like being eaten.

"Just thinking ahead," she said, forcing herself to lie back. "Lot of work to be done."

"I know," Fayez said with a sigh. "Break time's over. Now we have to actually earn our keep. Still, it was fun while it lasted. I mean apart from burning at a full g."

"New Terra's a little over that, you know."

"Don't remind me," he said. "I don't know why we couldn't start with some nice balsawood planet with a civilized gravity well."

"Luck of the draw," Elvi said.

"Well, as soon as we get papers for a decent Mars-like planet, I'm transferring."

"You and half of Mars."

"I know, right? Someplace with maybe a breathable atmosphere. A magnetic field so we don't all have to live like mole rats. It's like having the terraforming project done already, except I'm alive to see it."

Elvi laughed. Fayez was on the geology team and the hydrological workgroup both. He'd studied at the best universities outside Earth, and she knew from long acquaintance that he was at least as frightened and delighted as she was. Eric Vanderwert came by, easing himself into the couch beside Elvi. She smiled at him politely. In the year and a half out from Ceres, there had been any number of romantic or if not romantic at least sexual connections made between members of the science teams. Elvi had kept herself out of that tangle. She'd learned early that sexual entanglements and work were a toxic and unstable mixture.

Eric nodded to Fayez, then turned his attention to her.

"Exciting," he said.

"Yes," Elvi said, and across from her, Fayez rolled his eyes.

Murtry walked through, stepping between the crash couches. His gaze flickered over everything—the couches, the belts, the faces of the people preparing for drop. Elvi smiled at him, and he nodded to her sharply. It wasn't hostile, just businesslike. She watched him size her up. It wasn't the sexual way that a man considered a woman. It was like a loader making sure a crate's magnetic clamps were firing. He nodded to her again, apparently satisfied that she'd gotten her belts right, and moved on. When he was out of sight, Fayez chuckled.

"Poor bastard's chewing the walls," he said, nodding after Murtry.

"Is he?" Eric said.

"Had us all under his thumb for a year and a half, hasn't he? Now we're going down and he's staying in orbit. Man's petrified that we're all going to get ourselves killed on his watch."

"At least he cares," Elvi said. "I like him for that."

"You like everyone," Fayez teased. "It's your pathology."

"You don't like anyone."

"That's mine," he said, grinning.

The tritone alert came and the public-address system clicked.

"Ladies and gentlemen, my name is Patricia Silva and I'm your pilot on this little milk run."

A chorus of laughter rose from the crash couches.

"We're going to be detaching from the *Israel* in about ten minutes, and we're expecting the drop to take about fifty. So an hour from now, you're all going to be breathing entirely new air. We've got the governor on board, so we're going to make sure this all goes smooth and easy so we can put in for a performance bonus."

Everyone was giddy then. Even the pilot. Elvi grinned and Fayez grinned back at her. Eric cleared his throat.

"Well," Fayez said with mock resignation. "We came all this way. I suppose we should finish it."

The pain didn't have a location. It was too large for that. It spread everywhere, encompassed everything. Elvi realized that she'd been looking at something. A massive, articulated crab leg, maybe. Or a broken construction crane. The flat ground of the lake bed stretched out toward it, and then grew rougher until it reached the thing's base. She could imagine it had pushed its way out of the dark, dry soil or that it had crashed down into it. Her agonized mind tried to make it into debris from the shuttle and failed.

It was an artifact. Ruins. Some arcane structure left from the alien civilization that had designed the protomolecule and the rings, abandoned and empty now. Elvi had the sudden, powerful and disjointed memory of an art exhibit she'd seen as a girl. There had been a high-resolution image of a bicycle in a ditch outside the ruins of Glasgow. The aftermath of disaster in a single image, as compressed and eloquent as a poem.

At least I got to see it, she thought. *At least I got to be here before I died.*

Someone had dragged her out of the ruined shuttle. When she turned her head, she could see construction lights burning yellow-white and the others laid out on the flat ground in rows. Some were standing. Moving among the injured and the dead. She didn't recognize their faces or the way their bodies moved. After a year and a half on the *Israel*, she knew everyone on sight, and these were strangers. The locals, then. The squatters. Illegals. The air smelled like burning dust and cumin.

She must have blacked out, because the woman seemed to appear at Elvi's side in the blink of an eye. Her hands were bloody and her face smeared with dirt and gore not her own.

"You're banged up, but you're not in any immediate danger. I'm going to give you something for the pain, but I need to you stay still until we can splint your leg. All right?"

She was beautiful, in a severe way. Her dark cheeks had dots of pure black scattered across them like beads in a veil. Threads of white laced the black waves of her hair like moonlight on water. Only there was no moonlight on New Terra. Only billions of strange stars.

"All right?" the woman asked again.

"All right," Elvi said.

"Tell me what you just agreed to."

"I don't remember."

The woman leaned back, her hand pressing gently against Elvi's shoulder.

"Torre! I'm going to need a scan on this one's head. She may be concussed."

Another voice—a man's—came from the darkness. "Yes, Doctor Merton. Soon as I'm done with this one."

Doctor Merton turned back to her. "If I get up right now, are you going to stay where you are until Torre gets here?"

"No, it's all right. I can come help," Elvi said.

"I'm sure you can," the beautiful woman said with a sigh. "Let's just wait for him, then."

A shadow loomed up from the darkness. She recognized Fayez by the way he walked. "Go ahead. I'll sit with her."

"Thank you," Doctor Merton said, and then vanished. Fayez lowered himself to the ground with a grunt and crossed his legs. His hair stood out from his slightly oversized head at all angles. His lips were pressed thin. Elvi took his hand without intending to, and she felt him pull back for a second before permitting her fingers to stay touching his.

"What happened?" she asked.

"The landing pad blew up."

"Oh," she said. And then, "Do they do that?"

"No. No, they really don't."

She tried to think through that. *If they don't, then how could it have happened?* Her mind was clearing enough for her to notice how compromised she was. Unnerving, but probably a good sign.

"How bad is it?"

She felt Fayez's shrug more than saw it. "Bad. Only significant good news is that the village is close, and their doctor's competent. Trained on Ganymede. Now, if our supplies weren't all on fire or smashed under a couple tons of metal and ceramics, she might be able to do something."

"The workgroup?"

"I saw Gregorio. He's all right. Eric's dead. I don't know what happened to Sophie, but I'll go look some more once they get to you."

Eric was dead. Minutes before, he'd been in the couch beside her, trying to flirt and being annoying. She didn't understand it.

"Sudyam?" she asked.

"She's back on the *Israel*. She's fine."

"That's good then."

Fayez squeezed her hand and let it go. The air felt cool against her palm where his skin had abandoned it. He looked out over the rows of bodies toward the wreckage of the shuttle. It was so dark, she could hardly make him out except where he blotted out the stars.

"Governor Trying didn't make it," he said.

"Didn't make it?"

"Dead as last week's rat. We're not sure who's in charge of anything now."

She felt tears forming in her eyes and an ache bloomed in her chest that had nothing to do with her injuries. She recalled the man's gentle smile, the warmth of his voice. His work was only starting. It was strange that Eric's death should skip across the surface of her mind like a stone thrown over water and Governor Trying's should strike so deep.

"I'm so sorry," she said.

"Yeah, well. We're on an alien planet a year and a half from home with our initial supplies in toothpick-size splinters, and the odds-on bet for what happened is sabotage by the same people who are presently giving us medical care. Dead's not good, but at least it's simple. We may all envy Trying before this is over."

"You don't mean that. It's going to be okay."

"Elvi?" Fayez said, with a sardonic chuckle. "I believe that it isn't."

Chapter Three: Havelock

Hey," the engineer said blearily from the cell. "Havelock. You're not still pissed, are you?"

Not my job to be pissed, Williams," Havelock replied from where he floated beside his desk. The internal security station of the *Edward Israel* was small. Two desks, eight cells, a space as much brig as office. And with the ship in high orbit, the loss of effective gravity made it seem even smaller.

"Look, I know I got out of line, but I'm sober now. You can let me out."

Havelock checked his hand terminal.

"Another fifty minutes," he said, "and you'll be free to go."

"C'mon, Havelock. Have a heart."

"It's policy. Nothing I can do about it."

Dimitri Havelock had worked security contracts for eight different corporations over thirteen years. Pinkwater, Star Helix, el-Hashem Cooperative, Stone & Sibbets, among others. Even, briefly, Protogen. He'd been in the Belt, on Earth, Mars, and Luna. He'd done long-haul work on supply ships heading from Ganymede to Earth. He'd dealt with everything from riots to intimate violence to drug trafficking to one idiot who'd had a thing for stealing people's socks. He hadn't seen everything, but he'd seen a lot. Enough to know he'd probably never see *everything*. And enough to recognize that how he reacted to a crisis was more about the people on his team than with the crisis itself.

When the reactor had gone on Aten Base, his partner and supervisor had both panicked, and Havelock remembered the overwhelming fear in his own gut. When the riots had started on Ceres after the ice hauler *Canterbury* had been destroyed, his partner had been more weary than fearful, and Havelock had faced the situation with the same grim resignation. When the *Ebisu* had been quarantined for nipahvirus, his boss had been energized—almost elated—running the ship like a puzzle that had to be solved, and Havelock had been caught up in the pleasure of doing an important thing well.

Humans, Havelock knew from long experience, were first and foremost social animals, and he himself was profoundly human. It was more romantic—hell, more masculine—to pretend he was an island, unaffected by the waves of emotion around him. But it wasn't true, and he'd made his peace with that fact.

When the word came that the heavy shuttle's landing pad had exploded and the reports of casualties started coming in, Murtry's response had been an efficient and focused rage, and so Havelock's had been too. All the activity was on the planetary surface, so the only outlet had been on the *Edward Israel* itself. And how things went on the *Israel* were firmly in Havelock's wheelhouse.

"Please?" Williams whined from the cell. "I need to get some clean clothes. It's not going to make any difference, is it? A few minutes?"

"If it's not going make any difference, it won't matter if you see it through," Havelock said. "Forty-five minutes, and you're on your way. Just sit back and try to enjoy them."

"Can't sit back when you're floating in orbit."

"It's a metaphor. Don't be a literalist."

The *Edward Israel* assignment had been a great contract. Royal Charter Energy was the first real expedition out into the new systems that the rings had opened up, and the importance the company put on the mission's success were reflected in the size of the benefit package they were willing to put together. Every day on the *Israel* had been paid a hazard bonus, even when they were just loading on supplies and crew from Luna. And with almost a year and a half out, a six-year stretch before the scheduled return to Earth, and another eighteen months back—all at full pay—it was almost less a contract than a career plan.

And still, Havelock had hesitated before he signed up.

He'd seen the footage from Eros and Ganymede, the bloodbath in the so-called slow zone when the alien defenses had stopped the ships suddenly enough to slaughter a third of the people in them. With the massive density of scientists and engineers packed into the *Israel*, it was impossible to forget that they were going into the unknown. Here there be monsters.

And now Governor Trying was dead. Severn Astrapani, the statistician who'd sung Ryu-pop classics in the talent competition, was dead. Amanda Chu, who'd flirted with Havelock one time when they were both a little tipsy, was dead. Half the men and women on the first team were injured. The supplies on the heavy shuttle—and the heavy shuttle itself—were gone. And the quiet that came over the *Edward Israel* was like the moment of shock between the impact of a blow and the pain. And then the rage and the grief. Not only the crew's. Havelock's too.

His hand terminal chimed. The message was tagged for security services. Murtry, Wei, Trajan, Smith, and himself. Havelock opened it with a sense of pleasure. He might be the least senior person in the room, but he was still in the room. Being included made him feel like maybe he'd have some control over events after all. It was an illusion, but that didn't bother him. He took in the message quickly, nodded to himself, and keyed the release code for the cell.

"You're in luck," he said. "I've got a meeting I have to be at."

Williams pulled himself out of the cell. His salt-and-pepper hair was disarrayed and his skin looked grayer than usual. "Thank you," he said sullenly.

"Just don't do that again," Havelock said. "Things are going to be hard enough without people who should know better making it worse."

"I was just drunk," the engineer said. "I didn't mean anything by it."

"I know," Havelock said. "Just don't let it happen again. All right?"

Williams nodded, not making eye contact, then pulled himself along the handholds and launched himself up the tube toward the crew quarters and clothes that weren't ripped or stained with vomit. Havelock waited until he'd gone, then shut down the security station and headed toward the meeting room.

Murtry was already there. He was a small man, but with an energy that seemed to radiate from him like heat. Havelock knew that the security chief had worked corporate prisons and high-end industrial security his whole career. Between that and the simple fact that he'd been put in charge of the *Israel*, he didn't have to work for respect from the team. Floating beside him, information specialist Chandra Wei and ground operations second Hassan Smith looked serious and grim.

"Havelock," Murtry said.

"Sir." Havelock nodded back, taking hold of a handhold and turning himself so that his head was in the same basic orientation as everyone else's. A few seconds later, Reeve, Murtry's second, floated in.

Murtry nodded. "Close the door, Reeve."

"Trajan?" Wei asked, but from the bleak sound of her voice, she already suspected the answer.

"Trajan died in the shuttle," Murtry said. "Smith? You're getting promoted."

"Sorry to hear that, sir," Smith said. "Trajan was a good officer, and a professional. She'll be missed."

"Yeah," Murtry said. "So we're here to talk about the response plan."

"Drop a rock on the squatters?" Wei said, her voice joking in a way that had nothing to do with humor. Murtry smiled anyway.

"We're going to play it a little more by the book for now," Murtry said. "Besides, we still have people down there. I've sent back to the home office, and I've asked for latitude in how we engage the issue. I'm fairly sure, given the circumstances, we'll have cover from them if it comes to that."

"We're a year and a half from anywhere," Wei said. The implication—*No one can stop us from doing anything we choose*—hung in the air.

"We're also hours away from every screen and newsfeed from Earth to Neptune," Reeve said. "This sucks, but we've got the moral high ground. If we overreact, it'll be another round of the evil corporations oppressing the poor Belters. We're in a post-Protogen world. We don't win that."

"Didn't know they'd made you political officer," Wei said, and Reeve's jaw went tight. When Murtry spoke, his voice was calm and level and threatening as a rattlesnake.

"That. We're not doing that."

"Sir?" Reeve said.

"The thing where we start sniping at each other. We don't do that here."

Wei and Reeve looked at each other.

"I'm sorry, sir," Wei said. "I was out of line."

"Not a problem, because it's not going to happen again," Murtry said. "What action have we seen from the *Barbapiccola*?"

"Nothing," Wei said. "The Belters sent condolences and offers of aid, as if there was a damn thing they could do."

"Are they warming up the engines?"

"Not that I can tell," Wei said.

"We're keeping an eye on that," Murtry said. It was a statement and a question.

"We could take custody of the ship," Wei said. "It was Mao-Kwikowski before they got broken up. Its salvage status is very murky. Call it illegal, put a few people on her, and we could shut her down."

"Noted," Murtry said. "How is the crew, Havelock?"

"Shocked, sir. Scared. Angry. They're scientists. They looked on the squatters as an annoyance and a threat to their data. For most of them, this is outside their experience."

Murtry stroked his chin with the back of his hand. "What are they going to do about it?"

"So far? Get drunk. Yell at each other or at us. Design theoretical judicial systems. Most of them seem to want the whole thing to just go away so they can get on with their research."

Murtry chuckled. "God bless the eggheads. All right."

"We still have the two light atmospheric shuttles," Havelock went on. "I can get pilots for them, and we can evacuate the people we have on the ground."

"No evac. The squatters don't get to win this," Murtry said. "No one that goes down there comes back up. We put more people down there to support them. Whatever their research is, we make damned sure it's moving forward and everyone down there *sees* it's moving forward."

"Yes, sir," Havelock said, feeling vaguely embarrassed.

"Reeve, you're going down. Deal with the locals. Find out what you can. Keep our people safe. We want a show of force."

"But nothing strong enough they can use it for sympathy on the newsfeeds back home," Reeve said as if he were agreeing.

"Wei, I want your eyes on the enemy ship. If it starts warming up its drive, I want to know."

"Permission to put my comm laser upgrade into effect?"

The *Edward Israel* didn't have torpedo tubes or gauss guns. The closest they had to a weapon was an ancient comm laser that could be hacked to cutting strength. The ship had been designed when the dangers of space were all about radiation and air supply, not intentional violence. It was almost quaint.

"No," Murtry said. "Just monitor what they're doing, listen to the chatter, and bring it back to me. If someone needs to make the call, that's me. No initiative. Understood?"

"Yes, sir."

"Havelock, you're going to be up here coordinating with the team on the ground. Use the shuttles however they need to be used to get personnel and materials down to the surface. We're here to establish a base. We'll start establishing it."

"And if there's another attack, sir?" Wei asked.

"Then that's a decision the squatters will have made, and we'll respect their choice," Murtry said.

"I'm not sure what you mean, sir," she said.

Murtry's smile didn't reach his eyes. "There's a dignity in consequences."

Havelock's quarters were only slightly larger than the cells in the brig, but much more comfortable. He was webbed into his crash couch at the end of his shift when a soft knock came at the door and Murtry pulled himself in. The security chief was scowling, but no more so than usual.

"Anything up, chief?" Havelock asked.

"You've worked with Belters," Murtry said. "What do you think of 'em?"

"They're people," Havelock said. "Some are better than others. I still have friends on Ceres."

"Fine. But what do you *think* of Belters?"

Havelock shifted, the motion setting him drifting up against his restraints as he thought. "They're insular. Tribal, almost. I think what they have most in common is that they don't like inner planet types. A Martian can sometimes pass, though. They have the whole low-g physiology thing."

"So mostly they hate Earthers," Murtry said.

"That's what pulls them together. That thing where they're oppressed by Earth is just about the one thing they have in common. So they cultivate it. Hating people like us is what makes them them."

Murtry nodded. "You know there are people that would call you prejudiced for saying that."

"It's only prejudice when you haven't been there," Havelock said. "I was on Ceres Station just before it broke for the OPA. For me, it's all lived experience."

"Well, I think you're right," Murtry said. "That's why I wanted to talk to you. Off the record. Most of the people we've got on the ship are Earthers or at least Martian. But there are a few Belt types. Like that mechanical tech. What's his name?"

"Bischen?"

"Him. Just keep an eye on those ones."

"Is there something going on?"

"Just that the squatters are mostly Belt and outer planets, and the RCE is an Earth company. I don't want anyone getting their loyalties confused."

"Yes, sir," Havelock said. And then, more tentatively, "Is something happening, sir?"

"Not right away. But... well, you might as well know. I've had word from the home office. My request for latitude was respectfully declined. Apparently there's some politicking about how this gets handled. The OPA and the UN are talking about what they want to have happen. Want to make sure the squatters are treated well."

Murtry's anger was understated but profound, and Havelock found himself resonating with it.

"But *we* have the charter. We have a right to be here."

"We do."

"And we aren't the ones who started killing people."

"We're not."

"So what are we supposed to do? Sit on our hands while the Belters kill us and take our things?"

"The sale of the lithium from their illegal mining operations has been frozen," Murtry said. "And we are instructed not to do anything to incite further conflict."

"That's bullshit. How are we supposed to do our work if we're being all careful not to offend the bastards who are shooting at us?"

Murtry's shrug was an agreement. When he spoke, his calm, laconic tone barely covered his contempt.

"Apparently they're sending us a mediator."

Interlude: The Investigator

—it reaches out it reaches out it reaches out it reaches out—

One hundred and thirteen times a second, nothing answers and it reaches out. It is not conscious, though parts of it are. There are structures within it that were once separate organisms; aboriginal, evolved, and complex. It is designed to improvise, to use what is there and then move on. Good enough is good enough, and so the artifacts are ignored or adapted. The conscious parts try to make sense of the reaching out. Try to interpret it.

One imagines an insect's leg twitching twitching twitching. One hears a spark closing a gap, the ticking so fast it becomes a drone. Another, oblivious, reexperiences her flesh falling from her bones, the nausea and fear, and begs for death as she has for years now. Her name is Maria. It does not let her die. It does not comfort her. It is unaware of her because it is unaware.

But unaware is not inactive. It finds power where it can, nestled in a bath of low radiation. Tiny structures, smaller than atoms, harvest the energy of the fast-moving particles that pass through it. Subatomic windmills. It eats the void and it reaches out it reaches out it reaches out.

In the artifacts that are conscious, memories of vanished lives still flicker. Tissues that were changed without dying hold the moment that a boy heard his sister was leaving home. They hold multiplication tables. They hold images of sexuality and violence and beauty. They hold the memories of flesh that no longer exists. They hold metaphors: mitochondria, starfish, Hitler's-brain-in-a-jar, hell realm. They dream. Structures that were neurons twitch and loop and burn and dream. Images and words and pain and fear, endless. An overwhelming sense of illness. An old man's remembered voice whispering dry words that it is unaware of. *Full fathom five thy father lies. Of his bones are coral made.*

If there had been a reply, it could end. If there had been anyone to answer, it would have come to rest like a marble at the bottom of a hill, but nothing answers. The scars know that no answer will ever come, but the reflex triggers the reflex triggers the reflex and it reaches out.

It has solved a billion small puzzles already in cascades of reflex. It has no memory of having done so, except in its scars. There is only reaching out, delivering the message that its task is complete. Nothing answers, and so it cannot end. It reaches out. It is a complex mechanism for solving puzzles using what there is to be used.

Those are pearls that were his eyes.

And so it has the investigator.

Of all the scars, there is one that came last. That is most intact. It is useful and so it is used. It builds the investigator from that template, unaware that it is doing so, and tries another way of reaching out. And something answers. Something wrong and foreign and aboriginal, but there is an answer, so over the course of years it builds the investigator again and reaches out. The investigator becomes more complex.

It will not stop until it makes that final connection, and it will never make that final connection. It stretches, tries new combinations, different ways to reach out, unaware that it is doing so. Unaware that it exists. Empty, except in the insignificant parts.

The insectile leg will twitch forever. The scar that wails for death will wail forever. The investigator will search forever. The low voice will mutter forever.

Nothing of him doth fade but suffers a sea change
Into something rich and strange.

It reaches out.

Chapter Four: Holden

MCRN *Sally Ride*, this is independent vessel *Rocinante*, requesting permission to pass through the Ring with one ship. OPA heavy freighter *Callisto's Dream*."

"Transmit authorization code now, *Rocinante*."

"Transmitting." Holden tapped the screen to send the codes and stretched out his arms and legs, letting the motion pull him out of his chair in the microgravity. Several abused joints at various places on his skeleton responded with popping sounds.

"You're getting old," Miller said. The detective stood in a rumpled gray suit and porkpie hat a few meters away, his feet on the deck as though there were gravity. The smarter the Miller simulation had gotten—and over the last two years it had become damned near coherent—the less it seemed to care about matching the reality around it.

"You're not."

"Of my bones are coral made," the ghost said as if in agreement. "It's all about the trade-offs."

When the *Sally Ride* sent the go-ahead code, Alex took them through the Ring nice and slow, the *Callisto* matching speed and course. The stars vanished as the ship moved into the black nothingness of the hub. Miller flickered as they passed through the gate, started to resolidify, and vanished in a puff of blue fireflies as the deck hatch banged open and Amos pulled himself through.

"We landing?" the mechanic asked without preamble.

"No need on this trip," Holden said, and opened a channel to Alex up in the cockpit. "Keep us here until we see the *Callisto* dock, then take us back out."

"Sure could use a few days station-side, chief," Amos said, pulling himself over to one of the ops stations and belting in. His gray coverall had a scorch mark on the sleeve, and he had a bandage covering half of his left hand. Holden pointed at it. Amos shrugged.

"We've got a pair of soil ships waiting at Tycho Station," Holden said.

"No one's had the balls to try and rip off any of the ships on this route. This many navy ships hanging around? It'd be suicide."

"And yet Fred pays us very well to escort his ships out to Medina Station, and I like taking his money." Holden panned the ship's telescopes around, zooming in on the rings. "And I don't like being in here any longer than necessary."

Miller's ghost was an artifact of the alien technology that had created the gates and a dead man. It had been following Holden around for the two years since they'd deactivated the Ring Station. It spent its time demanding, asking, and cajoling Holden to go through the newly opened gates to begin its investigation on the planets beyond them. The fact that Miller could only appear to Holden when he was alone—and on a ship the size of the *Rocinante* he was almost never alone—had kept him sane.

Alex floated down from the cockpit, his thinning black hair sticking out in every direction from his brown scalp. There were dark circles under his eyes. "We're not landin'? Could really use a couple days station-side."

"See?" Amos said.

Before Holden could reply, Naomi came up through the deck hatch. "Aren't we going to dock?"

"Captain wants to rush back for those soil transports at Tycho," Amos said, his voice somehow managing to be neutral and mocking at the same time.

"I could really use a few days—" Naomi started.

"I promise we'll take a week on Tycho when we get back. I just don't want to spend my vacation time, you know"—he pointed at the viewscreens around them displaying the dead sphere of the Ring Station and the glittering gates—"here."

"Chicken," Naomi said.

"Yep."

The comm station flashed an incoming tightbeam alert at them. Amos, who was closest, tapped the screen.

"*Rocinante* here," he said.

"*Rocinante*," a familiar voice replied. "Medina Station here."

"Fred," Holden said with a sigh. "Problem?"

"You guys aren't landing? I'm betting you could use a few—"

"Can I help you with something?" Holden said over the top of him.

"Yeah, you can. Call me after you've docked. I have business to discuss."

"Dammit," Holden said after he'd killed the connection. "You ever get the sense that the universe is out to get you?"

"Sometimes I get the sense that the universe is out to get *you*," Amos said with a grin. "It's fun to watch."

"They changed the name again," Alex said, zooming in on the spinning station that had until recently been called *Behemoth*. "Medina Station. Good name for it."

"Doesn't that mean 'fortress'?" Naomi said with a frown. "Too martial, maybe."

"Naw," Alex said. "Well, sort of. It was the walled part of a city. But it sort of became the social center too. Narrow streets designed to keep invaders out also kept motorized traffic or horse-drawn carts out. So you could only get around by walkin'. So the street vendors gathered there. It turned into the place to shop and congregate and drink tea. It's a safe place where people gather. Good name for the station."

"You've put a lot of thought into this," Holden said.

Alex shrugged. "It's interestin', the evolution of that ship and its names. Started out as the *Nauvoo*. A place of refuge, right? Big city in space. Became the *Behemoth*, the biggest baddest warship in the system. Now it's Medina Station. A gathering place. Same ship, three different names, three different things."

"Same ship," Holden said, feeling a little surly as he instructed the *Rocinante* to begin the docking approach.

"Names matter, boss," Amos said after a moment, a strange look on his big face. "Names change everything."

The interior of Medina Station was a work in progress. Large sections of the central rotating drum had been covered with transplanted soil in preparation for food production, but in many places the metal and ceramic of the drum was still visible. Most of the damage the former colony ship had sustained during her battles had been cleaned up and repaired. The office and storage space in the walls of the drum was becoming the hub of efforts to explore the thousand new worlds that had opened up to humanity. If Fred Johnson, former Earth colonel and now head of the respectable wing of the OPA, was positioning Medina Station as the logical location for a fledgling League of Planets–type government, he at least had the good sense not to say it out loud.

Holden had watched too many people dying there to ever see it as anything but a graveyard. Which made it pretty much the same as any other government he could think of.

Fred had set up his new office in what had once been the colonial administration building back when Medina Station was still

called the *Nauvoo*. They'd also been used as the offices of Radio
Free Slow Zone. Now they were patched up, repainted, and deco-
rated with atmosphere-renewing plants and video screens of the
Ring space around the ship. To Holden it made for an odd juxta-
position. Sure, humans had invaded an extra-dimensional space
with wormholes to points scattered across the galaxy, but they'd
remembered to bring ferns.

Fred puttered around the office making coffee.

"Black, right?"

"Yep," Holden said, and accepted the steaming cup from him.
"I don't like coming here."

"I understand. I appreciate you doing it anyway," Fred said and
collapsed into his chair with a sigh that seemed excessive in the
one-third g of the station's spin. But then the pressures pushing
down on Fred had little to do with gravity. The five years since
Holden had met him hadn't treated the man kindly. His formerly
salt-and-pepper hair had gone entirely gray, and his dark skin was
lined with tiny wrinkles.

"No sign it's waking up?" Holden said, pointing his coffee cup
toward a wall screen that was displaying a blown-up image of the
spherical Ring Station.

"I need to show you something," Fred said, as though Holden
hadn't asked the question. At Holden's nod, Fred tapped on his
desk and the video screen behind him came to life. On it, Chrisjen Avasarala's face was frozen mid-word. The undersecretary of
executive administration had her eyes at half-mast and her lips in
a sneer. "This is the part that concerns you."

"—eally just an excuse to wave their cocks at each other,"
Avasarala said when the video started. "So I'm thinking we send
Holden."

"Send Holden?" Holden said, but the video kept playing and
Fred didn't answer him. "Send Holden where? Where are we
sending Holden?"

"He's close when he's out at Medina, and everybody hates

him equally, so we can argue he's impartial. He's got ties to you, Mars, me. He's a fucking awful choice for a diplomatic mission, so it makes him perfect. Brief him, tell him the UN will pay for his time at double the usual rates, and get him on New Terra as fast as possible before this thing gets fucked up any worse than it already is."

The old lady leaned in toward the camera, her face swelling on the screen until Holden could see the fine detail of every wrinkle and blemish.

"If Fred is showing this to you, Holden, know that your home planet appreciates your service. Also try not to put your dick in this. It's fucked enough already."

Fred stopped the recording and leaned back in his chair. "So…"

"What the hell is she talking about?" Holden said. "What's New Terra?"

"New Terra is the unimaginative name they gave to the first of the explored worlds in the gate network."

"No, I thought that was Ilus."

"Ilus," Fred said with a sigh, "is the name the Belters who landed there gave it. Royal Charter Energy, the corporation with the contract to do the initial exploration, call it New Terra."

"Can they do that? People already live there. Everyone calls it Ilus."

"Everyone *here* calls it Ilus. You see the problem," Fred said. He took a long sip of his coffee, buying himself time to think. "No one was ready for this. A shipful of Ganymede refugees commandeered a Mao-Kwik heavy freighter and blew through the Ring at high speed as soon as the first probe results came out. Before we'd had time to pick up the pieces from our initial incursion. Before the military blockade. Before Medina was ready to enforce a safe speed limit in the Ring space. They came through so fast we didn't even have time to hail them."

"Let me guess," Holden said. "The Ilus Gate is on the opposite side from the Sol Gate."

"Not quite. They were smart enough to come in at an angle to avoid slamming into the Ring Station at three hundred thousand kph."

"So they've been living on Ilus for a year, and suddenly RCE shows up and tells them that, oops, it's really *their* planet?"

"RCE has the UN charter for scientific exploration on Ilus, New Terra, whatever you want to call it. And they're there *because* the Ganymede refugees landed there first. The plan was to study these worlds for years before anyone lived on them."

Something in Fred's tone of voice tickled at Holden's mind for a second, and he said, "Wait. UN charter? When did the UN get to be in charge of the thousand worlds?"

Fred smiled without humor. "The situation is complex. We have the UN making a power grab to administrate all these new worlds. We have OPA citizens settling one without permission. We have an energy company getting the exploration contract on a world that also just happens to have the richest lithium deposits we've ever seen."

"And we have you," Holden said, "setting up to run the turnpike everyone has to take to get there."

"I think it's safe to say the OPA has fundamental disagreements with the idea that the UN is unilaterally in charge of handing out those contracts."

"So you and Avasarala are back-channeling this to keep it from turning into something bigger."

"There are about five more variables than that, but as a start, yes. Which is where you come in," Fred said, pointing at Holden with his coffee mug. Printed on the side of the mug were the words THE BOSS. Holden stifled a laugh. "Nobody owns you, but Avasarala and I have both worked with you, and think we can do it again."

"That's a really stupid reason."

Fred's smile gave away nothing. "It doesn't hurt that you have an atmosphere-rated ship."

"You know we've never actually used it, though, right? I'm not keen on the first in-atmosphere maneuver happening a million kilometers from the closest repair bay."

"The *Rocinante* is also a military design, and—"

"Forget it. No matter what your coffee cup says, I'm not going to be the boot on the colonists' neck. I won't do that."

Fred sighed, sitting forward. When he spoke, his voice was soft and warm as flannel. But it didn't hide the steel underneath it.

"The rules governing how a thousand planets are run are about to be made. This is the test case. You'll be going in as an impartial observer and mediator."

"Me? As a mediator?"

"The irony's not lost on me. But things have already started to go bad there, and we need someone keeping it from getting worse while three governments decide how the next one will work."

"You mean you want me to make it look like you're doing something while you figure out what to do," Holden said. "And going bad how?"

"The colonists blew up an RCE heavy lift shuttle. The provisional governor was on it. He's dead, along with a few scientists and RCE employees. It won't help our negotiations if Ilus turns into a full-blown war between Belters and a UN corporation."

"So I keep the peace?"

"You get them talking, and you keep them talking. And you do what you always do, you maintain absolute transparency. This is one time secrets won't help anyone. Should be right up your alley."

"I thought I was the galaxy's biggest loose cannon to you guys. Is Avasarala sending the match in to meet the powder keg because she *wants* this to fail?"

Fred shrugged. "I care less what she wants you for than what I do. Maybe the old lady likes you. Don't ask me to explain it."

Miller was waiting for Holden outside Fred's office.

"There are three thousand people on Medina Station right

now," Holden said. "How is it that not one of them is here to keep you from bugging me?"

"You going to take the job?" Miller said.

"I haven't decided," Holden said. "Which, since you are running a simulation of my brain, you already know. So you asking is really you telling me *to* take it. Stop me when I'm wrong."

Holden headed off down the corridor, hoping to run into another human and make the Miller ghost go away. Miller followed, his footsteps echoing on the ceramic floor. The fact that those echoes existed only inside Holden's mind made the whole thing even creepier.

"You're not wrong. You should take it," Miller said. "The man's right. It's important. Something like that goes from a few pissed-off locals to a meat grinder without much time in between. This one time, back on Ceres—"

"Okay, no. No folksy cop stories from the dead guy. What's on Ilus that you want?" Holden asked. "It might help if you just came out and told me what it is you want on the other side of those rings."

"You know what I'm looking for," the old detective said. He actually managed to look sad.

"Yeah, whatever weird alien civilization made you. And I already know you won't find it. Hell, *you* know you won't find it."

"Still gotta loo—" Miller vanished. A woman in a blue Medina Station security uniform walked by, looking at her hand terminal. She grunted something approximating a greeting without looking up.

Holden took the stairs up to the inner surface of Medina's rotating habitation drum. No chance Miller would surprise him there. The drum was full of activity, with some workers spreading imported soil for the eventual farms and others raising prefab buildings that would be houses and storage. Holden waved cheerily at them as he walked past. With his increasingly frequent Miller hauntings, he had come to appreciate the value of having other humans within line of sight. They made his life a little less weird just by existing.

He avoided the elevator to the engineering transition point that would take him out of the rotating drum and into the micro-gravity of the stern of the former colony ship. The *Rocinante* was docked at the airlock there. Instead, he walked up the long curl-ing ramp that kept him in sight of everyone in the rotating drum. The last time he'd climbed that ramp, people had been shooting and dying all around him. It wasn't a pleasant memory, but it was better than being trapped alone in an elevator car with Miller. The universe was getting a little thick with his personal history.

Before he passed through the transition point and into the engineering decks, he floated for a moment and looked out across the inside of the habitation drum. From his elevation the plots of soil looked like checkerboard squares of dark brown against the gray of the drum's skin. Equipment moved across them like metal insects, busy at unguessable tasks. Turning a bubble of metal into a tiny self-contained world.

We'll forget how to do this, Holden thought. Humanity had only just started learning how to live in space, and now they'd forget. Why develop new strategies for surviving on tiny stations like Medina when there were a thousand new worlds to con-quer, with air and water free for the taking? It was an astounding thought, but it also left Holden just a little melancholy.

He turned his back on the workers busy at their obsolete work, and returned to his ship.

"So," Naomi said as the crew sat together in the *Rocinante*'s gal-ley. "Are we going to Ilus?"

Holden had spent several minutes explaining what Fred John-son and Chrisjen Avasarala wanted from them, and then just sort of trailed off. The truth was he didn't know the answer to Naomi's question.

"There are a lot of reasons to do this," he finally said, tapping out a quick rhythm on the metal tabletop. "It is a really big deal. It's the test case for a thousand worlds to follow. And I admit there's some attraction to the idea that we'd get to help set the perspectives. Maybe get to help create the template for everything that follows. That's pretty damn exciting."

"And the money's good," Amos said. "Don't forget the money's good."

"But," Naomi prompted, putting her hand on his arm and smiling. Letting him know it was okay to share whatever his fears were. He smiled back and patted her hand.

"But I have one pretty compelling reason to say no," he said. "Miller really wants me to go."

They were silent for a long moment. Naomi was the first to speak.

"You're going to take it."

"Am I?"

"You are," she said. "Because you think you'll be able to help."

"You think we can't?"

"No," Naomi said. "I think you can. And even if we're wrong, not trying would make you cranky."

"Other thing to consider?" Amos said. "Money's really good."

Chapter Five: Basia

Jesus wept, Basia my child," Coop said. "We're *winning*. How much of a sister are you turning into if it gets rocky?"

The others all looked at him, waiting. Scotty and Pete, but also Loris and Caterine. Ibrahim and Zadie. Basia crossed his arms.

"They find out who killed their governor—" Basia began, but Coop waved a hand like shooing flies.

"Won't. If they haven't now, it's just going down as one of those things that happened. Hell, I don't remember who did it. You remember, Zadie?"

Zadie shook her head. "Ne savvy mé," she said like the Belter that she was. That she'd been before. Coop gestured toward her like he'd proved a point.

"I don't like how it came out either," Pete said. "But if we hadn't done it, they'd have been here this whole time instead of just dribs and drabs. Holden'd be here with a domed city already up, and then what would we be looking at?"

"Ex*act*ly," Coop said. "Slow them down, we wanted, and slow them down we did. Question now is what to do with the time we've got left."

"Could kill them all and drop their bodies down the mine pits," Loris said, her smile making it clear that she was mostly joking.

"I was thinking we could pooch their transmitter," Ibrahim said. "All their signal goes through one repeater in their technical hut. Something happened to that, they'd be choked for bandwidth like the rest of us."

"Would it take their hand terminals down too?" Coop asked.

"Might," Ibrahim said. "It would certainly make them local and line of sight."

"Worth considering," Coop said.

The ruins where they met were a half hour's fast walk from the town itself. Great towers of strange, bonelike material rose up out of the ground, leaning against one another in patterns that seemed almost random until he caught them at just the correct angle and some ornate symmetry revealed itself. The lower structures were soft at the edges, curved like vertebrae or the gears of some unimaginably nimble machine.

A soft breeze shifted through the ruins with a sound like reed flutes playing in the distance. Something had lived here once, but it was gone now, and its bones were a hiding place for Basia and his cabal. He had the sudden memory of a video he'd seen once of brine shrimp living in the bones of a dead whale.

"Question I have," Basia said, "is what we're aiming for. We knock out their bandwidth. What does that get us?"

"Makes it harder for them to show value," Loris said. "I've read the charter same as everyone else. Yes, it's got a lot of conservation and basic science riders and requirements, but let's all be clear. RCE is here to make a profit. If we can make it clear that they won't be able to..."

"That doesn't matter," Ibrahim said. "What we need to do is establish our own claim to the planet. Profit and loss comes later."

"I don't agree, Bram," Loris said. "If you look at the history of colonialism, legal precedent and title claims are almost always rationalized after the fact. What you see is—"

"What I see," Coop cut in, "is the time until the joint OPA/ UN observer gets here and changes the game getting shorter. Basia? You want to weigh in?"

Basia cracked his knuckles. "What he needs to see is that RCE isn't organized and we've got a ship full of refined lithium ready for market."

"So let's make that happen," Coop said, smiling his vicious smile.

After the meeting, they left one by one or in pairs, so as not to attract attention. First Pete and Ibrahim, together because they were lovers. Then Scotty, puffing on his pipe. Loris and Caterine. Then, usually, Zadie and Coop. But not today. Today, Coop nodded Zadie on ahead. She made the one-handed nod, the physical idiom of Belters who had to communicate in vacuum suits, and strode out, her too-long limbs giving her a gait that was awkward and graceful at once. Like a giraffe.

"Having a hard time with this, you," Coop said.

Basia shrugged. "Got off to a bad start. That's all."

"You were one of them before. Didn't fight," Coop said.

"Didn't," he said bitterly.

They had lived together on the ship with all the others for years after Ganymede. They had argued together, the two of them, for the exodus to the new planets that the ring gates had opened. Basia knew Coop. Knew he'd fought with a splinter of the OPA that had never accepted compromise with the inner planets. The split circle of the Outer Planets Alliance was etched in the man's skin, just over his left shoulder blade. It occurred to Basia, not for the first time, that *outer planets* had taken on a very new meaning in the last couple years.

"Can be hard," Coop said. "Especially on the big stations. Ceres. Eros, before. Ganymede. All kind of inners there. You live around them. Work with them. Come to like some of them maybe. And then the order comes, and you have to pop a seal and let someone die. Can't pass, because then they can start looking for the pattern. Who lived that shouldn't. Compromises the cell."

Basia nodded, but his mouth tasted sour. "That what we are? An OPA cell?"

"Resisting Earth's corporate power grab, ne? There's worse models."

"Yeah," Basia said. "I get your point."

"You do? Because what I'm seeing is you putting a lot of questions in a lot of heads. Thinking about whether we're on the path we should be."

Basia bristled. "That a problem for you?"

"Problem's for you, mate. Because the more you wonder, the more they wonder. And no matter what I pretend, we all remember who mashed that button."

The walk back from the meetings always left Basia upset. Everywhere, there were little reminders of what the group of them—his cell—had done and also what they hadn't. The little hydrology lab down by the wash with its geodesic dome and its drills, like the mining pits in miniature. The exobiologists' hut out alone on the edge of the township. The unfamiliar faces in the square, the clothing that had been fabricated with RCE templates.

On the flats north of the town, a soccer game was kicking up dust, townsmen including his own son Jacek playing with the corporation's people. At least they were still on different teams. Basia looped around, entering the town proper on the path that led to the mining pits. The breeze was rising toward a wind, stirring dust devils. High above in the blue arc of sky, a wedge of vast creatures like aerial jellyfish trailed golden streamers from pale white bodies. Lucia said each one was as large as the ship, but he couldn't bring himself to believe that. He wondered whether any-one had given the creatures a name.

"Basia!"

"Carol," he said with a nod as the big woman fell in step beside him. Carol Chiwewe had been everyone's first choice for coordi-nator when they'd landed. Smart and focused and strong-minded without being bullish. She almost certainly guessed that he was involved in what had happened at the landing pad, but it didn't matter. Some secrets stayed secrets because nobody knew them. Some because nobody told.

"I'm putting together a maintenance crew to head out for the pits. Going out tomorrow. Probably stay for five, six days. You in?"

"There a problem?"

"No, and I think we should keep it that way. Only a few more loads to get up the well before we can ship out."

"Be good to have a full hold before the observer arrives," Basia said.

"Wouldn't it just," Carol said with a smile. "Glad you're in. Meet at the square at nine."

"Okay," Basia said, and she clapped him on the shoulder, turn-ing back to whatever errand she'd been on when she saw him. It was another twenty minutes before he noticed that he hadn't ever exactly said yes. That was why she ran things, he figured.

His own home was near the edge of the town. They'd made the bricks from the local earth, processed through some of the mining equipment and fired in a kiln powered by combustion. It could only have been more primitive if they'd dug a cave and painted bison on the walls. Lucia was on the little porch area, sweeping the bricks with a broom made from a local grass analog that smelled like manure and peppermint and turned from black to gold when you cut it.

"You don't know what that thing's off-gassing," he said. It was a little joke between them. How she answered would tell a lot about where they stood. A litmus test for the pH of his marriage.

"A third of it's carcinogenic, a third's mutagenic, and a third we don't know what it does," she said with a smile. So things were good. Basia felt a knot loosen in his belly. He kissed her cheek and ducked into the cool of the house.

"You might as well stop that," he said. "Wind is just going to push it back."

Lucia made a few more desultory passes, the grass hissing against the brick, then followed him in. By the standards of Ganymede or the ship, the house was massive. A sleeping room for each of the children and a shared one for them. A room dedicated entirely to food preparation. The captain's suite on the *Barbapiccola* boasted fewer square meters than Basia's home. It was a barbarian palace, and it was his. He sat on a chair by the front window and looked out at the plain.

"Where's Felcia?" he asked.

"Out," Lucia said.

"You sound just like her."

"Felcia is my primary source of information about Felcia," Lucia said. She was smiling. Laughing a little, even. It was as good a mood as she'd been in for weeks. Basia knew it was a choice. She needed him in a good mood for something, and if he was wise, he'd fight against the manipulation. He didn't want to, though. He wanted to be able to act for a while as if everything were fine. And so he played along.

"I blame your side of the family. I was always very compliant as a boy. Do we have anything worth eating?"

"More ship's rations."

Basia sighed. "No salad?"

"Soon," she said. "The new crop is doing well. As long as we don't find anything strange in them, you'll be able to have all the carrots you want starting next week."

"Someday we'll be able to grow in the soil here."

"Maybe north of here," Lucia said, and rested her hand on his shoulder as she looked out the window with him. "Even the native fauna have a hard time around here."

"North. South. Ilus is all *here* as far as I'm concerned."

She turned, walking to the kitchen. Basia felt a tug of longing for her, a nostalgia of the body that belonged to a time when they'd been younger, childless, and horny all the time. He heard the pop and hiss of the rations canisters. The smell of sag aloo wafted through the air. Lucia came back in with a palm-sized plate of food for each of them.

"Thank you," he said.

Lucia nodded and sat in her own chair, her leg curled up under her. Gravity had changed her. The muscles of her arms and shoulders were more pronounced now, the curve of her back when she sat was at a different angle. Ilus was changing them in ways he had never expected, though perhaps he should have. He took a forkful of the sag aloo.

"Going to the mines tomorrow," he said.

Lucia's eyebrows rose a fraction. "What for?"

"Maintenance," he said, and then, because he knew what she was thinking, "Carol asked me."

"That's good, then." Meaning that it was Carol who had asked him to go and not Coop. He felt a stab of shame and then an annoyance that he was ashamed. He pressed his lips together a little more tightly.

"The observer's coming," Lucia said, as if she meant nothing by it. "James Holden."

"I'd heard. It's good. Gives us leverage against the RCE."

"I suppose so."

He could remember a time when they'd laughed together. When Lucia had come from the hospitals on Ganymede full of stories about the patients and the other doctors. They'd eat vat-grown steak as tender as anything harvested from an animal and drink beer fermented there on the little moon. They'd talked for hours, until it was long past time to sleep. Now their conversations were so careful, it was like the words all had glass bones. So he changed the topic.

"It's strange to think about it," he said. "I'll probably never

weld in a vacuum again. All those years apprenticing and working, and now everything I do has air around it."

"Tell me about it. If I'd known how it would all play out, I'd
have spent my rotations in the general clinics."

"Well, you're the best hand surgeon on the planet."

"The best hand surgeon on the planet is doing a lot of reading
on digestive disorders and gynecological exams," Lucia said dryly.
Her eyes went hard, distant. "We need to talk about Felcia."

And here it was. The gentleness, the calm, the soft memories.
This was where it had been leading. He sat forward, his eyes cast
on the ground.

"What's to say?"

"She's been talking about what happens next. For her."

"Same as happens for any of us," Basia said.

Lucia put another bite in her mouth, chewing slowly, though
the food hardly required it. A gust of hard wind pressed in at the
window with the soft ticking of grit against the glass. When she
spoke, her voice was soft, but implacable.

"She's thinking of university," Lucia said. "She's done the tuto-
rials and examinations on the network. She needs us to give permission before the applications move forward."

"She's too young," Basia said, knowing as the words came out
that it was the wrong tack. Frustration knotted his throat and he
put his dinner, half eaten, on the armrest.

"She won't be by the time she gets there," Lucia said. "If she
went with the first shipment and transferred at Medina, she could
be on Ganymede or Ceres Station in nineteen months. Twenty."

"We need her here," Basia said, his tone hard and definitive.
The conversation was over. Except that it wasn't.

"I don't regret coming here," Lucia said. "And you didn't force
me to come. The months after Ganymede when we were all living
like rats packed too tight? All the ports that wouldn't take us in?
I remember that. When Mao-Kwikowski was dissolved, I was the
one who helped Captain Andrada draw up the salvage papers. I
made the *Barbapiccola* our ship."

"I know."

"When we took the vote, my voice was with yours. Maybe living so long as refugees made us wild or brave. I don't know, but to come here. To begin everything again under a sky. Under some new star. I thought it was as obvious as you did, and I don't regret coming."

Her tone was fierce now. Her dark eyes glittered and flashed, daring him to disagree. He didn't.

"If we spend the rest of our lives mining lithium and trying to grow carrots, I will be delighted with that," she went on. "If I never reattach another ligament or regrow a lost thumb, then fine. Because I chose it. Jacek and Felcia didn't make that choice."

"I'm not sending my children back," Basia said. "What would they get back there? With all the work that needs to be done *here*, with all the things there are to be learned and discovered *here*, how is going backward a good idea?" His voice was getting louder than he'd meant, but he wasn't shouting. Not really.

"Being here is our choice," Lucia said. "Felica's choice is where her choice is. We can stand in the way or we can help."

"Helping her back into *that* isn't helping," Basia said. "She belongs here. We all belong here."

"Where we came from—"

"We came from here. Nothing that happened before matters. We are from here now. Ilus. I will go down dying before I let them bring their wars and their weapons and their corporations and their science projects here. And I will be damned if they get any more of my children."

"Dad?"

Jacek stood in the doorway. He had a soccer ball on his hip and an expression of concern in his eyes.

"Son," Basia said.

The moaning of the wind was the only sound. Basia stood up, took his canister and then Lucia's. Taking her leavings to the recycler was a small olive branch, but it was all he had. The sense of impotent rage and shame boiled up in his throat and found to release there. Katoa, the landing pad, the concern in Jacek's eyes. The years they had spent fleeing only to land in a brick palace that his daughter wanted to leave. All of it mixed into a single emasculating anger as hot as solder.

"Is everything okay?" Jacek asked.

"Your mother and I were just talking."

"We aren't from here," Lucia said as if Jacek hadn't come in, as if the adult conversation could go on with the boy there. "We're making it that way, but it isn't true yet."

"It will be," Basia said.

Chapter Six: Elvi

Elvi sat in the high meadow, her legs stretched out before her, and watched quietly. The plant analogs—she couldn't really call them plants—lifted up above the dry, beige soil, straining toward the sunlight. The tallest stood hardly more than half a meter with a flat corrugated top that shifted to follow the sun and glittered the iridescent green of a beetle's carapace. A gentle breeze shifted the stalks and cooled Elvi's cheek. She didn't move. Four meters away, a mimic lizard cooed.

This time, the answering coo was closer. Elvi fought not to bounce with excitement. She wanted to wave her hands in glee, wanted to giggle. She stayed still as a stone. The prey species waddled closer. About the size of a sparrow, it had a soft rill of something like feathers or thick hair that ran down its sides. It had six long, ungainly legs, each ending in a doubled hook. She wanted to see them as fingers or toes, but she hadn't seen any of the little things use the hooks to manipulate anything. It cooed again, a soft guttural chuffing halfway between a dove's call and a tambourine. The mimic lizard waited a moment, its wide-set eyes shifting toward the little animal. Elvi watched for the tremor in the lizard's side, an almost invisible fluttering of its scalelike skin.

With the speed of a gun, the lizard's mouth unhinged and a mass of wet pink flesh shot out. The prey animal didn't so much as squeak as the lizard's inverted stomach drove it to the ground. Elvi's fists wriggled in delight as the mimic lizard began hauling its internal organs back across the dry ground. The prey species was dead or paralyzed, adhering to the pink flesh. Dirt and small stones stuck to the stomach too. Eventually the whole mass reached the mimic lizard's too-wide jaw, and it began the long process of drawing the messy complex back through its mouth. From her previous observations, Elvi knew it would take the better part of an hour before the mimic lizard's newly concave sides filled out again. She stood up, dusting herself off, and hobbled over.

Her foot was still in the cast she'd gotten on that terrible first night. The pain from the broken bone was only a dull ache now, more an annoyance than a problem, but the cast made mobility an issue. She opened her satchel, the black lattice fabric ticking under her fingers, then gently lifted the feeding lizard into it. Its gaze flickered across her, untrusting. That was fair.

"Sorry, little one," she said. "It's in the name of science."

She closed the satchel and triggered the collection sequence. The lizard died instantly, and the internal assay sequence began, cataloging the gross structures of the animal's body, firing hair-thin needles through the corpse to gather samples at every boundary between tissues and feeding the data up to the dedicated system in the satchel's strap. By the time she got back to her little hut and took the corpses out for storage and cataloging, the mimic lizard and its prey would be modeled in her computer, terabytes of information ready to stream up to the *Edward Israel* and from there back to the labs on Luna. It would take the signal a few hours to travel the distance that had taken her eighteen months, but for those hours, she and her workgroup would be the only people in all the billions of humans scattered throughout the planets who would know this little being's secrets. If God had come and offered her the Library of Alexandria in exchange, she wouldn't have taken the trade.

As she tramped down the gentle slope toward her hut, the mining village spread out before her. It was tiny. Two parallel streets with a gap in the middle that passed for a town square. The buildings were cobbled together from the supplies they'd brought and what they could find on the planetary surface. Everything stood at slightly wrong angles, like a handful of dice had been scattered there. She was used to the strict rectilinear architecture that came from living where space was precious. That didn't apply here, and it made the little town seem more organic, like it had simply grown there.

Fayez was sitting on the small porch outside her hut. His skin had darkened in the weeks since the crash. The preliminary hydrological study had kept him and several of the others from the team out in the field for almost two weeks.

"You know what I love about this planet?" Fayez said instead of hello.

"Nothing?"

He scowled at her, feigning hurt feelings. "I love the period of rotation. Thirty hours. You can get in a full day's work, stay up getting drunk at the saloon, and still get a full night's sleep. I don't know why we didn't think of this back home."

"There are advantages," Elvi said, unlocking her door and stepping into the hut.

"Of course it means we've been here almost six weeks in the past month," Fayez said, "but thank God we didn't get one of those little spinning tops with sundown every six hours. Now if they can just fix the gravity."

The unit was a single four-by-six-meter room with bed, shower, toilet, kitchen, and workstation all hunched together. As she put the satchel into the archiving unit, it struck her how much her work was about inferring things from design. As soon as she'd seen the mimic lizard's forward-facing eyes, she'd assumed it was a predator. Anyone looking at her hut would know it had been made with the assumption that space would be at a premium. Everything was an artifact of its function. That was what made evolution so gorgeous. She looked in the mirror over her little sink. Her skin was covered in a thin layer of beige dust, like stage makeup.

"I don't want to do this," she said, wiping her cheeks with a damp tissue.

"Look on the bright side," Fayez said. "They've only tried to kill us once so far."

"You aren't helping."

"I'm not trying," he said, then winced at the unintentional reference to the dead man.

They had cremated Governor Trying and the other casualties of the crash. Apart from one villager who'd arrived with non-responsive bone cancer, they had been the first human deaths on the world. Certainly they were the first murders.

But after that, the people from the village had been nothing but kind. Lucia Merton, the doctor who'd come to help them after the crash, had followed up with each of the survivors. A Belter from Ceres named Jordan had brought Elvi food that his wife had cooked for the injured. The holy man had invited her to the services at the village temple. Everything about the inhabitants of New Terra said that they were kind, gentle, authentic people. Except that someone had killed the governor and almost a dozen others.

The RCE encampment stood south of the village proper. With Elvi and Fayez included, a little less than half the RCE employees on the surface had chosen to attend the village's community meeting. The others were involved in their work or still too badly injured. If she hadn't felt it was part of her job to educate everyone about the contamination hazards, Elvi would probably have stayed back at her hut too.

Most of the RCE personnel were field scientists. They dressed for comfort, herself included. The only ones in formal clothes were the security team. Hobart Reeve, Murtry's second, led three armed guards in RCE uniforms that made them look like soldiers or police. They hadn't been on the big shuttle, but had arrived on a light shuttle almost immediately. When the order had come in from RCE that no new personnel were going planetside until the UN observer arrived, Reeve had already been investigating what he always called "the incident."

The community hall was one side of the village's central square, set across the bare dirt and stone from the temple. Apart from the collection of religious iconography at the temple's eaves, the two were hard to tell apart.

The chairs were made from industrial cowling and modified crash couches. If the village had been in a more temperate part of the planet, there would have been more local flora, some sort of wood analog, to use. But this was where the lithium was nearest the surface, and lithium was what would bring money to the community. So like a microorganism moving along a concentration gradient, all of humanity had come to these twenty square kilometers.

Elvi sat at the back with the other RCE employees, except Reeve and the security detail, who sat closer to the front with the locals. She watched them all segregate without a word. No one enforced the separation, but it was there. Michaela, an atmospheric physicist, sat beside her with a smile. Anneke and Tor, both geoengineers, sat on her other side, hand in hand. Fayez in the couch beyond her, talking with Sudyam, who had come down with the first small shuttle after the accident. The incident. The attack. Anneke leaned in and murmured something to Tor. He blushed and nodded a little too vigorously. Elvi tried to ignore the sexual byplay.

The mayor of First Landing was a thick-featured Martian woman with a broad accent and finger-cut hair named Carol Chi-wewe, only they called her the coordinator, not the mayor. She called the meeting to order, and Elvi felt her heart starting to beat faster. The Belters had set the agenda, and so it started off with issues that were more important to them than to Elvi or RCE: the maintenance schedule for the water purification systems, whether to accept a credit line from an OPA-backed bank at unfavorable terms or wait until the first load of lithium came back and try for better. Everything was talked about in calm, considered terms. If there was anger or fear or murder, they had buried it so deeply that the mound didn't show.

Reeve's turn came, and he stepped smartly to the front of the room. His lips made a thin, forced smile.

"Thank you, madam coordinator, for inviting us to speak," he said. "We have confirmation that the independent observer is on the way with a commission from the UN, the Martian congress, and the OPA to assist with moving the development of the colony forward. It is our hope to have the security issues addressed before they arrive."

We hope to hang the bad guys on a rope before anyone gets here and says we can't, Fayez translated quietly enough for the words to reach Elvi's ears and no farther.

"We have definitively identified the explosive used in the attack, and we are looking into which individuals had access to it."

We don't have a goddamn clue who did it, and since you hicks store mining explosives in an unlocked shed, we aren't going to fig-ure it out anytime soon.

"I don't have to explain the gravity of this situation, but Royal Charter Energy is committed to the success of this colony for both our employees and this community. We're all in this together, and my door is always open to anyone with questions or concerns, and I hope that we can rely on the same kindness and collaboration that you've extended to us since we came."

So since we've got nothing, we'd really appreciate it if those of you who know who set the charges would just tell us. And also please consider not murdering us in our sleep. Thanks for that.

Sudyam coughed to hide her laughter and Fayez flashed a grin. At the front of the room, Reeve nodded and stepped down. The coordinator stood up, looking toward the back of the room. Elvi felt the sudden, powerful need to urinate.

"Doctor Okoye?" the coordinator said. "You wanted to speak?"

Elvi nodded and rose to her feet. It was about ten meters to the front of the room, and Elvi walked forward with her nerves screaming. The heat of the crowd's bodies seemed suddenly oppressive, the smell of sweat and dust overwhelming. Her tongue felt sticky and thick in her mouth, but she smiled. At an estimate, two hundred people sat before her, their eyes on her. Her heart ticked over so fast she had to wonder whether there was enough air in the room. She remembered someone telling her once to look for a friendly face in the crowd and pretend she was only speaking to them. Four rows in on the left, Lucia Merton was sitting with her hands folded in her lap. Elvi smiled, and the woman smiled back.

"I just wanted to take a minute," Elvi said, "to talk about how we can limit cross-contamination with the environment? Because we lost the dome? The hard perimeter dome?"

Lucia looked grave. Elvi chanced a look at the rest of the crowd and then wished she hadn't.

"Part...um. Part of the RCE's agreement with the UN was that we do a complete environmental study. We're in just the second biosphere that we've ever seen, and there's so much we don't know about it that the more we can keep it pristine, the better we'll be able to understand it. Ideally, we'd have a totally enclosed system here on the surface. Tight as a ship. Airlocks and decontamination rooms and..."

She was babbling. She grinned, hoping that someone would smile back. No one did. She swallowed.

"Every time we breathe, we're taking in totally unknown microorganisms. And even though we've got different proteomes, we're still big blobs of water and minerals. Sooner or later one of the indigenous species is going to find a way to exploit that. And it goes the other way too. Every time we defecate, we're introducing billions of bacteria into the environment."

"So now you're going to tell us how we can shit?" a man's voice said.

Elvi felt the sudden heat of a blush in her neck and cheeks. Even Lucia's expression had gone cold and distant, the woman's gaze fixed on nothing.

"I only meant that if we were doing this right, we'd have a protected, sterile environment and we wouldn't be going out into the ruins or cultivating crop plants in the open air because—"

"Because you think we did it wrong," the man sitting at Lucia's side said. He was a big man with a dusting of gray at his temples and in the stubble of beard and a permanently angry face. "Only you don't get to decide that."

"I understand that we're working with a complex situation here," Elvi said, her voice getting rough with desperation. "But we're all living in this massive Petri dish already, and I have a list of a few little sacrifices that we can all make that, from a scientific perspective—"

The man beside Lucia Merton flushed, and he leaned forward, his fists on his thighs. His eyes fixed on her like a predator's.

"I'm done sacrificing things to science," he said, and the buzz in his voice was a promise of violence. Lucia put a restraining hand on the man's wrist, but others around the room had taken up the man's disdain. The sounds of their bodies shifting in the seats, the murmur of voices in small conversations of their own filled the air. *Whoever killed Trying is probably in this room*, she thought. And then, immediately after that, *What the hell am I doing here?*

Carol Chiwewe stood up, her expression pained. Embarrassed on Elvi's behalf.

"Maybe we better come back to that another time, Doctor Okoye," she said. "It's late and people are tired, ne?"

"Yes," Elvi muttered. "Yes, of course."

Her skin burning with shame, she walked back toward her seat, and then past it, out into the street and alone in the deepening night toward her hut. Her shoes scraped in the gravel and dirt. The air was cool and smelled like coming rain. She wasn't more than halfway there, moving slowly in the near-black starlight, when a voice stopped her.

"I'm sorry about my dad."

Elvi turned. The girl was little more than a deeper darkness in the night. A slightly more solid shadow. Elvi found herself thankful that the voice wasn't a man's.

"It's okay," she said. "I don't think I did that very well."

"No, it's him," the girl said, stepping closer. "You couldn't have done right with him. My brother died, and now Dad's not that kind of man anymore."

"Oh," Elvi said. And then, "I'm sorry."

The girl nodded, shuffled with something, and a pale green light no brighter than a candle bloomed in her palm, casting shadows up over the girl's face. She was pretty the way youth is always pretty, but when she got older, Elvi thought she might be beautiful the way her mother was.

"You're Doctor Merton's daughter," Elvi said.

"Felcia," the girl said.

"Good to meet you, Felcia," Elvi said.

"I can walk you home. If you don't have a light."

"I don't," Elvi said. "I should have brought one."

"Everyone forgets sometimes," the girl said, setting off. Elvi trotted a little to catch up with her. For a dozen meters, they walked in silence. Elvi sensed that the girl was building up to something. A confession or a threat. Something dangerous. Elvi hoped that she was just being paranoid, and was certain that she wasn't.

When the girl spoke at last, her voice was tight with anxiety and longing, and her words were the last thing Elvi would have guessed.

"What's it like going to a real university?"

Chapter Seven: Holden

There should be fanfare, Holden thought.

Passing through a ring into another star system, halfway across the galaxy from Earth, should be a dramatic moment. Trumpets, or loud alarms, tense faces locked on viewscreens. Instead, there was nothing. No physical sign that the *Rocinante* had been yanked fifty thousand light-years across space. Just the eerie black of the hub replaced by the unfamiliar starfield of the new solar system. Somehow, the fact that it was so mundane made it stranger. A wormhole gate should be a massive swirling vortex of light and energy, not just a big ring of something sort of like metal with different stars on the other side.

He resisted the urge to hit the general quarters alarm just to add tension to the moment.

The new sun was a faint dot of yellow-white light, not all

that different from Sol when viewed from the Ring sitting just outside Uranus' orbit. It had five rocky inner planets, one massive gas giant, and a number of dwarf planets in orbits even farther out than the Ring. The fourth inner planet, sitting smack dab in the middle of the Goldilocks Zone, was Ilus. New Terra. Bering Survey Four. RCE charter 24771912-F23. Whatever you wanted to call it.

All those names were too simple for what it really was. Mankind's first home around an alien star. Humans kept finding ways to turn the astonishing events of the last few years mundane. A few decades from now, when all the planets had been explored and colonized, the hub and its rings would just be a freeway system. No one would think twice about them.

"Wow," Naomi said, staring at Ilus' star on the display with wide-eyed awe. Holden felt a rush of affection for her.

"I was just thinking that," he said. "Glad I'm not the only one." He opened a channel up to the cockpit.

"Yo," Alex said.

"How fast can you get us there?"

"Pretty damn fast, if you're willin' to be uncomfortable."

"Put us on a fast burn schedule and get some dirt under my feet," Holden said with a grin.

"High burn'll get us on the ground in 'bout seventy-three days."

"Seventy-three days," Holden said.

"Well, seventy-two point eight."

"Space," Holden said, trading his grin for a sigh, "is too damn big."

Five hours into their burn, the messages started to come in. Holden had Alex bring them down to one-third g for dinner, and played the first recording on the galley screen while he helped Amos make pasta.

An older man, brown-skinned and gray-haired, stared out of

the screen at him. He had the thin features and large cranium of a Belter, and just a hint of a Ceres accent.

"Captain Holden," he said once the recording started. "Fred Johnson notified us you were coming, and I wanted to thank you for your help. My name is Kasim Andrada, and I'm captain of the independent freighter *Barbapiccola*. Let me fill you in on the situation as it stands."

"This should be good," Amos grunted, dumping steaming spaghetti noodles into a colander to drain them. Holden handed him the pot of red sauce he'd been stirring, then leaned against the counter to watch the rest of the broadcast.

"The colony finally got a working mining operation running about four months ago. In that time, we've brought up several hundred tons of raw ore from our mine. At the purity levels we're seeing, that should translate to almost a dozen tons of lithium after refining. It's enough to buy equipment, medicine, soil and seeds, everything this colony needs to get a real toehold."

Naomi came into the galley, tapping away furiously at her hand terminal. "Smells good, I—" She stopped when she saw the video playing and sat down to watch.

"The *Edward Israel*," Captain Andrada continued, "has stated that they will not allow us to leave orbit until the arbitration is complete. Royal Charter's position being that they own this lithium until someone says they don't. One of your first priorities will be to get the *Israel* to lift the blockade and let us take this ore to the Pallas refineries, where we already have buyers lined up and waiting."

"Oh," Amos said, dumping the pasta and sauce into a large bowl and putting it on the table. "Is *that* our priority?"

Holden passed the playback. "Did come across as an order, didn't it?"

"He's OPA," Naomi said. "He thinks you're here as Fred's mouthpiece."

"This guy is going to give me indigestion," Holden said, killing the recording. "I'll watch the rest of this crap after we eat."

Five more broadcasts were queued up for viewing by the next day. The captain of the *Edward Israel*, an older Earthman named Marwick with flaming red hair and a British accent, demanded that Holden enforce the RCE charter by disabling the engines of the *Barbapiccola* if it tried to leave the system. Fred sent along encouragement and a reminder that Avasarala was shotgunning threats about the consequences for screwing the mission up. Three different news organizations asked for interviews, including a personal request from Monica Stuart for a live interview when he returned.

Miller watched them over his shoulder until Naomi came into their room and the detective disappeared in a blue shower of sparks.

"I think Monica likes you," Naomi said with a grin, then flopped down onto the double-sized crash couch they used as a bed. "Alex is taking us back up to high burn in twelve minutes, and I want to die."

"Monica would flirt with a lizard if she thought it would get her a good interview, tell Alex to give us another half hour so I can send a few responses, and hold on I'll get my gun."

Naomi pushed herself up with a groan. "I'll get some coffee while you find your bullets."

"Don't leave," Holden said, reaching for her arm. "I don't want to record these broadcasts with Miller standing behind me."

"He's only in your head," she said, but she sat back down anyway. "He won't show up on the recording."

"Do you think that makes it *less* uncomfortable? Really?"

Naomi crawled across the bed and curled up next to him, putting her head on his chest. He tugged on a lock of her hair and she let out a long contented sigh.

"I like long flights when we aren't doing these bone-crushing mad dashes," she said. "Nothing to do but read, listen to music, stay in bed all day. You being famous sucks."

"It's also the reason we're sort of rich now."

"We could sell the ship, go get jobs at Pur'N'Kleen again. Do the Saturn ice run…"

Holden stayed silent and played with her hair. It wasn't a serious suggestion. They both knew there was no going back to the people they used to be. Him the XO and her the chief engineer on an ice hauler that no one in the universe cared about unless it was late for a delivery. Anonymous people living anonymous lives. Would anyone even need Pur'N'Kleen anymore, with a thousand new worlds full of water and air?

"You going to be okay without me down there?" Naomi said.

The Belter colonists from Ganymede had spent months on the *Barbapiccola* prepping for landing on Ilus. Loading up on bone and muscle growth hormones, working out under a full g until their bodies would be able to handle the slightly heavier-than-Earth gravity of the planet. Naomi didn't have the time or inclination to radically alter her physiology for this one job. Holden had argued that she would have then been able to come to Earth with him after. She replied that she was never going to Earth, no matter what. They'd left it at that, but it was still a sore spot for him.

"No, I won't," he said, deciding not to revisit the argument. "But there it is."

"Amos will look after you."

"Great," Holden said. "I'll land in the middle of the tensest situation in *two* solar systems, and instead of the smartest person I know, I'll bring the guy most likely to get in a bar fight."

"You might need that," she said, her fingers tracing some of the scars he'd picked up over the last couple years. She stopped at a dark spot on his stomach. "You still taking your cancer meds?"

"Every day." *For the rest of my life*, he didn't add.

"Have their doctor look at this after you land."

"Okay."

"They're using you," she said as if they'd been talking about it all along.

"I know."

"They know this is all going to go wrong. There's no solution that doesn't leave someone angry and out in the cold. That's why they're sending you. You're an easy scapegoat. They hired you because you won't hide anything, but that's the same thing that makes you easy to blame for the inevitable failure of these talks."

"If I thought it was inevitable I wouldn't have taken the job," Holden said. "And I know why they hired me for this. It's not because I'm the most qualified. But I'm not quite the idiot they think I am. I think I've learned a few new tricks."

Naomi reached up and pulled a hair out of his temple. Before he could say "ouch" she held it up in front of him. It was the gray of damp ashes.

"Old dog," she said.

The flight to Ilus was grueling in more ways than just the long periods at high g. Every time the *Rocinante* dropped to a tolerable rate of acceleration for meals and maintenance, Holden would have dozens of messages waiting to be viewed and responded to. The captain of the *Edward Israel* became increasingly forceful in his demands for Holden to issue threats to the captain of the *Barbapiccola*. The colonists and their Belter compatriots in orbit were increasingly demanding that the *Barbapiccola* be released from lockdown. Both sides accused the other of escalating the conflict, though in Holden's opinion the fact that only the colonists had so far shed blood lessened their claim in that regard.

Their argument that only the sale of their lithium ore could make them a viable colony, and that the blockade of the shipment was effectively starving them out, was, however, a compelling one. RCE continued to insist that since they had the UN charter, the mining rights and the load of lithium in orbit were theirs.

"A thousand new worlds to explore, and we're still fighting over resources," Holden said to no one after a particularly long and angry message from the RCE legal counsel on the *Israel*.

Alex, who was lounging at the ops station nearby, answered

anyway. "Well, I guess lithium is like real estate. Nobody's makin' any more of it."

"You did hear the part about a thousand new worlds, right?"

"Maybe some of 'em have more lithium, but maybe they don't. And this one definitely does. People used to think gold was worth fightin' over, and that shit gets made by every supernova, which means pretty much every planet around a G2 star will have some. Stars burn through lithium as fast as they make it. All the *available* ore got made at the big bang, and we're not doin' another one of those. Now *that's* scarcity, friend."

Holden sighed and aimed an air vent at his face. The cool breeze from the recyclers made his scalp tingle. The ship wasn't hot. The sweat had to be coming from stress.

"We're astonishingly shortsighted."

"Just you and me?" Alex said, exaggerating his drawl to make a joke of it.

"A vast new frontier has opened up for us. We have the chance to create a new society, with untold riches beyond every gate. But *this* world has treasure, so instead of figuring out the right way to divide up the damned galaxy, we'll fight over the first crumbs we find."

Alex nodded, but didn't reply.

"I feel like I need to be there right now," Holden continued after a moment. "I'm worried by the time we land everyone will be so locked into their positions that we won't be able to help."

"Huh," Alex said, then laughed. "You think we're going there to help?"

"I think I am. I'll be down in engineering if anyone needs me."

"One hour to burn," Alex replied to his back.

Holden kicked the deck hatch release and it slid open with a hiss. He climbed down the ladder past the crew decks to the machine shop, where Amos was taking apart something complex-looking on one of the benches. Holden nodded to him and kicked open the final hatch into the reactor room. Amos shot him a questioning look, but Holden just shook his head and the mechanic turned back to his work with a shrug.

When the hatch slid closed above him, the reactor room flashed with blue light. Holden slid down the ladder to the deck, then leaned back against the wall.

"Hey," Miller said, coming around the reactor that dominated the center of the room as though he'd been standing on the other side of it waiting for Holden to arrive.

"We need to talk," Holden replied.

"That's my line." The detective gave him a sad, basset-hound smile.

"We're doing what you wanted. We've come through a ring into one of the other systems. You'll get to, I assume, ride me to the planet and take your look around."

Miller nodded, but didn't speak. *How much of what I'm about to say does he already know? How predictive is the brain model they've made of me?* Holden decided wondering that was the path to madness.

"I need to know two things," Holden said, "or this trip ends right now."

"Okay," Miller said with a palms-up, Belter version of a shrug.

"First, how are you following me around? You first showed up on this ship after Ganymede, and you've been everywhere I go ever since. Am I infected? Is that how you stay with me? I've gone through two gates without ditching you, so either you're inside my head or you're a galaxy-wide phenomenon. Which is it?"

"Yeah," Miller said, then took off his hat and rubbed his short hair. "Wrong on both counts. First answer is, I live here. During the Ganymede incident, which is a stupid name for it, by the way, the protomolecule put a local node inside this ship."

"Wait. There's protomolecule stuff in the *Roci*?" Holden said, fighting down the surge of panic. If Miller wanted to hurt him and had the means to do so, it would already have happened.

"Yeah," Miller said with a shrug, like it wasn't a big deal. "You had a visitor, remember?"

"You mean I had a half-human monster," Holden said, "that almost killed Amos and me. And that we vaporized in our drive trail."

"Yeah, that'd be him. To be fair, he wasn't exactly running a coherent program, that one. But he had enough of the old instructions left that he placed some material on the ship. Not much, and not what you'd call live culture. Just enough to keep a connection between the Ring Station's processing power and your ship."

"You infected the *Roci*?" Holden said, fear and rage briefly warring in his gut.

"Don't know I'd use that verb, but all right. If you want. It's what lets me follow you around," Miller said, then frowned. "What was the other thing?"

"I don't know if I'm done with *this* thing," Holden said.

"You're safe. We need you."

"And when you don't?"

"Then no one's safe," Miller said, his eerie blue eyes flashing. "So stop obsessing. Second thing?"

Holden sat down on the deck. He hadn't wanted to ask how Miller was in his head, because he was terrified the answer would be that he was infected. The fact that he wasn't, but his ship was, was both a relief and a new source of fear.

"What will we find down on Ilus? What are you looking for?"

"Same thing as always. Who done it," Miller said. "After all, something killed off the civilization that built all this."

"And how will we know when we've found it?"

"Oh," Miller said, his grin vanishing. He leaned toward Holden, the smell of acetate and copper filling the air or else only his senses. "We'll know."

Chapter Eight: Elvi

The sandstorms tended to start in the late afternoon and last until a little after sundown. They began as a softening of the western horizon. Then the little plant analogs in the plain behind her hut would fold their photosynthetic surfaces into tight puckers like tiny green mouths that had tasted lemon, and twenty minutes later the town and the ruins and the sky would all disappear in a wave of dry sand.

Elvi sat at her desk, Felcia at the foot of the bed, and Fayez with his back against the headboard.

Felcia had become a regular visitor, more often than not to talk with Elvi or Fayez or Sudyam. Elvi liked having her around. It made the division between the township and the RCE teams seem...not less real, but less terrible. Permeable.

Today, though, felt different. Felcia seemed more tightly wound than usual. Maybe it was the fact that the UN mediator's ship was getting close. Maybe it was the weather.

"So, our solar system only has one tree of life," Elvi said, moving her hands in the air as if to conjure it up. "It started once, and everything we've ever found shares that ancestry. But we don't know why."

"Why we all share?" Felcia asked.

"Why it didn't happen twice," Elvi said. "Only one kind of Schrödinger crystal. One codon map. Why? If all the materials were there for amino acids to form and connect and interact, why wasn't there one schema that started in one tide pool, and then another someplace else, and another and another? Why did life arise just the one time?"

"So what's the answer?" Felcia asked.

Elvi's let her hands wilt a little. A particularly strong gust drove a wave of hard grit against the side of the hut. "Which answer?"

"Why it only happened once?"

"Oh. I don't know. It's a mystery."

"Same reason there's only one tool-using hominid left. The ones that still exist killed all the competition," Fayez said.

"That's speculation," Elvi said. "Nothing in the fossil record indicates that there was more than the one beginning of life on Earth. We don't get to just make things up because they sound good."

"Elvi is very comfortable with mysteries," Fayez said to Felcia with a wink. "It's why she has a hard time relating with those of us who feel anxious with our ignorance."

"Well, you can't know everything," Elvi said, making it a joke to hide a tinge of discomfort.

"God knows I can't. Especially not on this planet," Fayez said. "There was no point sending a geologist here."

"I'm sure you're doing fine," Elvi said.

"Me? Yes, I'm wonderful. It's the planet's fault. It's got no geology. It's all manufactured."

"How do you mean?" Felcia asked.

Fayez spread his hands as if he were presenting her with the whole world. "Geology is about studying natural patterns. Nothing here's natural. The whole planet was machined. The lithium ore you people are mining? No natural processes exist that would make it as pure as what you're pulling out of the ground. It can't happen. So apparently, whatever built the gates also had something around here somewhere that concentrated lithium in this one spot."

"That's amazing, though," Elvi said.

"If you're into industrial remediation. Which I'm not. And the southern plains? You know how much they vary? They don't. The underlying plate is *literally* as flat as a pane of glass. Somewhere about fifty klicks south of here, there's some kind of tectonic Zamboni machine about which I am qualified to say absolutely nothing. Those tunnel complexes? Yeah, they're some kind of old planetary *transport* system. And yet here I am—"

"I need a letter of recommendation," Felcia blurted, then looked down at her hands, blushing. Elvi and Fayez exchanged a glance. The wind howled and muttered.

"For what?" Elvi asked gently.

"I'm going to apply for university," the girl said. She spoke quickly, like the words were all under pressure, and then more slowly until at last she trailed away. "Mother thinks I'll probably get in. I've been talking with the Hadrian Institute on Luna, and Mother arranged that I can get back to Pallas when the *Barbapiccola* takes the ore, and then take passage on my own from there, only the application needs a letter of recommendation, and I can't ask anyone in the town because we haven't told Daddy, and..."

"Oh," Elvi said. "Well. I don't know. I mean, I've never seen your academic work—"

"Seriously?" Fayez said with a snort. "Elvi, it's a letter of recommendation. You're not under oath for it. Cut the kid a break."

"Well, I just thought it would be better if I could actually say something I know about."

"When I went to lower university, I wrote my own letters of recommendation. Two of them came from people I made up. No one checks."

Elvi's jaw dropped a centimeter. "Really?"

"You are an amazing woman, Elvi, but I don't know how you survive in the wild." Fayez turned to Felcia. "If she won't, I will. You'll have it by morning, okay?"

"I don't know how I can repay you," Felcia said, but she already looked calmer.

Fayez waved the comment away. "Your undying gratitude is thanks enough. What's your field of study going to be?"

For the next hour, Felcia talked about her mother's medical career, and her dead brother's immune disorder, and intracellular signaling regulation. Elvi began to realize that she'd unconsciously thought of the girl as younger than she really was. She had the long, slightly gangly build and comparatively large head of a Belter, and somewhere in Elvi's mind, she'd mistaken it for youth. Felcia would have fit right in at the commons of lower university. The light shifted from beige to deep brown to a burnt umber, and then darkness. The wind calmed. When Elvi opened her door, two centimeters of fine dust covered the walkway and the stars glimmered in the sky. The air smelled like fresh-turned earth. Some sort of actinomycete analog, Elvi thought. Maybe one that was actually carried by the wind. Or maybe something else. Something stranger.

Felcia headed back for the town, Fayez for his own hut. As far as she could tell, Fayez was one of maybe two or three other people on the science team who was still sleeping alone. Sudyam and Tolerson were the latest pairing. Laberge and Maravalis had just broken off the relationship they'd started on the journey out, and each of them was already involved with someone else.

Sex wasn't a strange thing among the scientific teams. That it was unprofessional behavior was set in balance against the fact that—especially on a years-long field expedition like this—the pool of potential mates was both very restricted and generally fairly high-value. People were people. If she felt any jealousy at all, it wasn't for any of the particular relationships, but for intimacy itself. It would be nice to have someone to walk with in the darkness after the storm. Someone to wake up with in the morning. She wondered what the sexual politics were among the families of First Landing. If RCE had thought to send a social science team, it might have made a good paper.

Ahead of her and to the right, the alien ruins stood against the horizon, hardly more than a deeper darkness. Only a light was moving in them. It was small and faint. Less than a star, and only visible at all because it was moving. Someone was in the ruins again. Contaminating the site. She knew intellectually that she was letting herself be angry about it because it was better than feeling lonesome or guilty, but that didn't keep the rage from feeling real. She turned back to her hut, her lips pressed together. She scooped up a flashlight, checked the battery charge, and stalked out toward the ruins, the thin blue circle of light bobbing ahead of her and illuminating her way. The fine dust shifted under her feet like snow, and her thighs ached from the speed of her hike.

As she neared the ruins, she thought she saw a dim light heading the other way. Back toward the town. But when she called after it, no one answered. She stood in the darkness for almost a minute feeling first unsure of herself, then embarrassed, then angry at feeling embarrassed.

A path led into the ruins that even the recent dustfall couldn't conceal. Tracks as wide as a wagon where wheels had gone over the land often enough to leave ruts. Elvi shook her head and followed the path up, twisting around a high shoulder of land and into the huge alien structures.

Inside, the beam of her flashlight caught the walls and surfaces, sending off glittering reflections that seemed to shift whether she did or not. Where there was shelter from the wind, there were footprints. Lots of them. It wasn't just someone from town exploring on their own. They were treating the ruins like some sort of clubhouse. Any samples the science team took from the soil here would already be compromised. The microorganisms, a mixture of known and unknown and whatever emerged when the two encountered each other in a totally uncontrolled environment. That the same was true of the whole township seemed insignificant. These were alien structures. They'd been built by a vast, vanished civilization about which humanity still knew almost nothing. It wasn't some kind of *treehouse*.

"Hello?" she shouted. "Is anyone in here?"

Nothing answered her. Not even the wind. Shaking her head, she stalked deeper into the shadows. If anyone was here, she'd give them the talk she'd meant to give before. She would make them understand the issues, even if it took hectoring them all night.

The walls around her rose at strange and unsettling angles from the ground, organic and also not, like a machine that was built to pass for the product of nature. Arches rose, looking out over the bare, dark land. The deeper Elvi went, the more there seemed to be, until she had the illusion that the ruins were larger inside than out.

She was about to give up and turn back home when she saw something square. Simply being rectilinear made it stand out. The boxes were plastic and ceramic, functional gray where they weren't the bright red and yellow of warning labels. DANGER HIGH EXPLOSIVE. DO NOT STORE NEAR HEAT OR CLASS THREE RADIATION SOURCES.

"Oh no," Elvi said to herself. "Oh *hell* no."

"Doctor Okoye," Reeve said. "I'm hearing you tell me that you found explosives hidden outside of the town."

"Yes," Elvi said. "Of course that's what you're hearing me say."

"And that there is evidence of several people having been to this clandestine site."

They were sitting in Reeve's office now. The light from his lamp shone warm and soft, and his rough pants and untucked shirt suggested she'd rousted him out of bed. It felt like the middle of the night, though the extended rotational period meant the darkness would be stretching on for almost another ten hours.

"Yes," she said.

"All right," Reeve said. "It's all right. This is a good thing. I need you to tell me how to find this place."

"Yes. Of course. I'll take you."

"No, I need you to stay right here. Not back to your hut. Not out to the ruins. I need you right here where it's safe. You understand?"

"There was someone out there. I saw the light, and that's why I went. What if they'd still been there?"

"We don't have to worry about that, because it didn't happen," Reeve said in a carefully reassuring tone of voice that meant *You'd be dead*. Elvi dropped her head into her hands. "Can you give me directions?"

She did her best, her voice trembling. Reeve constructed a map on his hand terminal, and she was fairly sure it was accurate. Her mind seemed to be shifting on her a little, though.

"All right," Reeve said. "I'm going to have you stay here for a little while."

"But my work is all back at the hut."

The security man put a reassuring hand on her shoulder, but his gaze was already focused inward, planning some next step that didn't include her.

"We're going to see you're safe first," he said. "Everything else will come after that."

For the next hour, she sat in the little room or paced. The voices of Reeve and his security team filtered in through the wall, the tones serious and businesslike. And then there were fewer of them.

A young woman came to get her. Elvi had seen her before, but didn't know her name. It seemed wrong that they could have spent almost two years traveling out here together, and Elvi still didn't know her. It should mean something about populations and how they mixed. And how they didn't.

"Do you need anything, Doctor Okoye?"

"I don't know where to sleep," Elvi said, and her words seemed thin. Fragile.

"I've got a bunk ready," the girl said. "Please come with me."

The rooms were empty. The others gone out into the alien darkness to face a terribly human threat. The girl leading her to the bunk had a sidearm strapped to her belt. Elvi glanced out the front window as they passed. The street was the same one she'd walked down the day before, and it was also wholly changed. A sense of threat hung over everything like the promise of a storm coming. Like the haze on the horizon. She saw Felcia's brother walking down the street, not looking at her or anything else. Her fear was cold and deep.

Chapter Nine: Basia

Basia had volunteered for the night shift at the mine. Fewer people to hide from. Less open sky to make him jittery. The work, as backbreaking as it was, was a relief. The fabricator they'd brought down from the *Barbapiccola* was building tracks and carts as fast as they could load raw material into it. His team was trying to keep up with its output by assembling the rail system that would move ore from the pit to the sifters to the silos. There, it would wait for the *Barbapiccola*'s shuttle to take it up into orbit. Everything they'd mined so far had been moved with wheelbarrows by hand. A motorized cart system would increase production by an order of magnitude.

So Basia and his team worked the metal rails, pulling them out of the fabricator gleaming and new in the harsh white lights. They loaded them on handcarts and dragged them into the mining pit. Then unloaded them by hand and welded them into the growing railway system. It was the kind of physical labor people had mostly stopped doing in their mechanized age. And the process of welding inside an atmosphere was totally unlike welding in vacuum, so he had a new skill set to develop. The combination of mental challenge and physical toil left him exhausted. His world narrowed to the next task, the ache in his hands, and the distant promise of sleep. There was no time to dwell on other things.

Like being a murderer. Like the corporate security forces sniffing around for him and Coop and the others. Like the guilt he felt every time Lucia lied to them and said she didn't know anything that would help.

Later, when he sat in the crew hut with his muscles twitching and cramping with fatigue, trying to sleep with the daylight streaming in through the windows, then he could revisit the death of the shuttle over and over again. Think about what he could have done to disable the explosives faster than he did. How he could have tackled Coop, taken the radio away from him. If his mood was especially bad, he would think about how if he'd just listened to his wife, none of it would have happened in the first place. On those days he felt such shame that he hated her a little for it. Then hated himself for blaming her. The pillow he pressed to his eyes kept the sunlight out, but not the images of the shuttle exploding over and over again, screaming like a dying beast as it went down.

But during the night, while he worked, he had some measure of peace.

So when Coop appeared at the work site, sauntering into the pit like he didn't have a care in the world, Basia almost hit him in the face.

"Hey, mate," Coop said. Basia dropped his hammer, shoulders slumping.

"Hey," he said.

"So we got a thing," Coop continued, throwing one companionable arm around Basia's shoulders. "Need mi primero on it."

That couldn't be good. "What thing?"

Coop guided him away from the work site, smiling and nodding at the few other night-shift crew they passed. Just two chums out for a walk and a conversation. When they were out of earshot of everyone, he said, "Seen that RCE girl going up to the ruins. Sent Jacek to check on it."

"Sent *Jacek*," Basia echoed. Coop nodded.

"Good kid. Reliable."

Basia stopped, pulling his arm away. "Don't—" *Involve my son in this.* Before he could get the words out, Coop waved it off and kept talking.

"Está important." Coop stepped close, voice lowering. "She went up to the ruins, then went straight to the RCE goons. Jacek says they're planning to wait for us up there. Catch the resistance red-handed."

"Then we don't go back," Basia said. It seemed so simple. No reason to panic.

"You crazy, primo? Toda alles been up there. Trace evidence up the ass. They wait long enough, they get bored and bring a real crime scene team down, we all done. All of us, y veh unless you stopped shedding skin when you were there."

"Then what?"

"We go up first. A flare on that blasting powder, boom. No more evidence."

"When?"

Coop laughed. "What you think? Next week some time? *Now*, coyo. Got to go now. Mediator's landing in hours-not-days. Don't want this to be what he sees when he steps off the ship, do you? You a team lead, you can take one of the carts. We got to get that shit and get gone." Coop snapped his fingers impatiently. "Jetzt."

Coop spoke about insanity like blowing up their stash of mining explosives with such an air of self-assurance and certainty, Basia found it hard to argue. Sure, blowing up the alien ruins was crazy. But Coop was right. If they found the explosives and traced them back to Basia, they'd know. He didn't want to, but he had to. So he would.

"Okay," he said and walked toward the cart charging station. Only one was left, and because the universe was a cruel and mocking place, it was the same one he'd been driving the night of the bombing. It still had the dents and scorch marks it had picked up that night. The scorch marks everyone in the colony was careful not to ask about.

Coop waited impatiently for him to unlock it and back it out of the stall, then hopped in and started tapping out a fast drumbeat on the plastic dashboard. "Let's go let's go let's go."

Basia went.

Halfway to the alien ruins, they came across four more of Coop's inner circle. Pete and Scotty and Cate and Ibrahim. No Zadie. Her little boy had come down with a nasty eye infection, and she wasn't around much lately. Cate had a duffel bag she threw into the back of the cart with a metallic thump, then the four of them climbed in after it.

"That the stuff?" Coop asked, and Cate nodded and slapped the side of the cart to let Basia know he could drive. Basia didn't ask what the stuff was. Too late to start questioning.

The ruins looked as dark and deserted as they ever did, but Coop made Basia drive the long way round to come at the site from the side opposite the town. "Just to be safe," he said.

When Cate pulled open the duffel, Basia wasn't surprised to see it filled with guns. The *Barbapiccola* hadn't been a warship. They hadn't left Ganymede with a great store of weapons, but what there was had come down to the surface when First Landing was begun. This looked like most of them. Cate pulled out a shotgun and started loading fat plastic shells into it. She was a tall, rawboned woman with a wide jaw and a permanent frown line between her eyes. She looked natural holding a gun. Like a soldier. When Basia picked one up, a short-barreled automatic pistol of some kind, he felt like a child playing dress-up.

"You'll need this, killer," Ibrahim said and tossed him a narrow metallic object. It took Basia several seconds to realize it was the magazine for his pistol. It only took two tries to slide it in the correct way. Blow the explosives. Clear the site. Destroy the evidence. That had never really been the plan, and somewhere in his gut, he'd known.

While the rest of the group finished readying their weapons, Basia stood a few meters from the cart, staring up at the night sky. One of the points of light was the drive tail of the *Rocinante*, the ship Jim Holden was flying in on. The mediator. The one who was supposed to keep the colonists and RCE people from killing each other. He wondered how far out Holden was. He wondered if the man knew he was already too late. Too late for the second time. Holden had been too late on Ganymede too.

Basia's son Katoa hadn't been the only one who was sick. Whose immune system had faltered and failed under the thousand different stressors of life outside a gravity well. There had been a group of them who'd come to Doctor Strickland. The man who was supposed to know the answers. Katoa, Tobias, Annamarie, Mei. Mei, who had lived. Who James Holden had rescued from the labs on Io.

Holden had been there when they found Katoa too. Basia had never met the man. Had only ever seen him on news broadcasts. But Mei's father had been a friend. He'd sent a message telling Basia what had happened, and that he'd been with Holden when they found the boy's body.

Why one and not the other? Praxidike's Mei, but not his Katoa. Why did some people die and others live? Where was the justice in it? The stars he looked up at didn't have any answers for him.

Holden had been too late to stop what was happening on Ilus right now before anyone had ever set foot on it. Before the rings opened. Before Venus bloomed. If Katoa were still alive, Basia wouldn't have come here, and if he had, he wouldn't have stayed.

It was a strange thought. Surreal. Basia tried to picture the man he'd be in that other timeline, and couldn't. He looked down at the ugly black gun in his hand. *I wouldn't be doing this.*

"Game's on," someone said. Basia turned around. It was Coop. "Get back in it, coyo."

"Dui," Basia said, and took a deep breath. The night air was cold and crisp and tasted vaguely of dirt from that afternoon's dust storm. "Dui."

"Follow on," Coop said, then headed off to the ruins at a slow trot. Cate and Ibrahim and Pete and Scotty followed, clutching their guns in what they probably thought was a military style. Basia carried his pistol by the barrel, worried about getting his fingers anywhere near the trigger.

They entered the massive alien structure through one of the many openings in its side. Windows? Doors? No aliens left to say. Inside, the light coming off their flashlights and work lamps reflected off the smooth, strangely angled walls. The material looked like stone, was smooth as glass, and turned from black to a rosy pink where the light hit it. Basia trailed his fingers along it.

Coop waved for them to stop, and then ducked down and crab-walked over to a windowlike opening in one wall. He peeked over and dropped back down, motioning for the group to join him. Basia hunkered down with the rest.

"See?" Coop whispered, pointing at the next room beyond the window. "Knew they'd set up there."

Cate popped up for a second to look, then crouched down again with a nod. "I see five. Reeve, the boss, and four of his goons. Sidearms and stun guns. They're all looking the wrong way."

"Too easy, boss," Scotty whispered with a grin, and clicked off the safety on his rifle. Cate slid open the breech on her shotgun just far enough to make sure there was a shell loaded. Coop held up his big automatic pistol in one hand and yanked back the slide. Then on his other hand he raised three fingers and started silently counting down.

Basia looked at each of them in turn. They looked flushed and excited. All except Pete, who stared back at Basia, his skin looking a sickly green in the pale light, and his head shaking back and forth in a silent negation. Basia could practically hear the man thinking, *I don't want to do this.*

Something shifted in Basia's mind, and the world seemed to snap into focus with an almost physical sensation. He'd been following Coop in a daze since the moment the man showed up at the work site. And now they were about to shoot a bunch of RCE security people.

"Wait," he said. Coop answered by standing up, pointing his pistol into the next room, and firing.

Basia's mind stuttered. Time skipped.

Coop, yelling obscenities and firing his pistol over and over into the next room. Basia is lying on his back on the floor looking up as shell casings tumble out of Coop's gun and bounce across the ground next to him. They appear to be moving so slow that Basia can read the manufacturer's stamp. TruFire 7.5mm they say.

Skip.

He is standing next to Cate. He has no memory of getting up. She is firing her shotgun, and the sound of it going off in the tight space is deafening. He wonders if he will suffer permanent hearing loss. In the next room, three men and two women in RCE security uniforms are scrambling to take cover, or draw weapons, or return fire. They have looks of panic on their faces. They shout to each other as they move. He doesn't recognize any of the words. One of them fires a pistol, and a bullet slams into the wall near Cate. A piece of the bullet or a piece of the wall punches a small hole in her cheek. She continues to fire as if the injury is beneath notice.

Skip.

An RCE security woman clutches at her chest as blood fountains out of it. Her face is pale and terrified. He is just a meter away from her, standing next to Scotty. Scotty shoots her again, this time in the neck. She falls backward in slow motion, hands reaching up to the wound but going limp and lifeless halfway there, and she just looks like she's shrugging.

Skip.

He stands by himself in a corridor. He doesn't know where it is or how he got there. He hears gunfire behind him, and screams. An RCE security man is a few meters ahead of him, holding a stun gun. The man has dark skin and bright green eyes, wide with fear. Basia suddenly remembers that the man's name is Zeb, though he can't remember why he knows that. Zeb throws the stun gun at him and reaches for the pistol he still has in a holster on his hip. The stun gun bounces off Basia's head, opening up a three-centimeter gash that begins bleeding heavily, but he doesn't feel it. He sees Zeb pulling his pistol, and without thinking about it he points his own gun at him. He's surprised to see that he's holding it correctly, by the handle, with his finger on the trigger. He doesn't remember doing that. He pulls the trigger. Nothing happens. He's about to pull it a second time when there is a loud bang from behind him, and Zeb begins to fall, blood gushing from his forehead. He waits for the blackout.

There was no skipping. No respite. No escape.

"Good job," Coop said behind him. "That one almost got away."

Basia turned slowly, still in a dream. A fugue. A dissociative state. The impulse to lift his hand one more time, to let the violence carry him just one step farther and shoot Coop almost lifted his arm. Almost, but not quite. Zeb bled out on the floor. The sounds of gunfire stopped.

Behind him, the rest of his group whooped and hollered in happy and excited voices. Basia looked at his gun, remembering how they work in action videos. You put the magazine with the bullets in it in the gun, and then you have to put a bullet in the chamber. He remembered Cate pulling back the breech on her shotgun. Coop pulling back the slide on his automatic. Basia's gun wouldn't have fired no matter how many times he pulled the trigger.

Zeb stopped bleeding. *That was almost me,* Basia thought, but the thought had no emotional content yet. No weight. It was like a puff of acrid smoke passing through his mind, and then gone again.

"Help us drag these bodies out back, primo," Coop said, patting him on the back. "Zadie's washing the place down with corrosives and digestive enzymes, kill the evidence, but they ain't gonna eat the big chunks, eh?"

Basia helped. It took them several hours to bury the corpses of the five women and men in the hard-packed dirt behind the alien ruins. Coop assured them that the next dust storm would remove all signs that anyone had dug there. The RCE people would just disappear without a trace.

Scotty and Pete dragged the rest of their explosives out of the ruins and loaded them on the cart. Then they walked back to town with Cate and Ibrahim. Cate carried her duffel of guns over one shoulder. Basia's pistol was in it again, never having been fired.

"We had to do this," Coop said once they'd left. Basia didn't know if he was telling Basia that or himself. Basia nodded anyway.

"You set this up. You knew you were going to kill them, and you made me part of it."

Coop gave him a Belter shrug and a cruel smile. "You knew that coming out, coyo. You maybe pretended not to, but you knew."

"Never again," Basia said. "And if anyone in my family is hurt because of this, I will kill you myself."

He drove back to the mine, then walked to his house. The sun was just coming up when he finally stumbled into his tiny bathroom. The man in the mirror didn't look like a killer, but his hands were covered with blood. He started trying to wash them off.

Chapter Ten: Havelock

About five hours before—when Havelock had been halfway through his ten-hour shift—a man dressed in an orange-and-purple suit so ugly it approached violence sat down on a couch in a video studio on Mars. Havelock floated against his restraints, considering him. Strapping in was second nature now, even though it felt a little silly. The orbital space around New Terra was essentially empty, and the chance of a sudden acceleration was almost nil. It was just a habit. On the little monitor set into the cabin wall, the young man shook the feed host's hand and smiled at the camera.

It's been a while since you came by, Mister Curvelo," the host said. "Thank you so much for coming back."

"Good to be here, Monica," the man said, nodding like he'd been caught at something. "Good to be back."

"So I got a chance to play the new game, and I have to say it seems like a *real* departure from your previous work."

"Yeah," the man said shortly. His jaw was tight.

"There's been a certain amount of controversy," the host said. Her smile was a little sharper. "You want to talk about that?"

It was physically impossible for Havelock to sink back into his couch, but psychologically it was a snap.

"Monica, look," the man in the ugly suit said, "what we're exploring here are the *consequences* of violence. Everybody's looking at that first section, and they don't think about how everything comes after."

Havelock's hand terminal chimed. He muted the newsfeed and took the connection.

"Havelock," Murtry said, "I have a call I need you to take."

His voice was so calm and controlled, Havelock felt his breath go shallow. It was the sound of trouble, and his mind clutched at the first fear that came. The *Rocinante* and Jim Holden, the UN mediator, was about ten hours from the end of its deceleration burn. Almost here. If something had gone wrong with it…

"Something happened downstairs," Murtry said. "I've got Cassie on the horn, and I need you to keep her from melting down while I talk to the captain."

"Is it bad?"

"Yeah. Take the call. Be the calm one. You can do that?"

"Sure, boss," Havelock said. "Cool as November, smooth as China silk."

"Good man."

The picture froze for a fraction of a second, and then Cassie was looking out at him. For a year and a half, they'd been on the ship together, part of the same team, familiar if not intimate. He'd been aware vaguely when she'd struck up a romance with Aragão and then when they'd broken it off. He thought of her as a friend because he didn't think about her much at all.

In the image, her skin had an ashy color, and her eyes were lined with red.

"Cassie," Havelock said, his voice falling into the comforting register he'd trained for in the hostage negotiation workshop he'd taken after the Ceres riots. "Hear things are a little rough down there."

Cassie's laugh shifted the camera, shaking her on the screen like an earthquake. She looked away, and then back.

"They're gone," she said. In the pause afterward, her gaze shifted like she was looking for something. More words to say, maybe. "They're gone."

"Okay," he said. A thousand different questions pressed forward, wanting to be asked. *What happened? Who's missing? What happened?* But Murtry hadn't asked him to find out, and Cassie didn't need an interrogator. "Murtry's talking to the captain."

"I know," Cassie said. "We had a lead. We found a hideout. Reeve took them out. I stayed back with the witness."

"Is the witness there?"

"She's sleeping now," Cassie said. "I'm a security systems consultant, Havelock. I'm supposed to be figuring out optimal shift schedules and building the surveillance network. I don't shoot people. That's not my fucking pay grade."

Havelock smiled, and Cassie smiled with him, a tear leaking out the side of her eye. For a moment they were both laughing, the horror and the fear transforming into something like exasperation. Something a little bit safer.

"I'm scared as hell," Cassie said. "If they come for me too, I won't be able to stop them. I've got the office locked down, but they could cut through the walls. They could blow the place up. I don't know why we thought it was a good idea to be down here at all. After they blew the heavy shuttle, we should have hauled our butts back up the well and stayed there. We should have dropped rocks on them from fucking orbit."

"The thing now is keeping you and the witness safe."

"And how are you going to do that?" Cassie asked. Her voice was a challenge, but one that wanted to be answered. *You can't* and *Tell me that you can* all at the same time.

"We're working on that," Havelock said.

"I don't even have food in here," Cassie said. "It's all at the commissary. I'd kill for a sandwich. I really would. I'd kill for it."

Havelock tried to remember what they'd said in the workshop about talking with people who'd been traumatized. There was a list. Four things. The mnemonic was BEST. He couldn't remember what any of the letters stood for.

"So," he said. "I bet you're pretty freaked out right now."

"I'm not holding it together."

"Yeah, it feels like that, but actually, you're doing good just by not making it worse. That's how people usually get it wrong when things go to hell. Overreact, escalate. All goes pear-shaped. You're holed up and talking to us. Means you've got good instincts for this."

"You're making that shit up," Cassie said. "I'm just this side of going catatonic."

"Stay on this side, and that makes it a win. Seriously, though, you're doing the right thing. Stay cool, and we'll get on top of this. I know it feels like it's all going to hell, but you're going to be all right."

"If I'm not—"

"You will be."

"But if I'm not. *If*, right?"

"Okay," Havelock said. "If."

"Do me a favor. There's a guy back on Europa. Hihiri Tipene. He's a food engineer."

"Okay."

"Tell him I said I was sorry."

She thinks she's going to die, Havelock thought, *and she may be right*. The bright, coppery taste of fear flooded his mouth. The locals were killing RCE security, and she was the last one standing. He didn't know anything about the state of play down there. For all he knew, there might be three tons of industrial explosive about to turn Cassie into a memory. Any moment, she could die, and he could watch her die and not be able to do anything about it.

"You're going to tell him yourself," he said gently. "And after this, it won't even be scary."

"I don't know. You've never met Hihiri. Promise me?"

"Sure," Havelock said. "I've got your back on this one."

Cassie nodded. Another tear streaked down her cheek. He didn't feel like he was doing a great job of keeping her from meltdown.

A tiny inset window appeared on the feed. Murtry's security override.

"Hey there, Cass," Murtry said. "I've talked to Captain Marwick, and we're dropping a team to you. It's going to take us a couple hours, though. Your job is to keep that civilian safe."

Cassie's voice trembled when she spoke, but it didn't break. "There are forty of our people on the planet and two hundred of *them*. I'm one person. I can't protect everyone."

"You don't have to," Murtry said. "I've sent the lockdown notice. I'm coordinating the science teams. That's on me. Your job is Doctor Okoye. You just keep her breathing until we're down there, okay?"

"Yessir."

"All right," Murtry said. "Two hours. You can do this, Cass."

"Yessir."

"Havelock, we're doing a briefing in the security office right now. If you could pop by?"

"On my way," Havelock said. He undid his straps, pulled himself out of his couch, and launched for the hallway. The *Edward Israel* had corridors that were built as elongated octagons, like something his grandfather would have traveled in. The straps and toeholds along the walls had no directionality. He moved quickly down the hall, his brain flipping from telling him that he was climbing up a massive steel-and-ceramic well to falling headlong down it to—oddly—crawling upside down, as if he were on the ceiling of a drainage pipe. Belters, he'd been told, had a natural sense of themselves divorced from set ideas of up and down, but he'd only heard that from Belters, and always in the context of how they were better than him. Maybe it was true, maybe it was exaggeration. Either way, by the time he pulled himself into the security office, he felt a little woozy, and missed the false gravity of thrust.

Ten people clung to the walls, all oriented the same way. Men and women with radically different facial structures and skin tones, and all with the same expression. It was almost eerie. Murtry had broken out the riot gear, and the blue-gray body armor with the high neck-protecting collars made them all seem like huge, human-shaped insects. Even Murtry was wearing it, so apparently he was going on the drop too.

"—I have left," Murtry was saying from his place at the front of the room. "And you're *all* I have left. The cavalry's not going to come in and save our butts. We are the cavalry, and that means I have already lost everyone I'm going to lose. We are the security team for this whole planet, right here in this room. And we can do it, but not if we're making sacrifices. While we're down there, if you feel threatened, you do whatever it takes to protect yourself and your team."

"Sir?"

"Okmi?"

"Does that mean we have authorization for lethal response?"

"That means you have authorization for *preemptive* lethal response," Murtry said, then waited a moment for the words to sink in. Havelock sighed. It was ugly, but there wasn't a choice. If the heavy shuttle had been just a crime, they could have dealt with it like police. But the locals hadn't stopped there, and now more RCE people were missing or dead. So now it was more like a war.

Well. At least they'd tried the peaceful way first. Not that the Belters would give them any credit for it.

"We're dropping in twenty minutes," Murtry said. "It's a long, fast drop, and some of it'll be choppy. I'm bringing us down just east of the Belter camp. Smith and Wei are squad leads. Our first priority is reaching and reinforcing the office down there."

"What about the *Barbapiccola*?" someone asked.

"Screw the *Barbapiccola*! What about the *Rocinante*?"

Murtry lifted his hand, palm out.

"Don't any of you spend your time worrying about what's happening up in orbit or back at home. That's on me, and I'll take care of it. Me and Havelock." Murtry flashed a quick smile at him, and Havelock nodded, almost a little bow. "You have your orders, and you have my trust. Let's get downstairs and get this clusterfuck under control."

The security force broke, bodies moving through the air in a fast, efficient stream toward the hangar and the light shuttles. Havelock felt a thin stab of regret, watching the others head down without him. He remembered something from his childhood, a flash of memory here and gone, about a lame child and the Pied Piper.

Murtry floated through the air toward him, moving against the flow.

"Havelock, good to see you. I'm going to need a minute."

"Yes, sir."

Murtry nodded toward his private office. It was a tiny room, smaller even than a sleeping cabin, with a crash couch on old-style gimbals that arced up and over it. Murtry closed the door behind them.

"So I'm putting you in charge of the ship."

"Thank you, sir."

"I wouldn't go that far. I'm leaving you in a crap position," Murtry said. "We've got a full crew on the *Israel* that are mostly eggheads with their petticoats in a bunch because we're not letting them do science, and the captain's been fighting hard to keep them up here. Now there's trouble, they won't be pushing so hard to go down, but the pressure's got to go someplace. I'm leaving you a skeleton crew to deal with it."

"We'll get it done, sir."

"Good man. The biggest threat we've got on the board is the *Rocinante*. Used to be Martian military before it went OPA. *Israel* is huge, but we're a science ship. If the *Rocinante* knocks us down, we're going down."

"Why would they shoot us down?"

Murtry shrugged. "I think less about why and more about if. So...there's something I need, and it's going to play hell with your shuttle schedules, but I want you to do it anyway."

"Of course."

"We're taking one of the light shuttles for the drop," Murtry said slowly, as if he were thinking it through while he spoke, even though that clearly wasn't the case. "The one that's left? I want you to weaponize it. Take off anything that'd keep its reactor from overloading, and set it with a hardened remote ignition. Lock out all the standard nav controls and put in something that just you and me have access to."

"Captain Marwick too?"

Murtry's smile was an enigma. "Sure, if you want."

"Give me half a day, I'll get it done," Havelock said.

"Good."

"Sir? Who are you thinking we'd be using this against? The Belter camp?"

"We're just buying options, Havelock. I hope not to use it at all," Murtry said. "But if I decide I'm going to, I'll want it fast."

"You'll have it."

"I feel better knowing that," Murtry said, and put his hand on the desk to push off.

"Sir?"

Murtry lifted his eyebrows. Havelock felt a sudden flush of embarrassment, and almost didn't go on. And then he did.

"I know it's a small thing, sir, but when I was on the call, Cassie said she was hungry. I told her we'd bring her a sandwich."

Murtry's expression was empty as stone.

"I was wondering if you could take her a sandwich, sir."

"Might could manage," Murtry said, and Havelock couldn't tell if the man was amused or annoyed. Maybe both.

Havelock floated at his desk. The cells of the brig were all empty. His skeleton crew—the four most junior security staff and a technician they'd borrowed from the ship's maintenance crew—were quietly modifying the one remaining light shuttle. Making the bomb. On his monitors, the shuttle drop and the *Rocinante*'s final deceleration burn, and the internal monitors of the station with Cassie and Doctor Okoye, each had their own window. Havelock watched them all, waiting for the next thing to go wrong. Every minute seemed to stretch. The air recycler hummed and clicked. He chewed his thumbnail.

When the incoming message chime sounded, he started and had to put his hands to the console to keep from drifting off. He shifted to his message queue. The new one came from the RCE corporate offices on Luna, and the subject was listed as POSSIBLE STRATEGIES FOR DEESCALATING CONFLICT ON NEW TERRA: CALL FOR INPUT. The timestamp was five hours ago.

Somewhere out near the ring gates, the radio signals had passed each other, waves of electromagnetism passing through the void with human meanings coded into them. The distance it had taken a year and a half to travel in person, the message had managed in five hours.

Five hours, and still too goddamn slow.

Chapter Eleven: Holden

The *Rocinante* did the last of its deceleration burn on a tail of white fire and dropped into a high orbit around Ilus. Below, the planet looked enough like Earth that the fact that it didn't look like Earth was unsettling. Holden had looked down on alien worlds before. The rust red and white of Mars, the swirls and eddies of Saturn and Jupiter. They were totally unlike Earth's blue and brown and white. But Ilus had open sea and sky with puffs of cloud, all the markers that Holden's brain connected with his home world.

Except that there was only one large continent, and thousands of islands strung across its one giant ocean like brown beads on a necklace. The mix of alien and familiar made his head hurt.

"*Rocinante*," the *Edward Israel* broadcast at them. "Why are you target locking us?"

"Uh..." Holden slapped at the comm panel until he opened a

channel to them. "No, that's just standard range finding, *Israel*. Nothing to worry about."

"Roger that," a not quite convinced voice replied from the other ship.

"Alex," Holden said, switching to the internal channel. "Please stop poking the bear."

"Roger that, Cap," Alex said, exaggerating his drawl and stifling a laugh. "Just lettin' the locals know there's a new sheriff in town."

"Stop it. Give us an hour for the final check and get us dirtside."

"Okey dokey," Alex said. "Long time since I landed one of these."

"Is it going to be a problem?"

"Nope."

Holden climbed out of the ops chair and floated to the crew ladder. A few minutes later he was on the airlock deck with Amos. The mechanic had laid out two suits of their Martian-made light combat armor, a number of rifles and shotguns, and stacks of ammunition and explosives.

"What," Holden said, "is all this?"

"You said to gear up for the drop."

"I meant, like, underwear and toothbrushes."

"Captain," Amos said, almost hiding his impatience. "They're killing each other down there. Half a dozen RCE security vanished into thin air, and a heavy lift shuttle got blown up."

"Yes, and our job is not to escalate that. Put all this shit away. Sidearms only. Bring clothes and sundries for us, any spare medical supplies for the colony. But that's it."

"Later," Amos said, "when you're wishing we had this stuff, I am going to be merciless in my mockery. And then we'll die."

Holden started a snarky reply, then stopped himself. Had anything *ever* gone the way he planned? "Okay, one rifle each, but disassembled and in a duffel. Nothing visible. And light torso armor only. Something we can hide under our clothes."

"Captain," Amos said with mock surprise. "Have you actually *learned* from your past? Is this a new thing you do now?"

"Why do I put up with your shit?"

"Because," Amos said, starting to strip an assault rifle down to its component parts, "I'm the only one on the ship that can keep the coffee maker running."

"I'm off to get underwear and a toothbrush."

The *Rocinante* would have lit the night sky of Ilus during the final part of her deceleration burn. When she landed in a field outside of the colony's ramshackle town, she'd kicked up a dust cloud a kilometer across, and the noise of her descent should have rattled windows twice that far away.

So Holden was a little surprised and disappointed when no one was there to greet them.

He *was* the joint OPA and Earth mediator, personally selected by Chrisjen Avasarala of the UN and Fred Johnson, leader of the OPA as much as the OPA could be led, to oversee the settlement talks. In other places, that would merit a formal greeting by the planetary governor and possibly a marching band. Holden would have settled for a ride into town.

He hefted his two heavy bags and started to trudge toward the settlement. Amos carried three. The third was the one he called his *everything has gone to shit* bag. Holden sincerely hoped they never had to open it.

When they were far enough away, Holden sent the signal to Alex and the *Rocinante* blasted off again, kicking up a massive dust storm for a few seconds.

"You know," Amos said conversationally, "we landed so far from town to avoid blowing dust on the locals, and they couldn't even be bothered to send out a cart to pick us up? Seems ungrateful."

"Yeah. A little annoyed at that myself. Next time I have Alex land right in the damn town square."

Amos gestured with his head at a massive alien structure rising in the distance. It looked like two thin towers of glass twisted together, like a pair of trees growing beside each other.

"So, there's that," he said.

Holden had no reply. It was one thing to read about "alien ruins" on the location report. It was another thing entirely to see a massive construct built by another species towering over the landscape. How old was it? A couple billion years, if Miller could be believed on how long the protomolecule masters had been gone. Had humans ever built anything that would last that long?

"According to the security wonks on the *Israel*, that's where they think their people were massacred," Holden said after they'd walked together for several minutes.

"Oh good," Amos replied. "Somebody got killed there. That's how we claim stuff, you know. This planet is officially ours now."

Other than the admittedly hard-to-ignore alien tower, the rest of the landscape could have been the North American southwest. Hardpan dirt, with small shrublike plants. Small creatures scurried away at their approach. For a few moments they were surrounded by a cloud of biting insects, but after a number of them bit, drank their blood, and dropped dead, the rest seemed to pick up that humans weren't food and lost interest.

The colony itself looked like a shantytown. A ramshackle mix of prefab buildings and lean-tos made out of scrap metal and brick. A few were made of mud, so someone had decided to try using adobe. Something about the idea of humans traveling fifty thousand light-years and then building houses using ten-thousand-year-old technology put a smile on Holden's face. Humans were very strange creatures, but sometimes they were also charming.

A mob had gathered at the center of town. Or, more accurately, at the intersection of the only two dirt roads. Fifty or so colonists were facing off with a dozen people in RCE uniforms. They were shouting at each other, though Holden couldn't make out the words.

Someone on the edge of the crowd noticed them walking into

town and pointed. The arguing died down, and then the entire crowd surged toward Holden and Amos. Holden dropped his bags and waved, smiling. Amos smiled too, though he casually rested his hand on the butt of his pistol.

A tall, stocky woman a few years older than Holden rushed over to him and grabbed his hands. Holden was almost certain she was Carol Chiwewe, but if that were true, she'd changed a lot since the picture in his briefing files had been taken.

"Finally! Now you need to tell these goons—"

Before she could finish or Holden could respond, the rest of the crowd started shouting at him all at once. Holden could hear snatches of their demands: that he drive off RCE, that he give them food or medicine or money, that he let them sell their lithium, that he prove that the colony had nothing to do with the disappearance of the security officers.

As Holden tried to quiet the mob, an older man in an RCE security uniform strolled slowly toward him, the rest of the corporate security people following in a wide V, like a flock of geese.

"Please, stop. I'll hear out each and every one of your requests once we get settled in. But we can't do anything if you all yell at—"

"Chief Murtry," the RCE man said, moving through the crowd like it wasn't there, sticking his hand out and smiling. "Royal Charter Energy, head of expedition security."

Holden shook his hand. "Jim Holden. Joint UN/OPA mediator."

The crowd hushed and moved away, creating a small circle of calm with Holden and Murtry at its center.

"Those were your people that disappeared," Holden continued.

"They got murdered," Murtry corrected him, not losing his smile. The man made Holden think of a shark. All bared teeth and cold black eyes.

"My understanding is that that was not proven."

"It's true they cleaned up the scene. But I have no doubt."

"Until *I* have no doubt, no punitive action is to be taken,"

Holden said. He felt Amos move up closer behind him, a silent threat.

Murtry's smile didn't reach his eyes. "You're the boss."

"Mediator," Holden said, his tone letting Murtry know that as far as he was concerned, it meant the same thing.

Murtry nodded and spat to one side.

"Sure."

The dam broke, and the crowd rushed back in toward them, a tall woman pushing her way to the front. She jabbed her hand at Holden in an angry demand for a handshake. If Murtry had gotten one, she was going to get one too.

"Carol Chiwewe, colony coordinator," she said giving his hand two firm pumps. So that first woman had to have been someone else.

"Hello, madam coordinator," Holden started.

"This man," she continued, stabbing her fingers at Murtry, "is threatening us with martial law! He claims that the charter gives RCE the right to—"

"Enforce the laws of the UN charter, and keep the peace," Murtry said, somehow managing to talk over the top of her without raising his voice.

"Keep the peace?" Carol said. "You gave your people a shoot-first directive!"

The crowd rumbled in disapproval at this, and the shouting started up again. Holden waved his arms to calm them back down. He hoped it looked more dignified and commanding than it felt. When Murtry spoke, his voice was calm but hard.

"I have a hard time seeing how we'd be shooting first. Everybody that's died so far, your people killed. I won't tolerate any further threats against RCE employees or property."

A tall man with the large cranium of someone raised in the Belt pushed his way to the front. "Sounds like a threat right there, mate."

"Coop, please, don't make this worse," Carol said with a

resigned sigh. *Ah, Coop is a troublemaker,* Holden thought, making a note to remember the face.

"Just seems to me," Coop said, turning to look back at the mob with a grin, raising his voice to play to the crowd. "Just seems to me that the only one making threats right now is *you*."

The crowd rumbled encouragement, and Coop grinned from ear to ear, enjoying the power that came from giving the mob a voice.

Murtry nodded at him, still smiling. "There isn't anything I won't do to protect the lives of my team, that's true. And we've lost too many already to take further chances."

"Hey, don't blame us, mate, if you can't keep track of your people." Someone in the crowd laughed.

"Don't worry," Murtry said, his smile still didn't change, but he stepped in close to Coop. "I'll find out what happened to them."

"Maybe *you* should be careful," Coop said, looking down at the shorter man, his grin turning feral. "Or, you know, it might happen to you too."

"That," Murtry said, drawing his gun, "was definitely a threat."

He shot Coop in the right eye. The Belter man went limp and dropped like a machine that had been unplugged. Holden's own gun was in his hand and pointed at Murtry even before he fully processed what had just happened. Amos stepped up next to him, his pistol trained on the RCE security chief. The entire RCE team pulled weapons and aimed them back at Holden. The crowd was deathly silent.

"What the *hell*!" Holden said. "I just said no punitive action. I mean, I just *said* that."

"You did. That wasn't punitive action, it was a response to a direct verbal threat." Murtry put his pistol away and turned back to Holden. "We've established martial law here, under article 71 of the UN charter for exploration of this world. Any threat to RCE personnel will be dealt with swiftly and with prejudice."

He stared at Holden for several long seconds, then said, "Might should put your gun away, Captain."

Amos took a half step forward, but Holden put a hand on his arm. "Put it away, Amos." He holstered his own gun, and a second later the RCE team did the same.

"I'm glad we could establish this working rapport so quickly. I'd recommend you get settled in," Murtry said. "I'll come by for a visit later."

The coordinator had set aside rooms for Holden and Amos in the large, boxy prefab warehouse structure that had been converted into a combination of general store, commissary, and pub. The rooms in back were furnished with a cot, a table, and a water basin for washing.

"They gave us the presidential suite, I see," Amos said, dumping his bags on the floor of his tiny room. "I need a drink."

"Give me a second," Holden said, then went into his own room and called up to the *Rocinante*. He delivered a full report of the landing and the shooting of Coop. Naomi promised to beam it back to Fred and Avasarala for him, and told him to be careful.

The bar, such as it was, consisted of four shaky card tables and twenty or so chairs scattered near the commissary corner of the building. Amos was waiting with two bottles of beer when Holden finished up his report.

"That went well."

"Get the feeling we may be in over our heads here?" Amos asked after a few companionable sips of beer.

"Feels about normal to me," Holden replied.

"Yep."

They were on their second beer each when Murtry arrived. He talked to the bartender for a minute, then sat down across from Holden and put a bottle of whiskey and three glasses on the table.

"Have a drink with me, Captain," he said, pouring out three shots.

"You're going to go to prison for what you did today," Holden said, then tossed back his shot. The whiskey had the sour moldy taste of Belter distillations. "I plan to make sure of that."

Murtry shrugged. "Maybe. My plan is to make sure all my people survive long enough for prison to be an issue. I've lost almost twenty now, between the attack on the shuttle and the murder of my ground team. I won't lose any more."

"You're a corporate security detail. You don't get to declare martial law and shoot people who don't cooperate. I wouldn't put up with that from legitimate governments, much less a rent-a-cop like you." Holden poured himself another drink and sipped at it.

"What's the name of this planet?"

"What?"

"The planet. What's its name?"

Holden leaned forward, the word *Ilus* on his lips. He paused. Murtry's smile was thin.

"You've spent a lot of time working for the OPA, Captain Holden. And you're on record as harboring a deep-seated dislike of the kind of business that employs me. I have some reservations about your ability to address the situation here in an unbiased manner. Threatening me and calling me names doesn't do much to reassure me."

"You undermined my authority by killing a Belter within five minutes of my arrival," Holden said.

"I did. And I understand that could make you feel that I'm not taking your role here seriously. But your friends in the UN are a year and a half away," Murtry said. "Think about that. It takes between eight and eleven hours to have the first two exchanges of a conversation, and almost nineteen months to get here from there at civilian speeds. Our local governor has been murdered by terrorists. My people have been killed for trying to enforce our legal rights. Do you honestly think I'm going to wait for you to fix what's wrong here? No, I'll shoot everyone who threatens the RCE expedition or its employees, and I'll sleep well afterward. That's the reality of where you are now. Better get used to it."

"I know who you are," Amos said.

The big man had been so quiet that both Murtry and Holden started with surprise.

"Who am I?" Murtry asked, playing along.

"A killer," Amos said. His face was expressionless, his tone light. "You've got a nifty excuse and the shiny badge to make you seem right, but that's not what this is about. You got off on smoking that guy in front of everyone. You can't wait to do it again."

"Is that right?" Murtry asked.

"Yeah. So, one killer to another, you don't want to try that shit with us."

"Amos, easy," Holden warned, but the other two men ignored him.

"That sounded like a threat," Murtry said.

"Oh, it really was," Amos replied with a grin.

Holden realized both men had their hands below the table. "Hey, now."

"I think maybe one of us is going to end bloody," Murtry said.

"How about now?" Amos replied with a shrug. "I'm free now. We can just skip all the middle part."

Murtry and Amos smiled at each other across the table for an endless moment while Holden ran though contingencies in his mind: *What if Amos gets shot, what if Murtry gets shot, what if I get shot.*

"You fellas have a nice day," Murtry said, standing slowly. His hand was not on his gun. "Keep the bottle."

"Thanks!" Amos replied, pouring another drink.

Murtry nodded at them, then walked out of the bar.

Holden let out an exhalation that he'd been holding for what seemed like an hour. "Yeah, I think we are in way over our heads here," he admitted.

"I'm gonna need to shoot that guy at some point," Amos said, then tossed back another shot.

"I wish you wouldn't. This is already looking like a train wreck, and in addition to chewing up a few hundred colonists and scientists, which is bad enough, it will also be my fault when it all falls apart."

"Shooting him might help."

"I hope not," Holden said, but he was worried that Amos was right.

Interlude: The Investigator

—it reaches out it reaches out it reaches out it reaches out—

One hundred and thirteen times a second, nothing answers and it reaches out. It feels no frustration, though parts of it do. It is not designed to incorporate consciousness or will, but to use whatever it finds. The minds within it are encysted, walled off. They are used when they are of use, as is everything and it reaches out.

It is not a plan. It is not even a desire, or it is only a desire without knowledge of that longing's object. It is a selective pressure pressed against chaos. It does not think of itself this way because it does not think, but the environment changes, a new branch of possibilities opens, and it forms the investigator and leans into the new crack. The new space. The minds within it interpret this differently. As a hand reaching up through graveyard soil. As finding a door in a room where no door had been before. As a breath of air to a drowning woman. It is not aware of these images, but awareness of them is part of it.

The investigator puts pressure on the aboriginal, and the aboriginal takes action. The environment changes again. Patterns begin to match patterns, but there can be no recognition because it is not conscious to recognize. It would be aware of the aboriginal accelerating, of it slowing, the vectors shifting zero to one to a different zero in a different location, if it were aware, but it is not aware. It reaches out.

Patterns match, and it reorients and reaches out. Cascades of implicit information bloom, and the conscious parts of it see a lotus opening forever, hear a shout that is made of other shouts that are made of other shouts in a fractal constructed of sound, pray to God for a death that does not come.

It reaches out, but the ways in which it reaches change. It improvises, as it always has, the insect twitch, the spark closing the gap it reaches out.

It touches something, and for a moment, a part of it that can feel, feels hope. It is unaware of hope. The reply does not come. It is not over. It will never be over. It reaches out, and finds new things. Old things. It flows into places that are comfortable for it to flow. There are responses, and the responses feed the impulses that caused them, and there are more responses. All automatic and empty and dead as it is. Nothing reaches back. It feels no disappointment. It does not shut down. It reaches out.

It does not experience the wariness, but the wariness is part of it. It reaches out, rushing into the new possibility space, and something deep in it, wider than it should be, watches it reach.

Doors and corners. It reaches out it reaches out it reaches out. Doors and corners.

This could get ugly, kid.

Chapter Twelve: Basia

James Holden came too late.

Along with everyone else in the colony, Basia watched the drive plume of the *Rocinante* light the sky of Ilus. For him, maybe, it was already too late. He'd made the bombs that destroyed the RCE shuttle and killed the UN governor. He'd been there when Coop and the others murdered the RCE security team. And maybe there was no coming back from that. Maybe he was already a dead man, or a man destined for life in prison, the same thing really. But looking up at the line of white fire in sky, he couldn't help but feel a spark of hope. Jim Holden had saved the Ganymede children, too late for Katoa, but he'd saved the others. He'd brought down the evil corporation that had killed Basia's little boy. Neither Mao-Kwikowski nor Protogen existed anymore because of Holden. And while Basia had never met the man in person, he'd watched him on video casts and read about him in newsfeeds. It created a strange sense of intimacy, to watch the man who'd avenged Katoa on-screen, talking and smiling.

And that man was coming to Ilus. Perhaps he could save Basia too?

So when the bright line in the sky vanished, and Basia knew Holden and his crew were in orbit, he let himself feel a swell of hope. The first he'd felt in a long time.

And when he heard the thunderclap of a descending shuttle, he ran outside just like all the other colonists, watching to see where it would land. *The UN mediator is coming!* they shouted to each other. The man who saved Earth, they meant. The man who saved Ganymede. The man who will save us.

A small shuttle dropped out of the sky and settled on the hard-packed earth to the south of First Landing, and half the town's population ran to meet it. Basia ran too.

The shuttle sat on five squat legs, ticking with heat. The town waited in silence, too excited to talk. Then a ramp lowered to the ground, and a squat Earther with gray hair and a deeply lined face walked down it. It wasn't Holden. One of his crew, maybe? But the man was wearing armor with the RCE logo on it, and Holden was supposed to be an impartial mediator.

The man stopped halfway down the ramp and smiled a humorless smile at them. Basia realized he was holding his breath, then realized everyone else was too.

"Hello," the man said. "My name is Adolphus Murtry. I'm chief of security for Royal Charter Energy."

Was it another RCE ship they'd seen braking into orbit? The man walked down the ramp, still smiling that predator's smile, and as one the crowd backed away. Basia backed up with them.

"Because of the attack on the shuttle that claimed the lives of many RCE employees *and* UN officials, I am taking direct control of security on this world. If that sounds like martial law, that's because it is." Murtry whistled, and ten more people in security armor descended the ramp. They carried automatic weapons and slug-throwing sidearms. Not a non-lethal deterrent in sight.

"Please be aware," Murtry continued, "that because of the attack on the first security team—"

"No one proved they were attacked!" someone shouted from the crowd. Coop, it was Coop. Standing at the back with his arms crossed and a smug smile on his face.

"Because of that attack," Murtry continued, "I have given my people 'shoot first' authorization. They may, if they feel threatened, utilize lethal force to defuse the threat."

Carol pushed through the crowd to confront Murtry at the bottom of the ramp, and Coop followed her.

"You're not the government here," Carol said, anger making the tendons in her neck stand out. Her hands were in fists, but she kept them at her sides. "You can't just land here with a bunch of guns and tell us you have the right to shoot us. This is *our world.*"

"That's right!" Coop yelled and turned to face the crowd, inviting them to join in.

"No," Murtry said, his smile not changing, "it is not."

The air was split with thunder as another ship dropped into the atmosphere and landed on the western side of town. Murtry barely glanced up at it. *More troops dropping in*, Basia thought.

Murtry began walking toward town, his people trailing out behind him, and the crowd moving in a loose cloud around them. Carol kept talking, but her words had no effect. Murtry just smiled and nodded and didn't break stride. The ship that had landed on the other side of town blasted off on a column of white vapor and vanished from sight. The roar of its engines filled the world.

When they reached the center of town, Basia saw Jacek hanging around at the edge of the crowd. He grabbed his son by the arm, pulling him harder than he intended, and the boy gave a frightened squeak.

"Papa," he said as Basia dragged him away, "am I in trouble?"

"Yes," Basia shouted, then when he saw tears welling up in the boy's eyes stopped and dropped to his knees next to him. "No. No, son. You're not. But I need you to go home."

"But—" Jacek started.

"No buts, boy," Basia gave him a gentle shove toward their house. "Go home."

"Is that man going to kill us?" Jacek asked.

"What man?" Basia asked, but it was a delaying tactic. He knew what man. Even his little boy could smell the death coming off of Murtry and his people. "No one's going to kill us. Go home."

Basia watched Jacek walk home, waiting until he saw the boy go inside and close the door. Basia was just starting to walk back toward the crowd when the shot rang out.

His first thought was, *Jacek was right. They are killing us.*

Not *us*, though, once he got back to the crowd. Just Coop, lying in the dust with a red hole where his eye should be, blood pooling under his head.

And Holden, jaw clenched and eyes wide.

Too late, Basia thought. *Too late again.*

People with machine guns walked the streets of First Landing.

Basia and Lucia sat on their tiny front porch and watched them pass by in the fading sunlight of early evening. A man and a woman, both in body armor with the red-and-blue RCE company logo on it. Both carrying automatic weapons. Both with hard expressions on their faces.

"I did this," Basia said.

Lucia squeezed his hand. "Drink your tea, Baz."

Basia looked down at the cup of tea cooling on his lap. All the tea the little colony might ever have had come down on the shuttles with them. To waste such a luxury was unthinkable. He sipped at the lukewarm cup and didn't taste it.

"They'll kill me, next."

"Maybe."

"Or put me in jail forever, take me away from my family."

"You," Lucia said, "took yourself away when you joined with

those stupid violent people who blew up the shuttle. You drove them out to the ruins when they killed the RCE people. You made every choice that took you to this place. I love you, Basia Merton. I love you till my chest aches. But you are a stupid, stupid man. And when they take you away from me, I will not forgive you for it."

"You're a harsh woman."

"I'm a doctor," Lucia said. "I'm used to giving people bad news."

Basia drank off the rest of his tea before it could finish getting cold. "I could get some rope or chain from the dig site. Maybe hang a bench here. Then we could rock while we sit."

"That might be nice," Lucia said. The pair of RCE guards reached the end of the street and turned around to come back. With the sun about to dip below the horizon, their shadows were almost as long as the town itself.

"We've been focusing on lithium mining to get money," Basia continued. "But we need to start thinking about our own energy needs."

"This is true."

"We can't have the *Barb* bringing us power cells forever. And someday the ship will fly back to Pallas to sell the ore. So we won't have her for a couple years."

"Also true," Lucia said. She swirled the last of her tea and stared up at the stars. "I miss having Jupiter in the sky."

"It was beautiful," Basia agreed. "I have to go meet with Cate and the others tonight, after it gets dark."

"Baz," Lucia started, then just stopped with sad sigh.

"They'll want revenge for Coop. It will only make it worse."

"What," Lucia said, "does worse look like, I wonder?"

Basia sat quietly, thinking of the rocker he could build on their porch. Of adding a bigger water heater for hot baths. Of building a larger kitchen and dining area on the back of the house. Of all the things he wouldn't get to do now.

The guards were at the end of the town's long street, almost invisible in their dark armor and the fading light. Basia got up to leave.

"Can you stop them from killing anyone else?" Lucia asked, as though she were asking if he wanted more tea.

"Yes," Basia replied. It felt like a lie.

"Then go."

They met at Cate's house. Pete and Scotty and Ibrahim. Even Zadie came, her wife Amanda staying home to look after their boy and his infected eye. That wasn't a good sign. Of all of them, Zadie was the angriest. The one with the hottest head. Basia had worked with her on Ganymede, and more than once she'd shown up in the morning with a black eye or a busted lip from some bar fight she'd picked the night before. They were all upset, all standing on the ledge about to jump, but Zadie would be the hardest to talk off of it.

"They shot Coop," Cate said when Scotty, the last of them to arrive, finally came in. It wasn't a statement of fact. They'd all been there. They'd all seen it. No, it was the beginning of a justification.

"In cold blood," Zadie said, and punctuated it with a fist to her palm. "We all saw it. Just shot him in the face in front of God and everyone."

"So I have a plan," Cate continued. "The RCE people are holed up in—"

"Who put you in charge?" Zadie asked.

"Murtry did."

Zadie narrowed her eyes, but let it drop. Basia fidgeted on one end of Cate's couch. It was a handmade frame, covered with padding stripped from the ship and badly stitched remnants of the cloth they had the fabricator crank out once a month for clothing and other needs. Cate had made a small table out of the local wood analog to sit next to it. It wasn't quite level, and Basia's glass of water was at a noticeable tilt. Pictures of Cate's family, two sisters who still lived back in the Belt and their kids, hung on the walls. There was a pottery vase on the floor with sticks and branches in it that Basia thought was meant as decoration, not kindling.

It was too domestic a location for the kind of meeting they were having. It all felt unreal, that he and five people he knew were discussing the murder of a dozen corporate security guards in Cate's living room next to her vase full of sticks.

Scotty was talking, telling them to wait. Not the voice of reason, the voice of fear. Pete was on his side, arguing against escalating. Cate and Zadie shouted them down. Ibrahim said nothing, just pulled on his bottom lip and frowned at the floor.

"I think we wait for Holden," Basia said when there was a pause in the conversation.

"Holden's been here a day. What are we waiting for?" Cate asked, dripping angry sarcasm.

"He needs time to meet with us, get the lay of the land," Basia said, the words sounding feeble even in his own ears. "But he's the mediator. And he can talk directly to the OPA governing board and to the UN. His recommendations will have real weight. We need him on our side."

"The OPA?" Zadie spat. "The UN? What exactly are they going to do for us? Send a tersely worded letter? Murtry and his thugs are right there!" Zadie stabbed her fingers at the wall, at the street beyond, at the guards with machine guns. "How many of our people do they get to kill before we defend ourselves?"

"We killed them first," Basia said, then regretted it immediately. Everyone started shouting, mostly at him. Basia stood up. He knew he was an imposing figure, stocky and thick-necked. Bigger than anyone else in the room. He stepped forward, a physical challenge. He hoped his size would be enough. He was fairly certain Cate could beat him to death if she decided to. "Shut up!" They did. "We have a chance here," he continued, quieting his voice with an effort. "But it's so fragile. We killed the RCE people."

"I wasn't—" Zadie started, but Basia hushed her with a gesture.

"They killed Coop. Right now, they feel like they've made a point, so they won't kill anyone else unless we provoke them. So, right now, we are at a balance. If no one does anything to tip it one way or another, Holden can do what they sent him here to do. He can help us resolve this without more violence."

Cate snorted and looked away, but Basia ignored her. "I'm in this with you. I have just as much to lose as any of you. But we want this man on our side. He saw Murtry murder one of us. He's never seen us do anything. We have the advantage of seeming like the victims right now. Let's not change his mind on that."

There was a long moment while Basia stood in the middle of the room, panting with emotion, and no one spoke.

"Okay," Ibrahim said. He'd been a soldier once. The others respected him. When he finally spoke, it was with a tone of authority. Cate frowned, but said nothing.

"Okay?"

"Okay, big man," Ibrahim said. "We play it your way for now. Go talk to this Holden. Get him on our side. He's the one found your boy, sa sa? Use that."

Basia felt a rush of anger and shame at the mention of Katoa, of using him as an in with Holden, but he pushed it down. Ibrahim was right. It would give Basia something to talk to Holden about, and it would make him seem sympathetic.

"I'll talk to him tomorrow," Basia said, swallowing the sudden nausea he felt.

"It's on you now, big man," Ibrahim said. It sounded like a threat.

Basia walked home in the pitch black of the Ilus night. He wished he'd thought to bring a light. He wished he'd never blown up a shuttle full of people and helped Coop murder the RCE guards. He wished his wife wasn't angry with him, and that she wasn't right. He wished that Katoa were still alive and that they all still lived in their home on Ganymede and that no one had ever come to Ilus in the first place.

He tripped on a rock and fell to his knee, skinning it. No way to fix the other things, but at least he could have thought to bring a light.

Lucia had left a light on in the house. Without it, Basia might have walked right past it without realizing. At least she wanted him to come home. She left lights on to make it happen. For the first time in a long time, Basia felt himself smile.

A shadowy figure darted through the dim light around the house to the back door. Before he had time to think, Basia was at a dead run. The figure at the door cowered, smaller than him and terrified.

Felcia.

"Papa! You scared me!"

"Oh, baby, I'm so sorry. I didn't see it was you. Just saw someone sneaking around the house and came running."

Felcia smiled up at him, eyes damp and lip trembling, but being brave.

"Okay, going in now."

"Felcia," Basia said, putting his hand against the door to hold it closed. "Why are you sneaking up to the house in the middle of the night?"

"I was out, walking." She looked away, not able to meet his eyes.

"Please, baby, tell me it was a boy."

"It was a boy," she said, still not looking at him.

"Felcia."

"I'm going up on the next shuttle, Papa," she said, looking him in the eye finally. "I'm going up. When James Holden gets them to let the *Barbapiccola* go, I'm going with it. From Pallas I can catch transport to Ceres. Mama is calling her old mentor at CUMA to get me an interview for the pre-med program at the Hadrian on Luna."

Basia felt like someone had punched him in the solar plexus. The pain in his stomach kept him from breathing.

"I'm going, Papa."

"No," he said. "You're not."

Chapter Thirteen: Elvi

Elvi's grandfather had remarried late in life. His new husband had been a German man with a merry laugh, a snow-white beard, and a cheerful cynicism about humanity. What she remembered best about Grandpa Raynard was how quick he was with an epigram or a quip. He had one for every occasion. She'd thought they made him sound worldly and wise, in part because she was so often unsure what exactly he meant by them.

One thing he'd said was *Once is never. Twice is always.*

When the shuttle went down, she'd known—they'd all known—that someone had put the explosives there, but her experience of the Belter colonists beginning that same night had been so different that the knowledge and the emotional impact of it had become detached. Someone among the Belters had done a terrible thing, but that person was faceless, anonymous, unreal. Doctor Merton doing everything she could to save the wounded and soothe the injured was real. Her daughter, Felcia, who was at the farthest point humanity had ever been from Earth and whose ambitions were drawing her back toward Luna, was real. Anson Kottler and his sister Kani who'd helped Elvi set up her hut. Samish Oe with his goofy half smile was real. Carol Chiwewe. Eirinn Sanchez. They had all been so kind that Elvi had shelved the death of the governor as an outlier, something so rare it would never happen again.

But the disappearance of Reeve and the security crew was twice, and the way Elvi saw the colony and the RCE scientists and her own little hut out on the edge of the plain was different now. Because the threat of violence wasn't *never* anymore. It was *always*.

"Did you see anything else?" Murtry asked.

"No," Elvi said. "I don't think so."

"Doctor Okoye, I know this has been unpleasant for you," the chief of security said, "but I need to you try to remember if there was anything else you saw while you were out there. The person you saw coming back. Can you say if it was a man? A woman?"

That wasn't how memory worked, of course. Just willing herself to remember something, pushing herself, was much more likely to generate a false recollection and add bad data to the set than it was to haul up some telling detail she'd failed to mention. It seemed rude to explain that to Murtry, so Elvi only shook her head.

"I'm sorry," she said.

"It's all right," he said in a tone of voice that hinted strongly at his disappointment. "If anything else occurs to you, please do bring it to me."

"I will."

"Are you feeling okay?"

"I guess so. Why?"

"The UN mediator's asked to talk with you too," Murtry said.

"You don't have to if you don't want, though. Just say the word, and I'll tell him to go piss up a rope."

"No, I don't mind," she said, but she was thinking, *James Holden wants to talk to me?* "Should I...I mean, is there anything I should particularly tell him? About the work, I mean?"

The truth was, she just wanted to get out of the security offices. The extended thirty-hour day of New Terra made it hard to feel exactly how long she'd been there, but she'd come to Reeve in darkness, she'd slept in one of the cells that night. She'd stayed there while Murtry and the security team came down and made the town safe, and now it was morning again. So two days, New Terra. Maybe three back on Earth. What exactly *day* meant wasn't intuitive anymore.

"Captain Holden needs to understand exactly how bad our situation here is," Murtry said. "He came out here thinking there's two sides to this, so he's wanting to split some kind of difference. Anything you can do to help him understand why that's not the solution here, I would very much appreciate."

"Oh," she said. "Yes, of course."

"Thank you," Murtry said.

"One thing?"

Murtry raised his eyebrows and tilted his head toward her. He didn't quite say, *Yes, ma'am?* but it was physically implied.

"My research is still in my hut," she said. "I have some studies that were in progress when I came to talk to...when I came in. Is my hut off-limits, or will I be able to get back to them?"

"You'll go back," Murtry said. "The one thing that is not going to happen here, Doctor? We're not giving back a goddamn centimeter of our ground. Whoever did this doesn't get to win."

"Thank you," Elvi said.

Murtry's expression hardened for a moment. His eyes became flat in a way that Elvi associated with lab animals being sacrificed. He looked dead.

"You're welcome," he said.

Walking down the street of the town, Elvi felt a pang of unease, but less so than she'd expected. The little siege she'd suffered in the security office waiting for the relief team to come had been a bleak and frightening time. But now familiar faces had joined the townsmen. Two women in RCE security riot armor walked down the street across from her, their assault rifles resting easily in their hands. Just seeing them there left Elvi feeling safer. And then Holden had also arrived. Certainly, things weren't where they needed to be, but they were getting closer. They were getting better. That would have to be enough for now.

Another guard stood at the entrance to the general store, a rifle resting in his hands.

"Doctor Okoye," he said nodding her inside.

"Mister Smith," she said.

She'd been in the commissary building many times in the weeks since she'd landed on New Terra. Apart from little intimate get-togethers in the research huts and the formal town meetings in the community hall, it was the only place to go unless she found religion. She could see—*feel*—at once how the presence of James Holden had changed the nature of the space. It had been a community place before, public in the same way a municipal park might be, without any commanding human presence. Now a man sat at a table toward the back of the room, just as if he were a townsman getting a bowl of rice and a beer. Sitting there, leaning on his elbows and talking to Fayez, he commanded the space. He owned it. What had belonged to everyone was now the unquestioned domain of James Holden. Elvi's belly went a little tighter and anxiety sped her breath.

She had seen Holden on the newsfeeds and reports. At the beginning of the war between Mars and the Belt, he had been the most important man in the solar system, and the celebrity, while it had waxed and waned over the years, had never gone away. James Holden was an icon. For some, he was the symbol of the triumph of the single ship over governments and corporations. For others, he was an agent of chaos who started wars and threatened stability in the name of ideological purity. But whatever people thought he meant, there was no question that he was important. He was the man who'd saved Earth from the protomolecule. He was the man who'd brought down Mao-Kwikowski. Who'd made the first contact with the alien artifact and opened the gates that led to a thousand different worlds.

In person, he looked different than his image on the screen. His face was still broad, but not as much so. His skin had a warmth that even years in the sunless box of a ship couldn't erase. The dark brown hair had a dusting of gray at the temples, but his eyes were the same sapphire blue. As she watched, Holden rubbed a hand across his chin, nodding at something that Fayez was saying. It was an unconsciously masculine movement that left Elvi thinking of large animals—lions, gorillas, bears. There was no sense of threat in it, only of power, and she was profoundly aware that the man she had seen only as an image on a data feed was exhaling the same molecules that she was breathing in.

"You okay?"

Elvi started. The man who'd asked was huge, pale, and muscular. His shaved head and thick belly made him look like a gigantic baby. He put a hand on her shoulder as if to steady her.

"Fine?" she said, her inflection making it a question.

"You just looked a little weird there for a second. You sure you're feeling all right?"

"I was supposed to meet with Captain Holden?" she said, trying to pull herself back together. "My name's Elvi Okoye, and I'm with the RCE. I'm an exobiologist with RCE."

"Elvi!" Fayez called, waving her over.

She nodded to the pale man and walked over to the table where Fayez and Holden were sitting. James Holden's eyes were on her.

"This is Elvi," Fayez said. "We've known each other since upper university."

"How do you do?" Elvi said, her voice sounding false and tinny in her ears. She cleared her throat.

"Pleased to meet you," Holden said, rising to his feet and extending a hand. Elvi shook it just as if she were meeting anyone else. She was proud of herself for that.

"Sit," Fayez said, pushing out a chair for her. "I was just talking to the captain here about the resources problem."

"It's not an issue yet," Elvi said. "But it will be."

Holden sighed, clasping his fingers together. "I'm still hopeful that we can negotiate something that's equitable for everyone involved."

Elvi frowned and tilted her head. "How would you do that?"

Holden lifted his eyebrows. Fayez leaned in toward her.

"We were talking about resources like lithium and money," he said, then turned toward Holden again. "She was talking about water and nutrients. Different contexts."

"Is there not enough water?" Holden asked.

"There is," Elvi said, hoping that her blush didn't show. Of course they were talking about lithium mines. She should have known that. "I mean, there's enough water. And nutrients. But that's sort of the problem. We're here in the middle of a totally foreign biosphere. Everything about the place is different from what we're used to dealing with. I mean, it looks like life here is genuinely bi-chiral."

"Really?" Holden said.

"No one knows what that means, Elvi," Fayez said.

Holden politely pretended not to have heard him. "But the animals and insects here all look... well, they don't look familiar, but they've got eyes and things."

"They're under the same selection pressures," Elvi said. "Some things are just a good idea. Back on Earth, eyes evolved four or five different times. Powered flight at least three times. Most animals put the mouth near the sense organs. The degree of large-scale morphological similarities given the underlying biochemical differences is part of what makes this such an amazing research opportunity. The data I've been able to send back since we got here would be enough to fuel research for a generation, and I've barely scratched the surface."

"And the resources problem?" Holden said. "What are the resources you need?"

"It's not the ones we need," Elvi said, waving her hands. "It's the ones we *are*. From the perspective of the local environment, we're bubbles of water, ions, and high-energy molecules. We're not exactly the flavor that's around here, but it's only a matter of time before something figures out a way to exploit those."

"Like a virus?" Holden asked.

"Viruses are a lot more like us than what we're seeing here," Elvi said. "Viruses have nucleic acids. RNA. They evolved with us. When something here figures out how to access us as resources, it's probably going to be more like mining."

Holden's expression was dismayed. "Mining," he echoed.

"We have an advantage for the time being because we're an older biosphere. From what we can tell, things weren't really evolving here until sometime between one and a half and two billion years ago. We've got pretty strong evidence that we have a good billion-year head start on these guys, at least. And some of our strategies may work against them. If we can build antibodies against the proteins that the locals use, we might be able to fight them off like any other infection."

"Or we might not," Fayez said.

"Part of the reason I came out here, part of the reason I agreed to this, was that we were going to do it *right*," Elvi said, hearing the stress coming into her voice. "We were going to get a sealed environment. A *dome*. We were going to survey the planet and learn from it and be responsible about how we treated it. The RCE sent scientists. They sent researchers. Do you know how many of us have sustainability and conservation certifications? Five-sixths. Five-*sixths*."

Her voice was louder now than she'd meant it to be. Her gestures were wider, and there was a tremble of outrage in her words.

Holden's unreal blue eyes were on her, and she could feel him listening like his attention could radiate. Intellectually, she knew what was happening. She was scared and she was hurt and she was guilty for having been the one to lead Reeve and the others into danger. She'd been able to ignore it all, but it was bubbling up. She was talking about the biology and the science, but what she meant was *Help me. It's all going wrong, and no one can help me. No one but you.*

"Only when you got here, there was already a colony," Holden said. His voice was like warm flannel. "And a colony made up of a bunch of people who have a lot of very good reasons to distrust corporations. And governments."

"It looks calm here," Elvi said. "It looks beautiful. And it is. And it's going to teach us things we never dreamed before. But we're doing it wrong."

Fayez sighed. "She's right," he said. "I mean, I like talking about lithium and moral rights and legalities as much as the next guy. But Elvi's not wrong about how weird this place is when we start looking close enough. And it's got a lot of very dangerous edges that we're not paying any attention to. Because we're, you know, killing each other."

"I hear what you're saying," Holden said. "I'm going to need to look at it. The part where people are killing each other has to be my first focus. But I promise you both that I will put creating a closed, safe planetary dome on the list as soon as we've got the crisis under control. No matter who winds up being in control."

"Thank you," Elvi said.

"Most of the people here are good," Fayez said. "The Belters? We've been here for months, and I swear most of these people aren't monsters. They're just poor bastards who thought starting over was a good idea. And Royal Charter is a very, very responsible corporation. Look at their history, and you won't find any more graft and corruption than an average PTA. They're really trying to do all this right."

"I know," Holden said. "And I wish to hell that made it easier."

"Uh, Captain?" the huge baby-man said.

"Amos?"

"There's another mess of legal crap just came through from the UN for you."

Holden sighed. "Am I supposed to read it?"

"Don't see how they can make you," Amos said. "Just thought you'd want to ignore it intentionally."

"Thank you. Sort of," Holden said, then turned back to them. "I'm afraid I have to deal with bureaucracy for a while. But thank you both very much for coming. Please always feel free to come talk to me."

Fayez stood, and Elvi followed half a second later. He shook each of their hands in turn, then retreated to a room in the back. Fayez walked out to the street with her. Hassan Smith and his rifle acknowledged them again as they passed by.

The sun glowed in the oxygen-blued sky. She knew it was a little too small, the spectrum of light from it a little slanted toward the orange, but it was familiar to her now. As right as thirty-hour days and her close, familiar hut. Fayez fell into step beside her.

"Heading back to your place?" he asked.

"I should," she said. "I haven't been out since I came to see Reeve. I'm sure all my datasets are finished. I probably have a bunch of angry messages from home."

"Yeah, probably," he said. "So are you all right?"

"You're the third person to ask me that today," Elvi said. "Am I acting like there's something wrong with me?"

"A little," Fayez said. "You've got a right to being a little freaked out."

"I'm fine," Elvi said. Her hand still tingled a little where Holden had held it. She massaged her skin. At the end of the street, a Belter girl was walking fast with her head down and her hands shoved deep in her pockets. Murtry and Chandra Wei stood behind her, watching her suspiciously, their rifles in their hands. The wind coming off the plain lifted swirls of dust in the corners of the alleys. She wanted to go back to her hut, and she didn't. She wanted to go back up the well, onto the *Edward Israel* and home again, and she wouldn't have left New Terra for all the money in the world. She remembered being very, very young and terribly upset about something. Crying into her mother's shoulder that she wanted to go home, except that she was home when she said it. That was what she wanted now.

"Don't do it," Fayez said.

"Don't do what?"

"Fall in love with Holden."

"I don't know what you're talking about," she snapped.

"In that case, *really* don't do it," Fayez said with a cynical laugh, and turned away.

Chapter Fourteen: Holden

This is the first colonial arbitration meeting," Holden said, looking into the camera at the end of the table. "My name is James Holden. Representing the colony of New Terra—"

Ilus," Carol said.

"—is Carol Chiwewe, colony administrator. Representing Royal Charter Energy is chief of security, Adolphus Murtry."

"How exactly did that happen?" Carol said. She stared at Murtry when she said it, her expression unreadable. Holden had a feeling Carol might be a very good poker player.

Murtry smiled back at her. His face was equally unreadable. "What's that?"

"You know exactly what I mean," Carol snapped back. "What are you doing here? You're hired security. You have no authority to—"

"You put me in this room," Murtry said, "when you killed the colonial governor. You do remember that? Big explosion? Crashing ship? It would have been hard to miss."

Holden sighed and leaned back in his uncomfortable chair. He would let the two of them bicker a bit, release some of the venom they'd been storing up, then put his foot down and drag the discussions back on topic.

RCE had offered to host the talks on their shuttle or the *Edward Israel*, which would have been a lot more comfortable. But the colony had demanded that the meeting be held in First Landing. Which meant that instead of contour-fitted gel filled chairs, they were sitting on whatever metal and plastic monstrosities the colony had lying around. The table was a sheet of epoxied carbon weave sitting on four metal legs, and the room they were using was barely large enough for the table and three chairs. A small shelf on one wall held a coffee pot that was hissing to itself and throwing a bitter scorched smell into the air. Amos leaned against the room's one door, arms crossed, and with an expression so far beyond bored that he might actually have been asleep.

"—endless accusations without evidence to bolster your own *criminal* claims of property rights—" Carol was saying.

"Enough," Holden cut in. "No more outbursts from either of you. I'm here at the request of the UN and OPA to broker some sort of agreement that can let RCE do the scientific work they're authorized to do, and to keep the people already living on New Terra—"

"Ilus."

"—Ilus from being harmed in the process."

"What about RCE employees?" Murtry asked softly. "Are they allowed to be harmed?"

"No," Holden said. "No, they are not. And so the mandate of these meetings has changed somewhat in light of recent events."

"I've only seen one person murdered since Holden arrived, and that one is on you," Carol said to Murtry.

"Madam coordinator," Holden continued, "there can be no further attacks on the RCE personnel. That's non-negotiable.

We can't work out any sort of deal here unless everyone knows they're safe."

"But he—"

"And you," Holden continued, pointing at Murtry, "are a murderer, and one I intend to see prosecuted to the fullest extent of the law—"

"You have no—"

"—once we return to a region of space that actually *has* laws," Holden said. "Which brings us to our first real discussion point. There are two competing claims regarding who has the right to administrate this expedition. We have to establish who makes the laws here."

Murtry said nothing, but pulled a flexible display out of his coat and unrolled it on the table. It began slowly scrolling through the text of the UN charter giving RCE the scientific mission on New Terra. Carol snorted and pushed it back across the table at him.

"Yes," Holden said. "RCE has a legal mandate from the UN placing them in control of this planet for the duration of their scientific mission. But we can't ignore the fact that people had been living on New Terra, or Ilus, for months before that charter was drafted."

"No, we can't," Carol said.

"So we work out a compromise," Holden said, "that allows RCE to do the work they came here to do. Work which will, we hope, benefit everyone, including the colonists. This is a new world. There may be any number of dangers here we are unaware of. But this compromise must also allow for the possibility that the final decision of the home governments will be to grant Ilus self-governing status."

Amos snorted and his head jerked up, eyes wide open for a moment and then slowly narrowing back toward closed.

"Yeah, so," Holden said, "that's the long boring explanation. The short version is, I want RCE to move forward with doing the science, and I want the colonists to continue living their lives, and I don't want anyone getting killed. How do we make that happen?"

Murtry tilted his chair back on two legs and stretched out with his hands behind his head. "Well," he said, "you make a big point of telling me you plan to arrest me once we get back in civilized space."

"Yes."

"But by my count the *colonists*"—he sneered the word—"have racked up about two dozen kills."

"And when we figure out who the perpetrators are," Holden said, "they too will go back to Sol system to face trials."

"You're a detective now?" Murtry snorted. Holden felt a weird chill run down his spine and looked around as if Miller might somehow have appeared.

"I think that the RCE security force, working in conjunction with Mister Burton and myself, should continue its investigation of those crimes."

"Wait," Carol said, leaning forward suddenly in her chair, "I won't let him—"

"Investigation only. No trials can be held here, so no penalties can be meted out beyond protective detention, and that only with my express consent."

"Your express consent?" Murtry said, speaking slowly, like he was tasting the words. He smiled. "If they'll let my team keep looking into the killings while we continue the negotiations here, permit us the right to protect ourselves, and guarantee that anyone with strong evidence against them will be held against future trial, I'm fine with that."

"Of course he is!" Carol said. "Delay is all he needs to kill us."

Holden frowned at that. "Explain."

"We're not self-supporting yet," Carol said. "We've got the *Barb* up in orbit. She can bring us fuel cells charged from her drive, and she dropped us with all the food and seeds she had, but we can't really plant here yet. Soil has the wrong microorganisms in it. We desperately need food stores, soil enrichments, medical supplies."

"All of which RCE is happy to—" Murtry started.

"But what we do have is the richest lithium vein any of us have ever seen. And with that ore, we can buy everything else we need. The *Israel* is keeping the *Barbapiccola* from sending down her shuttle to pick up the rest, and she's threatened to stop the *Barb* if she tries to leave orbit."

"The mineral rights on New Terra are not yours," Murtry said. "Not until the UN says they are."

Carol slapped the table with her palm; it was as loud as a gunshot in the small room. "See? It's a waiting game. If he can just block us from taking our ore up to the ship long enough, then it won't matter who gets those rights. Even if they're awarded to us, we'll be so behind in moving the ore to the ship that we'll all starve to death before we ever get to market."

"So," Holden said. "You're asking for the right to keep loading the ore onto the *Barbapiccola* while the rights are negotiated."

Carol opened her mouth, closed it, and folded her arms.

"Yes," she said.

"Okay," Holden said with a nod. "Sounds fair to me. No matter who winds up selling that ore, they'll need a transport to move it, and the *Barb* is as good as anything else."

Murtry shrugged. "Fine. We'll allow the shuttle to land and begin transporting ore again. But mining operations come with some problems for me."

"Explain?" Holden said again.

"They're using explosives. The same type of explosive that was used to bring down the shuttle and kill the governor. As long as these people have unrestricted access to it my people are at risk."

"What's your solution?" Holden asked.

"I want to control access."

"So you'll let us move the ore you won't let us mine?" Carol said. "Typical corporate doublespeak."

"I'm not saying that," Murtry said, patting the air in a *calm down* gesture that struck Holden as intentionally patronizing. "I'm saying we hold the explosives when not in use, and your mining crews sign them out when needed. That way nothing goes missing and shows up later as a pipe bomb."

"Carol, does that seem fair to you?" Holden asked.

"It'll slow the process down, but it's not a deal breaker," she replied.

"Okay," Holden said, standing up. "We'll stop there for now. We'll meet again tomorrow to go over the UN proposal on colony administration and start hammering out details. We also need to talk about environmental controls."

"The OPA—" Carol started.

"Yes, I have the recommendations from Fred Johnson as well, and those will be discussed. I'd like to transmit a revised plan to the UN and OPA by the end of the week, and get their feedback. Acceptable?"

There were nods from both Murtry and Carol. "Great. I'll want you two with me when I present today's agreement at the town hall meeting tonight. Our first show of goodwill and solidarity."

Murtry rose and walked past Carol without looking at her or shaking hands.

Goodwill and solidarity indeed.

"So," Amos said when Holden exited the town hall meeting that night. "How'd it go?"

"I must have done it right," Holden replied. "*Everyone's pissed.*"

They walked along the dusty street together in companionable silence for a while. Amos finally said, "Weird planet. Walking in open air at night with no moon is breaking my head."

"I hear you. My brain keeps trying to find Orion and the Big Dipper. What's weirder is that I keep finding them."

"That ain't them," Amos said.

"Oh, I know. But it's like my eyes are forcing those patterns on stars that aren't really lined up the right way to make them."

There was another moment of silence, then Amos said, "That's, like, one of them metaphors, right?"

"It is now."

"Buy you a beer?" Amos said when they reached the doors of the commissary.

"Later, maybe. I think I'm going to take a walk. The night air is nice here. Reminds me of Montana."

"Okay, see you when I see you. Try not to get shot or abducted or anything."

"I'll do my best."

Holden walked slowly, the dirt of the planet puffing up around his ankles at every stride. The buildings glowed in the darkness, the only human habitation on the planet. The only civilization in the wilds. He put his back to it and kept on going.

He was far enough outside of town that he could no longer see its dim lights when a faint blue glow appeared beside him. The glow was both there and not there. It lit the air around it while also illuminating nothing.

"Miller," Holden said without looking.

"Hey kid."

"We need to talk," Holden finished for him.

"That's less funny the more you do it," the detective said, his hands in his pockets. "Did you come out here to find me? I admit, I'm a little flattered, considering your other problems."

"Other problems?"

"Yeah, that shantytown full of future corpses you're trying to treat like grown-ups. No way that doesn't end bloody."

Holden turned to look at Miller, frowning. "Is that the former cop talking? Or the creepy protomolecule skin doll."

"I don't know. Both," Miller said. "You want a shadow, you got to have light and something to get in its way."

"Can I borrow the cop for a minute?"

The gray, jowly man hoisted his eyebrows just the way he had in life. "Are you asking me to use your brain to make these monkeys stop killing each other over rare dirt?"

"No," Holden sighed. "Just advice."

"Okay. Sure. Murtry's a psycho who's finally in a spot where he can do the creepy shit he's been dreaming about doing all his life. I'd just have Amos shoot him. Carol and her gang of dirt farmers are only alive because they're too desperate to realize how stupid they are. They'll probably die of starvation and bacterial infections in a year. Eighteen months tops. Your pals Avasarala and Johnson have handed you the bloody knife and you think it's because they trust you."

"You know what I hate about you?"

"My hat?"

"That too," Holden said. "But mostly it's that I hate everything you say, but you're not always wrong."

Miller nodded and stared up at the night sky.

"The frontier always outpaces the law," Holden said.

"True," Miller agreed. "But this place was already a crime scene when you got here."

"Bombing the heavy shuttle was—"

"Not that," Miller said. "I mean all of it. All the places."

"I seem to spend a lot of time asking people to explain themselves lately."

Miller laughed. "You think somebody built those towers and structures and then just left? This whole planet is a murder scene. An empty apartment with warm food on the table and all the clothes still in the closets. This is some Croatoan shit."

"The North American colonists who—"

"Except," Miller said, ignoring him. "The people who vanished here? Not dumbass Europeans in way over their heads. The things that lived here modified planets like we remodel a kitchen. They had a defense network in orbit that could have vaporized Ceres if it wandered too close."

"Wait, what defense network?"

Miller ignored him. "An empty apartment, a missing family,

that's creepy. But this is like finding a military base with no one on it. Fighters and tanks idling on the runway with no drivers. This is bad juju. Something *wrong* happened here. What you should do is tell everyone to leave."

"Yeah," Holden said, "sure, I'll get right on that. This argument about who gets to live here really needed a third party both sides could hate."

"No one lives here," Miller said, "but we're sure as shit going to play with the corpses."

"What the hell is that supposed to mean?"

Miller tipped his hat back, looking up at the stars.

"I never stopped looking for her. Julie? Even when she was dead, even when I'd seen her body, I never stopped."

"True. Still creepy, but true."

"This is like that too. I don't like it, but unless something happens, we're going to keep reaching and reaching and reaching until we find what did all this."

"And then what?"

"And then we'll have found it," he said.

A man Holden didn't recognize was waiting for him at the edge of town. Belter tall, stocky and thick-necked. Big meaty hands he was rubbing together nervously. Holden consciously forced himself not to drop his hand to the butt of his gun.

"Thought you got lost out there," the man said.

"Nope, all good." Holden held out his right hand. "Jim Holden. Have we met?"

"Basia. Basia Merton. From Ganymede."

"Yeah, all of you are from Ganymede, right?"

"Pretty much."

Holden waited for the man to speak. Basia stared back, wringing his hands again.

"So," Holden finally said. "Mister Merton. How can I help you?"

"You found my son. Back...back there. You found Katoa," Basia said.

It took Holden a moment to make the connection. "The little boy on Ganymede. You're Prax's friend."

Basia nodded, his head moving too fast, like a nervous bird. "We'd left. Me and my wife and my two other kids. We got a chance to get out on the *Barbapiccola* and I thought Katoa was dead. He was sick, you know."

"Same thing Prax's daughter had. No immune system."

"Yeah. Only he wasn't dead when we left. He was still alive in that lab where you found him. I left my son behind."

"Maybe," Holden said. "There's no way to know that."

"*I* know that. I know it. But I brought my family here. So I could keep them safe."

Holden nodded. He didn't say, *This is an alien world filled with dangers you couldn't possibly anticipate, on top of which you didn't actually own it, and you came here to be safe?* It didn't seem helpful.

"No one can make us leave," the man finished.

"Well—"

"No one can make us leave," Basia repeated. "You should remember that."

Holden nodded again, and after a moment Basia turned and walked away. *If that's not a member of the resistance, he at least knows who they are,* he thought. Someone to keep an eye on.

His hand terminal chimed an incoming connection request at him.

"Jim?" Naomi said. There was a nervous edge to her voice.

"Here."

"Something's happening down there. Massive energy spike in your location, and, uh—"

"Uh?"

"Movement."

Chapter Fifteen: Havelock

Slowly, New Terra was taking on a sense of familiarity. The planet's one big continent and long strings of islands turned under the *Edward Israel* every ninety-eight minutes, orbital period and the rotation of the planet conspiring to make a slightly different image every time Havelock looked. The features of the planet had started developing names for him, even though they would never be the ones that the official records showed. The largest southern island was Big Manhattan, because the outline reminded him of the North American island. The Dog's Head islands were scattered in the middle of the planet's one enormous ocean, and looked like a collie's face if he squinted. What he thought of as the Worm Fields were actually a massive network of rivers on the big continent, any one of them longer than the Amazon or the Nile. In the north was Crescent City, a massive network of alien ruins that sort of looked like a cartoon moon.

And there, in the flat beige sweep of what he thought of as the Plate, was the black dot of First Landing, like the first lesion of a rash. It was tiny, but when the ship passed over it at night, it was the only spot of light. There were more places and ecosystems down there, more discoveries to make and resources to use, than there had ever been on Earth. It seemed bizarre that they were fighting and dying over that one tiny piece of high desert. And it also seemed inevitable.

Murtry looked out from the display, listening to Havelock's report. Gravity changed the shape of his face, pulling down at his cheeks and eyes. It actually looked pretty good on him. Some people just belonged down a well.

"We had one incident with Pierce and Gillett."

"Those are the two in marine biology?"

"Gillett is. Pierce is actually a soil guy. It didn't amount to anything more than a little domestic spat, but...well, tempers are fraying. All these folks came out here to work, and instead, they're stuck here. We're doing sensor sweeps and dropping the occasional high-atmo probe, but it's like giving starving people a cracker when they can smell the buffet. It's starting to come out at the seams a little."

"That makes sense," Murtry said.

"Plus which they hate null g. The autodoc's been pumping out antinausea drugs like there's no tomorrow. I'm surprised we aren't just putting that shit in the water at this point."

Murtry's smile was perfunctory. Havelock wanted to float the idea of a second colony. Maybe something in the temperate zone near a river and a beach. The kind of place someone might, for example, string up a hammock. It would let the expedition's crew get working, and the problems with the squatters could work themselves out without putting anyone else in harm's way. The words hovered at the back of Havelock's throat, but he didn't say them out loud. He already knew the arguments against it. You treated a tumor when it was small, before it spread. He could even hear it in his boss's voice. Havelock cracked his knuckles.

"The shuttle?" Murtry asked.

Havelock looked over his shoulder, even though he knew the office was empty apart from him. When he spoke, his voice was quieter.

"I got some pushback because it meant halving the supply schedule, but people got over it. I thought of having the hold stacked with high-density ceramics for shrapnel, and putting in a few pallets of the geology survey's shaped charges, but I don't have anything that's going to make a bigger explosion than the shuttle's reactor would. I've taken out all the safety overrides the way you asked, though. Physical and software. Honestly, it's a little scary going on it anymore, just knowing that it *could* go off."

"And the controls."

"The standard protocols are all stripped out. You can fly it or I can. Anyone else is talking to a brick."

"Good man."

"Captain Marwick's not happy about it."

"He'll cope," Murtry said. "Better to have it and not need it than need it and not have it."

"And we have the ship's drive," Havelock said. "If we pointed the *Israel*'s ass at the *Barbapiccola* and fired it up, we could slag it."

"Right range, we could take out the *Rocinante* too," Murtry said. "Except that they could say the same, and they've got missiles. No, we're just getting ready for contingencies. Which brings me to the point. I've got the solution to one of your problems."

"Sir?"

"All those bored scientists. We've lost a lot of the security team, and we're in a more hostile environment than we'd expected. I need you to do some cross training."

"You mean hire them into security?"

"Nothing official," Murtry said. "But if we had a dozen people who were familiar with the riot gear and had some practice in low g, it wouldn't hurt my feelings."

Havelock nodded. "A militia, then."

"I established that we're in de facto control of First Landing.

Holden thinks he's some kind of fucking Solomon. I'm fine letting him go with it for now, but when the time comes, we may need to put boots on the ground here. Or on the *Barbapiccola*. I'm happy if we don't, but I want the option. Can you do that?"

"Let me look into it," Havelock said. "I'm pretty sure it would mean bending corporate policy. The home office is pretty touchy about liability."

"They sent us to the ass end of nowhere and let a bunch of squatters take their best shot at us," Murtry said. "I don't particularly care what they think. It doesn't need to be official. Make it a club. Just a few folks enjoying a shared hobby for low-g tactics. Fabricate them a few paint guns. Just make sure they're ready."

"In case we need them."

"Right," Murtry said with his dragging, full-gravity smile. "In case."

Technically, Havelock could have spent the time in the main security office, strapped into Murtry's couch and using his desk. Instead, he tended to stick to his own familiar place beside the brig. He told himself it was because the system was already customized with his preferences and access codes, but he also knew it was more than that. Murtry had a way of claiming space even if he wasn't occupying it, and Havelock wouldn't have been comfortable. So when the second shift ended, the chief of the engineering workgroup came to him at the brig.

Chief Engineer Matthu Koenen was a thick man with short, bottle-brush white hair and a birthmark on his neck that he'd never bothered to have removed. He floated in the air by Havelock's couch, arms folded across his chest and legs crossed at the ankles like a dour, angry ballet dancer.

"Thank you for coming by," Havelock said.

"There trouble?" Koenen snapped.

"No," Havelock said, his voice automatically taking on the gruff tone he used when he was on duty. "I wanted to ask you about putting together a team. A dozen people for small-group tactics exercises."

The chief engineer's brows furrowed and the lines around his mouth deepened. Havelock stared him down. He'd spent too many years as a cop on too many Belter stations to be intimidated by a scowl.

"Small-group tactics?"

"Null-g exercises," Havelock said. "With the riot gear. Just to keep mind and body in condition."

Koenen lifted his chin, his gaze still fixed on Havelock. It was the kind of thing a Belter never did. Havelock didn't know why the gesture so clearly belonged to someone who'd lived planetside, but it did. He found it reassuring. "You're talking about military action? Are we expecting something?"

Havelock shrugged against the couch restraints. The couch shifted a few millimeters on its gimbals. "I want the option," he said, not realizing he was quoting Murtry until he'd already done it.

"Sure, then. I can find another eleven people. When do you want us?"

"How long will it take?"

Koenen tapped his hand terminal with two fingertips. *I can call them right now.* Havelock smiled.

"We'll meet in the shuttle bay at oh seven hundred. I'll go over the equipment. Then an hour drilling every day before shift for the foreseeable future."

"I'll put it on the schedule."

They nodded to each other, and the chief engineer put out his foot, pressing it against the face of one of the cells to launch himself to the ladder. Havelock felt something uneasy shift in his mind. He was forgetting something. Something important.

When it came to him, he grunted. "Chief!"

The man looked over from the ladder. The plane of his body was orthogonal to the desk, and Havelock's sense of balance shifted as his brain made one of its occasional panicked flailing attempts to determine up from down. He closed his eyes as a wave of nausea passed over him.

"Yes?"

"When you pick out your team," Havelock said between clenched teeth. "No Belters."

For the first time, Koenen smiled. It seemed genuine. "No shit," he said.

As the acting head of security, he was expected to eat in the officers' mess. It was one of those small gestures that gave the ship a sense of continuity, of rules and customs being followed. And there were some benefits for him. The lines were shorter, alcohol was available, and the wall screen was usually set to something interesting. Right now, a UN official in an uncomfortable-looking gray suit was folding his hands on a wide, glassy desk. The camera operator was framing it to be seen on hand terminals, and so the man's face was so large on the wall that Havelock could see his pores and the streaks where the technicians on Earth had dabbed on makeup.

"We are at the beginning of a new golden age," he said. "The scale of this is immense. Everything we have done, from the first stone tools to the domes on Ganymede, we have done in essence with the resources of one planet. Earth. Yes, the need for minerals and rare earths took us to Mars and Luna. And the Belt. And the need for infrastructure made the Jovian system much more than we had imagined. But we are looking at an expansion that is not one or two but *three* orders of magnitude more than we have had in the history of our species."

Havelock peeled back the foil from the top of his meal. The beef and peppers had been designed for null g: hard nuggets of protein and vegetable that resisted breaking apart in the air, but turned soft and pleasant in his mouth. It wasn't as sanitary as tubes of goo, but it was better eating. He popped the first cube into his mouth. It sponged up his saliva, clinging to his tongue. The camera on Earth flickered to a young, serious-faced woman.

"But the designers of the protomolecule," she said. "The species who sent it here on Phoebe in the first place?"

"It has been billions of years since that happened," the man in the suit said. "None of our probes have found any signs of advanced life still functioning. We have seen what appear to be ruins. We have seen what appear to be living biospheres. Honestly, there are mornings it takes my breath away."

Havelock sipped at the bulb of water, and the food bloomed into a rich mouthful, almost like it had been cooked in a normal kitchen instead of an industrial processor.

"So what's the catch?" the woman said.

The catch is that the first thing we did once we got here was let a bunch of Belter terrorists claim squatting rights and start shooting at us, Havelock thought as he plucked another cube from the pack. On the screen the UN man unfolded his hands.

"We are processing a bit over four thousand applications *already* for the rights to explore and develop these systems. We have to do this carefully if we are to get things done right. And it does not help that the OPA has used this to make what is essentially a power grab."

"Bloody Belters," a voice said. Havelock turned to see Captain Marwick floating in the air behind him. The man's close-cropped red hair and beard had more gray in them than when they'd left Earth. Havelock nodded.

"D'ye mind if I join you, Mister Havelock?"

"Not at all," Havelock said, blinking back surprise.

The captain pulled himself to the table and strapped into a crash couch. Behind him, the wall screen shifted from the UN man to the woman interviewing him, but Havelock only registered the change as shifts of lighting and background. His attention was on Marwick.

"How've things been going on the surface?" the captain asked, cracking open the box containing his own dinner. He made the words seem like nothing more weighty than polite conversation. Between other people, it probably would have been.

"You've seen the reports," Havelock said.

"Ah, reports, though. Written for posterity and the judge as often as not. Still, I was a bit surprised to see that our mutual friend Mister Murtry had taken quite such a firm hand just when the mediator arrived."

"Situation called for it," Havelock said. "We've lost a lot of good people down there by being restrained and patient."

Marwick made a humming sound that could have meant anything and ate a bite of his meal. His gaze fixed somewhere over Havelock's left shoulder.

"And of course we're in a position of relative power here, aren't we?" Marwick said. "I hope our friend on the ground is keeping in mind that won't always be the case."

"I'm not sure I know what you mean."

"Well, I am not, strictly speaking, a part of the expeditionary force, am I? The *Israel* is my domain. I use my rank as captain to make the demands and requests the home office prefers me to, though in truth I'm just the lorry driver. But I'll be driving my lorry back through that gate at some point, and Fred Johnson and his well-armed base will be waiting on the other side of it. I'd rather he not think of me first and foremost as a target."

Havelock chewed slowly, frowning. A dull anger tightened his jaw. "We're the ones who followed the rules here. We came with science teams and a hard dome. We hired them to build our landing platform, and they killed us. We're the good guys here."

"And the moral high ground is a lovely place," Marwick said, as if he were agreeing. "It won't stop a missile, though. It won't alter the trajectory of a gauss round. What our mutual friend does planetside has consequences that go a long way out from here. And there are those among us, myself included, who'd like to go home one day."

Marwick took another bite of his dinner, smiled ruefully, and nodded as if Havelock had said something. He undid the crash couch straps.

"Keeps body and soul together, these little boxes, but they don't really satisfy, do they? Give my left nut for a real steak. Well, it was a pleasure, Mister Havelock. As always."

Havelock nodded, but the anger in his chest rode the ragged edge between annoyance and rage. He knew that it was at least in part because that was the reaction Murtry would have had in his place, but knowing that didn't change the emotion. His hand terminal chimed. Chief Engineer Koenen had sent a message. He tapped it open.

we've got a full team. one of the boys is fabbing up a little logo for the club. just something to keep morale up.

Havelock considered the image. It was a stylized male form, squat and featureless, holding up a fist larger than its head. It was a cartoon of the Earther body type, and of violence. Havelock looked at it for a long time before he answered back.

looks great. make sure you get one for me.

Chapter Sixteen: Elvi

What do you mean *movement?*" Elvi asked.

"After we saw the power spike," Holden said, "the *Roci-nante* did a sweep of the location. Several of them, actually."

He held out his hand terminal, and Elvi took it. She tried to look serious, not to seem impressed. She was a scientist, for God's sake, facing a serious question, not a girl who'd get on her family's shared feed and burble about how James Holden had been in her hut. She flipped the images back and forth. Human brains were wired to see movement, and so the shifting shadows were easy to spot when she went quickly.

"Something's moving," she agreed. "Can we see what it is?"

"Not a lot of imaging satellites up there yet," Holden said. "The *Roci*'s built for ship-to-ship combat more than ground visualization."

Anywhere in the solar system, it wouldn't have been like this.

There were so many cameras of such exquisite sensitivity, almost nothing could happen in the vast emptiness inside the orbit of Neptune that couldn't be seen if someone wanted to look for it. It was another reminder of how far from home they were, and how many axioms of daily life didn't apply here.

"What does the *Israel* see?" she asked.

"Nothing that's a lot better," Holden said. "That's why we're going out. It's right at the range of the vehicles. It's going to take the better part of the day to get out there."

"Why?" she asked. "I mean, I see it's decently large, but there are likely to be any number of large organisms in the ocean and colder environments."

"Organisms don't make power spikes," Holden said. "All sorts of things are moving on this planet. All the time. This just started."

Elvi touched the image, expanding it until the shadows blurred.

"You're right. We should check it out," she said. "Let me get my instruments."

An hour later, she was in the back of an open loader, Fayez at her side. Holden sat in front of them, in the passenger's seat, while Chandra Wei drove. A vicious-looking rifle jounced at Wei's side, in easy reach if violence came on them unexpectedly. The loader's engines whined, and the wheels ground against the stones of the wind-paved desert.

"Why didn't Sudyam come?" Elvi asked, shouting to be heard over the loader and the wind.

Fayez leaned close to her shoulder. "Wei thought it would be good to have someone on the exobio workgroup still alive if this went poorly."

Elvi's felt her eyes go wide, and she glanced at the woman in the driver's seat. "Really?"

"She phrased it more gently," Fayez said.

There was no demarcation of the border, no fence or road to show that they had left First Landing. The stone-and-dirt hills rose and fell, organisms like grass or fungus clinging to the land

and being crushed under the loader's wheels. Slowly, the ruins that had become Elvi's landmark on New Terra thinned and shrank and fell out of view. She leaned her head against the loader's roll bar, letting the vibrations of the land translate themselves through her skull. Wei looked over her shoulder, and Elvi smiled at her. The memories of a hundred field excursions in graduate school left her body expecting beer and marijuana, and the anxiety of the actual errand tugged at her. Every day for weeks, she had found some new organism or fact that humanity had never seen before, and now she was going to something possibly even more alien. No one had said the word *protomolecule*, but the implication was thick as cement. Animals didn't make a power surge. The aliens did.

In the wide, bright sky above them, high-altitude winds pulled a huge green-and-pink cloud into thin streamers. The speculation on Luna was that the strange cloud coloration meant an organism was present in them, something that packed its own minerals up into the sky and used the vapor the way salmon used spawning pools. It was only a hypothesis. The truth could be a thousand times stranger. Or it could be utterly mundane. Elvi watched the bright fleece of cloud stretch, and the sun track a little too slowly past it. Fayez was typing furiously on his hand terminal. Wei drove with a focus and intensity that seemed to be her signature ever since she'd come to the surface. Which meant ever since Reeve and the others had gone missing.

Elvi wondered what it meant that she could go out into the absolute unknown, tracking across a planet with no idea what the local dangers might be, and it was thoughts of the people back in First Landing that frightened her. New Terra was supposed to be dangerous and wild and unknown. It was only living up to expectations. The dangers that the people posed were worse because she hadn't seen it coming. And so she was afraid she wouldn't next time either.

She wasn't aware of drifting into a doze until Fayez put his hand on her shoulder and shook her gently back to herself. He pointed up. A bright spot lit the blue of the sky like Venus seen from Earth. It grew slowly brighter as it tracked west. A thin white contrail formed behind it, the only perfectly straight line in the organically twisting sky. A shuttle. Elvi frowned.

"Were we expecting the shuttle?" she asked.

"That's not ours," Fayez said. "That's the *Barbapiccola*'s. The mining operation's under way again."

Elvi shook her head. It was all one stupid, shortsighted mistake after another, strung together so that each one seemed inevitable. The colony would sell the ore, get lawyers, make deals. The containment dome would never be set up. What should have been clean, solid biology would turn into a salvage job of *correcting for* this and *discarding the impurities* that. Fayez seemed to know what she was thinking.

"No research protocol survives contact with the subject population," he said. "That's not just this. It's everything."

The sun had dipped to half a hand above the horizon when the loader topped another rise like a thousand before it. Wei braked and shut off the engines. Fayez stood up in his seat, his elbows resting on the roll bar. Holden said something obscene under his breath.

"Well," Fayez said, his voice hushed. "At least it wasn't hard to find."

The thing hunkered down in the depression between two hills. Its vast carapace was the nacreous white that she'd seen in the walls of the ruins, but there was nothing architectural about this. It had an insectile form, long articulated limbs like legs pressing weakly out into the hardpack. Two larger appendages emerged from its back, one gray and splintered, the exoskeleton empty of anything but dust, the other swinging awkwardly. Five black circles on its abdomen recalled eyes, but didn't shift to focus on them. At least not as far as Elvi could tell.

"What is it?" Wei asked. Elvi noticed that the rifle had made its way to the woman's hands. She hadn't seen that happen.

"I don't know," Elvi said. "I haven't seen anything like it before."

"I have," Holden said. "It's one of their machines. Whatever designed the protomolecule had...things like this on the station between the rings. They were smaller, though. I saw one of them kill someone."

"You're telling me," Wei said, her voice even and calm, "that thing is a couple billion years old?"

"That would be my guess," Holden said.

Fayez whistled low. "That is not dead which can eternal lie. Or, y'know, whatever."

The monster from the desert shifted drunkenly, its legs awkward. Its one functioning arm twisted toward them, then collapsed to the ground. Its body shifted and trembled as it tried to lift it again.

"Look," Elvi said. "Back there."

All along the contour line at the bottom of the valley between hills, the stones had been scraped clean. None of the quasi-fungal grasses remained. No lizards or birds. It was like a vast hand had come down with a sponge and wiped the landscape clean. Now that she knew to look, she saw the thing's legs were pulling the native life up and feeding into tiny, chitinous orifices along its underbelly.

"It's...eating?" she said.

"On the station," Holden said, "soldiers tried to kill one with a grenade. The machines killed the man who threw it and used his body. Reprocessed it right there. Turned him into paste and used him to repair the damage."

"That makes sense," Elvi said. "The protomolecule repurposed biological systems during the Eros event as well."

"Glad you approve, Doctor Okoye," Wei said dryly. "In your scientific opinion, could this pose a threat to the expedition?"

"Sure, maybe," Elvi said, and Holden made a gurgling sound in the back of his throat. The thing lurched forward, lost its footing, and scrambled back. It was like watching a broken toy or a car-struck dog that hadn't quite died yet. It was fascinating and frightening, and she couldn't look away.

"I think we need to leave now," Holden said, fear making the words come fast. "Like now now. Not later now."

"Isn't what we came here for," Wei said, raising the rifle to her shoulder.

"What are you doing!" Holden shouted. "Did you not hear me about the putty making?"

In reply, Wei opened fire. Tracer rounds drew bright red lines through the air, and small explosions lit every place they struck. The thing staggered back, swinging its arm, but Wei pulled a fresh clip from her pocket when the first one went dry and resumed firing. The thing tried to push in toward Wei, and then to move away from her. A green-gray liquid poured from the wounds in its side. The report of the rifle was deafening.

The thing lurched one last time, and let out a high, teeth-clenching keen. It collapsed, legs splayed, in the pool of liquid. Wei let the gun's barrel drift down until it pointed at the ground. When she looked at Holden, her eyes were hard. Holden hands were on the loader's dash, the knuckles white. His face was gray.

"I hope that's not a problem, sir," Wei said.

"You are out of your fucking mind?" Holden said, his voice high and tight. "That thing could have killed you!"

"Yes, sir," Wei said. "That's why I killed it."

"Did you?" Holden said, his voice continuing to climb. "Are you sure? What if it's not all the way dead? Can we...burn it or something?"

Wei smiled.

"Yes," she said. "Yes, we can."

An hour later, the great ruddy disk of the sun touched the horizon. The flames danced around the thing's corpse, rising up higher than a bonfire. Greasy black smoke spiraled up toward the clouds, and the whole world seemed to reek of accelerants. Wei had taken a small tent from the loader's storage, and Fayez had set it up. Elvi stood, the heat of the sun and the fire pressing against her face. The night was going to be long. They all were, here.

"You all right?" Fayez asked.

"I'm fine. I wish I'd gotten some samples, though."

In the heart of the fire, the thing glowed. Its shell was white-hot, and thin cracks had started to show, radiating out from its joints. It was beautiful in its way, and she was sorry to see it destroyed and relieved in almost equal measures. It wasn't an emotional mixture she was used to.

Wei insisted on setting up watches through the night, and Holden volunteered to take the first of them. He seemed uneasy in a way that Elvi wouldn't have thought James Holden, captain of the *Rocinante*, was capable of. Vulnerable. Elvi lay in the tent, her head poking out. Fayez snored softly beside her. Wei, curled in the back of the loader with a thin blanket, was silent as stone. Elvi watched Holden and listened while he hummed to himself, a lonely human sound in the vast inhuman planet. Sleep didn't come. After two hours, she gave up, rose from her uncomfortable bed, and went to sit at the man's side. In a world without moonlight, there was only the orange glow of the alien's dying pyre and a thin silver highlight of stars. It reduced him to a few lines and a sense of mass and warmth.

"I couldn't sleep," she said.

"I don't think I will either," he said. "I hate the way those things scare me."

"I'm surprised to hear you say that."

"You were expecting me to enjoy it?" She could hear the smile. Far above them, a falling star streaked across the sky, bright, and then gone.

"I'm not used to hearing men admit to having emotions," she said. "You were on Eros when the outbreak came, weren't you? I'd think after that, nothing would frighten you."

"Doesn't work that way. After Eros, everything frightened me. I'm still trying to calm down." He chuckled. When he spoke again, his voice had sobered. "Do you think that thing was a machine? Or was that an animal?"

"I don't think that's a distinction they would have made."

"You mean the designers? Who the hell knows how they would have seen anything?"

"Oh, we can say some things," Elvi said. "What they cared about was in what they designed. And still is, in a way. We know that they respected the power of self-replicators and knew how to harness it."

She felt him turn toward her more than saw it. She was profoundly aware of being a woman in a dark wilderness with a man beside her. It made the vast night seem intimate.

"How do we know that?" he asked.

"Where they sent the protomolecule," she said. "The universe has some things that are fairly consistent. The elements are the same. Carbon is always carbon. Nitrogen's always nitrogen. They make the same bonds and can build the same structures. All the systems we've surveyed have at least one planet that has the possibility of generating organic replicators."

"Meaning things with DNA?"

"Or things that act like DNA. They sent out bridge builders to use those basic biological replicators, whatever their form. They can take a biosphere and turn it into a massively networked factory. It's probably how they spread. Target the places that can be hijacked into making the things that let you get there. Also, they really built structures to last. They seem to have taken the long view on galactic colonizing."

She leaned back, letting her hand rest on the front of the loader. Not reaching out to him, but putting her fingers where, in the darkness, he might accidentally brush against them. To the north, some small animal called, its voice high and chirping.

"It was there for billions of years," Holden said. "And we killed it with a rifle and some mineral spirits."

"In our defense, it wasn't looking healthy. But yes. It wasn't expecting anything as advanced or aggressive as we are. They built structures that lasted billions of years. The ruins. That thing. The rings. All of it."

"They sound like gods sometimes. Angry spiteful gods, but still."

"No," Elvi said. "Just organisms that we don't understand. And with their own constraints. They were specialized for their ecosystem, just like we are. Thirteen hundred worlds seems a lot when you've only ever had the one, but it's a raindrop in the ocean compared with what's out there, just in our galaxy."

"They had more."

Elvi made a small inquiring sound.

"They had more," Holden said. "But something attacked them, and they tried to stop it. They burned up entire solar systems. A lot of them. Then, when that didn't work, they shut down the whole network. Quarantined themselves and died anyway."

"I didn't know that."

"I saw it. Sort of. A guy I used to know is kind of looking into it."

"I'd like to talk to him," she said.

"Yeah, he's less helpful than you'd expect."

Wei shifted in her sleep. Elvi yawned, though she wasn't particularly tired.

"Why did it wake up?" he said, nodding toward the alien corpse. "Was it because of us? Did it know we were here?"

"Maybe," she said. "Or maybe they cycle up and down every so often. We've only seen one. There may be a lot of these and seeing them will be common. There may be a few and it will be rare. There could only have been one. Not enough data yet."

"I guess not. Still, I wish I knew what was going to happen."

"I don't. So much of my life has been better than what I imagined, I've come to enjoy being surprised. When I was doing my undergraduate at Kano, I was imagining I'd be doing environmental assays on Europa for my whole career. Instead, this."

"Kano?"

"I spent a lot of time in the West African Shared Interest Zone when I was growing up. Northern Nigeria. I went back there for university."

"Really?" Holden said, his voice bright. "One of my fathers had family in Nigeria."

"One of them?"

"I have several," he said. "Extended parental group."

"Oh. I've heard of those."

"Makes for a big nuclear family, and a *huge* extended one. We might be cousins."

"I hope not," Elvi said, laughing, and then wished she could suck the words back. The silence was terrible. She couldn't see his face clearly, but she could imagine it. The surprise. The embarrassment. She pulled her hand back and put it in her lap.

"I—" he said.

"If you'd like, I'll take the rest of the watch," Elvi said. The lightness in her voice sounded forced, even to herself. "I don't think I'll be sleeping much tonight anyway."

"That would be...great," Holden said. "Thank you."

"Just be careful of Fayez. He steals the blankets."

James Holden slid off the loader. She heard his footsteps tracking back to the tent, heard the rustle of the plastic as he bedded down. She hunched over, arms around her belly. The thing from the desert was nothing more than embers, glowing dull orange in the night but illuminating nothing. The humiliation sat with her, bright and painful as a paper cut.

"Stupid," she said softly. "Stupid, stupid, *stupid*."

The alien darkness didn't disagree.

Chapter Seventeen: Basia

Coop and Cate had been old-school OPA, back when the Outer Planets Alliance was just a shared opinion with guns. They'd come up the ranks together when even wearing the OPA's split circle on your sleeve was an arrestable offense. They'd learned their craft sneaking past armed Earth-Mars Coalition checkpoints, planting bombs, smuggling guns, and generally acting like the terrorists the inner planets had accused them of being. The only reason they hadn't both gone to prison camps forever was because by some standards, the OPA had won. After Eros, the inner planets had begun treating the OPA like an actual government, and many of the OPA warriors had received the de facto amnesty that non-enforcement brought.

Cate was just a miner now, like the rest of them, but she could use words like *tactical advantage* and actually sound like she knew what she was talking about.

"The terrain and numerical superiority are our tactical advantages," Cate said to the small group assembled in her house. "But we're outgunned. No way around that. We have maybe a dozen firearms total. We can still get explosives, but the deal Holden struck with RCE makes it much riskier."

"Fucking Holden," Zadie said.

"We'll deal with him soon enough," Cate replied.

Her audience was made up of the usual gang. Zadie's son had taken a turn for the worse with his eye infection, and her wife was staying home with him full-time now. Basia had the impression that Zadie was looking for someone to punish for her family's pain. Pete, Scotty, and Ibrahim were there as well, the veterans of their one skirmish with the RCE security people. It gave them a degree of status in the group that they'd latched on to. But there were a few new people as well. Other members of the colony who might have been on the fence before about the best way to deal with RCE, but had been pushed into the revolutionary camp by Murtry's brutal tactics. By the martyring of Coop.

"How?" Scotty asked. "How do we deal with Holden?"

"I think we remove all of our problems in one multi-front operation," Cate said. "Murtry and his team, Holden and his thug, everyone at once. The key to this kind of war is money."

"Make us too expensive to occupy." Ibrahim nodded. He'd been OPA too.

"Exactly. That's how we got the inners off our asses in the Belt. If it's not economically viable to occupy us, they won't. Every one of them that goes home in a body bag is one more nail in the corporate coffin." Cate punched one large fist into her other hand to punctuate.

"I don't follow. How does killing them help us with that?" Basia asked. He'd agreed to come in the hope he might be able to help cooler heads prevail. That was looking less and less likely the longer the meeting went on.

"It's an eighteen-month trip to send new troops to the front," Cate answered. "That's a long-flight freighter tied up for over three years. That's expensive. And for the year and a half they're flying out here, we're fortifying our position. Making camps in the hills. Branching out. In order to win, they'll need to do a full military program. Medina Station won't support that, even if they get pissed at us for pushing the issue."

"Coercive alliance," Ibrahim added, nodding.

"By the book," Cate said.

The room was quiet for a moment as everyone there mulled over her words. The metal roof rattled and scraped as the wind outside blew sand across it. The windows creaked, cooling with the night. A dozen people breathed the alien air.

"They're here already," Basia said, clearing his throat to break the silence. "Isn't that exactly what they'll do?"

"What who will do?" Scotty asked.

"The *Rocinante*," Basia replied. "They're in orbit right now. A warship, with guns and missiles and who knows what else. If we kill Holden, can't they just bomb us?"

"Let's hope they do!" Cate thundered at him. "By God let's hope so. A few videos of dead colonists, murdered by UN ships in orbit, and the public opinion war is over."

Basia nodded as though he were agreeing, while what he was really thinking was, *I'm on the wrong team.*

"So, we move on both groups at once," Cate said. Her voice had taken on the same cadences Coop used to have. It was as if the man were still in the room, haunting the place. "They keep two people on roving patrol at all times, so we'll need a team shadowing them until the signal goes out. We'll put a second team on the security building where Murtry and the rest of his people will be. The third team will go to the commissary where Holden and his crewman are holed up at night. I'm thinking Scotty and Ibrahim for team one. I'll lead..."

Cate rattled on, laying out the insanity of multiple murder like a puzzle to be solved or a game to be won. Coordinating the attacks so all three happened at once, so no one could raise the alarm. Using phrases like *fields of fire* and *maximum aggression* as if they meant anything other than gunning down a dozen women and men while most of them slept. The little group nodded and followed along. Basia was astonished by how easily the unthinkable became the routine.

"My children live here," Basia said, interrupting.

"What?" Cate said, looking genuinely puzzled. She'd been mid-sentence when he spoke up. "I don't—"

"The bodies that we take pictures of to send to the newscasts," Basia continued. "Those are our children. My children."

Cate blinked at him, too puzzled to be angry yet.

"Como?"

"I wanted to come here and maybe talk you out of doing something stupid," Basia said, standing up and addressing the room. "I thought maybe with Coop gone, we could put an end to this. But this isn't just stupid anymore. Not when you can talk about dead friends and family as media tools. That's evil. And I can't be part of it."

The room was silent again, except for the sand and the cooling windows and the breathing.

"If you try to get in our way—" Ibrahim started, but Basia wheeled to face the man.

"What?" he said, getting close enough that his breath stirred the whiskers in Ibrahim's thin beard. "If I get in your way what? Don't make half a threat, macho."

Ibrahim was smaller than him. He lowered his eyes and said nothing. Basia felt a brief moment of shameful relief that it was Ibrahim who had chosen to press the issue, not Cate. Basia was afraid of Cate. He'd never have been able to stand up to her.

"Dui," he said, backing away and nodding to them all. "Gone now."

They began talking in hushed tones after the door closed behind him, but he couldn't hear what they were saying. It made the back of his neck itch. He wondered if he'd gone too far, and if they'd be content with just killing him and not Lucia too.

Halfway home he ran into two of the RCE security people

walking patrol. Two women in heavy body armor that made them look bulky and dangerous. One of them, a fair-skinned woman with raven-black hair, nodded at him as he walked past. Everything about her was a threat: the armor, the large assault rifle she cradled in her arms, the stun grenades and wrist restraints hanging on her belt. Her friendly smile looked wildly out of place. Basia couldn't stop himself from picturing her bleeding out in the street, shot in the back by one of his friends.

Lucia was waiting on their porch, sitting cross-legged on a large pillow and drinking something that steamed in the night air. Not tea. They had almost none of it left. Probably just hot water with a bit of lemon flavoring. But even the artificial flavorings would soon be gone unless they were given permission to begin trading their ore.

Basia sat down on the hard carbon fiber floor next to her with a thump.

"So?" Lucia asked.

"They won't listen." Basia sighed. "They're talking about killing the RCE people. All of them. And Jim Holden and his people too."

Lucia shook her head, a gentle negation. "And you?"

"At this point, they may be talking about killing me too. I don't think they will as long as I don't get in their way. But I can't take part. I told them so. I'm so sorry I let it get this far, Lucy. I'm a very stupid man."

Lucia gave him a sad smile, and put her hand on his arm. "Not doing anything now keeps you on their side."

Basia frowned. The night air still held the earthy smell of the recent dust storm. A graveyard scent. "I can't stop them by myself."

"Holden is here to do that. He's back from whatever he was doing out in the desert with the science teams. You could talk to him."

"I know," Basia said, admitting what he'd already been thinking. The fact that it was necessary didn't make it feel like any less of a betrayal of his friends. "I know. I will."

Lucia laughed her relief. At Basia's puzzled look, she grabbed him in her arms and pulled him close. "I'm so happy to know that the Basia I love is still in there."

Basia relaxed into her embrace, letting himself feel safe and loved for a moment.

"Baz," Lucia whispered in his ear.

Don't say anything that will ruin this moment, he thought.

"Felcia is leaving on the shuttle for the *Barbapiccola*. Now. Tonight. I gave her permission."

Basia pulled himself away, holding Lucia at arm's length. "She's doing what?"

Lucia frowned at him, and gripped his upper arms tightly. "Let her go." There was a warning in her voice.

Basia pulled himself free and leaped to his feet. Lucia called after him, but he was already running down the road toward the landing site as fast as his legs would carry him.

His relief when he saw the shuttle still sitting there was so powerful he almost collapsed. One of the colony's electric carts whizzed by, nearly running him over in the dark. The bed of the cart was filled with ore. They were still loading the shuttle. He had time.

Felcia stood a few meters from the airlock, a suitcase in each hand, chatting with the pilot. They were in a bright pool of illumination cast by the work lights surrounding the ship, and her dark olive skin seemed to glow. Her black hair hung about her face and down her back in loose waves. Her eyes and mouth were wide as she spoke on some topic that excited her.

In that moment, his daughter was so beautiful it made Basia's chest ache. When she spotted him, her face lit up with a smile. Before she could speak, Basia wrapped her in his arms and squeezed her tight.

"Papa," she said, worry in her voice.

"No, baby, it's okay," he shook his head against her cheek. "I didn't come to stop you. I only...I couldn't let you leave without saying goodbye."

His cheek felt wet. Felcia was crying. He held her by the shoulders and pushed her away to look at her face. His little girl, all grown up but crying in his arms. He couldn't help but see the four-year-old she'd once been, weeping when she fell and hurt her knee.

"Papa," she said, her voice thick. "I was worried you would hate me for going. But Mama said—"

"No, baby, no." Basia hugged her again. "You go, and when they let the ship leave, you go to Ceres and become a doctor and have a fantastic life."

"Why?"

Because the people here see your death as a tool for winning a public opinion battle. Because I've lost all the children I ever plan to lose. Because I can't have you see me when they finally arrest me.

"Because I love you, baby," he said instead. "And I want you to go be amazing."

She hugged him, and for that one moment, all was right in the universe again. Basia watched as she boarded, stopping just inside the airlock to wave and blow him a kiss. He watched as they loaded the last of the ore into the cargo compartment. He watched as the shuttle lifted off with a roar and wash of heat.

Then he turned back toward town to find Holden.

Holden and Amos were sitting in the commissary's tiny bar. Amos drank and watched everyone who came in through the door. He held his glass with his left hand, his right never far from the gun at his belt. Holden was typing rapidly on a hand terminal lying on the table. Both men looked tense.

Basia walked toward them, smiling and nodding his head and keeping his hands visible and away from his body. Amos smiled back. The big man's scalp looked pale and shiny under the commissary's white LEDs. When he leaned forward in his chair it looked perfectly natural and non-threatening, and Basia noted that it also put the gun closer to hand seemingly by accident.

They were not the sort of details he would have noticed before. Coop and Cate and the violence of the last few months had left him on edge, seeing the potential for violence everywhere. When he looked at Amos, he suspected his instincts were not wrong.

Raising his hands, he said, "Captain Holden, can I join you for a moment?"

Holden's head darted up, startled and frightened. Basia was pretty sure he was not the source of the man's fear, and wondered what was. Murtry and his corporate killers? Had Holden heard from someone else about the planned attack?

"Please," Holden said, the fear disappearing from his face as quickly as it had come. He gestured at one of their table's empty chairs. "What can I do for you?"

Amos said nothing, just kept smiling his vague smile. Basia sat, making sure to keep his hands on the table and in plain view. "Captain, I've come to warn you."

"About?" Amos said at once. Holden said nothing.

"There is a group here. The same group that attacked and killed the RCE security team prior to your arrival. They plan to kill the remaining security people sometime in the next few days. Maybe as early as tomorrow night."

Holden and Amos shared a quick look. "We've been expecting something like that," Holden said. "But that's not the important—"

Basia didn't let him finish. "They also plan to kill you."

Holden sat up a little straighter. He didn't seem angry so much as offended.

"Me? Why would they want to kill *me*?"

"They think it will send a message," Basia said, his tone apologetic. "Also, they're mad about the explosives inspectors."

"Told you," Holden said to Amos. "A good compromise pisses everyone off."

Without realizing he was going to do it, Basia grabbed the bottle off the table and took a long drink. It must have been something they had brought with them, because it was much better whiskey than anything the colony had access to. It warmed his throat and belly pleasantly, but didn't calm him as much as he'd hoped. He pushed the bottle back toward Amos, but the big man stopped him. "You keep that, brother. You look like you need it."

"What are you going to do?" Basia asked Holden.

"About the assassination? Nothing. It won't matter because we're all leaving."

"We're all—?"

"We're evacuating the planet. All of us. Everyone."

"No," Basia said. "No one's leaving. We can't go now." *I helped kill people to stay here.*

"Oh, we *really* are," Holden said. "Something very bad is happening on this planet, and it has nothing to do with obstinate Belters or sociopathic corporate security."

Basia took another long drink from the bottle. The alcohol was starting to leave him a little fuzzy, but not any less anxious. "I don't understand."

"Somebody used to live here," Holden said, waving one arm around. It took Basia's drink-addled mind a moment to realize Holden didn't mean the commissary. "Maybe they're gone, and maybe they aren't, but they left a lot of stuff behind and some of it's waking up. So before we wind up being Eros with a great big sky, everyone is getting the hell out of Dodge."

Basia nodded without understanding. Amos grinned at him and said, "The towers and robots, man. He means the alien shit. Looks like some of it's waking up."

"I'm sending a message up to the *Roci* right now to bounce it on to the UN and the OPA council," Holden continued. "My recommendation is that everyone get into orbit as soon as possible. I'm asking for emergency command of the *Israel* and the *Barbapiccola* to facilitate that."

"That isn't going to happen," Basia said, his voice soft.

"It's not an easy sell," Holden said, "but I can be persuasive. And once I have command—"

"They won't go," Basia said. "People already bled for this land. Died for it. We're willing to kill each other to stay here, we'll sure as hell stay and fight whatever else wants us gone."

"Providing there's anyone left," Amos said.

"Well, sure," Basia agreed. "Providing that."

Chapter Eighteen: Holden

Murtry and his security team had converted the small prefab security outpost into a fortress. The inner walls had been sprayed with energy-absorbing foam that looked like whipped cream but formed a ballistic barrier that could stop small-arms fire and light explosives. A large gun cage sat against one wall, secured with a biometric lock. It had only a few guns in it. Since Holden didn't know exactly how many the security team had brought with them, that was either a good thing or a bad thing.

Murtry sat behind a small desk with a hand terminal lying on it. He leaned back in his chair, hands behind his head, a vague smile on his face. He looked like a man with all the time in the world.

"Did you hear me when I said that people are planning to murder your team?" Holden asked.

"I wish you'd stop using that word," Carol Chiwewe said. She insisted on being present at any meeting between Holden and the RCE people, and it had seemed like a reasonable request. Now, with her own people plotting an attack, it felt like a security risk.

" 'Murder'?" Murtry said. " 'Terrorism' has a nice ring to it. 'Homicide' always sounded a bit legalistic to me. Pretentious."

"Wait," Holden cut in before Carol could respond to Murtry's baiting. "Cut that out right now. My capacity for giving a shit about your little tiff down here has hit its limit. This is no longer a negotiation of rights or a discussion of who attacked who first."

"No?" Murtry said. "And what is it, then?"

"It's about me telling you what's going to happen."

"Telling," Murtry said.

"You're not in charge here," Carol added. Holden squashed the irritation he felt at their only taking sides to make his life harder.

"Two things have changed recently, and one hasn't," he said, working to keep his tone pleasant. "The violence is about to escalate, with us teetering on the edge of an all-out shooting war between the colony and RCE. And, probably more importantly, the alien stuff left on this planet is waking up."

"What's the one that didn't?" Murtry asked.

"What?"

"The one thing that didn't change."

"Right," Holden said, leaning across the desk toward him. "I'm still the only guy in the system with a warship in orbit. So with those three things in mind, we're leaving this planet before you idiots can kill any more of each other, or before the aliens kill all of us."

"Threats now?" Carol said behind him.

Without looking away from Murtry, Holden said, "You bet, if that's what it takes. Start getting your people ready for evac. Get the *Israel*'s shuttles down here. Do it now. The *Israel* is leaving with me in thirty hours, and you'll want to be on it when we go."

"You can't," Carol said, and Holden spun around to face her.

"I can. We'll get the *Barb*'s shuttle back down here, and I suggest you have your people pack up everything they care about and start getting on it. Because the *Barb* is leaving."

Carol's mouth went tight and her hands curled into fists.

"You done?" Murtry asked, his voice light. "May I present my rebuttal?"

"There isn't one," Holden said, pulling a chair up to the desk and sitting down. Showing he didn't care about the trappings of control the security office gave Murtry.

"So, here's the price of fame," Murtry continued. "You are one of the most recognized people in the solar system. It's why they sent you. Fame gives you the illusion of power. But it's all just a façade."

"No, the fact that I own the *Rocinante*—"

Murtry patted the air again in the same condescending gesture he'd used on Carol. "You're famous for being the man who tries to save everyone. For being the solar system's white knight. Tilting at giants like Protogen and Mao-Kwik. Your ship's got the right name."

Murtry laughed at Holden's frown.

"Yeah, I've read a book," Murtry went on. "So that's why they send you here. No one will expect the great James Holden to take sides. Of secretly backing either the colonists *or* one of those nasty Earth corporations. You're the man without an agenda or subtext."

"Great," Holden said. "Thanks for the insight. Now call your people and—"

"But we're eighteen months from the closest legal remedy, and the only real power you have out here is violence."

"You're the violent man here," Carol said, making it an accusation.

"I am," Murtry agreed. "I understand its uses better than most. And the thing I know about you, Captain Holden, is that you are not. Now, if that brute you brought with you were in here making these threats, well, I'd have to take that seriously. But not from you. You've got a warship in orbit right now that could blow the *Israel* and the *Barbapiccola* into glowing slag, then rain down destruction on this planet that would wipe out every shred of human life in this solar system. *But* you're not the man to pull that trigger, and we both know it. So save your threats. They're embarrassing."

"You're out of control," Holden replied. "You're insane, and as soon as RCE finds out—"

"Finds out what? That the UN mediator got spooked because there was an alien artifact on an alien planet, and I didn't?" Murtry interrupted. "Send in a full report. I'm sure that with your reputation and the backing of the UN and OPA, your words will be given serious consideration. And maybe, *maybe* three years from now a replacement will arrive to relieve me of duty."

Holden stood up, dropping his hand to the butt of his gun. "Or maybe I relieve you right now."

The room went silent for a moment. Carol seemed to be holding her breath. Murtry frowned up at Holden, seemingly taken off guard for the first time. Holden waited, not breaking eye contact, angry enough to draw on Murtry and furious with himself for letting it get to that point.

Murtry smiled. It did nothing to break the tension. "If you'd brought the other one with you, that threat might have some weight. We both know who the killer on your crew is."

"If you think I wouldn't blow you out of that chair right this second to save everyone else on this planet, then you don't know me at all."

There were scratching sounds on the floor as Carol shuffled back toward the door and out of the potential firing line. Holden kept his eyes on Murtry. The man frowned up at him for several seconds, then shifted back to the vague smile. *Here we go*, Holden thought, and tried not to let the rush of adrenaline make his hand shake.

When the hand terminal on the desk squawked a connection

request, Holden was so startled that he half drew his gun before he could stop himself. Murtry didn't move. The terminal screeched again.

"May I answer that?" Murtry asked.

Holden just nodded at him, dropping his gun back into its holster. Murtry picked up the terminal and opened the connection.

"Wei here," a voice said.

"Go ahead."

"Team in position. Birds are all in the nest and tooling up. Are we a go?"

"Hold," Murtry said, then put the terminal down and looked back up and Holden. "You're still twitching over what happened on Eros. I get that. You're not rational about all this alien shit, and honestly, who would be? I forgive you for the threats. And I appreciate that your initial purpose in coming here was to warn me about the danger to my team. It says something to me that in spite of our differences, you're still trying to save my people."

"No one needs to die here," Holden said, hoping against hope that Murtry was backing down.

"Well, that's not strictly speaking true," Murtry replied. "I'm good at this job. Did you think I didn't know about this little uprising? I knew before you did."

The security teams constantly patrolling the town would never have gotten close enough to listen in. "You've been bugging the town."

"Every building in it," Murtry agreed. "So while I appreciate you coming here, I think I've got the situation handled."

"You bugged my town?" Carol asked, anger seeming to win out over her fear.

"What are you doing?" Holden said. "Don't do something stupid."

Murtry just smiled again, picked up his hand terminal, and said, "Strike team is go."

The gunshots outside were softened by the foam covering the

walls, and sounded like a rapid string of faint pops. Like distant
fireworks, or a bad hydraulic seal finally letting go.

"Oh no," Carol said, and rushed to the door. Holden followed
her, fumbling with his hand terminal to call Amos.

Outside, the sound was much louder. The staccato reports of
gunfire splitting the peaceful night air, the flashes a distant strobe
lighting up the far edge of the town. Holden ran toward the shots,
shouting into his terminal for Amos to come. He stumbled in the
dark, dropping it, but didn't stop to pick it up.

At the northern edge of town, he found the rest of Murtry's
security team firing on one of the houses. Shots were coming back
at them from inside. The security people were shouting at the people in the house to surrender, the people inside cursing and firing
in answer. Smoke poured out one of the house's broken windows,
something inside burning.

"Stop it!" Holden yelled as he ran toward the RCE people. They
ignored him and continued to pour fire into the house. Answering bullets hit one of the RCE people in the chest, the body armor
making a dull thud as it stopped the round. The security woman
fell on her back, yelling in pain and surprise. The rest of the team
opened up on the window the shot had come from, blasting the
frame and inside wall behind it into splinters.

The blaze inside the house spread suddenly with a wave of heat
and a whooshing sound. Someone inside screamed in panic or
pain. The front door, already just a mass of carbon fiber splinters
from gunfire, swung open. A woman rushed out, a rifle in her
hands. The security team shot her into a splatter of blood, and she
collapsed at the bottom of the steps, twitching.

"They're burning!" Holden yelled, grabbing the nearest RCE
person by the arms and shaking him. "We have to get them out!"

The man responded by shoving him away. "Stay back until the
area is cleared, sir!"

Holden shoved back, hard enough to put the RCE man on his
ass in the dirt, and ran toward the fallen woman at the front of

the house. Someone inside must have thought he was attacking, because a shotgun blast rang out and the ground a meter behind him flew up in a miniature explosion of dust. The RCE people opened up, and Holden found himself between two different firing lines.

Again, some distant and still calm part of his brain thought, marveling at how often this sort of thing seemed to happen.

He dove to the ground and rolled his body on top of the fallen woman, screaming for everyone to stop. No one listened. The fire in the house billowed out with another loud whump, and the heat scorched the exposed skin on Holden's face and hands. The gunshots from inside the house cut off all at once, and the RCE return fire soon after. Holden grabbed the fallen woman by the arms and dragged her away from the flames. He stumbled when he reached the RCE people, falling down at their feet.

"Help *her*," he croaked at the woman who reached down to help him up. He pushed himself up to his hands and knees, but stopped there, too dizzy to stand.

Another member of the security team was already bending over her. "This one's dead."

Holden collapsed back to the ground, suddenly robbed of strength. Too late. The big meat grinder he was trying to save these people from just kept chewing away relentlessly, and they kept lining up to throw themselves inside. The RCE people were helping up their fallen comrade, and she was insisting that she was fine, that the armor had stopped the round, that she'd just have a big bruise. Someone joked about idiots bringing slingshots to a gunfight, followed by laughter. All the while, the house burned, filling the air with acrid black smoke and the smell of hot epoxy and cooking pork.

The RCE people seemed to remember he was there, and several came over to look down at him. "Secure him," one said. Wei. The one who'd come out to look at the alien robot with them. The one who'd shot it. She stared down, nothing like compassion in her eyes.

"Fuck you," Holden said, trying to push himself back up to his feet. "You aren't securing shit."

Wei smashed him in the chest with her rifle butt, knocking him back to the ground. One of the other security people pointed his rifle at Holden. He found himself thinking it was very likely he was about to be shot.

"Hold on, now," a calm voice said. Murtry strode into view out of the darkness. "No one's shooting Captain Holden."

"He tried to help the terrorists," Wei said.

"Did he?" Murtry feigned shock. "You didn't, did you? That would be a violation of the neutrality of your position here, wouldn't it?"

"I tried to help a woman who'd been shot," Holden replied, slowly climbing to his feet. His sternum felt bruised. That was all right. It would only hurt when he breathed.

"That sounds reasonable," Murtry said. "Is that the extent of his aid to the terrorists?"

Wei nodded, then looked away, annoyed.

"Then there's no reason to detain you," Murtry continued, his voice full of good cheer. *He's insane*, Holden thought. *He's gone completely over the edge. I could kill him right now and end this.* In his mind, he could picture Miller nodding in approval at the thought.

"Sir," Wei said, bringing her rifle up to her shoulder and aiming into the darkness beyond the firelight. "Incoming."

"Hold your panties," Amos said from the dark and stepped into the light. He had Basia Merton and Carol Chiwewe and a number of other colonists with him.

"My God," Carol said, looking at the fire. "Did anyone get out?"

One of the security people pointed his rifle at the body lying on the ground. "She did."

"Zadie," Basia said. "They killed her."

Murtry stepped forward and cleared his throat. When everyone was looking at him, he said, "My team surrounded the house where a cell of known terrorists were actively preparing to murder myself, the entire RCE security detachment, and Captain Holden. They had firearms and possibly explosives. When the RCE security team demanded that they exit the building unarmed and with their hands up, they opened fire. All of the terrorists were killed by the *return* fire. It's possible that explosives the terrorists were planning to use acted as an accelerant when the house started burning. Everything done here was by the book and appropriate for protecting RCE personnel and the UN/OPA mediator from harm."

Carol looked at blazing house with a stunned expression. "Appropriate…"

"Mister Merton," Murtry continued. "So glad you could join us. Sergeant Wei, take Basia Merton into custody."

"What?" Basia said, raising his hands and backing up. "Why me?"

"No," Holden said, stepping in front of Wei and planting his hand on the breastplate of her armor. "Not happening."

"Mister Merton was a party to this conspiracy," Murtry said, speaking loud enough for the gathering crowd of colonists to hear. "He attended the secret meeting at which the attack was planned, and there is significant evidence that he was a participant in the attack which killed five of my people. Might have something to say about what happened to Governor Trying too." Lowering his voice, he said, "Out of the way, Holden, or we'll just go through you." Wei smiled at him without humor. One of the other RCE people walked around them toward Basia, a plastic wrist restraint in his hands.

Amos stepped in front of Basia and punched the RCE man in the face. It sounded like a hammer hitting a side of beef. The security man fell to the ground, a puppet whose strings had been cut.

"Nope," Amos said, then shook his right hand with a grimace and added, "Ouch."

The rest of the security team brought their rifles to bear on him. Holden saw Amos drop his right hand toward his gun, then stepped in front of him and yelled, "Stop!"

"We're taking him in," Murtry said, pointing at Basia. "One way or the other. We'll let the assault on one of my people slide for now. Emotions running hot, and all."

"We're all leaving anyway," Holden said, keeping his voice low, appealing to Murtry rather than the crowd.

"You have no authority to order anyone to leave," Murtry replied. "I hoped we were done with that."

"In the meantime," Holden continued as though Murtry hadn't spoken, "the UN is taking custody of this man. Basia. As part of our investigation. He'll be secure on my ship, he won't be a threat to your people down here, and when we all get back you can present your evidence and have him arrested."

" 'Get back,' " Murtry said with a lazy smile. "Just going to keep him in a holding cell for the next few years? Because I accused him of something?"

"If I have to," Holden said. "Because I don't believe for a second that you wouldn't kill him."

Murtry shrugged. "Okay. He's your baggage, then. Just keep him off my planet."

Basia looked stunned, his eyes focused on nothing in particular. The colonists began organizing a firefighting detail to put the blaze out. Murtry and his team stood and watched, not offering to help, a visible reminder of the threat they presented next to the violence of their handiwork.

Holden headed back into town, Basia and Amos in tow. He patted his pockets looking for his hand terminal before remembering he'd dropped it on the run out to the fight. He'd never find it in the dark, so he borrowed Amos' and called the ship.

"Naomi," he said once she'd picked up. "Bring the *Roci* down to the landing area. We're going to need you to offload our heavier armor and some bigger firepower."

"This doesn't sound good," she said.

"It's not. Have you heard back from the UN or Fred yet?"

"Nothing yet. I take it this means RCE and the Ganymede folks aren't in a big hurry to leave?"

"No," Holden said with a heavy sigh. "No, they'd rather stay here and kill each other right up until the alien shit starts turning them into spare parts."

"And you?" she said. She meant was he coming up the well too. It was the sane thing to do.

"Not yet," he said. "If it escalates any more, maybe."

" 'It' the aliens or 'it' the people?"

"Right?"

"Alex has seen a few more power spikes, and there's more movement, but it's pretty far south of you. If it starts looking more interesting, I'll let you know."

"Thank you. Oh, and you'll be picking up a passenger."

"Que?"

"It's complicated, but we're putting him on the *Roci* because he isn't safe down here anymore. I owe this guy, Naomi. He tried to save my life. Take good care of him."

"Okay."

"And honey?" Holden said, unable to keep the worry out of his voice. "When you get back up, keep a close eye on the *Israel*. I think things might be about to go all the way bad down here, and when they do, they may go bad up there too."

"Ha!" Naomi said, and he could hear the smile in her voice. "Let 'em try."

Chapter Nineteen: Havelock

The corridor stretched forty meters between the recycling tanks and the secondary machine shop with hatches inset every ten meters. Open lifts at either end led to environmental control fore and hydroponics aft. The age of the *Israel* showed not only in the design of the walls and the grating of the floor, but also in the green-gray finish of the ceramic. Harsh edges at the doorways marked where safety design had improved in the decades since the ship first flew out past the orbit of Mars. A white scar splashed across one wall where something drastic had happened in some previous era of the ship's history and been patched like painting over graffiti. Havelock fought the urge to press himself into the corner nearest the doorway.

It was hard. His species had evolved in the gravity well of Earth, had grown and developed in it. His hindbrain told him that pressure meant safety. The angry whispers of the men in the hall set his heart tripping over faster, and the wall, centimeters from his back, seemed to pull at him like a magnet. It was an error waiting to happen. Lean in, push against the wall, and it would push back, sending him out into the open air of the corridor. And the firing lines. The second law of thermodynamics as applied to gunfights.

"Clear," one of the engineers said, and Havelock was torn between pleasure and annoyance. *Not clear*, he thought. They hadn't seen him, so they thought he wasn't there. He held the gun at his leg, stayed still. Waited. Didn't hug the wall.

The first man who floated by didn't notice him until he'd already been shot. Havelock's paint round bloomed orange against the man's chest. The one behind him had already launched, his body sailing between one handhold and the next, unable to change his trajectory. Havelock hit him twice, once in the leg, then in the belly. In a real fight, there would be blood in the air now. Fine red droplets spinning into orbs and already coalescing and beginning to clot. The third man was still far enough down the corridor that Havelock didn't have a clear line of sight. Half a dozen blue paint rounds hissed past him, splattering the ceramic bulkhead. Suppressing fire. Not a bad plan, but there was no one left to exploit it.

Havelock pulled gently at the handhold behind him to keep from drifting out, reloaded his pistol, and counted incoming rounds. The "dead" engineer floated in the corridor, a sour expression on his face. Havelock counted fifteen rounds, then there was a pause and the slick metallic sound of the pistol ejecting the paint round magazine. Havelock pulled a few centimeters forward, looking down the hall. The last man—Williams—hadn't even taken cover while he fumbled to reload his gun. Havelock fired three times, hitting him only once. The accuracy on the pistols stank, but it was enough to make his point. The last engineer barked out an obscenity.

"All right," Havelock said into his hand terminal. "That's a wrap, guys. Let's get the cleanup crew out, and meet back in the conference room in thirty."

It was hard to judge the training sessions. On the one hand, they had been going for eight days now, and they were not ready for real action. The engineers weren't soldiers. The three who'd had some training earlier in life were so out of practice that they were worse than the absolute beginners. At least the novices knew they didn't know anything.

And on the other hand, they were getting better faster than Havelock had expected. With another week or ten days, they'd be at least as competent as a squad of rookies. Maybe more.

Security trainees were driven by any number of things—the need for a job, an idealistic view of helping people, sometimes just a narcissistic love of violence. The engineers weren't like that. They were more focused, more driven, and there was a palpable sense of the team against the enemy. Murtry's defeat of the terrorist cell downstairs left them at once excited and edgy, and Havelock didn't see anything wrong with the bloodthirst, so long as it was channeled and controlled.

For the next half hour, the engineers and the security team—Havelock and two others from this skeleton crew—went through the corridors, holds, and locks cleaning up the mess from the exercise. The paint polymerized quickly, peeling off the walls and grates without flaking much or leaving fragments on the float that someone could breathe in. The engineers had also manufactured sets of personal vacuuming systems that filtered everything from tiny particles of the paint casing to volatile molecules out of the air. They laughed and joked and traded friendly insults as they worked, like junior belts cleaning a dojang. Havelock hadn't intended the cleanup as a team-building exercise, but it worked well enough that he was starting to tell himself that he had.

The conference room where they had the orientation before the exercise and the postmortem afterward had been designed for the false gravity of thrust. An oblong table was bolted to the floor with crash couches around it that the engineers didn't use. Havelock didn't know how the decision had been made to ignore the table and rotate the consensus for up and down ninety degrees, but every meeting was like that now. The engineers and security floated against the walls or in the open air, the "floor" to their right, and Havelock took his place by the main doors.

"All right," he said, and the murmur of conversations stopped. "What did we learn?"

"Not to trust motherfucking Gibbs when he tells us the corridor's clear." Laughter bubbled after, but it wasn't angry or mean. Even the man being mocked was smiling.

"Wrong answer," Havelock said with a grin. "The right answer is don't hurry when you're clearing a space. We have a natural tendency to see an empty space and think it's safe. Doors and corners are always dangerous, because you're moving into something without being sure what's there. By the time you see the enemy, you're exposed to them."

"Sir?"

Havelock pointed to the woman with the raised hand. "Yes."

"Sir, is there an algorithm for this? Because if we could get some kind of best-practice flowchart that we could study when we're not here, I think it would help us a lot."

"We could classify them by the types of doors or corners," someone else said. "And what plane we could use to approach them. Seem to me like we'd be better off shifting the axis so that whatever we're coming to reads as down."

Havelock let them talk for a while. It was funny, hearing the tactics of small-unit assault analyzed in terms of engineering, but those were his crew now. They were learning to solve violence like an equation: not to eliminate it, but to understand it fully.

"What I don't understand," Chief Engineer Koenen said, "is why we're looking at the *Barbapiccola* at all."

The eyes of the assembled team turned toward Havelock, looking for an answer. Or at least a response. A surprising nervousness crawled up his throat, and he chuckled.

"They're the bad guys," he said.

"The *Barbapiccola* is an unarmed freighter with a standing crew of maybe a hundred people that requires a shuttle to transfer from the surface," the chief engineer said. "The *Rocinante* runs with less than a skeleton crew, half of which are already off the ship. It seems to me that we have a lower-risk, higher-value option here."

A murmur of agreement passed through the room. Havelock shook his head.

"No," he said. "First thing is just what you said. The *Barbapiccola*'s unarmed. If things don't go well, the worst we can expect in retaliation is a strongly worded letter. The *Rocinante* was a state-of-the-art Martian warship before Holden took her to the OPA. God knows what modifications they've made since then. She's got a full rack of torpedoes, PDCs, and a keel-mounted rail gun. If the crew on the *Rocinante* see us as a threat, they can end us, and there's really nothing we can do about it."

"But if we were the ones with that firepower—" Koenen began.

"We'd be fine as long as we stayed here," Havelock said. "But as soon as we go back through the ring gate, there's a whole mess of lawyers, treaties, and other ships with even bigger guns. If we have to commandeer the *Barbapiccola*, at least we have a legal argument to make."

The engineers groaned and shook their heads. Legal arguments were another phrase for *bullshit* to them, but Havelock pressed on.

"For one thing, the ore they're carrying is RCE property as long as the UN charter stands. For another, if they bring any of the colonists up from the surface, we can argue they're aiding and abetting murder."

"Argue?" one of the men in the back of the group said. The laughter that followed was bleak.

"Being true makes it a strong argument," Havelock said. "Go after the *Rocinante*, and we look like everything they say we are. If we stand tough, we can protect ourselves and still win the long game."

"Long game's great if you're around long enough to play it," the man at the back said, but his tone of voice told Havelock that they'd seen the sense in what he said. For the time being, anyway.

Ivers Thorrsen was a geosensor analyst with advanced degrees from universities on Luna and Ganymede. He made more in a month than Havelock would in a year of working security. Also, he was a Belter. Growing up in microgravity hadn't affected him as much as Havelock had seen in other people. Thorrsen's head was maybe a little big for his body, his spine and legs maybe a little long and thin. With enough exercise and steroids, the man could almost have passed for an Earther. Not that it mattered. Everyone on the *Israel* knew what everyone else was. Back when they'd left home, the differences hadn't mattered. Not much.

"In addition to the energy spikes, there are twenty heat upwellings that we've seen so far," he said, pointing to the rendered sphere of New Terra on Havelock's desk display. "They've all appeared in the last eighty hours, and so far we don't have any idea what they are."

Havelock scratched his head. The cells in the brig were empty, so there was no one to overhear them. No need to be polite.

"Were you expecting me to have a hypothesis? Because I was under the impression that we were here in order to find a bunch of stuff we didn't know what it was. That you've seen something you don't understand seems pretty much par for the course."

The Belter's lips pressed thin and pale.

"This could be important. It could be nothing. My point is that I have to find out. I'm busy with important work. I can't spend all my time dealing with distractions."

"All right," Havelock said.

"This is the third day running that someone has sprayed urine in my locker. Three *times*, you understand? I'm trying to get my gear not to smell like piss instead of running the numbers."

Havelock sighed and canceled out his display. New Terra and its mysterious hot spots vanished. "Look, I understand why you don't like it. I'd be cheesed off too. But you have to cut them a little slack. People are bored and they're under pressure. It's natural to get a little rowdy. It'll pass."

Thorrsen folded his arms across his chest, his scowl deepening. "A little rowdy? That's what you see? I am the only Belter on my team, and I am the *only* one getting—"

"No. Look, just no, all right? Things are tense already. If you want me to, I'll put a monitor on the locker and let people know they need to cool it, but let's not make this into a Belters against the inner planets thing."

"I'm not making it into anything."

"With all respect, I think you are," Havelock said. "And the more you try to make this into a big deal, the more it's going to come back and bite you on the ass."

Thorrsen's rage was palpable. Havelock shifted slightly, pushing himself higher in the direction that they'd temporarily chosen as up. It was an old trick he'd learned back when he'd worked with Star Helix. Humanity might have gone up out of the gravity wells, but the sense of being taller, of establishing dominance, was buried too deeply in the human animal for a little thing like null g to erase it. Thorrsen took a deep, shuddering breath, and for a moment Havelock wondered if he was going to take a swing at him. He didn't want to lock the analyst in a cell for the night. But if it came to it, he wouldn't mind.

"I'll put a monitor on your locker, and I'll send out a general announcement that people need to put a sock in it. No one'll piss on your stuff again, and you can get back to work. That's what you want, right?"

"When you write your announcement, is it going to say that they should stop pulling pranks, or that they should stop harassing Belters?"

"I think you know the answer to that."

Thorrsen's shoulders hunched, defeated. Havelock nodded. It struck him, not for the first time, that confrontations were like a dance. Certain moves required certain responses, and most of it happened in the lower parts of the brain that language might not even be aware of. Thorrsen's hunch was an offer of submission, and his nod accepted it, and Thorrsen probably didn't even know it had happened.

Certainly didn't, in fact, because his rational mind kept on dieseling even though everything that needed talking about was already decided.

"If you were the only Earther and it was Belters doing this, you'd feel different about it."

"Thank you for letting me know about the problem," Havelock said. "I'll see it's addressed."

Thorrsen pushed off from the desk and sailed gracefully through the air, vanishing into the corridor. Havelock sighed, opened his desk display again, and paged through the ship reports. The truth was that incidents were on the rise. Most of it was little things. Complaints of petty infractions of corporate policies. Accusations of hoarding or sexual misconduct. One of the organic chemists had been making euphorics. The ship psychiatric counselor was issuing increasingly strident warnings about something he called *internal stratification*, which just sounded like social politics as usual to Havelock. He signed off on all the reports.

If you were the only Earther.

The funny thing was that Havelock had been the only Earther in a Belter society, and more than once. When he'd been on a twenty-berth hauler from Luna to Ganymede for Stone & Sibbets, he'd been one of two Earthers, outnumbered and always subtly excluded. He'd worked for Star Helix on Ceres Station for the better part of a year, always getting the worst cases, the worst partner, the less-than-subtle reminders that he didn't belong. He'd been dealt more than his fair share of shit by Belters for not having the right-shaped body or knowing the polyglot mess that passed for a kind of outer planets cant. They hadn't pissed in his locker, mostly because it hadn't occurred to them.

Havelock set a monitor specifically on Thorrsen's locker, then pulled up a fresh security template. He looked at the empty field, asking him by its blankness what he wanted to say.

We're eight billion klicks from home and a bunch of half-feral terrorists want to keep on killing us, so let's stay calm.

Or maybe:

Damn near every Belter I've dealt with treated me like I was dipped in shit because of where I came from, but now that we're in the majority, let's all respect their tender little feelings.

He cracked his knuckles and started typing.

It has come to the attention of security that an increasing number of pranks have been played among the crew. While we all understand the need to keep things light in these stressful times, some of these have gone beyond the realm of good taste. As acting head of security

He paused.

Once, on Ceres, Havelock had been assigned to close down an illegal club up near the center of the station where the Coriolis had been vicious and the spin gravity at its least. When he'd gotten to the place, the combination of bright lights, shrieking dub, and his unaccustomed inner ear had left him vomiting in the carved corridors. An image of him had made its way onto the board back in the offices. He'd played along because objecting would have made it worse. He hadn't thought about that case in years.

If you were the only Earther.

"Fuck," Havelock said to the empty air. He cleared the screen.

It has come to my attention that some RCE employees and team members have been singled out for harassment because they are from the outer planets. It is critical under these stressful conditions that we not confuse our teammates with our enemies because of accidents of physiology and environments of origin. As such, I am taking the following actions:

"I'm gonna regret this," Havelock said to the screen, but by the time he'd finished the announcement, checked it for grammar, and sent it out, he felt almost good.

Chapter Twenty: Elvi

Sitting outside her hut, her hand terminal resting on her knees, the now-familiar sunlight warming her neck and back, Elvi waited for the reports from Luna to buffer. The comm laser on the *Edward Israel* was the only conduit back to the worlds she'd known, and it was swamped with technical data flowing out from the workgroups on the planetary surface and the sensor data from the *Israel*. It was sobering to realize that for all the tragedies and fear and death that wracked New Terra, most of the raw data going back home was still technical. And her slow connection was more than the townspeople of First Landing had. The *Barbapiccola* didn't even support a feed for them. Their hand terminals were strictly ad hoc, local, line-of-sight networks if they functioned at all.

A breeze lifted a whirl of sand, then set it gently down again. High above, the green clouds scattered apart and rejoined, lacing the blue sky like algae floating on the surface of a pond. The air smelled of heat and dust and the distant presentiment of rain. The reports finished loading and Elvi pulled them up and spent a long hour reading them, listening to the debates, putting together her perspective. It was harder than she liked. Her mind kept jumping around without her.

Everything was changing on the planet so quickly, everything was so different than she'd expected it to be, that just maintaining focus was hard. The voyage into the desert, seeing a two-billion-year-old mechanism actually still functioning, if only barely, had been revelatory. Then the exposure and destruction of the terrorists among the squatters, which should have been a relief, had left her oddly unsettled. And, though she hadn't mentioned it to anyone and never would, she'd been suffering recurring and intrusive dreams about James Holden.

On the screen, the research coordinator's report ended, and Elvi realized she hadn't heard any of it. She sighed, restarted it, and stopped it again before the woman back at the RCE labs on Earth could say anything. Elvi looked up at the sky, wondering where the *Rocinante* and the *Barbapiccola* and the *Edward Israel* were, hidden by the atmosphere-scatter of blue. One of the plant analogs beside the path leading back to the town let out a volley of rising clicks. It was something she'd wanted to investigate, but she hadn't had the time. Not yet. "Doctor Okoye," the research coordinator said from sixty AU away, or half a galaxy depending on how you looked at it, "I've just come from a meeting with the stats team, and I wanted to bring you up to speed on the plan for how we'd like to proceed with the data collection in the next weeks. The Luna group especially was hoping to request additional sampling on several of your initial subjects so that we can narrow our error bars…"

Elvi listened, focused, pushed away all her other thoughts and feelings. This time, she ended the report with a list of action items, a clear sense of how her work was changing the resources and plans of the labs back at home, and a half dozen questions about mineral sequestration that she wanted to ask Fayez. Protocol said she should record a reply and send it out right away. The hours it would take to reach home meant it would arrive before the morning meetings. But instead, she switched to her organizer and began listing her obligations. Water samples and soil samples. Samples of three different plant analog species. A report on the alien artifact...

She'd been thinking about possible triggers to the artifact's sudden activity, and since Holden had been there and was, after all, the mediator who was ultimately responsible for making the situation on New Terra better—sensible, sane—she thought maybe, if she could give a solid reason that the artifact in the desert wasn't moving in reaction to their presence, it would take something off his plate. Just as a kindness, and to help support him in making peace.

Certainly it wasn't just that she was generating excuses to see him again.

She went down the list of things to do, then paused. At the end, she wrote, *Letter of recommendation for Felcia Merton*. She sat for a long moment, looking at the words, trying to decide how she felt about them. She erased the line, waited, and then entered it in again.

Walking into the town was like entering another world, and a harder one. The dirt streets weren't empty, but the people who walked them stayed closer to the walls than they had before. The smiles and nods, the eye contact and simple greetings were all gone. The townspeople walked quickly, with their heads down. Elvi had the urge to stand in their way, block them with her body until they acknowledged that she was there.

The building where it had happened stood near the edge of town. The fire had melted what it hadn't burned. The bones of the structure still stood, charred and tilted in the afternoon sun. She paused before them. They reminded her of something, but she couldn't quite remember what. Something dead. Something about fire.

Oh. Of course. The artifact, burning in the desert.

Two of the RCE security force walked down the street in front of her, striding in the middle of the road. She couldn't make out their words, but the tone of the conversation was bright, loose, and celebratory. One of them laughed. Elvi turned, walking toward them. As they passed, one of them lifted a hand in greeting and Elvi returned it automatically. Across the street, one of the Belter women—Eirinn her name was—stepped out from a door, saw the security forces, and hesitated before she came out into the light. Elvi watched the woman walk, her head a little too high, her shoulders pulled a little too far back. Nothing proved fear like the effort of rejecting it. First Landing had belonged to that woman once.

Elvi stepped into the commissary, hoping to find Holden at his traditional table. The room was dim, and it took her eyes a moment to adjust. The other one, Amos Burton, was there instead, eating a bowl of brown noodles that smelled of fake peanuts and curry. In the back, Lucia Merton sat in a booth with someone. Elvi looked away before the doctor met her gaze.

Amos looked up at her as she came close.

"I was wondering if Captain Holden...I wanted to talk with him. About the artifacts? In the desert?"

"Something happen with it?"

"I had some theories about it that I thought might be...useful."

Oh good God, she thought. I'm stuttering like a schoolgirl. Thankfully, Amos didn't notice, or if he did he pretended not to.

"Captain's off getting ready to transfer the prisoner," Amos said. "Should be back around sundown."

"All right," Elvi said. "That's fine. If you'd tell him I was looking for him? I'll likely be in my hut by the time he's back. He can find me there."

"I'll let 'im know."

"Thank you."

She turned away, fists pushed into her pockets. She felt humiliated without being entirely certain why she should. She was just going to offer some perspective on the artifacts and the local ecosystem. There was nothing about it that was at all inappropriate or—

"Elvi!"

She felt her belly drop. She turned toward the back, toward the booth where Lucia Merton sat. Fayez had swiveled around in the chair and was waving at her. She looked at the door to the street, wishing there was some graceful way to get through it.

"Elvi! Come sit. Have a drink with us."

"Of course," she said, and walked toward the back of the commissary, regretting every step as she took it.

Doctor Merton looked pale except for the bags under her eyes. Elvi wondered if the woman was ill, or if it was just distress and grief.

"Lucia," Elvi said.

"Elvi."

"Sit, sit, sit," Fayez said. "You're standing there, I feel short. I hate feeling short."

Elvi smoothed the fabric of her pants and slid in next to Fayez. His smile was beery and amused. Lucia's glance at her was almost an apology. *You could have sat next to me*, she seemed to say.

"We were just talking about Felcia," Fayez said, then turned to Lucia. "Elvi is the smartest person on the team. Seriously, do you know that she's the one who wrote the first real paper on cytoplasmic computation? That's her. Right there."

"Felcia's told me about you," Lucia said. "Thank you for being a friend to my daughter."

Your family tried to kill me, Elvi thought. *You shared your bed every night with a man who wanted me dead.*

"You're welcome," she said. "She's a very talented girl."

"She is," Lucia said. "And God knows I tried to talk her out of being a doctor."

"You were hoping she'd stay?" Elvi asked, and her voice was more brittle than she'd intended.

"Not that, no," Lucia said, laughing. "That she's leaving this planet is the only good thing that's happened since we came. It's only that I'm afraid she's doing it because it's what I do. Better that she find her own way."

"It's a long way to Luna," Fayez said. "I mean, I had five major courses of study before I fell in love with geohydraulics. I was going to be a brewer. Can you imagine that?"

Elvi and Lucia said *Yes* at precisely the same time. Elvi smiled despite herself. Lucia stood.

"I should go get Jacek," she said.

"Is he all right?" Elvi asked. It was a reflex. A habit of etiquette. She wished she could take the question back even as the words left her mouth. The doctor's smile was wistful.

"As well as can be expected," she said. "His father is leaving today."

Taken prisoner on the Rocinante, Elvi thought, but said nothing.

"Your money's no good here," Fayez said. "It's on me."

"Thank you, Doctor Sarkis."

"Fayez. Call me Fayez. Everyone else does."

Lucia nodded and walked away. Fayez shook his head and stretched, his arm reaching behind Elvi's shoulders. She shifted to the opposite side of the table.

"What the hell are you doing?" she asked.

"What am *I* doing? You think that's the question?"

"You know that her husband—"

"I don't know a damned thing, Elvi. Neither do you. I'm rich in interpretation and poor in datasets, just the same as you."

"You think...you think it's not..."

"I think that building was filled with terrorists, and that Murtry killed them and saved us. That's what I *think*, though. I also think that the more the locals know and love me, the less likely it is that I'll be scalped in the next uprising. And...and what is civilization if it isn't people talking to each other over a goddamned beer?" Fayez said, then lolled his head back over his shoulder. "Am I *right*?"

"Fuckin' A," Amos called back. "That sure is whatever you were talking about."

"That's right," Fayez said.

"You're drunk."

"I've been doing this for a while," Fayez said. "I've probably had drinks with a third of the people in this shithole. What I want to know is where the rest of you are while I'm making peace."

For a moment, she could see his fear too. It was in the angle of his jaw and the way his half-closed eyes cut to the left, avoiding hers. Fayez who could laugh at anything, however tragic, was scared out of his wits. And why wouldn't he be? They were billions of klicks from home, on a planet they didn't understand, and in the middle of a war that had now killed people on both sides. And how odd and obvious that it would be a victory for their side—the nameless, faceless killers identified and killed or imprisoned—that would call up the panic.

Fayez was waiting. Waiting for the next escalation. The other shoe to drop. He was reaching out for whatever control he could find or hope for or pretend into being. Elvi understood, because she felt just the same, only she hadn't known it until she saw it in someone else.

He scowled down at the table, then, slowly, his gaze floated up to meet hers. "What *are* you doing here?"

"Sitting with you, apparently," she said.

Waiting for the other shoe.

Chapter Twenty-One: Basia

Basia stood at the edge of the landing area, steel shackles damp with his sweat and chafing his wrists and forearms. Murtry had insisted on restraints until Basia was off-planet, though he had given the key to Amos, and the big man had assured Basia he'd be uncuffed once the *Rocinante* lifted off. It was one last visible demonstration to the citizens of Ilus that Murtry could and would exert his will upon them. Jim Holden was still trying to play the peacemaker, and he'd agreed to the restraints in exchange for Basia being released into his custody without any further threats or considerations. Basia understood why everyone was doing what they were doing.

It didn't make it less humiliating.

Lucia and Jacek stood with him, waiting for the *Rocinante* to land. Jacek stood in front of him, back pressed to his father's stomach and Basia's cuffed hands on his shoulders. His wife's hand, gripping his own, rested on his son's shoulder. All three of them touching. He tried to draw strength from it. Tried to lock the sensation of having his wife and his son close to hand into his memory. He had the terrible sense that it was the last time he'd ever feel her touch. He felt both relief and sadness that Felcia was already gone. Bad enough that his son, too young to really understand what it all meant, had to see him in chains. He could not have stood his bright, beautiful girl seeing him that way.

The other townspeople—men and women he had lived with sharing air and water and sorrow and rage—avoided the spectacle of his departure as if his guilt were an illness they might catch. He'd become a stranger to them. He might almost have preferred to have them condemn him.

All I wanted was my freedom. All I wanted was my family with me, and not to lose another child to them. He was amazed and sick at heart that that had been too much to ask of the universe.

Amos, his nominal guard, stood a respectful distance away, arms crossed and staring up at the sky. Giving the family the space to say goodbye. Holden stood with Murtry and Carol, the triumvirate of power on Ilus. They weren't looking at each other. They were there to take the sting off of Murtry exerting his control by pretending they were part of the decision. His life was a pawn in their political games. Nothing more.

"Just a couple more minutes, chief," Amos said. A moment later came a high-altitude thunderclap. The *Rocinante*, dropping through the atmosphere faster than sound, descending on them all like the angel of judgment.

It seemed unreal.

"I'm happy having you two here with me right now," he told Lucia. It wasn't even a lie.

"Find a way to come back to us," she said.

"I don't know what I can do."

"Find a way," she repeated, making each word its own sentence. "You do that, Basia. Don't make me grow old on this world alone."

Basia felt something thick blocking his throat, and he had trouble breathing around the pain in his stomach. "If you need to find someone..."

"I did," Lucia said. "I found someone. Now he needs to find a way to come back to me."

Basia didn't trust himself to speak. Worried that if he opened his mouth it would turn into a sob. He didn't want Murtry to see that. So instead he put his cuffed arms around Lucia and pulled her tight and squeezed until neither of them could breathe.

"Come back," she whispered one last time. Anything she might have said after that was drowned out by the roar of the *Rocinante* landing. A wall of dust blew past, stinging the bare skin on Basia's neck. Lucia pressed her face into his chest, and Jacek clung to his back.

"Time to go," Amos shouted.

Basia let go of Lucia, hugged his boy to his chest one last time, *the* last time maybe, and turned away from them both to board his prison.

"Welcome aboard, Mister Merton," a tall, pretty woman said when the inner airlock door opened. She wore a simple jumpsuit of gray and black with the name Nagata stenciled over the breast pocket. Naomi Nagata, the executive officer of the *Rocinante*. She had long black hair pulled into a ponytail, the same way Felcia had worn hers when she was a young girl. On Naomi it looked more like a functional choice than an aesthetic one. She didn't appear to be armed, and Basia felt himself relax a degree.

He handed her the key to his restraints and she unlocked them. "Basia, please," he said as she worked. "I'm just a welder. No one has ever called me Mister Merton."

"Welder?" Naomi asked. It didn't sound like she was making pleasantries. She took the restraints, rolled them into a ball, and secured them in a locker. Shipboard discipline, where any free object became a projectile during maneuvers. "Because we always have a repair list."

The compartment they stood in looked like a storage room laid on its side. The lockers ran parallel to the ground, rather than vertically, and there was a small hatch on either wall, with what looked like a ladder running across the floor. Naomi tapped on a panel on one wall and said, "Strapping in down here, Alex, get us off this dustball before my knees start leaking."

A disembodied voice with a Martian Mariner Valley twang said, "Roger that, boss. Up in thirty ticks, so get belted in."

Naomi pulled on a strap on the floor and a seat folded out. It was designed so a person would have to lie on the floor on their back to put their butt on the seat. A variety of restraining belts folded out with it. She pointed at another strap in the floor and said, "Better get with it. We lift in thirty seconds."

Basia pulled out his own seat and awkwardly lay on the ground to get into the straps. Naomi helped him buckle in.

The Martian voice counted down from five, and the floor lurched as the ship lifted off. There was a disorienting rotation, and the floor became a wall behind him and he was actually sitting on the cushion he'd pulled out. He became very grateful for the straps holding him in place.

Then a giant roared at the bottom of the ship, and an invisible hand crushed Basia into his chair.

"Sorry," Naomi said, her voice given a false vibrato by the rumbling of the ship. "Alex is an old combat pilot, he only flies at full speed."

As always when flying out of a gravity well, Basia was surprised by how quickly it was over. A few minutes of crushing gravity and the roar of the engines, then with almost no transition at all, he was floating in his straps in silence.

"All done," Naomi said as she began unbuckling. "Might be a few short maneuvering bumps as Alex gets us into the orbit he wants, but those yellow lights on the wall will flash fifteen seconds before any burn, so just grab a strap and hang on."

"Am I a prisoner?" Basia asked.

"What?"

"I'm just wondering how this works. Am I restricted to my room or is there a brig or something?"

Naomi floated for a moment staring at him, forehead crinkling with what looked like genuine puzzlement. "Are you a bad guy?"

"Bad guy?"

"Are you going to try to hurt anyone on this ship? Destroy our property? Steal things?"

"Definitely not," Basia said.

"Because the way I heard it, you turned on your friends in order to save our captain's life."

For a moment, Basia felt something like vertigo and then pride or the promise of it. And then he remembered the concussion of the heavy shuttle rattling him and Coop's voice. *We all remember who mashed that button.* He shook his head.

Are you a bad guy?

Naomi Nagata waited for him to speak, but he didn't have words for the guilt and shame and anger and sorrow. In time she lifted a fist, the Belter's physical idiom for a nod. He lifted his in reply.

"Make yourself at home." She pointed at the hatch to his right. "That's aft. That way is the crew decks and the galley. The galley is open whenever. We've got a cabin set up for you, it's tiny but private. If you keep going aft and hit the machine shop you've gone too far. For safety reasons don't go into the machine shop or engineering."

"Okay, I promise."

"Don't promise, just don't go in there. The other way"—she pointed at the hatch on his left—"takes you up to the ops deck. You can come up there if you want, but don't touch anything unless we tell you to."

"Okay."

"I'm headed up there right now. You're welcome to tag along."

"Okay."

Naomi stared at him for a second, an unreadable expression on her face. "You're not our first, you know."

"First?"

"First prisoner transport," Naomi said. "Jim has this thing about fair trials. It means that we've done our share of taking people to court even when an airlock and mysteriously erased records made a lot more sense."

Basia couldn't stop himself from giving the airlock door a nervous look. "Okay."

"And," she continued, "you're the first one I can remember that he specifically told me to be nice to."

"He did?"

"He owes you one. I do too," Naomi said, then gestured at the ladder and the deck hatch in a you-first motion. Basia pulled himself up to the hatch and it whined open. Naomi pulled herself along behind him. "So you can get comfortable. But the terrified mousey thing you're doing right now will bug the shit out of me."

"Okay."

"Still doing it."

The deck above the storage and airlock area was a large compartment filled with gimbaled chairs and wall-mounted screens and control panels. A dark-skinned man with thinning black hair and a middle-aged beer belly was strapped into one of the chairs. He turned to face them as they floated into the room.

"All good?" he asked Naomi. He was the source of the Mariner Valley voice.

"Seems to be," Naomi said, and pushed Basia into the closest chair then strapped him in. He allowed it to happen, feeling like an infant being manhandled by his mother. "Didn't get any face time with Jim. He wanted this fellow off the ground as fast as possible."

"Well, can't say I was lookin' to stay longer."

"I know. Gravity wells," Naomi said with a shudder. "I don't know how people live like that."

"I was thinking more about the bugs all coming back to life. I got five more power spikes since the last time we checked."

"I was trying not to think about those."

"Should have gotten Holden and Amos both," Alex said. "And anyone else with sense."

"Just keep an eye. If anything gets close, I want them to know about it."

Once she'd finished belting him in, Naomi floated over to a different chair and pulled herself into it. She began calling up screens and tapping on them faster than Basia could follow, still talking to the Martian man as she worked.

"Alex," she said, "meet Basia Merton the welder."

"Welder?" Alex raised his eyebrows and grinned. "We got a pile of shit on the to-do list with Amos vacationing on the surface."

Basia opened his mouth to reply but Naomi said, "Basia, meet Alex Kamal, our pilot, and the solar system's worst vacuum welder."

"Hello," Basia said.

"Hello back," Alex said, then turned to Naomi. "Hey, while I'm thinkin' about it? You were right about that shuttle."

"Yeah?" Naomi pushed off her chair and floated over to look at the screen next to Alex. He scrolled through what looked like video on fast-forward for a few seconds.

"See there?" Alex said, pausing it. "They detach it and park it a few hundred meters from the *Israel* then send an engineerin' team out. They're inside for a couple hours, then back to the *Israel*. It hasn't moved out of that orbit since."

"They're doing all the shuttle runs with the other one," Naomi said, pulling up video on a second screen and fast-forwarding through it. "I knew it."

"Yeah, you're very clever. Want to keep the 'scopes recording that, or do I aim 'em at the bugs?"

"The shuttle," Naomi replied after a few more seconds of moving back and forth through the video.

Basia knew he'd been invited to sit with them. And it appeared they were talking about monitoring the RCE ship, which didn't strike him as a personal conversation. But he couldn't help but feel a bit out of place. Like an eavesdropper on a private moment. It was the comfortable shorthand the two members of the *Rocinante*'s crew had. They sounded like family discussing household matters. It was unsettling to think they were the only three people on the ship. It was too large. Too empty. He didn't want to be alone in the silence of an unfamiliar ship, but staying felt wrong too.

Basia cleared his throat. "Should I go to my cabin?"

"Do you want to?" Naomi asked without looking at him. "There is nothing to do in there. It's not even one of the ones with its own video display. All the good cabins are taken by crew."

"You can get access to the ship's library from there," Alex said, pointing at the screen closest to Basia. "If you're bored."

"I'm scared as shit," Basia said without knowing ahead of time he was going to.

Alex and Naomi both turned to look at him. The Martian's face was kind. He said, "Yeah. I bet. But nothin' bad is gonna to happen to you here. Until the captain says otherwise, treat this like home. If you want to be alone, we can—"

"No." Basia shook his head. "No, but you're talking to each other like I'm not here, so I thought...." He shrugged.

"Sorry. We've been together enough years we almost don't need to talk anymore," Naomi said. "I think the *Israel* has weaponized one of its shuttles. We've been monitoring the ship, and the activity around one shuttle was suspicious. I think they turned it into a bomb."

"Why would they do that?"

"Because," Alex answered, "that's an unarmed science ship and they flew into what they seem to see as a war zone. That shuttle could be used to attack another ship like a guided missile, or maybe as a bomb to flatten the colony."

"They want to attack you?" Basia asked. *Why would they do that? Wasn't the* Rocinante *and her crew here to solve the conflict?*

"I doubt it," Naomi said. "More likely the *Barbapiccola* if she tries to break orbit and run."

"Yeah," Alex said with a laugh. "The *Israel* takes a swing at us, it'll be the shortest dogfight in history."

"First Landing. They could flatten the colony?" Basia said. "They don't know that. You should warn them. My family is still down there."

"Trust me," Naomi said, "that won't happen. Now that we know, we'll keep an eye on that shuttle, and if it moves, we can stop it."

"Should probably tell the boss, though," Alex said.

"Yeah." Naomi tracked through the video a few more times, then shut it off.

Alex unbuckled his restraint and pushed off toward the ladder. "Or…shit, XO, I can take care of it right now. I had the *Roci* go over the shuttle specs and calculate a rail gun shot that'll cut her damn reactor in half."

Naomi stopped him with a shake of her hand. "No. Just once I'd like to find a solution that doesn't involve blowing something up."

Alex shrugged. "Your call."

Naomi floated quietly for a moment, then seemed to come to a decision and hit the comm panel. After a few seconds Jim Holden's voice said, "Holden here."

"Jim, I've got a problem and a solution I need to run past you."

"I like that we already have a solution," Holden replied. Basia could hear the smile in his voice.

"Two solutions," Alex called out. "I've got a solution too."

"We've been watching the *Israel* like you asked," Naomi said. "And Alex and I agree that the probability is high they've weaponized one of the two light shuttles. They're keeping it powered down and in a matching orbit about five hundred meters from the big ship. I think it's a last-ditch weapon to use if the *Barb* tries to run, but that doesn't mean they couldn't use it on the colony, as unlikely as that seems."

"You haven't met this Murtry character running RCE security," Holden said. "Or it would seem pretty damn likely. What's our best course of action?"

"We get everyone off the planet, go back home, and spend a few decades doing unmanned exploration before we even think of coming back," Naomi said.

"Agreed," Holden said. "And what are we actually going to do?"

"I figure you'd want us to take care of it. Alex thinks he can gut it with a rail gun shot, but that seems like a pretty obvious escalation to me. Shooting gauss rounds past the *Israel*, I mean."

"Things are escalating just fine on their own," Holden said. "But we'll keep that option on the table for now. What else?"

Naomi pulled herself closer to the comm panel and lowered her voice, as though the console were Holden himself and she was about to deliver bad news. "I take an EVA pack, fly over to the shuttle, and plant a cutout on the drive. If they run system checks, everything will come back functional, but if they try to move the shuttle I can kill it remotely. No explosions, just a dead shuttle."

"That seems risky," Holden said.

"Riskier than flinging rail gun shots through its reactor?"

"Not really, no."

"Riskier than leaving it out there and armed?"

"Oh, *hell* no. Okay, Naomi, this is your call. One way or the other, I want that threat off the board. We have enough shit to worry about down here."

Naomi smiled at the comm panel. "One dead shuttle, coming up."

She shut off the connection with a sigh. Basia looked from one to the other of them, scowling.

"Why?"

"Why what?" Naomi asked lightly.

"Why would you act directly against RCE? Aren't you supposed to be mediators? Neutral? Why take any action at all when you can stay out of it?"

Her smile had depth and complexity. Basia had the feeling she'd heard a more profound question than the one he'd meant to ask.

"Choosing to stand by while people kill each other is also an action," she said. "We don't do that here."

Chapter Twenty-Two: Havelock

Havelock's system filtered the newsfeeds from Sol—and it was still damned weird thinking "from Sol"—for four topics: New Terra, James Holden, contract security, and European league football. Strapped in his office crash couch, he tapped through the feed summaries. CHANGES TO COMPENSATION SCHEDULE REGULATIONS TIP THE BALANCE TOWARD EARTH-BASED CONTRACT SECURITY, STAR HELIX TO PROTEST. He deleted it. EARTHMAN'S BURDEN: FIFTY FAMOUS EARTHERS WHO SWITCHED SIDES FOR THE OPA. Holden was number forty-one. Havelock deleted it. LOS BLANCOS DEFEAT BAYERN 1–0. Havelock raised his eyebrows and put the highlights reel in his viewing queue. INCREASED VIOLENCE ON NEW TERRA. UN AND OPA REACT. MARS POSITIONING WITH OPA.

Havelock felt his belly go tight. The feed came from an intelligence analysis service with contacts in the governments of all three major powers. He opened it.

"This is Nasr Maxwell with Forecast Analytics, and this proprietary feed is intended solely for use by the subscribers and partners of Forecast Analytics. Any other distribution is in violation of MCR and UN intellectual property statutes and is subject to prosecution.

"Intelligence reports from the UN indicate that the violence on New Terra has escalated. The security forces of Royal Charter Energy discovered a new potential attack, and in thwarting it killed between seven and sixteen local insurgents. Reaction from the OPA to the attack itself has been muted, but the RCE and United Nations forces will be announcing this afternoon that a relief mission will be launched for New Terra. Initial reports suggest this will be a joint task force with both corporate assets and United Nations military escort.

"Representatives of the OPA have not responded to this plan, but are on record as being willing to use military force to control traffic through Medina Station. Given the tactical constraints of the ring gates, Forecast Analytics projects the possibility of a modest OPA military force being able to effectively blockade the UN and RCE efforts. Sources close to the Martian congress speaking with Forecast Analytics under condition of anonymity have suggested that the Martian government would support the OPA's action.

"Analysis suggests that this is not evidence of a long-term amity between the OPA and Mars, but a tactical alliance intended to forestall the UN and Earth-Luna corporate structures from establishing a greater foothold in these new worlds. Given the time it will take a UN and RCE group to be assembled and make the journey to Medina Station, we predict that the situation on New Terra will be evolving without immediate physical involvement from in-system players for the foreseeable future, and the greater question of how traffic through the gates will be regulated will be a source of high-level tension and probable military action in the coming months and years."

Havelock scratched his ear. Prior experience told him that

Forecast Analytics was usually about a day ahead of the mainline, non-proprietary feeds. Which would mean that in about thirty hours they'd be getting flooded with news and opinion pieces about themselves from people who'd never been farther than the Jovian system. Even if it only changed the stories that the people downstairs were telling about themselves, it could make things even worse. If the squatters knew there were more RCE ships coming—even if they weren't going to be here for years—maybe they'd get even more desperate. Or maybe Mars getting in bed with the OPA would make them think they had support back home. Either way, nothing good could come of it.

Havelock wished there was a way to shut down the communication to the ring, just as a way to keep the dramatics of national politics contained. Things were screwed up enough without getting the professional-class screwups at the UN involved. More than they already were, anyway. At least they hadn't picked up on the UN/OPA mediator deciding the planet was full of boojams and was telling everyone to run away and hide under their blankets. Or, on second thought, maybe it would have been better if they had. It would be a distraction, anyway.

His hand terminal squawked, and he accepted the connection.

"I think we're about ready," Chief Engineer Koenen said.

"I'll be right there," Havelock replied, releasing the couch straps. He pushed off toward the door and hauled himself hand over hand toward the airlock.

He slid into the storage deck where his little militia was waiting, his brain arbitrarily deciding that the bank of lockers was down, the airlock door up. Human brains needed an answer, even if they had to make up something they knew was bullshit. A dozen people floated in the space. Havelock started talking to them as he lifted his own vacuum suit out of the locker at his feet.

"Good to see you today, team. So we're going to do a practice breaching. It's going to be a lot like last time, except this time we're going to have a squad that's trying to stop you."

One of the men at the back shook a paint gun and hooted.

The others around him laughed. Havelock pulled on the vacuum suit and started working the seals. He left the helmet off for the moment so that he could speak through the free air.

"Do we have teams set up?"

"I'm taking Alpha and Beta," Koenen said. "Figured you could lead the Gamma on attack."

"That works," Havelock said. He shifted his paintball gun from side to side, getting a feel for its mass. "You have the emergency airlock?"

"Here," one of the Beta team said, twisting to show his backpack. The bright yellow box held a bubble of adhesive-backed polymer bound to a second sheet that was fitted with a seal and an inflating tank the size of Havelock's thumb. Laid out properly on the hull of a ship, it would look like a hemispherical blister and contain up to two atmospheres of pressure indefinitely or eight for a full tenth of a second. Havelock wasn't actually going to let the engineers cut through the hull of the *Israel*, but he was going to make sure they could get everything ready up to the moment when they'd fire up the torch welders.

"All right," he said. "Now before we get out there, remember we're on the outside of a ship, and the shuttle is on the planet. The chances of your drifting to where we can't get you back are non-zero."

The little bit of joking and whispering stopped. Havelock looked through the room, making eye contact with several of them as if his gaze were enough to make them safe.

"All these suits have mag boots," he said. "They only work for a few centimeters, so they'll keep you against the ship, but they won't pull you back to it. For that you have the grapnel lines. You've all trained with those?"

A murmur of general assent answered him.

"All right. If you're drifting, the grapnel line will adhere to any metal surface on the hull. They've got their own propellant, so there won't be any kick. Do not under any circumstances pass through or stop in any of the areas marked in red. Those are maneuvering thruster outlets, and while we aren't planning to make any adjustments, don't assume it. We're not doing this to lose anyone else.

"If you get out there and you start feeling too hot or like there's something wrong with your air feed, you're probably having a panic attack. Just let me or the chief know, and we'll pause the exercise and get you inside. If you start feeling wonderful and powerful and like you've seen the face of God, you're having a euphoric attack, and those are more dangerous than the panic. You aren't going to want to tell us about those, but you have to. All right?"

A ragged chorus of *Sir, yes sir* echoed through the room. Havelock tried to think of what else he should say. He didn't want to insult their intelligence, but he didn't want anything to go wrong either. In the end, he shrugged, fastened the helmet, and gave the order through the exercise frequency.

"Alpha and Beta teams, into the lock. You've got thirty minutes."

There were three exercise-specific settings on the suit radio. One was open to all the people going out. One was just for Havelock's team, and the last was between him and Koenen. The mom-and-pop channel, the chief engineer called it. Havelock opened all the channels, but all he could hear was the banter of his own group. The chief and his men weren't transmitting. After ten minutes, Havelock switched to the mom-and-pop channel.

"Okay," he said. "We're coming out."

There was a crackle as the chief switched.

"That wasn't thirty minutes."

"I know," Havelock said, and the chief chuckled.

"Okay. Thank you for the heads-up. I won't give it away."

Astronomy had never been a particular interest of Havelock's, and living in a ship or station, he'd seen actual stars less often than he did in his childhood on Earth. The starscape around New Terra was beautiful, familiar and unfamiliar at the same time. The few constellations he knew—Orion, Ursa Major—weren't there, but he still looked for them. The bright smear of the galactic disk was still part of the sky, and the local sun could pass for Sol. More or less, anyway. New Terra's ring of tiny moons caught the light, their low albedo making them hardly more than the stars behind them. The *Edward Israel* was moving at something like eight thousand kilometers a minute. That this stillness masked a velocity that was orders of magnitude faster than a rifle shot was intellectual knowledge. What he felt was motionless. He stood on the skin of the ship, rooted by his mag boots, shifting gently like seaweed on the ocean floor. To his right, New Terra's terminator seemed to inch across its vast ocean. To his right, the shuttle stood half a kilometer out, looking small and forlorn against the vast night. His strike force stood around him, craning their necks, in awe of the massive emptiness all around. He was almost sorry to pull his attention back to the small, vaguely intimate necessities of violence.

He checked to be sure he was speaking on the channel exclusive to his group. "All right. Their target area for setting up the emergency lock is aft of the main storage area. We're going around clockwise. In ten minutes, we'll be moving into eclipse. If we come up from between the primary maneuvering thrusters and hangar bay, we should have the sun behind us. So let's get moving."

The small chorus of excited *yessirs* told him they liked the idea. Coming out of the sun, raining death on the enemy. It was a pretty enough plan. The only things that kept it from happening were their unfamiliarity with the mag boots and the fact that Koenen had placed the emergency airlock a hundred meters farther away than Havelock had expected. The bright moment passed, and the sun shifted behind New Terra, where it would stay for almost twenty minutes.

"Okay," Havelock said, "Plan B. Everyone turn off your helmet lights."

"What about the indicators on our external batteries, sir?"

"We're going to have to hope they're dim enough that—"

One of the engineers to his left raised the paint gun and turned it on himself. The muzzle flash was like a spark.

"What the hell are you doing?" Havelock demanded.

"I figured if I got some paint on the indicator light, I could—" the man began, but it was too late. Koenen's men had seen the muzzle flash. Havelock tried to get his forces to hunker down close to the skin of the ship and fire across the ship's shallow horizon, but they kept rising up to see if they'd struck anything. In less than a minute, the last of his men reported an enemy hit and Havelock called the exercise to a halt. The massive dark bulk of the planet was almost above them now, the sunlight a soft ring where the atmosphere scattered it. The two groups gathered.

The airlock was only half attached, and three of his team's paintballs had smeared it. Two of the chief engineer's boarding party had been hit. The rest were elated. Havelock set his team and the wounded of the opposition to cleanup, and the disgraced soldiers started repacking the airlock.

"Nice work," Havelock said on the mom-and-pop channel.

Koenen grunted. His arms were crossed awkwardly over his chest, the bulk of the suit defying the pose. Havelock frowned, not that anyone could see him.

"Something the matter, chief?"

"You know," the chief engineer said, "I don't mind that the *Israel* has her own engineering crew. I understand that we've got separate mandates. But we're working with the same equipment and supplies, and as a courtesy, I would like to be kept in the loop when the ship crew are sending out a team."

"Okay," Havelock said. "I can talk to them when we get in. Is it something that's been happening often?"

"It's happening right now," the chief said, pointing out into the darkness.

It took Havelock a moment to see it. A flicker where no flicker should be. The weaponized shuttle brightened and dimmed. A welding torch, half a klick away in the darkness. Panic felt strange in null g, the blood flowing away from his hands and feet.

"Do you have enhanced magnification on your helmet?" Havelock asked.

"Yeah," the chief said.

"Could you take a look at who's out there?"

The chief engineer bent back. The surface of his helmet glittered for a moment, the HUD taking over. "Red EVA suit. Got a decent-sized pack on it too. Long-distance travel. And a welding kit."

Havelock said something obscene, then switched to the all-group channel. "Everyone stop. We have a problem. There's someone at the shuttle over there, and he isn't one of ours."

For a moment, no one spoke. Then one of the militiamen, his voice calm and matter-of-fact, said, "Let's go kick his ass."

It was exactly not what Havelock wanted to do. If the enemy had a rifle, he could pick half the team off before they got close. Even then, they had paint guns. But the alternative was to let whoever they were do whatever they were doing to the only ace up the *Israel*'s sleeve.

"Okay," Havelock said. "Here's the plan. Everyone sync up with the ship's computer. We're going to let the *Israel* calculate our burns. Turn off the mag boots." He plucked out his hand terminal, fed in the emergency security override, and coded in his request. Their vacuum suits had more then enough propellant to get them all to the shuttle and back again, provided nobody missed or tried to do something clever. Above them, the penumbra around New Terra grew lopsided, the sun preparing to reemerge. Another tiny dawn. The computer announced the burns were ready.

"Okay," Havelock said. "These are the bad guys. We don't know how many there are. We don't know how they're armed. So we're going to try to scare them off. Everyone get your gun at the ready. Look threatening, and *don't fire*. If they figure out our guns aren't real, we may be in for a bad time."

"Sir?" one of the men said. "You remember we're covered with target paint, right?"

Before Havelock could answer, the thrusters started, pushing compressed gas out behind them like a fog and smoke. All their suits rose together into the night. Or else fell. The acceleration pushed the blood into Havelock's legs, and the suit squeezed, pressing it back. It wasn't even a full g. It was hardly a third, but it felt like something much, much faster. Much more dangerous. Now that he knew to look for it, the welding flicker was obvious. It didn't stop. The main burn cut out, and the suits rotated, starting the braking burn. The perfect synchrony meant the *Israel* was still coordinating them.

This time, the intruder saw them. The welding torch died. Havelock looked down between his feet, his paint gun centered between his toes, waiting for the bullets to start streaming out and praying that they wouldn't.

They didn't.

"It's working!" one of the men shouted. "Motherfucker's running away!"

And there it was. A red EVA suit on the skin of the shuttle. It struggled with something, looked up toward Havelock and his militia descending upon him, and turned back. Whoever it was, there was only one of them. The braking thrust stuttered. They were almost at the shuttle now. Fifty meters. Forty. Thirty. Havelock opened a standard general-response channel.

"Attention unidentified welder. You will stand down."

The red suit stood, the EVA suit firing off. The person lifted at a ninety-degree angle, not going directly away from them, but diving down toward the planetary surface and whatever lower orbit would mean a safe rendezvous. Havelock felt the relief flooding him. They weren't shooting. His HUD promised him that the shuttle's basic functions were unchanged. It hadn't been set to detonate. And the militia boys weren't in charge of their own burns, so they wouldn't be taking off after the intruder.

He had underestimated them.

The first dark thread rose out toward the intruder and missed, but once the whole team had seen the grapnel fire, the idea was out there. A half dozen grapnels fired, their propellant flaring blue and orange as they flew like tiny missiles toward the fleeing welder. Then one made contact. The enemy and the man who'd fired the grapnel both jerked, and the engineer's suit started an emergency burn, trying to compensate. With the enemy encumbered and slowed, two more grapnels connected. Soon five of his people had lines attached to the saboteur, their collected thrusters holding the red suit's EVA pack in check. Havelock took control of his suit back from the *Israel* and dropped down toward the planet and the prisoner.

The red suit was twisting now, trying to bring its welding torch to bear on the lines. Havelock raised his gun, and the enemy paused. He was close enough now that he could see the face behind the helmet. A Belter woman, dark-skinned, with wavy dark hair clinging to her sweaty forehead. Her expression was pure chagrin.

He opened the general channel again.

"Hi," he said. "Don't panic. My name's Havelock. I'm acting security chief for the *Edward Israel*, and you have to come with me now."

Interlude: The Investigator

—it reaches out it reaches out it reaches out it reaches out—

One hundred and thirteen times a second, it reaches out, and the things it finds are not the signal that would let it end, but they are tools, and it explores then without knowing it is exploring them. Like water finding its mindless way through a bed of pebbles, it reaches out. What it can move, it moves, what it can open, it opens. What it can close, it closes. A vast network, ancient and dead, begins to appear, and it reaches into it. The parts of it that can think, struggle to make sense of it. Parts of it dream of a mummified body, its dry heart pumping dust through petrified veins.

Not everything responds, but it reaches out, presses, *moves*. And some things move back. Old artifacts awaken or don't. None of them are what it seeks. None ever will be. It experiments without awareness of experimenting, and a landscape begins to form. It is not a physical landscape, but a logical one—this connects to this connects to this. It builds a model and adds it to the model it already has, and does not know it has done so. It reaches out. One hundred thirteen times a second, it reaches out.

Something that worked once, stops working. It reaches out and what answered before answers less now. Something burns or fails or tries to rise up and breaks. Part of the map goes dark, dies, and it reaches out to the silent dead. Part of it feels frustration, but it is not aware of that part, and it reaches out. Part of it wants to scream, wants to die, wants to vomit though a mouth it imagines has been transformed into something else for years now. It does not experience these things, though parts of it do. It reaches out.

And it pulls back.

It is unaware of pulling back, but one time out of every seventeen million attempts, it touches something and will not touch it again. It is not aware of pulling back, because it is not aware of anything, but the failures accrue. A blank place forms, an emptiness. A void. Avoid. Jesus, an old woman thinks, now with the puns.

The map is not physical, but it has a shape. It is a model of part of the universe. It becomes more detailed, more concrete. Some things come alive and then die. Some do not answer ever. Some become tools, and it uses the tools to reach out, except not *there*.

The emptiness gains definition too. With every failed connection, with every pulling back its liminal borders become better defined. It struggles to make sense of the shape of the nothing that defies it. The structures of the minds that never died within it struggle with it. It is a cyst. It is a negative space. A taboo. It is a question that must not be asked. It is not aware that it thinks these things. It is not aware that the space exists, that when it reaches into that place, it dies.

It does not need to be aware of the problem. It has a tool for this. A thing that finds what is missing. A tool for asking questions that shouldn't be asked. For going too far. The investigator considers the cyst, the shadow, the space where nothing is.

That right there? The investigator thinks. Yeah, where I come from, we'd call that a *clue*.

Chapter Twenty-Three: Holden

Come on," Holden said to the empty desert and the man who wasn't there. "You show up every time I don't want you around. But I get something I want to talk to you about, and nothing."

The thing that had been Miller didn't answer. Holden sighed, hoped, and waited.

Ilus had lost some of its strangeness. The moonless sky still felt too dark, but no darker than a new moon on earth. His nose had become accustomed to the planet's strange scents. Now it just smelled like night and the aftermath of rain. His growing familiarity was both comforting and sad. Humans would go out to the thousand worlds of the gate network. They would settle down in little towns like First Landing, then spread out and build farms and cities and factories, because that's what humans did. And in a few centuries, most of those worlds would be very similar to

Earth. The frontier would give way to the civilizations that followed it. Remaking it in the image of their original home.

Holden had grown up in the Montana district of North America. A region filled with nostalgia for lost frontiers. It had held out against urban creep longer than most places in the former United States. The people there clung to their farms and ranches even when those things stopped making economic sense. And because of that, Holden couldn't help but feel the allure of the untamed place. The romantic notion of sights no one else had seen. Ground no one else had walked.

This new frontier would last throughout Holden's lifetime. Conquering and taming a thousand-plus planets was the work of generations, no matter how much of a head start the protomolecule's masters had given them. But in his heart, Holden knew that conquered and tamed they would be. And then there would be a thousand Earths with steel-and-glass cities covering them. Holden felt a shadow of that distant future's loss of mystery as though it were his own.

In the moonless black sky, a star moved too quickly. One of the ships. The *Israel* or the *Barbapiccola*. The *Rocinante* was too small and too black to reflect the light. Did the people up there think about how momentous what they were all doing was? Holden worried that they didn't. That the strangeness had already become normal, like the night scents of Ilus. That all they saw now was the conflict to be won and the treasure to be harvested.

With a sigh, Holden turned back toward the town and started walking. Amos would be wondering where he was. Carol, the town administrator, had asked for an after-dinner meeting so he needed to track her down too. A fat, dog-shaped thing with a bullfrog's head walked in front of him and made a sound like boots crunching on gravel. Mimic lizards, the locals called them. They were sort of scaled like a lizard, but to Holden the limbs looked all wrong. Holden took out his hand terminal and used it to shine a faint light on the creature. It blinked up at him and made the gravel noise again.

"You'd be a good pet if you didn't vomit your stomach up periodically," Holden said, crouching down to get a better look at the creature. It croaked back at him. Nothing like the words he'd used, but a surprisingly good imitation of his voice and tones. He wondered if the animals could be taught to speak words like a parrot.

The terminal in his hand buzzed. The lizard skittered away, buzzing back at him over its shoulder.

"Holden here."

"Yeah, Cap," Alex said. "I got some bad news."

"Bad like the zero-g toilet on the *Roci* is out of order, or bad like I should be looking at the sky for incoming missile trails?"

"Well…" Alex started, and then took a long breath. Holden looked up at the sky. Just stars.

"You've scared me now. Spit it out."

"Naomi," Alex started, and Holden felt his heart drop. "She was out installing the remote cutout on the shuttle, and they were doin' some kind of group exercise on the outside of the *Israel* and they spotted her. Just dumb luck, really."

"What happened? Is she okay?" Please be okay.

"They got her, Cap," Alex said. Holden felt his chest go empty.

"Got her. Like, *shot* her?"

"Oh! No. Captured. She's not hurt. The security guy on the *Israel* called to make sure I knew she was unharmed. But they're callin' it sabotage, and they locked her up."

"Fuck," Holden said, able to breathe again. He knew who'd have authorized that. Murtry. And now that the RCE security chief had a big bargaining chip he'd go all-in. "Does anyone else know?"

"Well, Amos called up looking for her a minute ago—"

Holden didn't hear the rest of what Alex said, because he was already running toward town. The longer he ran without hearing gunfire, the more hopeful he became that Amos had realized the sensitivity of the situation, had decided to wait and consult with his captain before taking any action. He hoped Amos wasn't already on the radio with the *Israel* and a pistol held to Murtry's head demanding Naomi's safe return.

He was half right.

When he burst into Murtry's security office he found the RCE security chief pressed to one wall with Amos' left hand around his throat and a pistol against his forehead. At least no one had called the *Israel* with demands. Likely because Amos didn't have a free hand to dial.

In addition to Murtry and Amos, four RCE security personnel stood around the room with drawn sidearms pointed at Amos' back. One of them, a raven-haired woman named Wei, said, "Drop the gun or we'll shoot."

"Okay," Amos said with a shrug. "Blast away, sweetie. I guarantee I take this piece of shit with me. I'm good. You good?" He leaned closer to Murtry, punctuating the question with a jab of the pistol against his forehead. A little trickle of blood had started to run down Murtry's face from the force of the barrel pressed against it.

Murtry smiled. "Keep barking, dog. We both know there's no bite coming. You shoot me, she's dead."

"You won't know," Amos said.

"Don't, Amos," Holden ordered.

"Oh, do," Murtry said, the words almost a whisper.

Holden held his breath, sure the next thing they heard would be a gunshot. Amos surprised him by not firing. Instead he leaned in even farther until his nose was touching Murtry's and said, "I'm gonna *kill* you."

"When?" Murtry replied.

"That is exactly the question that should stay on your mind," Amos said and let the man go.

Holden started breathing again with a gasp. "I've got this, Amos."

The big mechanic holstered his gun, to Holden's relief, but made no move to leave.

"Seriously. I've got it. I need you to go back to the rooms and get on the line with Alex. Get me a full report. I'll be back there in a minute."

For a moment, Holden thought Amos would argue with him. The mechanic stared back, face flushed with rage, his jaw clenched hard enough to crack his teeth. "Okay," he finally said and then left. The other four security people kept their guns trained on him the entire time.

"That was smart," Murtry said. He pulled a tissue out of a box on his desk and wiped the blood from his forehead. He had an ugly bruise forming around the cut Amos' pistol had left. "Your boy almost didn't make it out of this room, *mediator.*"

Holden surprised himself by laughing. "I've never seen Amos pick a fight he didn't plan to win. I'm not sure what he had in mind, but even at five to one my money would be on him."

"Everyone loses eventually," Murtry said.

"Words to live by."

"That's quite the killer you have working for you, as critical as you are of my methods."

"There's a difference. Amos is willing to lose face to protect something he loves. He doesn't need to win more than he needs to keep his friends alive. And that's why you're nothing alike."

Murtry agreed with a nod and a shrug. "So if you weren't here to save your man, then what?"

"We keep escalating," Holden said. "Some of that is my fault. *I* asked Naomi to deal with the shuttle."

"Sabotage—" Murtry started.

"But I did that in response to finding out you'd weaponized it. We keep reacting to what the person before us did, justifying ourselves like kids on a playground. 'He started it.'"

"So you'll be the first to break the cycle?"

"If I can," Holden said. "You've gone too far, Murtry. Disable the shuttle, give me Naomi back. Let's see if we can find a way to stop the escalation."

Murtry's vague smile shifted into an equally vague frown. The

man leaned back on his desk and touched another tissue to the cut
on his forehead. It came away with a single crimson spot. Then
he folded his arms, casual but immovable. Holden knew that it
was a deliberate affectation intended to look natural. He was
both impressed and worried by anyone who had that level of self-
awareness and control.

"I've acted entirely within the purview of my assignment here,"
Murtry said. "I've protected RCE assets and personnel."

"You've killed a bunch of colonists and kidnapped my XO,"
Holden replied, trying to keep the anger out of his voice and
failing.

"I've killed fewer squatters than they've killed of us, all of
which were actively engaged in plotting and carrying out attacks
on RCE assets and personnel. Which, as I said, is my job."

"And Naomi—"

"And I captured a saboteur and am holding her pending an
investigation. 'Kidnapping' is not only a provocative term, it's
inaccurate."

"You want this to blow up." Holden sighed. "You can't wait for
the next chance to make things worse, can you?"

The frown shifted back to the smile. Neither meant anything.
Just different masks. Holden wondered what it looked like inside
Murtry's head and shuddered.

"I've done the minimum necessary at each step," the man said
through his disquieting grin.

"No," Holden replied. "You could have left. You had the *Israel*.
After the first attack on the shuttle you could have pulled your
people out and waited for the investigation. A lot of people would
still be alive if you had."

"Oh no," Murtry said, shaking his head. He stood up and
uncrossed his arms. Every movement slow and deliberate and
conveying threat. "No, that's one thing we won't do. We won't
give up a centimeter of ground. These squatters can throw themselves against us until every one of them is shattered into dust, but
we're not going anywhere. Because that…"

Murtry's smile sharpened.

"...is also my job."

The walk from the RCE security shed back to his room at the community center wasn't a long one, but it was very dark. Miller's faint blue glow illuminated nothing, but it was oddly comforting anyway.

"Hey, old man," Holden said in greeting.

"We need to talk." Miller grinned at his own joke. He made jokes now. He was almost like a real person. Somehow that was more frightening than when he'd been insane.

"I know, but I'm kind of busy with keeping these people from killing each other. Or, you know, us."

"How's that working for you?"

"Terrible," Holden admitted. "I've just lost the only real threat I had to make."

"Yeah, Naomi being on their ship makes the *Rocinante* a non-factor. Letting her anywhere near that ship was a dumb mistake."

"I never told you about that."

"Should I pretend I'm not inside your head?" Miller asked with a Belter shrug. "I'll do it if it makes you more comfortable."

"Hey, Miller," Holden said. "What am I thinking now?"

"Points for creativity, kid. That'd be difficult to pull off and less fun than you might expect."

"So stay out."

Miller stopped walking and grabbed Holden's upper arm. Again he was surprised at how real it felt. Miller's hand felt like iron gripping him. Holden tried to pull away and couldn't. And all of it was just the ghost pushing buttons in his brain.

"Wasn't kidding. We need to talk."

"Spit it out," Holden replied, finally yanking his arm away when Miller let go.

"There's a spot a way north of here I need to go look at."

"By which you mean you need *me* to go look at."

"Yeah," Miller said with a Belter nod of one fist. "That."

Against his will, Holden felt his curiosity piqued. "What is it?"

"So, turns out our coming here caused a little ruckus with the locals," Miller said. "May have noticed. Lot of leftover stuff waking up all over the planet."

"Yeah, I wanted to talk to you about that. Is that you? Can you control it?"

"Are you kidding? I'm a sock puppet. Protomolecule's got its arm so far up my ass, I can taste its fingernails." Miller laughed. "I can't even control myself."

"It's just that some of it seems dangerous. That robot, for instance. And you were able to turn off the station in the slow zone."

"Because *it* wanted me to. You can order the sun to come up if you time it right. I'm not driving this bus. Making it do what I want would be like talking someone out of a seizure."

"Okay," Holden said. "We have got to get off this planet."

"Before that, though, there's this thing. This not-thing. Look, I've got a pretty good map of the global network. Lots of leftover stuff coming up, checking in. Except one spot. Like a big ball of nothing."

Holden shrugged. "Maybe it's just a place where there are no nodes on the network."

"Kid, this whole planet is a node on the network. There shouldn't be anyplace that's off-limits to me."

"So what does it mean?"

"Maybe it's just a spot that's really really broken," Miller said. "That'd be interesting but useless."

"And the useful thing?"

"It's a leftover bit of whatever killed this place."

They stood in silence for a moment, the cool evening wind of Ilus ruffling Holden's pants and not affecting the detective at all. Holden felt a chill start at the base of his spine and slowly climb his back. The hairs on his arms stood up.

"I don't want to find that," he finally said.

"And I do?" Miller replied with his best attempt at a friendly smile. "Free will left the conversation for me a while back. But that's where the clues are. You should come with. It's going to happen eventually anyway."

"Why is that?"

"Because real monsters don't go away when you close your eyes. Because you need to know what happened here just as bad as I do."

Miller's expression was still friendly, but there was a dread in it too. A fear that Holden recognized. And shared.

"Naomi first. I don't go anywhere until we get her back."

Miller nodded again and flew apart into a spray of blue fireflies.

Amos was waiting for him when he got back to the bar. The big man sitting alone at a table with a half-empty bottle of something that smelled like antiseptic and smoke.

"I'm guessing you didn't kill him after I left," Amos said as Holden sat down.

"I feel like I'm walking a tightrope so narrow I can't even see it," Holden replied. He shook his head when Amos offered him the bottle, so the mechanic took a long swig from it instead.

"This ends in blood," Amos said after a moment. His voice sounded distant, dreamlike. "No way around that."

"Well, since my job is pretty much exactly the opposite of that, I hope you're wrong."

"I'm not."

Holden lacked a compelling argument, so instead he said, "What did Alex have to say?"

"We put together a list of demands for the captain of the *Israel*. Make sure Naomi gets well taken care of while she's there."

"What will we give up in exchange?"

"Alex isn't blowing the *Israel* into its component atoms right this second."

"I hope they agree we're being generous."

"He is, however," Amos continued, "keeping a constant rail gun lock on the *Israel*'s reactor."

Holden ran his fingers through his hair. "So not too generous, then."

"Say pretty please, but carry a one-kilo slug of tungsten accelerated to a detectable percentage of c."

"I believe I've heard that said," Holden replied, then stood up. He suddenly felt very tired. "I'm going to bed."

"Naomi's in Murtry's goddamn brig, and you can sleep?" Amos said and took another drink.

"No, but I can go to bed. Then tomorrow I'm going to figure out how to get my first officer back from the RCE maniac holding her hostage, so that I can go find the scary alien bullet fragment embedded in the planet."

Amos nodded as if that all made sense. "Nothing in the afternoon, then."

Chapter Twenty-Four: Elvi

Elvi slept, and she dreamed.

In her dream she was back on Earth, which was also the corridors of the *Edward Israel*. A sense of urgency pressed at her, shifting quickly toward dread. Something was on fire somewhere because she hadn't turned in the right forms. She had to file the forms before everything burned. She was in the bursar's office at the university and Governor Trying was there too, only he was waiting for his death certificate and it was taking too long. She couldn't submit her forms. She looked at the onionskin papers, trying to find the submission deadline, but the words kept changing. First, the line at the bottom read, *Elvi Okoye, lead researcher and Argonaut,* and the next time she read it, *Fines to be paid directly at the temple: rabbits and hogs.* The urgency pushed at her, and when she shouted the onionskin started coming apart in her fingers. She tried to press the forms back together, but they wouldn't go.

Someone touched her shoulder, and it was James Holden, only he looked like someone else. Younger, darker, but she knew it was him. She realized she'd been naked this whole time. She was embarrassed, but also a little pleased. His hand touched her breast, and—

"Elvi! Wake up!"

Her eyes opened, the lids heavy and slow. Her eyes struggled to focus. She didn't know where she was, only that some dumb bastard was interrupting something she didn't want interrupted. The dark lines before her slowly became familiar. The roof of her hut. She shifted, reaching out for someone but already uncertain who. She was alone in her bed. Her hand terminal glowed dimly. Her analysis equipment flickered as data from her work flew up and out, through the vast darkness to the Ring and Medina Station, to Earth, and answering information flew back out to her. Which was all fine and as it should be, so why the hell was she awake?

A soft knock came at the door, and Fayez's voice. "Elvi! Wake up. You've got to see this."

Elvi yawned so deeply her jaw ached with it. She pulled herself up to sitting. The dream was already fading quickly. There had been something about a fire and someone touching her whom she had badly wanted to be touched by. The details lost all coherence as she sat up and reached for her robe.

"Elvi? Are you there?"

When she spoke her words were slow, heavy, a little slurred. "If this isn't important, I will rip your throat open and piss down your lungs."

Fayez laughed. There were other voices behind his. Sudyam saying something too low to make out the words. Yma Chappel, the geochemistry lead too. Elvi paused, threw off the robe, and pulled on her real clothes and work boots to go with them. When she stepped out of her hut, a dozen of the people in the research teams were standing in pairs or small groups all across the night-dark plain. They were all looking up. And in the high darkness, something larger than a star glowed a sullen red. Fayez, squatting on the ground, glanced over at her.

"What is that?" Elvi asked, her voice instinctively low, as if she might startle it.

"One of the moons."

She stepped forward, her neck back, scowling up at the night. "What's it doing?"

"Melting."

"Why?"

"Right?" Fayez said, standing up.

Sudyam, to their left, raised her voice. "Makes you wish we'd sent probes there, doesn't it?"

"We're one ship, and this is a whole damn planet," Fayez said. "Plus which, we've been focusing a lot of effort on killing each other."

"Point being?" Sudyam asked.

Fayez spread his hands wide. "We've been busy."

The moon shifted colors for a moment, turning from dull red to a bright orange to yellow-white, and then back down the spectrum again, waning as suddenly as it had waxed.

"Is anyone recording this?" Elvi asked.

"Caskey and Farengier aborted the high-altitude refraction study and started sucking down data from it is as soon as they saw it was happening. Mostly, it's visible light, heat, and about thirty percent more gamma particles than background. The sensor array on the *Israel*'s showing about the same thing."

"Is it dangerous?" Elvi asked, knowing the answer even as she spoke the words. Maybe. Maybe it was dangerous, maybe it wasn't. Until they knew what it was, all they could do was guess. In the starlight, Fayez's expression was difficult to make out. The apprehension at the corners of his mouth and in the curve of his eyes might only have been her imagination. Another kind of dream. "Do the others know?"

"I guess so," Fayez said. "Assuming they're not too busy taking each other prisoner and setting people on fire."

"You told Murtry?"

"I didn't. Someone probably did."

"And Holden? What about him? Does he know?"

"Even if he does, what's he going to do about it? Speak to it reassuringly?"

Elvi turned toward First Landing. The few lit houses were like a handful of stars fallen to the ground. She took out her hand terminal, setting its screen to white and using it as a torch.

"Where are you going?" Fayez called from behind her.

"I'm going to talk to Captain Holden," she said.

"Of course you are," Fayez said with an impatient grunt. "Because what would be useful for him is a biologist's perspective on it."

The words stung a little, but Elvi didn't let herself be drawn into the conversation. Fayez was a good scientist and a friend, but his habit of making fun of everything and derailing anything serious for the sake of humor also made him less useful than he should have been. One of the others should have made sure everyone knew that something was happening overhead. It shouldn't have had to be her. And still, she quietly did hope that she would be the one to bring the news.

The dry air smelled like dust and the tiny, night-blooming flower analogs. Where there had been a few tough, ropy plants, months of foot traffic had made paths, and Elvi followed them as easily in the near-darkness as she would have in the day. It occurred to her, not for the first time, that the scattering of huts, the ruins, and even First Landing itself had become as familiar to her as anyplace else she'd lived. She knew the land, the feel of the breezes, the smells that rose and fell at different times of day. Over the past month, she had been the ears and eyes of the whole scientific community back in the solar system. Even when the terrorists had killed Reeve, and Murtry had come down, at least a part of her day had been running samples and transmitting data back home. She had spent more time not just in but *with* this environment than anyone else.

Above her, the tiny red moon reminded her that she still didn't know much. Normally, that would have been a delight and a challenge. In the darkness of the New Terran night, it felt like a threat. Her steps took on a rhythm, her boots tapping against the wind-paved stones.

In the town, people were in the streets much like they had been out by the RCE huts. They stood in the streets and on their little cobbled-together porches, looking up at the glowing dot as it drifted toward the horizon. Elvi couldn't say if they were curious or apprehensive or just wanting something to think about that wasn't the conflict between RCE and the squatters. Between *us* and *them*.

Or maybe they were seeing it as an omen. The burning eye looking down on them all, judging them and preparing for war. She'd heard a folktale like that once, but she didn't remember where.

Wei and one of the other RCE security men were walking down the main street, rifles at the ready. Elvi nodded to them, and they nodded back, but no one spoke. Probably someone had told Holden. But she'd come all this way. She should at least be sure.

In the street outside the commissary where Holden was living, Jacek Merton was pacing. The boy's body leaned into the motion, his hands at his sides clenched in fists. His gaze was fixed about three feet in front of him like someone looking at a screen, and his shoulders were hunched in like he was protecting something. She was about to say hello, when a small warning bell chimed in her head.

Between one heartbeat and the next, she wasn't Elvi Okoye going in the middle of the night to see Captain Holden on pretenses that even she could see were pretty damned flimsy. That wasn't the son of Lucia and Basia Merton, brother of Felcia, in front of her. This wasn't even a town. She was a biologist in the field seeing a primate. And in that frame of reference, some things were perfectly clear. The boy was working himself up to violence.

She hesitated and started to turn back. Wei was only a few dozen meters and a corner or two away. If Elvi shouted, the security people would probably come at a run. Her pulse was quick. She could feel it in her throat. The long hours after Reeve's death came back to her like a recurring nightmare. She should scream. She should call for help.

Except the boy wasn't just a primate. Wasn't just an animal. He was Felcia's brother. And if she called for help, they might kill him. She swallowed, caught between fear and courage. Uncertain. What would Fayez do? she wondered. Offer the kid a beer?

He stopped and looked up at her. His eyes were empty. He wore a light jacket that pulled down a little on one side, like he had something heavy in his pocket.

"Hi," she said, smiling.

A moment later, Jacek said, "Hi."

"Weird, isn't it?" She pointed up at the red dot. It seemed more portentous than ever. Jacek glanced up at the sky, but didn't seem to react to it.

"Weird," he agreed.

They stood in front of each other, the silence rich and tense. The light spilling from the commissary windows left the boy half in light, half in shadow. Elvi struggled, trying to find something to say. Some way to defuse everything and make it all okay. Fayez would have made a joke, something that the boy could laugh at and that would put them both on the same side of the laughter, and Elvi didn't know what it was.

"I'm scared," she said instead, her voice breaking a little. It surprised the boy as much as it did her. "I'm just so scared."

"It's okay," Jacek said. "It's just some kind of reaction up there. It's not like it's doing anything but melting up in orbit."

"Still scared, though."

Jacek scowled at his feet, torn between the errand he'd been steeling himself for and the impulse to say something kind and reassuring to this obviously unstable, vulnerable, strange woman.

"It'll be okay?" he tried.

"You're right," she said, nodding. "It's just. You know. I mean, you do know, don't you?"

"I guess."

"I was coming to see Captain Holden," she said, and Jacek's eyes flickered like she'd said something insulting. "Were you too?"

She could see in his face as he tried to bring back the blankness he'd had before, the tightness and anger and emptiness. He wasn't someone for whom violence came naturally. He'd had to put effort into it. It was that effort she'd seen in him.

"He took my father away," Jacek said. "Mom worries we'll never see him again."

"Is that why you came? To ask?"

Jacek looked confused.

"Ask...what?"

"To talk to your father."

The boy blinked, and he took an unconscious step toward her. "He won't let me talk to him. He took him prisoner."

"People talk to prisoners all the time. Did someone tell you that you couldn't talk to your dad?"

Jacek was silent. He put his hand into his jacket pocket—the heavy one—and then took it out again. "No."

"Come on, then," Elvi said, moving toward him. "Let's go ask him."

Inside the commissary, Holden was pacing from the front of the room to the back to the front again. The big man—Amos—sat at a table with a pack of cards, playing solitaire with an unnerving focus. Holden's face was paler than usual, and the sense of barely restrained emotion gave his body a tension that she didn't picture him with. Amos looked up as she walked in, her hand on Jacek's shoulder. His eyes were flat and empty as marbles, and his voice was just as cheerful as ever.

"Hey there, doc. What's up?"

"Couple things," Elvi said.

Holden stopped. It seemed to take him a second to focus. Something was bothering him. His gaze locked on her and he tried to smile. An unexpected tightness came to her throat. She coughed.

"Jacek was wondering if there was any way he could talk with his father," Elvi said. There didn't seem to be much air in the room, she was having a hard time catching her breath. Maybe she was developing allergies.

"Sure," Holden said, then looked over his shoulder at Amos. "That's not a problem, is it?"

"Radios still work," Amos said. "Might want to give Alex the heads-up to expect it. His hands are kind of full right now."

"Good point," Holden said, nodding to himself as much as any of them. "I'll set that up. Do you have a hand terminal?"

It took Jacek a moment to realize the question was directed at him. "It doesn't work. We don't have a hub. It's all just line-of-sight."

"Bring it over when you can, and I'll see if I can't put it on our network. That'll be easier than setting up times for you to use mine. Will that work?"

"I... Yeah. Sure." She could feel the boy's shoulder trembling. Jacek turned and walked out without meeting anybody's gaze, but especially avoiding hers. The door closed behind him.

"Kid was packing, boss," Amos said.

"I know," Holden replied. "What did you want me to do about it?"

"Know. That's all."

"Okay, I know. But I really don't have time to get shot right now." He turned his attention to her. A lock of hair was dropping down over his forehead, and he looked tired. Like he was carrying the whole planet on his back. Still, he managed a little smile. "Is there anything else? Because we're a little..."

"Is this a bad time? Because I can—"

"Our XO got arrested by Murtry," Amos said, and the flatness of his eyes had gotten into his voice now. "May be a while before there's a really good time."

"Oh," Elvi said, her heart suddenly picking up its pace. *The XO is Holden's lover* and *Holden has a lover* and *Holden may not have a lover anymore* and *Jesus, what am I doing here* all collided somewhere in her neocortex. Elvi found she was very unsure what to do with her hands. She tried putting them in her pockets, but that felt wrong so she took them out again.

"I'd been thinking?" she said, her voice rising at the end of the word even though it wasn't a question. "About the thing. In the desert. And now with the moon?"

"Which moon?"

"The one that's melting down, Cap," Amos said.

"Right, that one. I'm sorry. I've got a lot of things going on right now. If it's not something I can actually do something about, it's not sinking in the way it probably ought to," Holden said. And then, "I'm not supposed to do anything about the moon thing, am I?"

"We can let the scientists tell us if we're supposed to freak out," Amos said. "It's all right."

"I've been thinking about hibernation failure rates, and that maybe what we were seeing was analogous."

Holden lifted his hands. "I couldn't tell you."

"It's just that hibernation is a really very risky strategy? We only see it when conditions are so bad that the usual kinds of survival strategy would fail. Bears, for instance? They're top predators. The food web in wintertime couldn't sustain them. Or spadefoot toads in the deserts? In the dry periods, their eggs would just desiccate, so the adults go dormant until there's rain, and then they come back awake and go out to the puddles and mate furiously, just this mad kind of puddle orgy and...um, anyway, and then they, they lay their eggs in the water before they can dry out again."

"Ok-ay," Holden said.

"My point is," Elvi said, "not all of them wake up. They don't have to. As long as enough of the organisms reactivate when the time comes, enough that the population survives, even if individuals don't. It's never a hundred percent. And shutting down and coming back up is a complicated, dangerous process."

Holden took a deep breath and ran his hands through his hair. He had thick, dark hair. It looked like he hadn't washed it in a while. Amos lost his game, scooped up the cards, and started shuffling them with slow, deliberate movements.

"So," Holden said, "you think that these...things we're seeing are artifacts or organisms or something trying to wake up?"

"And failing. At least sometimes," she said. "I mean, the moon melted. And that thing in the desert was clearly broken. Or anyway, that's what it was looking like to me."

"Me too," Holden said. "But just because it was moving, we kind of knew things were waking up."

"No, that's not the point," Elvi said. "There are always a small percentage of organisms that don't wake up, or wake up wrong. These things? If that's the model, they're the ones waking up *wrong*."

"Following you so far," Holden said.

"Failure rates are usually low. So why aren't we seeing a bunch of things waking up *right*?"

Holden went over to the table and sat on its edge. He looked frightened. Vulnerable. It was strange seeing a man who'd done so much, who'd made himself known across all civilization by his words and deeds, look so fragile.

"So you think there are more of these things—maybe a lot more—that are activating, and we're just not seeing it?"

"It would fit the model," she murmured.

"All right," he said. And a moment later, "This isn't making my day better."

Chapter Twenty-Five: Basia

Basia sat alone on the operations deck of the *Rocinante*. He was belted into a crash couch next to what he'd been told was the comm station. The controls were quiet, waiting for someone to request a connection, occasionally flashing a system status message across its screen. The messages were incomprehensible mixtures of acronyms, system names, and numbers. The text was in a gentle green font that made Basia think they weren't particularly urgent.

Alex was in the cockpit, the hatch closed. That didn't mean anything. The hatches closed automatically to seal each deck from the others in case of atmosphere loss. It was a safety measure, nothing more.

It still felt like being locked out.

The panel startled him with a burst of static followed by a

voice. The volume was just loud enough that Basia could tell it was a conversation between two men without understanding any of the words. A red RECORDING status blinked in one corner of the screen. The *Rocinante*, monitoring and recording all of the radio transmissions around Ilus. Maybe Holden was doing that on purpose to have a record of his mission when he returned to Earth. Or maybe warships did it by default. It wasn't something that a welder had to worry about. Or a miner. Or whatever he'd been with Coop and Cate.

Basia was looking for a way to turn up the volume and listen in when Alex's voice blared from the panel. "Got a call comin' in."

"Okay," Basia said, not sure if the pilot could hear him. He didn't know if he needed to press a button to respond.

The message on the comm panel changed, and a male voice said, "You don't need to do anything."

For a moment, Basia had the irrational feeling that the person speaking had read his mind. He was about to reply when another voice, younger, male, said, "Just talk?" Jacek. The second voice was Jacek. And now Basia recognized the older voice as Amos Burton. The man who'd guarded him at the landing field. "Yeah," Amos said. "I've opened a connection to the *Roci*."

"Hello?" Jacek said.

"Hey, son," Basia replied around the lump in his throat.

"They made our hand terminal work again," Jacek said. By *they* Basia guessed he meant Holden and Amos.

"Oh yeah?" Basia said. "That's real good."

"It only talks to the ship," Jacek said, his young boy's voice bright with excitement. "It doesn't play videos or anything like it used to."

"Well, maybe they can make it do that too, later."

"They said someday we'll be on the network, like everyplace in Sol system. Then we can do whatever."

"That's true," Basia said. Water was building up in his eyes, making it hard to see the little messages flashing by on the screen.

"We'll get a relay and a hub and then we can send data back and forth through the gates. We'll have everything on the network then. There's still going to be a lot of lag."

"Yeah," Jacek said, then stopped. There was a long silence. "What's the ship like?"

"Oh, it's pretty great," Basia said with forced enthusiasm. "I have my own room and everything. I met Alex Kamal. He's a pretty famous pilot."

"Are you in jail?" Jacek asked.

"No, no, I get to go anywhere I want on the ship. They're real nice. Good people." *I love you. I am so sorry. Please, please be all right.*

"Does he let you fly it?"

"I never asked," Basia said with a laugh. "I'd be scared to, though. It's big and fast. Lots of guns on it."

There was another long silence, then Jacek said, "You should fly it and blow up the RCE ship."

"I can't do that," Basia said, putting as much smile in his voice as he could. Making it a joke.

"But you should."

"How's your mom?"

"Okay," Jacek said. Basia could almost hear the shrug in his voice. "Sad. I started playing soccer more. We have enough for two teams, but we trade players a lot."

"Oh yeah? What do you play?"

"Fullback right now, but I want to play striker."

"Hey, defense is important. That's an important job."

"It's not as fun," Jacek said, again with the verbal shrug. There was a long silence while both of them reached for something to say. Something that could be said. Jacek gave up first. "I'm gonna go now, okay?"

"Hey, wait a minute," Basia said, trying to keep the thickness in his throat from changing his voice. Trying to keep his tone light, fun. "Don't run off yet. I need to ask you to do something."

"Got a game," Jacek said. "Pretty soon. They'll get mad."

"Your mom," Basia said, then had to stop and blow his nose into the sleeve of his shirt.

"Mom what?"

"Your mom will work too much, if you don't watch her. She gets to looking things up at night. Medical things. And she won't get enough sleep. I need you to make sure she gets some sleep."

"Okay."

"It's serious, boy. I need you to look after her. Your sister's gone, and that's good, but it just leaves you to help out. You gonna help out with this?"

"Okay," Jacek said. Basia couldn't tell if the boy was sad or angry. Or distracted.

"See you, son," Basia said.

"See you, Pop," Jacek replied.

"Love you," Basia said, but the signal had already died.

Basia wiped his eyes with the sleeves of his shirt. He floated against his restraints, breathing deep, ragged breaths for a full minute, then pulled himself over to the crew ladder. He moved aft, deck hatches opening at his approach and slamming shut behind him as he went, the sound echoing through the empty ship.

He changed shirts in his room, then spent a few minutes in the head cleaning his face with wet towels. They had a large shower unit—he couldn't remember the last time he'd had a real shower—but it only worked when the ship was under thrust.

When he no longer looked like a man who'd been bawling, Basia floated back along the ladder to the cockpit. He was considering whether or not it was polite to knock before entering when he drifted too close to the hatch's electronic eye and it snapped open with a hiss.

Alex was belted into the pilot's chair, the large display directly in front of him spooling out ship status reports and a rendering of Ilus, its single massive continent dotted with red and yellow marks. And one green dot that was First Landing. The pilot scowling at the screen tensely as though he could will the universe to do something. Like he could make it give his crew back.

Basia was turning to leave when the deck hatch banged shut and Alex looked up.

"Hey," he said and tapped out something on the panel.

"Hello," Basia said.

"How'd your call go? Everything okay?"

"Fine. Thank you for letting me use the radio."

"No problem, partner," Alex said with a laugh. "They don't charge us by the hour."

An uncomfortable silence stretched out that Alex pretended not to notice by pressing buttons on his controls. "Am I allowed to be up here?" Basia finally asked.

"I don't mind," Alex said. "Just, you know, don't mess with anything."

Basia pulled himself into the chair behind Alex and belted in. The armrests of the chair ended with complex-looking joysticks, so Basia was careful not to bump them.

"That's the gunner's seat," Alex said, turning his entire chair around to face Basia.

"Should I not—"

"Naw, it's fine. It ain't on. Push buttons there all you want. Hey, wanna see somethin' cool?"

Basia nodded and put his hands on the two control sticks. They were covered with buttons. The gunner's seat. Those sticks might control the *Rocinante*'s lethal weaponry. He wished Jacek could see him sitting there, holding the controls.

Alex turned around and did something on his own panel, and the screen in front of Basia came to life with a view matching Alex's own. Basia looked at the bright limb of his planet, trying to find the location of First Landing. Without the green dot overlay it was impossible in daylight. If they were on the night side he could have spotted them as a spark of light.

Alex did something else, and the view shifted to a dull red blob of molten rock. "That's the moon goin' meltdown. It wasn't a very big one, but still, kinda makes you wonder what could melt a hunk of rock that size."

"Do we know?"

"Hell no. Some kind of alien protomolecule shit'd be my guess."

Before Basia could ask for more details, the radio squawked at them. "Alex here," the pilot said.

"Kid's gone, wanted to check in," Amos' voice said.

"How's the captain doing?" Alex asked.

"Not great. And once again he stopped me from doing the obvious thing."

"Shooting the RCE chief in the face?"

"Awww," Amos said. "Warms my heart how well you know me."

"They got her, buddy," Alex said, his voice firm but gentle. "Don't do anything that makes it worse."

"Yeah, yeah."

"You just watch the captain's back down there," Alex continued. "I'll take care of our XO."

"If they hurt her?"

"Then it'll be rainin' RCE parts down on Ilus for a year."

"Won't actually help," Amos said with a sigh.

"No," Alex agreed. "No, it won't. It'll happen, though."

"All right. Gonna go find the captain. Amos out."

Alex tapped on his controls, and the view swung around away from the planet. For a moment, there was nothing, and then a tiny flicker of light, no more than a single pixel. The view zoomed in until it became a massive ship painted with the RCE colors. After a moment, it zoomed again, the rear of the ship swelling until it filled the screen, a small red crosshair glowing in the center of the view.

"Got my eyes on you," Alex said under his breath.

"What's that?" Basia asked, pointing at the crosshair.

"That's where the reactor sits. The *Roci*'s got a lock on that location. I can send a gauss round right through her heart faster than her first alarm bell can ring."

"Won't that...you know..." He made an explosive motion with his hands.

"No, it'll just vent. Probably kill a lot of their engineering staff."

"Do they know you're aiming at them?"

"Not yet, but I'm about to fill 'em in. That's what'll keep my XO breathin'."

"Nice that you can do something to protect her," Basia said, and meant to stop, but the words pressed out past his teeth. "My daughter is on the *Barbapiccola*. My wife and son are down on Ilus. I can't do anything to help them or protect them."

Basia waited for the empty words of reassurance.

"Yeah," Alex said. "You really fucked that one up, didn't you?"

Alex tapped something on his screen, and the words RAIL GUN ARMED glowed red for a second over the image of the *Edward Israel*.

"I need to call over to that ship in a sec," Alex said.

"Warn them."

"More like threaten them," Alex said. "Pretty much the shittiest thing we have to offer for someone we all love, but it's what we got left." He reached out and fiddled with something on the bulkhead and a stream of cool air shot out of the vent. It ruffled the pilot's thinning black hair and dried the sweat accumulating on his scalp. He closed his eyes and sighed.

"I don't even have threats," Basia said. It sounded like whining even to him. "I don't even have that."

"Yeah. So I flew for the Mars navy for twenty years," Alex said, his eyes still closed.

"Oh?" Basia said. He wasn't sure what the correct response was.

"I was married," Alex continued, moving his head around to let the cool air strike every part of his neck and face. Basia didn't reply. It had the feeling of a story, not a conversation. Alex would tell it or he wouldn't.

"Life for a naval spouse is, frankly, pretty shitty," Alex said after a few moments. "Typical tour on an MCRN boat can go from ninety days to four, maybe five hundred days. Depending on your MOS and fleet locations."

"MOS?" Basia asked before he could stop himself.

"Your job. Anyway, while you're out on a boat, your partner is back home, doin' whatever they do. Lot of folks do plural marriages, group partnerships, things like that. But I'm a one-woman kind of guy, and I guess she was a one-man kind of woman. So we did it the old-fashioned way."

Basia nodded, even though Alex couldn't see him. When they were building new domes Basia had done work that kept him at a surface camp for four or five days straight. His wife's medical practice wouldn't have let her travel with him, even if they hadn't had children. Those were long weeks. Basia tried to imagine stringing ten or twenty of those weeks in a row and failed.

"But that meant she stayed home while I flew," Alex said after a quiet moment. "She had her own work. Software engineer. Good one, too. So it's not like she was pinin' away at home for me. But still, if you love somebody you want to be with 'em, and we loved each other. Faithful to each other, if you can imagine that. My tours were tough on us both. I'd get home and we'd break the bed."

Alex reached out and turned down the air vent, then spun his chair to face Basia. His broad dark face held a sad smile. "It was a crap situation, but she stuck with me. Through twenty years of me bein' on ships she stuck with me. And when I was in port things were good. She'd work from home and I'd take a lot of leave, and we'd wake up late and make breakfast together. Work in the garden."

Alex closed his eyes again, and for a moment Basia thought he might have fallen asleep. "Ever been to Mars?"

"No," Basia replied. "But my wife has."

"The newer areas, the ones built after we had some idea of what folks need to feel happy, were built different. No more narrow stone corridors. They built wide corridors with lots of green space down the middle for plants."

"Like on Ceres," Basia said. "I've been to Ceres."

"Yeah, that's right. They do that on Ceres too. Anyway, you could apply for a permit to care for a section of that space. Plant what you wanted. We had a little chunk in the corridor outside our home. My wife planted an herb garden, some flowers, a few hot pepper plants. We'd work in it."

"Sounds nice," Basia said.

"Yeah." Alex nodded, eyes still closed. "I didn't know it at the time. But it really was. I kinda thought it was a pain in the ass, to be honest. Never been much for gardening. But she liked it and I liked her and back then that was enough."

"Did she die?" Basia asked.

"What? Goodness, no."

"So what happened?"

"What happened is that she waited twenty years for me to retire. And I did, and then we didn't have to spend time apart anymore. She went to part-time with her work, I took a part-time gig flying suborbital shuttles. We spent a lot of time in bed."

Alex opened his eyes and winked. He seemed to be waiting for a response, so Basia said, "And then?"

"And then one day I put into port at the Mariner orbital transit, and while they were unloadin' my cargo I almost walked into an MCRN recruiting office and signed up again."

"Do they take—"

"No, I didn't do it, and yeah, I was too damn old anyway. But when I landed we had a big fight over something stupid. I don't even remember what. Hell, I didn't know what we were fightin' about even at the time, except I sorta did."

"Leaving."

"No, actually, it was never about leavin' her. I never stopped wanting to be with her. But I needed to fly. She'd waited twenty years for me, and she'd done it thinkin' we'd have all the time in the world after I was through. She'd done her tour, just as much as I had, and she deserved the part that came after."

Basia felt what was coming like a punch in the stomach, unable to avoid comparing it to his own situation. "But you left anyway."

Alex didn't reply for a time, didn't move, just floated in the straps of his pilot's chair like a corpse in water. When he spoke again, his voice was strained and quiet, like a man admitting something shameful. Hoping no one will hear.

"One day I left work at the transit office and I walked across the street to the Pur'n'Kleen Water Company and I signed a five-year contract to fly long-haul freighters out to Saturn and back. That's who I am. I'm not a gardener, or a shuttle pilot, or—turns out—a husband. I'm a long-flight pilot. Pushing a little bubble of air-filled metal across an ocean of nothing is what I was born to do."

"You can't blame yourself for what happened," Basia started.

"No," Alex said, a deep frown cutting into his forehead. "A person can fail the people they love just by being who they are. I'm who I am, and it wasn't what my wife wanted me to be, and somethin' had to break. You decided to do what you did down on that planet, and it put you up here with me instead of with your family."

Alex leaned forward, grabbing Basia's hands in his own. "It's still on *you*. I will never live down not being the person my wife needed after she spent twenty years waitin' for me. I can never make that right. Don't go feelin' sorry for yourself. You fucked up. You failed the people you love. They're payin' the price for it *right now* and you demean them every second you don't own that shit."

Basia recoiled as if from a slap to the face. He bounced off the chair and back into the straps. A fly caught in a spider's web. He had to stop himself from ripping at the straps to get free. When he'd stopped struggling, he said, "Then what?"

"Shit," Alex said, leaning back. "I barely figured out my own mess. Don't ask me to figure out yours."

"What was her name?" Basia asked.

"Talissa," Alex said. "Her name *is* Talissa. Even just sayin' it makes me feel like ten kilos of manure in a five-kilo sack."

"Talissa," Basia repeated.

"But I can tell you this. I'll never let someone I care about down again. Never again. Not if I can help it. Speakin' of which, I need to make a call," he said with a bright, frightening smile.

Chapter Twenty-Six: Havelock

It was hard to say exactly what changed on the *Edward Israel* after they captured the saboteur, but Havelock felt it in the commissary and the gym, at his desk as he worked, and in the hallways as he passed by the crew members and RCE staff. Part of it was fear that someone had taken action directly against the ship, part of it was excitement that after months of floating and frustration, something—*anything*—had happened that wasn't at ground level. But more than that, it felt to him like the mood of the ship had clarified. They were the *Edward Israel*, the rightful explorers of New Terra, and everyone was against them. Even the UN mediators couldn't be trusted. And so, strangely, they were free.

The remaining crew of the *Rocinante* wasn't doing anything to change their opinions.

"If you try to break orbit," the man on the screen said, "your ship will be disabled."

His name was Alex Kamal, and he was the acting captain of the *Rocinante*. If RCE's intelligence was accurate, he was also the only remaining crew member of the corvette, and had the one remaining squatter terrorist on the ship with him awaiting transport back to Earth for trial. Havelock crossed his arms and shook his head as the list of threats went on.

"If we find that any harm has come to Naomi Nagata, your ship will be disabled. If she is subjected to torture, your ship will be disabled. If she is killed, your ship will be destroyed."

"Well, ain't that just ducky," Captain Marwick said. "You recall we were talking about *not* having people want to kill my ship?"

"It's just talk," Havelock said as Kamal went on.

"We have already sent our petition to the United Nations and Royal Charter Energy demanding Naomi Nagata's immediate and unconditional release. Until that petition is answered and she is back on the *Rocinante*, the *Edward Israel* and all RCE personnel and employees are advised to do everything in their power to avoid any further escalation of this situation. This message serves as final verbal notification before the actions I've outlined are taken. A copy of this message is being included in the packet to the UN and RCE's corporate headquarters. Thank you."

The round-faced, balding man looked into the camera for a moment, then away, and then back before the recording ended. Marwick sighed.

"Not the most professional production," he said, "but made his points effectively enough, I'd say."

"Sneeze, and he shoots us," Havelock said. "Look like we're going to sneeze, and he shoots us. Make sure his chief engineer doesn't catch cold, or he shoots us. Give her a blankie at night and a cup of warm milk, or he shoots us."

"Did have a certain sameness to his thinking, didn't he?" Marwick said.

Havelock looked around the cabin. The captain's rooms were smaller than the security station, but he'd placed steel mirrors at the sides and along the tops of the walls to make it feel big. It was an illusion, of course, but it was the kind of illusion that could make the difference between sanity and madness over the course of a few years in confined spaces. The screen set into the wall hiccupped and shifted to a starscape. Not the real one outside, but the one from Sol. Seeing the old constellations was disconcerting.

"Who's seen this?" Havelock asked.

"Sent to me and Murtry," Marwick said. "Don't know who Murtry's shown it to, but I've run it past you."

"All right," Havelock said. "What do you want me to do about it?"

"Want? I want you to pop the lady free and set her back home with a stern talking-to," Marwick said. "After that, I want to get my ship back under thrust and go the hell home the way my contract said. What I expect is that you find out whether this is really all talk, or if my ship's going to come under fire."

"They have the firepower."

"I'm deeply aware of that. But do they have the will and expertise to use it? I'm only asking because the lives of my crew are in threat here, and it's making me a bit nervous."

"I understand," Havelock said.

"Do you, now?"

"I do. And I'll find out what I can. But in the meantime, let's start by assuming that he means it."

"Yeah," Marwick said, running a hand through his hair. He sighed. "When I signed up for this, I was thinking it was a hell of an adventure. First alien world. No stations or relief ships if things went pear-shaped. A whole new system full to the top with Christ only knows what. And instead, I get this shite."

"Right there with you, sir," Havelock said.

Havelock's paintball militia, emboldened by the capture, had pressed for immediate action. They had the emergency airlock. The orbital mechanics of the *Rocinante* had clearly brought it close enough for a transit. Go now, they'd said, take the *Rocinante* when they weren't expecting it, and get the whole charade over with. Havelock had been tempted. If he hadn't seen what point defense cannons could do to a human body, he might have given the go-ahead.

Instead, they'd pulled power on the prisoner's suit and hauled her back to the *Israel* before she suffocated. Since then, she'd been in the drunk-tank cell in Havelock's office. With the security team down to less than a skeleton crew, he'd given the prisoner access to the privacy controls. He didn't have enough women left on the team to put one on guard duty full-time.

In fact, when he got back to his office, the place was empty except for Nagata in her cell. She looked over, greeting him with a little chin-lift. She wore a red paper jumpsuit and her hair floated around her head in a dark starburst. Enemy capture protocol didn't allow her hairband, a hand terminal, or her own clothes. She'd been in the cell for the better part of two days. Havelock knew from training exercises that he'd have been half crazed with claustrophobia by now. She'd gone from looking embarrassed to retreating into her own thoughts. It was a Belter thing, he assumed. A few generations living and dying without a sky, and enclosed spaces lost the atavistic terror of premature burial.

He sloped across the room to her.

"Nagata," he said. "I had some questions for you."

"Don't I have the right to an attorney or union representative?" she asked, her voice making it clear that she was at least half joking.

"You do," Havelock said. "But I was hoping you'd help me out of your kind and generous spirit."

Her laugh was sharp, short, and insincere. He pulled up the video file on his hand terminal and set it floating just outside the steel mesh of the cell door.

"My name is Alex Kamal, and I am acting captain of the *Rocinante*. In light of recent events—"

Havelock shifted back to his desk, strapping himself in at the couch from force of habit more than anything. He watched Naomi's face without actually staring at her. The woman had a great poker face. It was hard to tell whether she felt anything at all as she watched her shipmate of years threaten them all on her behalf. When the file ended, he reached out and pulled the hand terminal back to himself.

"Don't see what you need me for," she said. "He used small words."

"You're hilarious. The question I have is this: Are you really going to let your shipmates turn themselves into criminals and murderers so that you can postpone answering for your crimes?"

Her smile could have meant anything, but he had the sense he'd touched on something. Or close to it. "I feel like you're asking me for something, friend. But I don't know quite what it is."

"Will you tell the *Rocinante* to back off?" Havelock said. "It won't do you any damage. It's not like we're letting you go regardless. And if you cooperate, that'll speak well for you when we get back to Earth."

"I can, but it won't matter. You haven't shipped with those men. When you listen to that, you hear a list of threats, right?"

"What do you hear?"

"Alex saying how it is," Naomi said. "All that stuff he told you? Those are just axioms now."

"I'm sorry to hear you say that," Havelock said. "Still, if you'll record something for him assuring him that you're in good condition and aren't being mistreated, it'll only help."

She shifted, the microcurrents of air and the constant drift of microgravity bringing her back against the cell's far wall. She touched it gently, steadying herself.

"Alex isn't the problem," she said. "Let me tell you a little about Jim Holden."

"All right," Havelock said.

"He's a good man, but he doesn't turn on a dime. Right now, there's a debate going on in his head. On the one hand, he was sent out here to make peace, and he wants to do that. On the other hand, he protects his own."

"His woman?"

"His crew," Naomi said, biting the words a little. "It's going to take him a while to decide to stop doing what he agreed to do and just tip over the table."

Havelock's hand terminal chimed. It was a reminder to review the next week's schedules. Even in the depths of crises, minor office tasks demanded their tribute. He pulled up the scheduling grid.

"You think he will, though," Havelock said.

"He's got Amos with him," Naomi said, as if that explained everything. "And then they'll assault the ship and get me out."

Havelock laughed. "We're stretched a little thin, but I don't see how they can expect to get through to you."

"You're talking about the man who got a load of people off Ganymede when it was still a war zone," Naomi said. "And went onto the alien station at Medina by himself. And scuttled the *Agatha King* by himself when it had two thousand protomolecule zombies on it. He fought his way off Eros in the first outbreak."

"Rushing in where angels fear to tread," Havelock said.

"And making it through. I can't tell you how many last good-byes I've had with him, and he always comes back."

"Sounds like a rough guy to have for a boyfriend," Havelock said.

"He is, actually," she said with a laugh. "But he's worth it."

"Why?"

"Because he does what he says he's going to do," she said. "And if he says he's going to pop me out of this cell, then either that will happen, or he'll die."

Her expression was calm, her tone matter-of-fact. She wasn't boasting. If anything, he thought there was a hint of apprehension in her voice. It disturbed him more than the acting captain's list of threats.

He closed the scheduling grid, considered his hand terminal for a few seconds. It would be afternoon on the surface, a little over halfway through one of the long, fifteen-hour days.

"Excuse me," he said to the prisoner. "I've got to make a call."

He thumbed the privacy controls down, and the steel mesh of

the cage deformed into a pearly opacity. He requested a connection to Murtry, and a few seconds later his boss appeared on the screen. The sun had darkened his skin, and a tiny scab on his forehead looked almost like a caste mark. He nodded to Havelock.

"What can I do for you?" Murtry said.

"I wanted to touch base with you about the prisoner," Havelock said. "Check our strategy."

"Saw the pilot's little tantrum, did you?"

"You know, boss, all that you said before about how they have the biggest guns and if they want to take us down, they can? Because that's still true."

In the background of the feed a door slammed, and Murtry looked up, nodded, and refocused on Havelock. "Less an issue now than ever. As long as one of theirs is on the ship, they won't shoot."

"Won't?"

"Will be less likely to," Murtry amended.

"And what's the plan when RCE orders us to release her?" Havelock said. "It might be worth cutting her loose early. Get out in front of it, get some goodwill back."

"We're way past goodwill."

"I'm just not sure we have the authority to hold her, and if—"

"Are you in her brig?"

Havelock blinked. "Sorry?"

"Are *you* in *her* brig?"

"No, sir."

"Right. She's in yours. You have the jail and you have the pistol, that makes you the sheriff," Murtry said. "If the home office doesn't like what we're doing, we'll appeal the decisions. If we lose the appeal, they can send someone out and have a meeting face-to-face. By that time, all this will look so different they might as well not try. And the home office knows that, Havelock. What we've got here is a very free hand."

"Yeah. All right. I just wanted to check."

"My door's always open," Murtry said in a voice that meant

maybe Havelock shouldn't bother him with any more stupid ideas. The connection dropped, and Havelock considered the default screen for a few seconds before he pulled the grid back up. A few seconds later, he deactivated the privacy shield. Naomi was floating in the cage, pushing herself from side to side like a bored kid.

"Your privacy equipment sucks," she said.

"Really?"

"Really."

"You heard that, then?"

" 'A very free hand,' " she said.

"Sorry. That was supposed to be between me and him."

"I know, but it came right through. Honestly, can you hear me peeing in here?"

"Just that the vacuum comes on," Havelock said, feeling a little blush in his neck and a sharp embarrassment at being embarrassed. "It's pretty loud."

"Old ships," she said.

He went back to the business of running his staff. A report came in complaining of theft from one of the ship technician's personal lockers. He routed it to the woman on duty. As long as things stayed pretty calm and the crew was all focused on the dangers outside, he could hold the place together. Having a common enemy actually helped with that. A lot of common enemies. Naomi started humming to herself, a soft melody that hovered just on the edge of recognizable. Havelock let himself enjoy it a little. It was that or be annoyed.

"He wasn't the only one," he said.

"Sorry?" Naomi said.

"He wasn't the only one who got off Eros during the outbreak. My old partner was there. He got off too. Then he went back later. When it hit Venus."

"Wait. You knew *Miller*?"

"Yeah," Havelock said.

"Small universe."

"He was one of maybe six decent people working Ceres Station when Star Helix had the contract. Warned me to quit Protogen before they imploded too. I was sorry about it when he died."

"He'll be flattered," she said.

"We're not the bad guys here. RCE didn't start any of this. You said you liked Holden because he always does what he says he'll do? That's us. RCE are the ones who asked permission and made a plan and came out here to do what everyone agreed we should do."

"Not the people in First Landing. They didn't agree."

"No, because they were breaking the rules that we were following. I'm just...I know how weird and dangerous this all is, but before your friends start blasting rail gun rounds through our reactor, I want you to see that we're not the bad guys here."

His voice had gotten thinner and higher as he spoke. At the end, he was almost shouting. He pressed his hands together. Bit his lips.

"Under a little pressure," she said.

"Some," he agreed.

"Let me out, I'll put in a good word for you," she said. "And it'll keep Holden from doing anything stupid."

"Really?"

"It'll keep him from doing a couple particular stupid things," she said. "He may come up with something else. He's clever that way."

"I can't," he said.

"I know."

The ship passed invisibly into the planet's shadow, the decks clicking and groaning as the expansion plates adjusted to the change in radiant heat. Havelock felt a little rush of shame. She was his prisoner. He was the jailer. He shouldn't need her approval. If she thought he and his people were baby-killing fascist power freaks, it didn't change anything he had to do. Naomi went back to humming. It was a different song now. Something slow, in a minor key. After a while, she let it drift into silence.

"They weren't the only ones," she said as he finished the week's duty roster. "They were the only ones that were trapped in the outbreak, but the place was locked down before that. A bunch of thugs in stolen riot armor making sure everyone did what they were told, and shooting the ones who didn't. Getting ready for it. A few people made it past them."

"Really? Who?"

Naomi shrugged.

"Me," she said.

Chapter Twenty-Seven: Elvi

Elvi sat on the crest of the hill, looking west. The morning light behind her caught the wings of thousands of butterfly-like animals. She hadn't seen them before, but today they filled the air from the ground to twenty meters high. A vast school of tiny animals. Or insects. Or whatever other name humanity eventually assigned to this foreign kingdom of life. For her, right now, they were butterflies.

They moved together like a school of fish, independent and coherent. Bursts of color—blue and silver and crimson and green—flashed through them, seeming almost to come in patterns for a moment and then dissolving into chaos. The column of them rose, narrowing, then broadened and flattened. They moved past her in a rush, and for a few seconds she was inside the cluster, palm-sized wings fluttering gently against her with a sound like sheets of paper falling and a clean, astringent smell like mint without being mint.

She smiled and raised her arms up into the cloud of them, taking joy in the beauty and the moment, and then they passed, and she turned to watch them flow through the air, tumbling to the south as if they were going somewhere in particular.

She stood and stretched, adjusting her collection satchel against her hip. The sunlight pressed against her shoulders and the nape of her neck as she walked forward into the dusty, stone-paved field. The ruins rose to the north, with First Landing not even a smudge next to them, all human artifacts hidden by the curve of the planet and the shape of the hills. All except her.

Here and there, a few butterflies remained, possibly dead. Possibly quiescent. She squatted beside one, looking into the vibrant blue of its wings, the coppery complication of flesh where its body—what she thought of as its body—folded together, inter-articulated like a hinge. She put on her gloves and lifted the tiny body. It didn't so much as flutter. Even though it meant getting less physiological data, she hoped it was already dead.

"Sorry, little one," she said, just in case. "It's in the name of science."

She folded it into the black lattice, sealed it, and triggered the collection sequence. The array of sampling needles clicked and muttered to themselves. Elvi squinted up into the white-blue arch of the sky. The red dot floated about fifteen degrees above the horizon, bright enough to show through the thin, greenish clouds.

The satchel coughed, throwing out an error code Elvi hadn't seen before. She took out her hand terminal, connecting it to the satchel's output channel. The preliminary dataset was a mess. Elvi felt a deep, cold stab of fear. If the satchel was broken, it could take days before the one functioning shuttle could bring her a spare from the *Israel*. She wasn't even positive they had a spare in the toolkit or if they'd all been lost in the wreck of the heavy shuttle. The prospect of years going by collecting data by hand and spending her nights doing dissections like she was back in lower university reared up like a ghost. She took the butterfly out.

Its corpse looked almost the same as when she'd put it in. She sat cross-legged beside it and ran the satchel's system diagnostics, chewing her lips as she waited for a fresh error code.

The readout came up clean. She looked from the satchel to the butterfly, then back again. A second hypothesis formed, as chilling as the first. Maybe worse. She picked up the dead butterfly and marched back toward the huts. Fayez's was a small green geodesic design he'd constructed halfway down a thin hill, high enough that any storm runoff would pass it by, but not at the crest where the wind would catch it. He was sitting on a stool, leaning back against the hut. He was wearing a pair of polyfiber work pants, a T-shirt, and an open bathrobe. He hadn't shaved in days, and the stubble on his cheeks made him look older.

"This isn't an animal," she said, holding out the butterfly.

He let the stool come down, its legs tapping the ground. "Good to see you too," he said.

"This isn't two biomes coming together. It's three. This… whatever it is? It doesn't have any of the chemical or structural commonalities that you'd expect to see."

"Lucia Merton was up looking for you. Did you run across her?"

"What? No. Look, this is another machine. It's another thing like"—she pointed at the low red moon—"like *that*."

"All right."

"What if they're really not coming awake just because we're here? What if they're consistent? It complicates everything."

Fayez scratched his scalp just above his left ear. "You seem to want something here, Elvi, but I don't know what it is."

"How am I supposed to make any sense of this place when it keeps changing all the rules?" she said, and her voice sounded shrill even to her. She threw the butterfly down angrily, then immediately wished she hadn't. Not that it cared, just that the gesture seemed cruel. Fayez smiled his sharp little smile.

"You're preaching to the choir. You know what I've been doing all morning?"

"Drinking?"

"I wish. I've been going over surface data from the *Israel*. There's a chain of islands on the far side of the planet with what looks like a metric ass-ton of volcanic activity. Only so far as I can tell, this planet doesn't have, you know, tectonic plates. So what the hell is mimicking vulcanism? Do you know what Michaela's working on?"

"No."

"There's a pattern in the ultraviolet light that reaches the ground here, like it's some kind of carrier signal. Doesn't exist before the sunlight hits the exosphere, and by the time it comes here, complex, consistent patterning. She's got no idea where it's coming from. Sudyam's workgroup has what they think might be complex molecules that incorporate stable transuranics."

"How does that work?"

"I know, right?" Fayez said.

Elvi hung her hand on her shoulder, letting her elbow hang loose. Sweat trickled down her spine.

"I have to—"

"—tell Holden," Fayez said. "I know."

"I was going to say 'review my data.' See if maybe there's a common structure between that"—she nodded at the butterfly—"and the big thing in the desert. Maybe I can make sense of it."

"If you can't, no one can," Fayez said.

Something in his voice caught her attention, and she looked at him more closely. His fox-sharp face looked softer around the eyes and jowls. The flesh around his eyes was puffier than usual. "Are you all right?"

He laughed and spread his arms toward the horizon, gesturing at the whole planet—the whole universe—at once. "I'm great. Just spiffy. Thanks for asking."

"I'm sorry. I just—"

"Don't, Elvi," he said. "Don't be sorry. Just go on dealing with all of this the way that you do. Pile on another few layers of not thinking about it, and sail on, my dear, sail on. Whatever keeps you sane and functioning in a place like this, I will carry a flag for it. I'll even pray with Simon on Sunday mornings. That's how bad I've got it. Whatever works for you has my blessings."

"Thank you?"

"Afwan," he said, waving his hand. "Only before you bury your head back in your datasets again? Go see Doctor Merton. She looked worried."

The boy sitting on the clinic table was six years old. His skin was the same deep brown as Elvi's own, but with an ashy color to it. Not dryness, but something deeper. His eyes were bloodshot like he'd been weeping. Maybe he had been. His mother stood in the corner, her arms crossed and a vicious scowl on her lips. Lucia's voice was crisp and calm, but her shoulders rode high up beside her ears.

"So I'm seeing this here," she said, as her finger pulled down on the boy's cheek, opening a thin gap between the lower lid and the roughened surface of the eyeball. The discoloration was almost invisible in the redness, but it was there. The faintest hint of green.

"I see," Elvi said. She smiled at the boy. He didn't smile back. "So, Jacob—"

"Jason."

"Sorry. Jason. How long have you had trouble seeing things?"

The boy shrugged. "Right after my eyes started hurting again."

"And everything looks…green?"

He nodded. Lucia touched Elvi's arm. Silently, the doctor shone a light into the boy's eye. The iris barely reacted, and Elvi caught a glimpse of something in the fluid behind the boy's cornea, like a badly maintained aquarium. She nodded.

Lucia stood up, smiling at the woman. "If you'll wait with him here, Amanda. I'll be right back."

Amanda nodded once, sharply. Elvi let Lucia draw her through the examining room door and down a short hallway. Outside, a stiff breeze had picked up, rattling the clinic's doors and windows.

"He's the only one I've seen like this," Lucia said. "There's nothing in the literature."

"His mother doesn't seem to like me very much," Elvi said, trying to make it a joke.

"Her wife was shot and killed by RCE security," Lucia said.

"Oh. I'm sorry."

The testing array was good, but it was old. Ten years, maybe fifteen. A long scar ran across the bottom of its screen where something had gouged at it. Elvi could believe it had made the long trek from war-torn Ganymede to come here. She was surprised it still worked, but when Lucia thumbed in her access code, the screen came to life. The sample was beautiful in its way. A branching of elegant green like a pictogram meaning *tree*.

"It began in the extracellular matrix," Lucia said. "Low-level inflammation, but nothing worse than that. I hoped it would clear up on its own."

"Only now it's in the vitreous humor," Elvi said.

"I was wondering…" Lucia began, but Elvi had already taken out her hand terminal and started syncing it to the array. It only took a few seconds to find a match. Elvi tapped through the data.

"All right," she said. "The closest match is some of the rainwater organisms." Lucia shook her head, and Elvi pointed up. "You know how the clouds are greenish? There's a whole biome of organisms up there that have found ways to exploit the moisture and high ultraviolet exposure."

"Like plants? Fungi?"

"*Like* them," Elvi said. "It's not where we've been burning most of our cycles. But it looks like a pretty crowded niche. A lot of species fighting for resources. I'm guessing this little fella was in a raindrop that dropped into Jason's eye and found a way to live there."

"He's had several eye infections, but they all came from familiar organisms. This thing. Is it contagious, do you think?"

"I wouldn't guess so," Elvi said. "We're just as new to it as it is to us. It evolved to spread in open air through a water cycle. It's salt tolerant if it's living in us, and that's interesting. If his eyes were already compromised, he may have been vulnerable to it, but unless he starts throwing his tears at people, wouldn't think it would go too far."

"What about his eyesight?"

Elvi straightened up. Lucia looked at her seriously, almost angrily. Elvi knew it wasn't directed at her, but at the terrible ignorance they were both struggling under. "I don't know. We knew something like this was bound to happen sooner or later, but I don't know what we can do about it. Except tell people not to go out when it's raining."

"That isn't going to help him," Lucia said. "Can you ask the labs back home for help?"

A hundred objections filled Elvi's mind. *I don't control the RCE research teams* and *All the data analysis is planned out and running months ahead of where we are now* and *I just got another sample of a third biome this morning.* She tapped at her hand terminal, saving a copy of the array's data, then translating it into RCE's favored formats and sending it winging through the air back to the *Israel*, and then the Ring, and then Earth.

"I'll try," she said. "In the meantime, though, we need to let people know it's a problem. Has Carol Chiwewe heard about this?"

"She knows I'm suspicious and that I wanted to bring you in on it," Lucia said.

Elvi nodded, already trying to think what the best way would be to bring the issue to Murtry's attention. "Well, you let your side know, and I'll tell mine."

"All right," Lucia said. And then a moment later, "I hate that it breaks down that way. Your side and mine. One of my teachers back in school always used to say that contagion was the one absolute proof of community. People could pretend there weren't drug users and prostitutes and unvaccinated children all they wanted, but when the plague came through, all that mattered was who was actually breathing your air."

"I'm not sure if that's reassuring or awful."

"There's room for both," Lucia said. "This scares me as much as anything that's happened. This little...thing. What if we can't fix it?"

"We probably can," Elvi said. "And then we'll fix the next one. And the one after that. It's tricky and it's hard, but everything's going to be all right."

Lucia lifted an eyebrow. "You really believe that?"

"Sure. Why not?

"You aren't scared at all?"

Elvi paused, thinking about the question. "If I am, I don't feel it," she said. "It's not something I think about."

"Take what blessings you can, I suppose. What about the third side?"

Elvi didn't know what Lucia was talking about, and then she heard Fayez's mocking voice in her memory and her heart leaped. She hated it a little that her heart leaped, but that didn't stop her.

"I'll tell him," she said. "I'll tell Holden."

In the commissary, Holden sat hunched over his hand terminal. He'd shaved and his hair was combed. His shirt was pressed. *Cleans up pretty*, a voice in the back of her mind said, and she pushed it away.

A woman's voice came from the terminal, crackling and sharp. "—squeeze all the balls I can get my hands around until someone starts crying, but it will take time. And I know you're thinking of taking this public, because you're fucking stupid, and that is what you always think of. You and publicity are like a sixteen-year-old boy and boobs. Nothing else in your head. So before you even begin—"

Amos lumbered up from the side. His smile was as open and friendly as ever, but Elvi thought there might be a little edge to it. His broad, bald head always made her think of babies, and she had to restrain herself from patting it.

"Hey," Amos said. "Sorry, but the captain's a little busy."

"Who's he listening to?"

"United Nations," Amos said. "He's been trying to get your boss to let our XO out."

"Not my boss," Elvi said. "Murtry's security. It's a whole different organizational structure."

"That corporate stuff's not my strong suit," he said.

"I just needed to…" she began, and Holden drew himself up, looking into the hand terminal camera. His lips formed a hard little smile, and she lost her train of thought.

"Let me make it clear," Holden said, his voice low and solid as stone, "that this was done on my orders. If Royal Charter wants to put me on trial when I get back because I ordered my crew to disable their illegally weaponized shuttle I would be happy to—"

"Doc?" Amos said.

"What? Sorry. No, it's just that there are some things going on that I thought he needed to know about."

Amos shook his head in something that almost passed for sorrow. "No. Nothing's happening until the XO's clear."

"No, it is, though," Elvi said. "Not just one thing either. I found more artifacts waking up today. Some of them are passing for local animals, I think. If we'd been here long enough to build a catalog, we could tell which were which, but as it is, everything looks new. So we don't know."

"So some of the lizards are protomolecule stuff?" Amos asked.

"Yes. Maybe. We don't know yet. And there's more, because the local biome is starting to find ways to invade us. Exploit our resources. And the perimeter dome never got set up, and so all of our microfauna are just wandering around mixing with the local ecosphere and there's no way to get it back so we're contaminating everything and everything's contaminating us."

She was talking too fast. She hated this. When—if—she ever got back to Earth she was going to take some communications classes. Something that would keep her from rattling on like a can rolling down stairs.

"It's *all* accelerating," she said. "And maybe it is a reaction to us or to something we're doing. Or maybe it's not. And I know we're having trouble figuring out the politics and getting along with each other, and I'm really sorry about that." There were tears in her eyes now. Jesus. What was she? Twelve? "But we have to look at what's happening, because it's really, really dangerous and it's happening right now. And it's all going to hit a crisis point, and then something really, really bad will happen."

And then Holden was there, his eyes on her, his voice soothing. She wiped her tears with the back of her hand and wondered whether any of Jason's invading blindness-fungus had been on her hands when she did it.

"Hey," Holden said. "Are you all right?"

"I am," she said. "I'm fine. I'm sorry."

"It's okay," Holden said. "You said something about a crisis?"

She nodded.

"All right," he said. "What would that look like?"

"I don't know," she said. "I *won't* know. Not until it's happened."

Chapter Twenty-Eight: Basia

Basia floated above the world.

Seventeen hundred kilometers below, Ilus spun past at a dizzying pace. Alex had told him that the *Rocinante* had an orbital period just under two hours, but Basia couldn't feel it. Floating outside the ship in microgravity, his inner ear told him that he was drifting, motionless. So instead the universe appeared to spin far too quickly, like some giant child's toy. Every hour, moving from dark to light, and then an hour later back to darkness, the sun rising from behind Ilus, spinning around behind him, and setting again briefly. Basia had been outside long enough to see the change three times, the center of his own cosmos.

The planet's one vast ocean was in night. The string of islands that crossed it tiny black spots in a larger darkness. One of the islands, the largest of them, was outlined in a faint green light. Luminescence in the waves crashing against its beaches and cliffs.

The day-side was dominated by Ilus' single massive continent. The southwestern quarter was the enormous desert. First Landing would be just to the north of it. In daylight, it was far too small to see with the naked eye. Even the huge alien towers where he'd met with Coop and Kate and all the others in some previous lifetime were too small to find.

"You okay out there, partner?" Alex's voice said over the radio. "Been driftin' a while now. That hatch ain't gonna fix itself."

As he spoke, the *Edward Israel* passed into the daylight side of the planet and flashed like a tiny white spark. It was almost too far away to be seen, but, in orbital terms, very very close. Alex was holding the *Rocinante* locked in a matching orbit so he could keep his gun pointed at them.

"It's beautiful," Basia said, looking back down at the planet spinning by. "When we came in on the *Barb* I never took time to just look at it. But Ilus is beautiful."

"So," Alex said, his drawl adding an extra syllable to the word, "remember when we talked about the euphoria you can get on a spacewalk?"

"I'm not new at this," Basia replied. "I know what the happys are like, and I'm good. The hatch is almost done. Just taking a break."

They'd eaten all their meals together. Alex had shared his collection of twenty-second-century Noir Revival films with him. Just the night before they'd watched *Naked Comes the Gun*. Basia found noir too bleak, too hopeless to enjoy. It had led to a lengthy conversation over drinks about why Alex thought he was wrong to feel that way.

And, true to Naomi's promise, Alex had dug up a list of open repair projects for Basia to work on. One of which was a sticky actuator arm on one of the *Rocinante*'s two torpedo loading hatches.

The hatch lay open next to him, a door in the flank of the warship a meter wide and eight meters long. A massive white tube sat just below the opening. One of the ship's torpedoes. It looked too big to be just a missile. Almost a small spaceship in its own right.

It didn't look dangerous, just well crafted and functional. Basia knew that in its heart lay a warhead that could reduce another spaceship to molten metal and plasma. It was hard to reconcile that with the gentle white curves and sense of calmness and solidity.

The faulty actuator had already been cut out, and floated next to the ship at the end of a magnetic tether, waiting to be taken inside. With an effort, Basia turned away from the stunning view of Ilus and pulled the new actuator off the web harness on his back.

"Going back to work now," he said to Alex.

"Roger that," the pilot replied. "Be glad to have that working."

"Planning to need it?" Basia asked.

"Nope, but I'd like to have the option if it comes up." Alex laughed. He laughed, but he was also serious.

Basia began attaching the new arm to the hull mounts and the missile hatch. He knew almost nothing about electronics, and had worried that wiring up the new device would be beyond his skills, but it turned out that it had a single plug that went into a port inside the actuator housing. Which made sense when he thought about it. They would design warships around the idea that damage was inevitable. That repairs would sometimes take place in hostile environments. Making everything as modular and easy to swap out as possible wasn't just sensible, it was a survival trait. He wondered if the Martians had had a Belter on the design team.

"The *Barbapiccola* is on our side of Ilus," Alex said, still in that same lazy, sleepy voice.

"Can you show me?" Basia looked around, but could see nothing but the glowing planet below and the white spark of the *Edward Israel*.

"Hold on." A moment later, a tiny green dot appeared on Basia's heads-up display, drifting slowly.

"It's the dot?"

"Well," Alex said, "it's where the dot *is*. But it's too far away to see right now. Just a sec."

A green square appeared on Basia's HUD, then zoomed in like a telescope until the distant freighter was the size of his thumbnail.

"That's at 50X," Alex said.

"Space is too big," Basia replied.

"It's been said. And this is just the space in low orbit around one planet. Breaks the head a bit to think about."

"I try not to."

"Wise man."

The *Barbapiccola* looked like a big metal shipping container with the squat bell housing of a drive at one end, and the blocky superstructure of command and control on top. She was ugly and utterly functional. A thing of the vacuum that would never know the heat of atmospheric drag.

The large cargo bays that took up most of her interior would be full of the raw lithium ore they'd already pulled off of Ilus. Waiting to fly to the refineries on Pallas Station. Waiting to be traded for food and medicine and soil enrichments. All the things the fledgling colony needed to survive.

Waiting to take his daughter away.

"Can we talk to them?" he asked.

"Huh? The *Barb*? Sure. Why?"

"My daughter is over there."

"Alrighty," came the reply, followed by a burst of static. A few moments after that, a voice with a thick Belter accent replied.

"Que?"

"Sa bueno. Basia Merton, mé. Suche nach Felcia Merton. Donde?"

"Sa sa," the voice said, the tone a fight between curiosity and irritation. The connection stayed open but silent.

While he waited, Basia finished mounting the actuator arm and plugged it in. He called down on the ship channel to have Alex test it, and it opened and closed several times without binding or twisting the hatch. The motor made a smooth vibration in the hull beneath his magnetic boots that set his helmet to humming.

"Papa?" came a hesitant voice.

"Baby, Felcia, it's me, honey," he replied, trying to keep from babbling like an idiot and mostly failing.

"Papa," she said, delight coloring her voice. Deeper now, richer, but still the voice of the little girl that had squealed *Papa* when he came home from work. It still melted all the hard, angry, adult places in his heart.

"I'm up here with you, honey."

"On the *Barbapiccola*?" she said in confusion.

"No, I mean, in orbit. Over Ilus. I can see your ship, honey. Flying by."

"Let me find a screen! Where are you? I can look for you."

"No, don't worry about that. I'm pretty far away. Had to magnify a lot to see you. Just keep talking to me for a minute before you go around the planet again."

"Okay," she said. "Are they nice to you over there?"

Basia laughed. "Your brother wanted to know the same thing. They're fine. The best jailers ever. And you?"

"Everyone is nice, but worried. Maybe the RCE ship won't let us leave."

"Everything will be fine, honey," Basia said, patting at the empty space as if she could see him and take comfort from it. "Holden's working it out."

"He made you a prisoner, Papa."

"He did me a favor, Felcia. He saved me," Basia said, and realized it was true as he said it. Murtry would have killed him. And his son and wife were still down on the planet. "I just wanted to say hello. Not talk about that stuff."

"So hello, Papa," she replied with her grown-up little girl's voice.

"Hello, podling," he replied, calling her by a nickname he hadn't used in years.

She made a strange noise, and it took Basia a moment to realize she was crying. "Never going to see you again, Papa," she said, her voice thick.

He started to reply with objections, with reassurances. But his conversation with Alex came back to him, and instead he said, "Maybe, podling. That's nobody's fault but mine. Remember that, okay? I tried to do what I thought was right, but I messed up and it's on no one but me if I have to pay for it."

"I don't like that," Felcia said, still crying.

Me either, honey, he thought, but said, "Is what is, sa sa? Is what is. Doesn't change that I love you, and your mama, and Jacek." *And Katoa, who I left to die.*

"They say I have to go," Felcia said. The tiny green dot that hid the massive spaceship his daughter lived on was moving away, toward the horizon, into radio blackout. He could see it happening. Watch the unimaginable distance between them getting wider until a planet came between them.

"Okay, honey," he said. "Bye now. I love you."

Whatever she might have said in reply was lost, as the *Barbapiccola* slipped behind Ilus and the channel broke up into static and died. No relay satellites in orbit around the new world yet. Back to line of sight, like nineteenth-century primitives bouncing radio around inside their atmosphere. Basia thought of his home, really just a shack in a tiny village with two dusty roads. Maybe that was appropriate.

Seventeen hundred kilometers below, his world spun. Beneath his feet, a spaceship capable of flying across the solar system hummed to itself with barely restrained power.

Maybe not *just* like a nineteenth-century primitive.

"You ready to come back in?" Alex said, breaking into his reverie.

"In a minute," Basia replied. "Can you find First Landing and point it out?"

"Sure. It's moving away, but you can still see it."

Another tiny green dot appeared on his HUD over a spot just north of Ilus' great southern desert. Knowing where to look, Basia thought he could detect the open bowl of the mining operations north of the village, but that might just have been wishful thinking.

Lucia would be down there, seeing patients, looking after Jacek. It was daylight in the village, so Lucia would definitely still be working. Basia tried to imagine what she was doing at that moment. The temptation to have Alex call down to the village so he could talk to her was almost overpowering. But he'd been self-ish enough already, calling Felcia. He was a source of pain to his family now. The only comfort to be had came at their expense.

So instead he began packing up his tools and the damaged actuator.

If he never came back, would Lucia find someone else? He tried to tell himself that he was the sort of man who'd want that for her. That her happiness was more important than his fears about los-ing her. He tried the idea on like a new outfit. Seeing if he could find a way to make it fit.

It didn't. He saw with clarity as perfect as if Alex were zooming his HUD in on the idea that he was *not* that sort of man. It was hard to tell if that was a flattering testament to his commitment to his marriage, or a scathing commentary on his own insecurities and selfishness. Like almost everything else that had happened to him over the last months, it was murky and difficult to navigate.

He would go back with Holden, probably to the UN complex on Luna. The OPA would claim he was their citizen, but Gany-mede had originally been a UN colony. The legality of which people were citizens of which government was still being worked out, and would be for decades. Plenty of time to try him as a UN citizen for crimes against a UN-based company and throw him in prison for all eternity.

Years of trials, probably.

Basia began slowly walking across the hull of the *Rocinante*, dragging his webbed-together bundle of tools and spare parts behind. At the stern of the ship he stopped and planted both feet, waiting for the bundle to float past him and stop at the end of its line. The weight pulled his arms out painfully for a moment as he killed its momentum.

"Open the cargo bay hatch," he said.

"Roger," Alex replied, and the ship started to vibrate under Basia's feet. The two heavy doors of the cargo bay slowly slid open. When they were about halfway, he yanked down on the line and the bundle of tools swung around the edge of the ship and into the cargo bay. He let go of the line and let them sail inside without yanking him off the edge after them.

In the corner of his vision, there was a bright burst of light, like the flash of a distant camera. Basia turned to look, expecting to see one of the other two ships moving into the sunlight. Instead, there was a growing point of white light centered over Ilus' largest island. It was bright enough to overpower the faint green luminescence of its beaches, and rapidly expanding.

In seconds, the dark side of the planet was lit up as brightly as if a second sun had risen. The other islands in the chain suddenly visible in stark black and white, casting long shadows across the ocean as the white spot grew. He felt his heart start to race.

"Alex?" he said.

The ocean around the big island heaved up, bulging out beyond the curve of the planet in what must have been a tsunami miles high. But before Basia could grasp the enormity of the forces involved in such an uprising, it was gone. The island, the massive upwelling of the ocean, the smaller nearby islands, they all disappeared in a column of white fire and a rapidly rising mushroom cloud.

Basia's visor darkened dramatically, and he had a sense that if it hadn't the light coming from the planet below might have blinded him. But even through the welder's shield darkness of the helmet, he could see the column of fire growing, hurling white vapor up until it broke free of the planet's atmosphere and became glittering crystals of ice speeding away from the gravity well like a shower of glass from a bullet-shattered window.

A massive ripple, like wind across a field of grass, sped away from the growing pillar of fire through the surrounding ocean. Intellectually, Basia knew the ripples had to be waves, hundreds or thousands of feet high, rushing away from the blast. But the intellectual part of his brain was rapidly disappearing behind the screaming primitive who was relieving his bladder into the suit's condom catheter in fear.

Basia had grown up in the Jupiter system. He'd seen video of Io up close more than once. Io was famous for having the most massive volcanoes ever seen by man. Gigantic geysers of sulfur blasting out of the surface of the moon until particles were flung into Jupiter's plasma torus and faint ring system. They made Io an almost insanely inhospitable place.

The explosion Basia was looking at from orbit dwarfed those eruptions. It looked like half the planet was being flattened by the force of the blast.

His initial thought was that it was a very good thing First Landing was on the other side of the world. His second, that the shock wave was heading that direction, and not even traveling around the planet was going to slow it down much.

"Jesus Christ!" Alex yelled across the radio. "Are you seein' that shit!"

"Call down," Basia tried to yell back. It came out as a panicky whimper. "You have to warn them."

"Warn them to do what?" Alex asked. He sounded dazed.

What do you do when the planet you're standing on tries to kill you?

Basia didn't know.

Chapter Twenty-Nine: Holden

Holden stood on a low hill overlooking First Landing trying to enjoy the beauty of the planet while his brain chewed on the half dozen insoluble problems that he was somehow supposed to solve. The usual dust had been tamped down by the recent run of gentle rains. It made the town look clean, well-tended. Peaceful. Above, the sky was a stunning indigo blue with just the faintest streamers of high-altitude clouds breaking it up. His hand terminal was reporting the temperature as 22 degrees Celsius with a gentle four-knot wind coming out of the northeast. The only thing that would have made it better was Naomi there with him, or at least back safe on the *Roci*. But that would have made it a lot better.

I miss planets," Holden said, closing his eyes and facing the sun.

"I don't," Amos replied. He'd been so quiet during their afternoon walk that Holden had sort of forgotten he was there.

"You never miss a breeze? The sun on your skin? A gentle rain?"

"Those are not the parts of planetary life that imprinted on my memory," Amos replied.

"Want to talk about it?" Holden asked.

"Nope."

"Okay." Holden didn't take the mechanic's refusal personally. Amos had, as he described it, a lot of past in his past. He didn't like people digging around there, and Holden was the last person to pry. Holden already knew more about Amos' brutal upbringing on Earth than he wanted to.

"Better head back, I guess," Holden said after a few more pleasant moments in the breeze. "Might have an RCE reply to my requests."

"Yeah." Amos snorted. "If the RCE bigwigs sent a reply seconds after receiving your message, they should be arriving just about now."

"I won't let your facts about light delay get in the way of my optimism."

"Not much does."

Holden was silent for a long moment. He licked his lips.

"If they say no," he said. "If they're committed to letting Murtry hold on to her. I'm going to have to make a decision about whether she's more important than keeping this place from devolving into a shooting war."

"Yup."

"I'm pretty sure I know what I'm going to pick too."

"Yup."

"There will be people who think I'm very selfish."

"True," Amos said. "But also, fuck 'em. They're not us."

"That us-and-them thing is the problem at the base of all this—" Holden started, but his hand terminal interrupted, a high-priority alarm sounding. It was the alert reserved for crewperson in danger. *Naomi*, he thought. *Something happened to Naomi.*

Amos took a few steps toward Holden, he brow furrowing and hands clenching into fists. His mind had gone to the same place. If something had actually happened to Naomi, there was no way he'd be able to stop Amos from killing Murtry this time. Probably, he wouldn't even try.

"Holden here," he said, trying to keep his voice level.

"Cap, we got a problem," Alex replied. His voice was shaky, terrified. Holden had flown with Alex through half a dozen battles. Not even when the missile trails filled the sky around them had he ever heard his pilot panic. Whatever it was, it was bad.

"Is she hurt?"

"What? Who? You mean Naomi? Naomi's fine, far as I know," Alex replied. "You're in deep shit, Captain."

Holden looked around. First Landing looked quiet. A new shift of Belters were boarding the carts that would take them to the mine. A few people walked the streets, going about their business. The two RCE security people on patrol were chatting amiably with a local and sipping some sort of hot drink from a thermos. The only violent thing happening within line of sight was a mimic lizard slowly dragging a stomach-engulfed bird back through its gullet.

"Okay?" Holden said.

"Something blew up on the other side of the planet," Alex said, talking fast enough to stumble over his words, most of his drawl disappearing. "Absolutely flattened an island chain over there. I mean it's like someone dropped a rock. Kill-the-dinosaurs kind of thing. Shock wave is heading around the planet right now. You have about six hours. Maybe."

Amos had traded his angry face in for one of genuine surprise. It wasn't an expression he wore often, and it made him look vaguely childlike.

"Six hours until what, Alex?" Holden said. "Details, please."

"Figure two-, three-hundred-kilometer-an-hour winds, lightning, torrential rains. You're far enough inland to avoid the three-kilometer-high tsunami."

"Basic wrath of God package, minus drowning," Holden said, reaching for humor to hide his rising fear. "How certain is this?"

"Uh, Captain? I'm watching the other side of the planet rip itself to shreds right now. This isn't a prediction. This is thousands of klicks of planet between you and the apocalypse disappearing fast."

"Got some video to send?"

"Yep," said the pilot. "Got fresh underwear for after you watch it?"

"Send it anyway. I may need it to convince the locals. Holden out."

"So, Cap," Amos said. "What's the plan?"

"I haven't got a clue."

"Run it again," Murtry said after Holden played the apocalyptic video Alex had shot with the *Rocinante*'s telescopes. Holden, Murtry, and Carol Chiwewe were in the town hall, Holden's terminal synced up to the big screen hanging on one wall.

Holden obliged and played through the recording a second time. Again, the big island disappeared in a flash of light and a column of fire. Again, the other islands vanished under a massive wall of water and then the spreading clouds of steam and ash. Again, the shock wave raced away from the center of the explosion, dragging massive waves behind it.

As the video played, Murtry talked quietly on his hand terminal with someone. Carol shook her head gently, as though it were possible to deny the evidence playing on-screen.

The video ended, and Murtry said, "This is matching our data. The geoengineering group thinks there was some kind of fission reaction down near the bottom of the ocean." Holden prickled at the implication he might be lying about something so serious, but held his tongue.

"Like a bomb?" Carol Chiwewe said.

"Or an alien power plant failing out," Murtry said. "Can't really speculate."

"How quickly can we evacuate?" Carol said, her voice surprisingly firm for a person who'd just looked Armageddon in the eye.

"That's what we're here to talk about," Holden said. "What's our best plan for protecting the colony? Evacuation is one option, but we're down to a little over five hours now."

"Evacuation won't work," Murtry said, "at least using our shuttle. The window's too tight. We'd be taking off in the face of that shock wave, with turbulence and atmospheric ionization doing its best to knock us out of the sky. Better to survive down here and still have a shuttle available afterward for relief."

Holden frowned and nodded. "I hate to admit it, but I agree. Alex says he can't put the *Roci* down and get it back off the ground before the blast. And if we do try to evacuate, we'll probably have riots on our hands. How do you tell someone that their kid doesn't get to leave on the shuttle?"

"Riots won't be a problem," Murtry said. The calm of his voice was chilling.

"How do we protect everyone? The entire colony?" Holden said, again choosing to ignore the provocation.

"There's mines," Amos said. He hovered over Holden like an anxious parent. He'd started doing that whenever Murtry was around.

"No." Carol shook her head. "It's low ground. It'll flood if we get too much rain."

"I think we should count on anything that can go wrong doing so," Holden agreed. "So no pits and caves that can fill up with water. I'm thinking the ruins."

Murtry leaned back in his chair, frowning. "What makes you think those'll hold up to three-hundred-kilometer-an-hour winds?"

"Honestly? I have no good reason to believe that," Holden said. "But they've been there a very long time. That's what I've got.

Hope that if they made it this far, they can make it through what's coming."

"Better'n those huts you guys are living in," Amos added with a beefy shrug. "I can kick down any building in this town in ten minutes."

Murtry leaned back even farther in his chair, staring up at the ceiling and making clicking noises with his tongue. After a few seconds he said, "Okay. That's as good a plan as any I have. We just need to outlive that initial shock wave. What comes after will be bad, but we'll be able to take any survivors off through it. So let's play it your way. I'll get my people moving. Better get the word out."

"Carol, find as many people as you can to spread the news," Holden said. "Make sure everyone brings as much food and water as they can reasonably carry, but *nothing* else. The planet's on fire. Can't stop to save mementos."

"I'll give her a hand," Amos said.

"We're on the clock," Holden reminded them, punching an alert into his hand terminal as he said it. "I want to see all of you inside the structure in four hours, not a minute later."

"We'll try," Carol said.

It took longer to move the colonists than Holden had hoped. Each person told had to express shock and disbelief. Then they had to have a conversation about their surprise. Then they had to have a conversation about what items they'd bring with them. Some argued about bringing personal items, each one sure that their particular case was unique. Every time Holden heard it happen, he wanted to start shouting.

It was the blue sky and gentle breeze. The disaster just wasn't real to them. Not when they could look out across the sky and see nothing but wisps of cloud. They were playing along, because Holden and Carol and Murtry were in charge, and you did what the people in charge asked you to do unless there was a compelling reason not to. But Holden could see the disbelief in their eyes, hear it in every silly delay and argument.

Across the street, a man was clutching a bundle of clothing under one arm while he dragged a large plastic container of water behind him. Amos walked over and traded a few smiling words with the man. The man vigorously shook his head and tried to walk off. Amos grabbed the bundle of clothes out of his hands and threw them on top of a nearby hut, then picked up the water and shoved it into the man's arms. The man started to argue, but Amos stared him down with a vague smile, and eventually the other man turned and left, trudging after the others headed to the alien ruins.

"Captain?" a tentative voice said to his back. He turned around to find Elvi Okoye smiling up at him, a large sack thrown over one shoulder.

"Hello," he said. "What've you got there?"

"It's blankets. Fayez and Sudyam and I are bringing all the blankets we had at the compound. The temperature's sure to drop significantly once the debris cloud covers us. The nights will get cold."

"Good thinking. We should probably tell some more people to bring blankets."

"So," she added, still with her unsure half smile, "I wanted to ask for some help for the chemical sciences group."

"Help?"

"The chemical analysis deck is pretty heavy, and they're having trouble moving it. One or two more people would make the job a lot easier."

Holden laughed in disbelief. "We won't be doing science up there, Elvi. Tell them to ditch it and carry water or food instead."

"It makes water," she said.

"They can carry—It makes what?"

"It can sterilize and distill water," she said, nodding as if by doing so she could make him agree faster. "We might need it. For when, you know, the bottles run out."

"Yes," he said, feeling like an idiot.

"Yes," she agreed, smiling helpfully.

"Amos!" he yelled. When the big man came over he pointed at Elvi and said, "Find someone to help you, then follow her. There's a big piece of equipment they need help moving."

"Equipment?" Amos frowned. "Wouldn't food or water be—"

"It makes water," Holden and Elvi said at the same time.

"Roger," Amos said and left in a hurry.

Holden noticed that a subtle darkening of the sky had begun. The sun was still high. It was barely past midday and into the early afternoon. But the sunlight was shifting toward red and the world was darkening along with it, as though a beautiful sunset were starting about five hours early. Something about the change sent a shiver up his spine.

"Get up there," Holden said, giving Elvi a gentle push toward the alien towers. "Go now. Tell your people to hurry."

To her credit, she didn't argue, just took off at a dead run back toward the RCE science compound. All around him the colonists were moving faster, arguing less, and casting the occasional frightened glance at the sky.

Holden hadn't been inside the alien structure since he'd looked it over as a crime scene. It had the same eerie and inhuman aesthetic sense he'd seen before, first on Eros after the infection, and later on the Ring Station at the heart of the gate network. Curves and angles that were subtly wrong and yet weirdly beautiful at the same time. He tried to imagine what use the protomolecule masters had made of the buildings, and failed. He couldn't picture them housing machines like a factory, nor could he picture them as dwellings, scattered with furniture and personal items. It was as if, standing empty as they were, they still fulfilled whatever alien function they'd always been meant to serve.

It was also where Basia Merton and the others had hidden their explosives. Where they'd killed the security team. The bloodiest crimes that had been committed on the planet had all been centered right here, where they were all going now.

"Give me another recount," Carol Chiwewe said to her aides. "Who are we missing? Find out who we're missing."

She'd been doing head counts of the colonists ever since she'd arrived, almost the last person in. They kept coming up with new numbers over and over as stragglers drifted in and people milled around. It was an impossible task, but Holden respected her commitment to ensuring they left no one behind.

The RCE science team huddled together in one rounded corner of the building's large central room, Elvi among them. Several scientists were fiddling with a large machine. Getting it ready to purify large quantities of water, Holden hoped. Lucia drifted across the room to exchange a few words with Elvi, her son Jacek in tow. Holden breathed a sigh of relief they'd both made it. Basia would be up on the *Rocinante* going out of his mind with worry, and Holden was happy he'd be able to report that they were as safe as he could make them.

"Hey, Cap," Amos said, coming out of a side room with several colonists trailing. "We got a problem."

"Another one? Worse than the cataclysmic storm heading our way?"

"Related, I guess you'd say," Amos replied. "We've been going through the head counts and looks like the Dahlke family is missing."

"We're sure about that?"

"Pretty," Amos said with a shrug.

Carol saw them talking and made her way through the crowded room toward them. "One hundred percent sure," she said. "Clay Dahlke was in town picking up supplies when we warned him. He headed out to get his wife and daughter. They've got the house farthest outside of town. I should have sent someone along but I was stupid—"

"You had plenty to do," Holden reassured her. "How far from here is the Dahlke place?"

"Three klicks," Amos said. "I'm about to head out with these guys and see if we can find them."

"Wait a minute," Holden said. "I'm not sure you can make a six-kilometer round trip with the time we have left, let alone look for someone."

"Not leaving that little girl out there, chief," Amos said. He kept his voice carefully neutral, but Holden could hear the barest presentiment of a threat hiding in it.

"All right," Holden said, giving in. "But let me call up to the *Roci* and get an update. At least let me do that."

"Sure," Amos said agreeably. "Someone's looking for a poncho for the kid right now anyway."

Holden headed out of the main room and through the confusion of smaller chambers around it, trying to find the entrance. The alien building was a maze of connecting passages and rooms. As he walked, he pulled out his hand terminal. "Alex, this is Holden, you listening?"

The sound coming out of the terminal was filled with static from the atmosphere's heavy ionization, but Holden could still hear Alex when he said, "Alex here. What's the word?"

"Give me an update. How close are we?"

"Oh, boss, you just need to look west." The fear in Alex's voice was audible even over the heavy static.

Holden stepped out of the alien tower's main entrance and looked toward the slowly setting sun.

A curtain of black covered the horizon as far as the eye could see. It was moving so quickly that even from dozens of kilometers away it appeared to hurtle toward him, a black roiling cliff shot through with lightning. The ground beneath his feet trembled and shook, and Holden remembered that sound moved more quickly through a solid than through the air. The vibration he felt now was the sound of all that fury, coming through the earth like an early warning. Even as he thought it, a rising roar started in the west.

"What's it look like?" Amos had come into the antechamber

and was pulling a light backpack on. His colonist friends stood behind him, their faces a mixture of hope and fear.

"It's too late, big man," Holden said, looking west and shaking his head. "It's way too late."

He wasn't sure as he said it if he meant for the Dahlkes, or for all of them.

Chapter Thirty: Elvi

The storm front came, seeming slow at first—a tall purple-black churn higher than skyscrapers with only the slightest stirrings in the warm air to show that it was real—and then between one breath and the next, hit with the violence of a blow. Air and water and mud jetted through the windows, archways, and holes in the ruin like the stream from a firehose. It did not simply roar; it deafened. Elvi curled with her back against the wall of the ruin, her arms wrapped around her knees, and endured. The walls shuddered against her spine, vibrating with the hurricane gusts.

Across from her, Michaela had her hands over her ears, her mouth open in a shriek that Elvi couldn't hear. She had thought the rain would be cold, but it wasn't. The slurry that soaked up on the ruin's floor was warm and salty, and somehow that was worse. She laced her fingers together, squeezing until her knuckles ached. The mud-thick water filled the air until the spray made it hard to breathe. Someone lurched through the archway to her left, but she could no more make out who than stop the catastrophe by willing it. She felt certain that the ruins would fail, the more-than-ancient walls snap apart, and she and all the rest of them would be thrown into the storm, crushed or drowned or both. All she could think of was being in the heavy shuttle, the confusion and the panic when it was going down, the trauma of the impact. This felt the same, but it went on and on and on until she found herself almost missing the sudden impact of the crash. That, at least, had ended.

She knew that it was daytime, but the only lights were the cold white of the emergency lights and the near-constant barrage of lightning that caught people's faces like a strobe. A young man, his face set and stony like an image of suffering and endurance. A child no more than eight years old, his head buried in his mother's shoulder. Wei and Murtry in uniform, standing as close as lovers and shouting into each other's ears in the effort to be heard, their faces flushed red. The vast shifts of barometric pressure were invisible, but she felt them in the sense of overwhelming illness, of *wrongness*, that washed through her body. She couldn't tell if the shaking came from the walls of the storm-battered ruins, more little earthquakes, or her own overloaded nervous system.

At some point, her perception of time changed. She couldn't say if the storm had been hours or days or minutes. It was like the half-awareness of trauma, the doomed patience of being assaulted and knowing the only thing that would end it was the mercy of the attacker. Now and then, she would feel herself rising to some fuller consciousness, and will herself back into the stupor. Shock. Maybe she was going into shock. Her awareness seemed to blink in and out. She was curled against Fayez, both her hands squeezing at his elbow, and didn't remember how she'd gotten there. The dark slurry of mud was ankle high all through the ruins, brown and green. She was covered in it. They were all covered in it.

When this is over, I'm going to go back to my hut, take a long bath, and sleep for a week, she thought. She knew it was ridiculous. Her hut would no more have withstood this than a match could stay lit underwater, but she still thought it and some part of her believed it was true. A blinding-bright flash and crackling detonation came almost simultaneously. She gritted her teeth, closed her eyes, and endured.

The first change she noticed was a baby screaming. It was an exhausted sound. She shifted, her shirt and pants soaked and cold and adhering to her skin with the muck. She craned her neck, trying to find where the grating noise was coming from. She felt the thought shifting at the base of her skull before she knew what it was, a surreal lag between the realization and being conscious of it. She could hear a baby crying. She could hear something—*anything*—that wasn't the malice and venom of the storm. She tried to stand up, and her legs buckled under her. Kneeling in the muck, she gathered herself, squared her shoulders, and tried again. The rain slanted in through the windows of the ruin, but only at about twenty degrees. It still fell in buckets out of a black sky. The wind gusted and pushed and howled. In any other context, it would have been the teeth of a gale. Here and now, it meant the worst was over.

"Doctor Okoye?"

Murtry's face was lit from below, the emergency lantern hung over his shoulder. His expression was the same polite smile over sober, focused attention. Her battered mind wondered whether there was anything that could shake the man's soul, and thought perhaps there wasn't. She wanted to be reassured by his predictability, but her body wasn't able to feel comfort. Not now.

"Are you all right, Doctor?" he said, his hand on her shoulder.

She nodded, and when he started to step away, she clutched at him. "How long?"

"The front hit a little over sixteen hours ago," he said.

"Thank you," she said, and turned back to the window and the rain. The lightning still played among the clouds and lanced down to the ground, but not so often now. The flashes showed her a transformed landscape. Rivers flowed where yesterday had been desert hardpan. The flowers, or what she thought of as flowers, were churned into nothing. Not even sticks remained. She couldn't imagine how the mimic lizards could have survived. Or the bird-like animals she'd thought of as rock sparrows. She'd meant to go to the wash east of First Landing and collect samples of the pink lichen that clung in the shadows there. She wouldn't get to now.

The sense of loss was like a weight on her throat. She had glimpsed an ecosystem unlike anything anyone had ever seen before, a web of life that had grown up apart from anything she had known. She and her workgroups had been the only people ever to walk in that garden. And now it was gone.

"The usual state of nature is recovering from the last disaster," she said. It was a truism of ecological biologists, and she said it the way a religious person might pray. To make sense of what she saw. To comfort herself. To give the world some sense of purpose or meaning. Species rose in an environment, and that environment changed. It was the nature of the universe, as true here as it had been on Earth.

She wept quietly, her tears indistinguishable from the rain.

"Well, there's something I wasn't expecting," Holden said. She turned to look at him. The dimness of the ruins rendered him in monochrome. He was a sepia print of James Holden. His hair was plastered back, clinging to his head and the nape of his neck. Mud streaked his shirt.

She was too tired to dissemble. She took his hand in hers and followed his gaze toward the back of the ruins. His hand was solid and warm in hers, and if there was some stiffness and hesitation in it, at least he didn't flinch away.

Carol Chiwewe and four other squatters were bailing the storm muck out the window with stiff plastic utility panels, streaks of green-brown staining the pale gray. Behind them, twenty or thirty of the squatters from First Landing were clumped in groups, huddled together under blankets. RCE security moved among them with bottles of water and foil-packed emergency rations. Fayez and Lucia were standing together, talking anima-tedly. Elvi couldn't make out the words.

"I don't see it," she said. "What weren't you expecting?"

He squeezed her fingers and let go of her hand. Her palm felt colder without his in it.

"Your security people helping the Belters," he said. "I guess nothing brings people together like a disaster."

"That's not true," Elvi said. "We would always have helped. We came out here planning to help. I don't know why everyone thinks that we're so awful. We didn't do anything wrong."

Her voice cracked on the last word, and she started weeping in earnest. She felt oddly distanced from her grief, as if she were watching it from the outside, and then Holden put his hand on her shoulder, and she felt the pain. For a time, it washed her away. Flooded her. Three lightning strikes came close by, loud and bright and sudden, the thunder from them rolling away in the distance.

"I'm sorry," she said, when she could say anything. "There's just been...so much."

"No, I should apologize," Holden said. "I didn't mean to make you feel worse. It's just..."

"I understand," she said, reaching for his hand again. Let him laugh at her. Let him turn her away. She didn't care now. She just wanted to be touched. To be held.

"Hey, Cap," Amos said, looming up out of the darkness. He had a clear plastic poncho over his shoulders, the hood straining to fit the thick neck. "You going to be all right for a while?"

Holden stepped back, retreating from her. She felt a brief, irrational flash of rage toward the big man for intruding. She bit her lip and scowled up at him. If he noticed, he gave no sign.

"I don't actually know how to answer that question," Holden said. "I don't see any reason I'd die right away. That's about the best I've got."

"Beats the alternative, anyway," Amos said. "So that Dahlke family that didn't make it here before the shit hit the fan? Yeah, some of us are gonna go have a looksee."

Holden scowled. "You sure that's a good idea? It's still pretty bad out there. And this is more water than I'm guessing this place has seen in ever. There'll be a lot of flooding, and there's no good way to get help out if something goes south."

"They had a little girl," Amos said. The two men exchanged a long look that seemed to carry the weight of some earlier conversation. Elvi felt like a stranger watching two family members communicate in the half-code of long familiarity.

"Be careful," Holden replied after a long moment.

"That ship may have sailed, but I'll do what I can."

Wei walked toward them. She'd taken off her armor, but she still had an automatic rifle strapped to her back. She nodded at Amos. "I've got a couple more who want to tag along."

"Don't matter to me if it don't matter to you," Amos said. Wei nodded. There was a darkness in her eyes that seemed to echo Amos'.

Elvi looked over. A half dozen other people were struggling into the same kind of poncho Amos wore. In the dimness and the wreckage, it was hard to tell which of them were squatters and which were RCE. Even Belters and Earthers were hard to differentiate now. Elvi didn't know if that was an artifact of the darkness or if some deeper part of her brain was changing her perceptions, making anything human into something like her. Minds could be tricky that way.

Among them, she caught a glimpse of Fayez and her mouth went coppery with sudden fear. "Wait," she said, hopping across the space. "Fayez, wait. What are you doing?"

"Helping out," he said. "Also, getting out of this sardine can. I've gotten used to having a couple feet of social distance. Just being around all these people stresses me out."

"You can't. It's dangerous out there."

"I know."

"You stay here," she said, grabbing at his poncho and tugging it up, trying to get it back over his head. "I can go."

"Elvi," he said. "Elvi! Stop it."

She had a double handful of plastic sheeting in her fingers. It was already wet.

"Let them go," she said. "They're professionals. They can take care of this. We...people like us..."

"We're past us and them at this point. We're just people in a bad place," Fayez said. And then a moment later, "You know what I am, Elvi."

"No. No, you're a *good* man, Fayez."

He tilted his head. "I meant that I'm a geologist. It's not like they need me to talk about plate tectonics. What were *you* thinking?"

"Oh. Ah. I just..."

"Come on, Professor," Wei said, tapping Fayez on the arm. "Time to go for a walk."

"How can I refuse?" Fayez said, gently taking the plastic sheeting out of Elvi's hands. She stood watching as six of them walked together toward the entrance. Amos, Wei, Fayez, and three of the squatters—no, two squatters and Sudyam—one-use chemical lanterns glowing in their hands. They walked out into the gale. She stood at the window, ignoring the rain that soaked her. Amos and Wei took the lead, their heads down, their ponchos blowing out behind them. The others followed close behind, clustered like ducklings. The night around them was black and violent, and they moved into the downpour, growing fainter with every minute until she couldn't make them out at all. She stood there a while longer, her mind empty and exhausted.

She found Lucia and Jacek in one of the larger chambers. Two Belters were struggling to place a wide plastic panel over one of the windows to block the rain now that the wind wasn't so violent that it would simply shatter. A half dozen others were scraping out the muck. They'd already done so much work, Elvi could see pale strips of the ground. Everywhere people were sleeping, curled into and against each other. The sound of the storm was still enough to drown out their moans. Or most of them.

Lucia looked up at her. The woman seemed to have aged a

decade, but she managed a smile. Elvi sat down beside her. They were both covered in salt mud, and the muck was starting to reek a little. Putrescence or something like it. All the small life forms living in the planet's great ocean that had been broken and thrown to the sky, starting to decay. It broke her heart to think of the scale of the death that surrounded them, so she didn't.

"Can I help you?" Lucia said.

"I came to ask the same thing," Elvi said. "Tell me what I can do."

The long, terrible night went on, the rain slackening only slightly. No light came through the clouds. No rainbows promised that the disaster was ended. Elvi moved from one group to another, talking and checking. Some were the squatters, some were RCE. All had the same stunned expressions, the same sense of amazement that they were still alive. The scent of the muck was getting richer and more pungent as whatever organic structures it had held broke down. Elvi hated to imagine how the world would stink when the last of the rains fell and the sun came back to warm the landscape. That was a problem for another time.

She didn't notice it when she fell asleep. She'd been at the window, looking out in hopes of catching a glimpse of the search party's return. She remembered very clearly hearing Holden's voice behind her and a woman replying to him. She'd meant to turn back, find him, ask if she could help. If she could do something to stay in motion, to keep from thinking or feeling for another hour more. But instead she woke up.

For a moment, she didn't know where she was. Her exhaustion-drunk mind tried to make the close quarters into her cabin on the *Israel*, as if she were still on the journey out to New Terra. As if none of this had ever happened. Then the present reasserted itself.

She was in the corner of a smaller chamber. Eight other people were stretched out on the damp ground around her, heads pillowed by their arms. Someone was snoring, and a body was pressed up against hers. Lightning stuttered in the distance, and she saw the body beside hers was Fayez. The thunder came a long time later, and softly. Then there was only the patter of rain. She touched his shoulder, shaking him gently.

He groaned and shifted, the poncho still on him crackling with the motion. "Well, good morning, Doctor Okoye," he said. "Imagine meeting you here."

"Is it?"

"Is it what?"

"A good morning."

He sighed in the dark. "Honestly, I don't even think it's morning."

"Did you find them?"

"We didn't find anything."

"I'm sorry."

"I mean we didn't find anything at all. The huts are gone. First Landing's gone. The mine pit's gone or else the landmarks are so different we couldn't find it. The roads are gone."

"Oh."

"You know those pictures you see of a natural disaster where there's nothing but mud and rubble? Imagine that without the rubble."

Elvi lay back down. "I'm sorry."

"If we only lose them, it'll be a miracle. We managed to get a signal through to the *Israel*. The atmospheric data make it look like we'll be going without a sunrise for a good long time. No one said the words 'nuclear winter,' but I think it's safe to say things aren't going to be business as usual around here for a nice long while. We've got the battery power we carried in with us, but no hydroponics. Only as much fresh water as the chemistry deck will pump out. I was hoping that some of the storage buildings might have made it. They were pretty well built, some of them."

"Still. Maybe some good can come out of it."

"I admire your psychotic optimism."

"I'm serious. I mean look at us all. You went out with Amos

and Wei and the locals. We're all here together. Working together. We're taking care of each other. Maybe this is what it takes to resolve all the violence. There were three sides before. There's only one side now."

Fayez sighed. "It's true. Nothing points out shared humanity like a natural disaster. Or a disaster, anyway. Nothing on this mudball of a planet's even remotely natural if you ask me."

"So that's a good thing," she said.

"It is," Fayez agreed. And then a moment later, "I give it five days."

Chapter Thirty-One: Holden

Holden had witnessed the aftermath of a tornado as a child. They were rare in the Montana flatlands where he'd grown up, but not entirely unheard of. One had touched down on a commercial complex a few miles from his family's farm, and the local citizens had gathered to help with the cleanup. His mother Tamara had taken him along.

The tornado had hit a farmers' market at the center of the complex, while totally avoiding the feed store and fuel station on either side of it. The market had been flattened as if by a giant's fist, the roof lying flat on the ground with the walls splayed out around it. The contents of the store had been scattered in a giant pinwheel that extended for hundreds of meters around the impact point. It was young James Holden's first experience with nature's fury unleashed, and for years afterward he'd had nightmares about tornadoes destroying his home.

This was worse.

Holden stood in what his hand terminal told him had been the center of First Landing, the constant rain sheeting off his poncho, and turned in a slow circle. All around there was nothing but thick mud occasionally cut by a rivulet of water. There were no flattened buildings. No wreckage strewn across the ground. With the fury and duration of the winds, it was entirely possible that the detritus of First Landing was hundreds or even thousands of kilometers away. The colonists would never rebuild. There was nothing *to* rebuild.

A ripple of lights danced through the heavy cloud cover overhead, and a second later the booming of the thunder, like a barrage of cannon fire. The rain intensified, reducing visibility to a few dozen meters, and swelling the little streams cutting gullies across the muddy ground.

"I'd say 'what a mess,' but it's actually kind of the opposite of that," Amos said. "Never seen anything like this, Cap."

"What if it happens again?" Holden said, shuddering either at that thought or at the cold rainwater trickling down his back.

"Think they have more than one of whatever blew up?"

"Anyone know what the first one was yet?"

"Nope," Amos admitted with a sigh. "Big fusion reactor, maybe. Alex sent an update, said it tossed a lot of radiation up around the initial blast."

"Some of that will be coming down in the rain."

"Some."

The mud at Amos' feet moved, and a small, sluglike creature pushed its way up out of the ground, desperately trying to get its head above water. Amos casually kicked it into one of the nearby streams where the current whisked it away.

"I'm running low on my cancer meds," Holden said.

"Radioactive rain ain't gonna help with that."

"Was my thought. Bad for the colonists too."

"Do we have a plan?" Amos asked. His tone suggested he didn't expect an answer.

"Get off this hell-planet before the next catastrophe."

"A-fucking-men," Amos replied.

They walked back toward the alien towers, trudging through the thick mud and occasionally having to leap across a newly formed arroyo filled with fast-moving water. The ground was covered with small holes where brightly colored worm-slugs had pushed their way to the surface, and shiny trails of slime radiated in all directions showing their recent passage.

"Never seen these before," Amos said, pointing at another of the creatures slowly making its way across the wet ground. They weren't much bigger than Holden's thumb, and eyeless.

"Forced up by the rain. This was pretty arid land before. There's a lot of subterranean life drowning right now I'd bet. At least these guys have a way to get out of it."

"Yeah," Amos said, frowning down at one, "but, you know, gross. One of those things climbs into my sleeping bag, I'm gonna be pissed."

"Big baby."

As if in response to Amos' worries, the ground shifted and dozens more of the slugs pushed their way up. Wrinkling his nose in disgust, Amos picked his way through them, trying not to get their slime on his boots. The trails they left were quickly washed away by the rain.

Holden's had terminal buzzed at him, and he pulled it out to find that a message had been downloaded. The terminal had been trying to connect to the *Roci* for hours. There must have finally been a break in the storm long enough for it to send and receive updates.

He tried to open a channel to Alex, but got only static. Whenever his window had happened, he'd missed it. But the fact that there were occasional breaks in the atmospheric clutter was a hopeful sign that they'd get comms back soon. In the meantime, he could keep sending messages and hoping they'd slip through the static a bit at a time.

The update waiting for him was a voice message. He plugged the bud into his ear and hit play.

"This is a message for Captain James Holden, from Arturo Ramsey, lead counsel for Royal Charter Energy."

Holden had sent dozens of requests to the various senior vice presidents and board members of RCE for Naomi to be released. Getting a reply back from the company's top lawyer was not a good sign.

"Captain Holden," the message continued, "Royal Charter Energy takes your request for the release of Naomi Nagata from detention on the *Edward Israel* very seriously. However, the legal landscape we're navigating with this situation is murky at best."

"It's not murky, give me my damn XO back, you smug bastards," Holden muttered angrily. At Amos' questioning look he shook his head and continued the recording.

"Pending further investigation, we're afraid we're going to have to follow the advice of the security team on site and hold Naomi Nagata in protective custody. We hope you understand the delicate—"

Holden turned off the recording in disgust. Amos raised an eyebrow.

"That's the legal wonk at RCE telling me they plan to keep holding Naomi," Holden said. " 'Following the advice of the security team on site.' "

"Murtry," Amos grunted.

"Who else?"

"Sort of wondering why you haven't let me off the leash on that, Cap," Amos said.

"Because, before *this*"—Holden waved an arm at the mud and rain and worms around them—"we had a job to do that would not have been aided by murdering the RCE security chief."

"Would've loved to give it a try, though. You know, just to see."

"Well, my friend, you might still get your shot," Holden said. "Because I am about to order him to do something he really isn't going to want to do."

"Oh," Amos said with a smile, "goody."

When they returned to the ruins, the camp was in chaos. People were frantically sweeping something out of the tower entrance using blankets and sticks and other makeshift implements. An agonized howl echoed out of the structure, like someone in terrible pain.

Doctor Okoye spotted them from the tower opening and ran to meet them. "Captain, we have a serious problem." Before he could reply, she kicked one of the worms away from his feet with a squeal. "Look out!"

Holden had watched her capture and sacrifice a number of the local fauna during their association. She'd never struck him as squeamish. He couldn't picture a few slimy slug analogs being the thing that broke her.

"What's going on?" he asked when she'd finished kicking slugs away from him.

"A man died," she said. "The one who was married to the man and woman who took care of the carts. The taller one. Beth is her name, I think. The wife's name. That's her crying inside."

"And that relates to the worms how?"

"That slime they secrete is a neurotoxin," Elvi replied, wide-eyed. "He touched it, and it was almost instant paralysis. Full respiratory failure. One of the worms was climbing up a wall near their sleeping area and he grabbed it to throw it outside. By the time we realized what was happening, he was dead."

"Jesus," Amos said, staring down at the worms surrounding them, something like respect mixed in with his disgust.

"Some kind of defense toxin?" Holden asked.

"I don't know," Elvi replied. "It might just be slime to aid in locomotion, like a terrestrial slug. It might not be toxic to the other life forms on New Terra. We've never even seen them before. How can we know anything? If I had my collection equipment, I could send the data back to Luna, if I could send the message back to Luna, but—"

Elvi's voice was rising as she spoke. When she ended, she was almost in tears. "You're right," Holden said. "It was a stupid question, and it doesn't matter anyway."

"Why doesn't it—" Elvi started, but Holden pushed past her.

"Where's Murtry," he asked.

"Inside, organizing the people to find and remove all the slugs from the structure."

"Come on, Amos," Holden said. "Let's change his priorities."

Inside, the fear was so pronounced it was almost an odor. Half of the colonists were in almost frantic activity, building slug-sweeping implements and clearing the structure. The other half sat on the floor, many wrapped tight in blankets, empty expressions on their faces. The human mind could only take so much threat. Everyone had a different limit, and he couldn't really blame the people who had been broken by the last thirty hours. It was actually sort of amazing that it hadn't happened to all of them.

He was, however, unsurprised to see Basia's wife and son busily at work with the chemical sciences team.

"Doctor Merton," he greeted her with an apologetic smile.

"Captain," she replied. Her returning smile was thin, and very tired. As the colony's only doctor, she'd had a very long day.

"I've heard about the death," he started, but she cut him off with a sharp nod and a gesture toward the chemical analysis deck.

"We're analyzing the toxin right now," she said. "It's unlikely we'll be able to make a counter-agent with the tools available, but we're going to try."

"I appreciate the effort," Holden said. "But I'm hoping to make it unnecessary."

"Are we being forced to leave?" she said, a look of sad resignation replacing her wan smile. "After all this…"

"Maybe not forever," Holden said, putting his hands on her shoulders. She felt very thin.

She nodded slowly, looking around them at the dirty, frightened people filling the room. "I can't argue. There's nothing left to fight over."

Oh, Holden thought, *some people can always find a reason to fight, speaking of which.* "I need to find Murtry."

Lucia gestured at an opening behind her, and Holden left with one last squeeze of her shoulders and what he hoped was an encouraging smile.

In the next room, Murtry was down on his haunches looking at something on the floor. Wei stood behind him, nose wrinkled in disgust and her rifle in her hands.

"Wei," Amos said with a nod.

"Amos," the security officer replied with a grin.

Holden wondered what was going on there. They couldn't have a thing, could they? When would they have found time to have a thing? But they definitely acted like they were sharing a private joke.

"Captain Holden," Murtry said, standing up, not giving him more time to think about possible Amos-and-Wei dalliances. On the floor behind the RCE security chief was a clear plastic bowl inverted over one of the slugs. The creature was nuzzling its prison with its pointed eyeless face.

"Made a friend," Holden said, pointing at the slug.

"They say it's a good idea to know your enemy," Murtry replied.

"They say a lot of stuff."

"Yes. Yes, they do. How did the recon go?"

"About how you'd expect," Holden said. "Initial reports are correct. There isn't a single standing structure. Not even the remains of one. All the colony supplies are lost. We can make potables out of ground water until the chem lab runs out of supplies. But what's raining out of the sky is radioactive, and probably has things living in it."

"All right," Murtry said, scratching his ear with one thick fingernail. "Can we agree that at present, the insurgent colony might not be viable?"

"You don't have to sound happy about it."

"I'm going to have some relief flown down as soon as comms

clears up. RCE is happy to share these needed supplies with the refugees."

"Very magnanimous," Holden said. "But RCE is going to do me a bigger favor."

"Oh," Murtry said, his face shifting into a smile. "We are?"

"Yeah. Go ahead and bring the supply shuttle down. Evacuation is going to take some time, and we'll want plenty of medicine, food, and shelter to keep these people healthy until everyone is off-world."

"Off-world? Sounds like you're doing *us* a favor there, Captain."

"I'm not done," Holden said, and took a step forward, deliberately moving into Murtry's space. The security man stiffened, but didn't step back. "When the shuttle leaves, it's going to take some of the colonists with it. The sick and vulnerable first. And as soon as your people can de-weaponize the second shuttle, it'll start making runs too. I'm giving the same orders to the *Barbapiccola* and the *Rocinante*. We're leaving this planet, and if I can't stick everyone on the *Roci* and the *Barb*, the *Edward Israel* will be taking the rest."

Murtry's smile cooled. "Is that right?"

"It is."

"I fail to see why the ship that brought the squatters here can't also take them away," Murtry said.

"One, it no longer has the room," Holden started.

"Then they should dump the ore they illegally stole from this world," Murtry said.

"And two," Holden continued as if he hadn't interrupted, "she's down to the last of her supplies. I won't stick hundreds of people on that ship that may not make it back to Medina. I doubt it's RCE policy to ignore a humanitarian crisis. And even if it is, it's sure as hell going to make for terrible press."

Murtry took an answering step toward Holden, crossing his arms and shifting his smile into an equally meaningless frown.

Plan B is that I have Amos kill you right now and just take what

I want when the shuttle lands, Holden thought, but worked to keep it off his face.

Almost as if he could sense the thought, Amos shuffled forward and put one hand on the butt of his pistol. Wei shifted to his right, still gripping her rifle.

We are so close, Holden thought, *to all of this going completely off the rails.* But he couldn't back down. Not with a couple hundred people living or dying on the outcome of the confrontation. Wei cleared her throat. Amos grinned back at her. Murtry cocked his head to one side, his frown deepening.

Here we go, Holden thought, and suppressed the urge to swallow a mouth suddenly full of saliva.

"Of course," Murtry said. "We'd be happy to assist."

"Uh," Holden replied

"You're right. We can't leave them here," Murtry continued. "And there isn't room for them anywhere else. I'll let the *Israel* know they're taking on passengers as soon as we get comms up."

"That would be great," Holden said. "Thank you."

"Doctor Okoye," Murtry said. Holden turned to find the diminutive scientist had come in, her usual tentative smile on her face.

"Sorry to interrupt," she said. "But we've gotten the radio back up. We're on with the *Israel* right now. You said to tell you as soon as we got through."

"Thank you," Murtry said and started to follow her out of the room. He paused, as though something had suddenly occurred to him, and turned to Holden. "You know, we're only in this situation because these people came down and built a shantytown. We'd brought much better structures with us on the heavy shuttle. Much of this could have been avoided."

Holden started to reply, but Elvi said, "Oh, no. I'm unhappy about the loss of the dome and the permanent structures too. But we clocked gusts of three hundred and seventy kilometers an hour out there. Nothing we set up would have withstood that."

"Thank you, Doctor Okoye," Murtry said with a tight smile, "for correcting me. Let's go call the ship, shall we?"

Elvi blinked in puzzlement as Murtry left. "Is he mad at me?"

"Sweetie," Amos said, clapping her on the back, "that just means you're not an asshole."

Chapter Thirty-Two: Havelock

After they'd lost radio contact with Murtry, Havelock had tried to sleep. He *should* have slept. There was nothing he could do. Not yet, anyway. Not until it was over. He floated in his couch, the straps keeping him centered over the gel, and willed his consciousness to fade. His mind wouldn't rest. Were they still alive down there? What if the explosion was just the first of several? What if the planet detonated and took out the *Israel*? Should he have Marwick pull the ship into a higher orbit? Or even away from the planet entirely? And if the *Barbapiccola* tried to do the same...then what? He wasn't supposed to let them break orbit with a full load of RCE's lithium ore.

He closed his eyes again, but they opened as soon as he stopped consciously willing them shut. After three hours, he gave up, took off his straps, and went to the gym instead. His float-atrophied muscled complained with every set, and he put the feed of the planet below on the screen. The contours of New Terra were gone. The whole planet had become a flat and uniform gray, clouds obscuring whatever violence was happening beneath them. After the exercise round, he bathed, changed into a fresh uniform, and went to his office. His incoming message queue was filled with requests for comments from every news organization there was, and several he doubted were real. He forwarded them all to the RCE corporate headquarters on Luna. Let them answer if they wanted to. At this point, they knew as much as he did.

He checked on comms from the planet, but the signal wasn't getting through. So he checked again. And again. The gray planet was silent.

"Any word?" the prisoner asked.

"Nothing," Havelock replied. And then, a moment later, "I'm sorry."

"Me too," she said. "They'll be all right."

"I hope so."

"Are *you* all right?"

Havelock looked over at her. For a detained saboteur who'd been in the box for days now, she looked calm. Almost amused. He found himself smiling back at her.

"Might be a little stressed," he said.

"Yeah. Sorry about that."

"Not your fault," Havelock said. "You aren't the one calling the shots around here."

"There's someone calling the shots around here?" Naomi asked, and a man cleared his throat behind him. Havelock shifted his couch, the bearing hissing, to look back at the hatch. The chief engineer floated there. He wore the militia armband over his uniform sleeve.

"Hey there, chief," he said, pulling himself into the room. "Wondering if we could have a talk. Alone, maybe."

"You can put up the privacy shield if you want," Naomi said. "I'll still hear everything."

Havelock undid his straps and pushed off. "I'll be back," he said over his shoulder.

"You shall always find me at home," Naomi said.

The commissary was between rushes. The chief engineer grabbed a bulb of coffee for himself and another for Havelock. They floated together near a table bolted to the deck. Force of habit.

"So we've been talking," Chief Engineer Koenen said. "About the event."

"Yeah, it's been pretty much the only thing on my mind too."

"How sure are we that it's...well...*natural*?"

"I'd have gone pretty much a hundred percent it wasn't," Havelock said with a grim laugh. The chief engineer's expression seemed to close, and Havelock pressed on. "But maybe that depends on what you mean by natural. Is there something bothering you?"

"I don't want to sound paranoid. It's just that the timing on this seems pretty convenient. You and me and the boys catch the UN mediator red-handed. Throw the bitch in the brig. And then this big disaster comes out of nowhere, takes everyone's attention off her."

Havelock sipped at the coffee.

"What are you thinking, chief? That it was rigged?"

"Those squatters got here before we did. We don't know what they found and just never told us about. And Holden worked for the OPA. He worked for Fred fucking Johnson, right? Hell, everything I heard says he's been sleeping with that Belter girl we brought in. His loyalty isn't to Earth. And he was the one who went on the alien whatever-the-hell-it-is that Medina Station's floating around and came back out. I've been following some independent casts. The Martian marines that went there after him? There's some pretty weird shit that's gone on with all of them since then."

"Weird shit like what?"

The chief engineer's eyes brightened and he hunched forward, a posture of intimacy and complicity that was a habit of gravity. For the next half hour, he ran down half a dozen strange occurrences. One of the marines had died of an embolism during a heavy-g burn just before she'd been scheduled to talk with her cousin who ran a popular newsfeed. Another had quit the military and wasn't talking about anything that had happened. There had been rumors of a secret report that suggested—strongly suggested—that James Holden had been killed on the station, and a doppelgänger put in his place. It stood to reason with all the other changes the protomolecule could make to a human body that recreating one wouldn't be hard for it. Only the report had never been made public, and the people who had read it had been targets of whisper campaigns to discredit them.

Havelock drank his coffee and listened, nodding and asking the occasional question—usually for the sources of the information the chief engineer was reporting. When they were done, Havelock promised to look into the issue, then hauled himself back to his desk. On the readout, the planet was still covered in clouds.

"Everything okay?" Naomi asked.

"Fine," he said. And then a moment later, "Just scared people trying to find a version of events where someone has control over everything."

She chuckled. "Yeah. I'm doing the same."

"You are? How?"

"Chewing down my fingernails and praying," she said. "Mostly praying."

"You're religious?"

"No."

"Are you and Holden secretly alien spies that blew up the planet as part of a Belter conspiracy to distract the media?"

Naomi's laughter was deep. "Oh, was that what it was? I'm so sorry."

Havelock chuckled too, feeling a little guilty as he did. Koenen was one of his people. Naomi Nagata was a saboteur and the enemy. And still, it was a little funny, and there wasn't anyone else to talk with.

"It's not that bad. Conspiracy theories come up whenever people feel like the universe is too random. Absurd. If it's all an enemy plot, at least there's someone calling the shots."

"Belters."

"This time, yeah."

"Are they going to break in here and throw me out the airlock?"

"No, they're not like that," Havelock said. "They're good guys."

"Good guys who think I destroyed a planet."

"No, that your alien doppelgänger boyfriend did to keep people from thinking about you. Don't worry. You'll be fine. No one's really thinking you're in league with the protomolecule. They're just scared."

Naomi went quiet. Her fingertips pressed against the cage and she hummed quietly to herself. It wasn't a melody Havelock knew. He checked his incoming queue again. Another half dozen requests for comment. A note from one of the security team that the Belters on the *Israel* had started sitting together in the commissary and exercising together in the gym. It seemed suspicious to the man making the report. It sounded like circling the wagons to Havelock. He'd have to think about what to do about that. If anything. The radio signal to the planet still didn't go through. The analysis of the IR sensors that could see through the cloud cover was that First Landing was being destroyed by the storm. He turned his attention to the sensor array data as it streamed back to Earth. Maybe someone there could make something of it. The first-report newsfeeds were already speculating that it had been a fusion core overloading. Having just heard about how Jim Holden was a shapeshifting alien left him a little skeptical about everything.

When, six hours later, his hand terminal lit up with an incoming request from Murtry, Havelock felt a huge weight lifting from his shoulders. He accepted the connection, and a low-res Murtry fuzzed to life on the screen. The feed jumped and hopped, but the audio quality was all right apart from a little static.

"Good to see you, Havelock. How're things holding together up there?"

"No complaints, sir. Mostly we were waiting to hear from you. That looks like a hell of a rainstorm you've got going down there."

"Loss of life was minimal," Murtry said. "A few of the squatters didn't bother getting to shelter in time, and the floodwaters pulled some local bugs out from the ground that'll kill you if you touch them. They lost another one to that. Our people are fine. The camp's a loss."

"Ours or theirs?"

"Ours *and* theirs. Everyone down here's going to be starting over from scratch."

"I'm sorry to hear that."

"Why?"

Havelock blinked. His smile felt nervous. "Because we just lost everything."

"We didn't lose as much as they did," Murtry said. "That makes this a win. We're going to need to pack the shuttle with relief supplies and get it down here. Food. Clean water. Medical supplies. Warm clothes. No shelters, though. Or if they are, make 'em those cheap laminate ones that won't hold up for more than a week."

"Are you sure? I can get some emergency prefabs worked up—"

"No. Nothing like permanent shelter comes down here until our people are the only ones using it. And we'll be hauling up some of the squatters. Can you start setting something up for an extra hundred or so people? It doesn't need to be comfortable, but it has to be something we can control."

"We're bringing the squatters on the *Israel*, sir?"

"We're getting them off the planet and putting them under our thumbs," Murtry said with a smile. "His Holiness, Pope Holden, thinks he bullied me into it. That man is about as smart as a dead cat."

Havelock was suddenly acutely aware that Naomi's privacy

shield was down and every word of his conversation was carrying to her. He tried to think of a way to trigger it that wouldn't let Murtry know that he'd forgotten protocol up to now.

"There a problem, Havelock?"

"Just thinking where we can put them, sir," Havelock said. "We'll come up with something."

"Good man. This thing was a lucky break. Play this right, and we'll get all the squatters off the planet. Even if we can't, they're going to have hell's own time claiming they've got a viable settlement." Murtry's smile was thin. "This last sixty hours, we've probably made more progress toward straightening this mess out than all the time since we came out here."

Naomi rapped against the cage with her knuckles, the grate clacking softly enough that the hand terminal's mike didn't pick it up. Her eyebrows were raised in query, but she didn't speak. Havelock made the smallest possible nod.

"What about the mediation team?" he asked. "Holden and his people?"

"Holden and Burton are fine. Burton almost got his ass caught out in the worst of it, but it didn't quite happen," Murtry said with a shrug and a smile. "Can't have everything."

Havelock winced, thinking how callous Murtry's words would sound to someone who didn't know him. "Well, let them know we'll put together relief supplies and get them down there as soon as we can get through the cloud cover."

"No permanent structures."

"No, sir. I understand."

"I'm going to want to get some of our science team up when the shuttle goes back too. The ones that're going a little too native. I'll work up an evac list."

"Do you want me to get the...ah...other shuttle ready to return to normal duty?" Havelock said, hoping that Murtry wouldn't tell him to keep the weapon live. There was silence on the connection. "Sir?"

"We'll have to, won't we?" Murtry said. "Yeah, all right. But be ready to put it back in play as soon as the evacuation's done. I don't like giving up our advantages for nothing."

"No, sir," Havelock said. "I'll see to it."

"Good man."

The connection died. Havelock started pulling up the duty roster and inventory lists. It was almost a minute before he risked glancing over at Naomi. She looked like she'd eaten something unpleasant.

"That's who you work for?"

"He's the chief of security," Havelock said.

"That man is a snake."

"He just came off badly," Havelock said. "He didn't know you could hear him."

"If he had, he might have hissed a little different," she said. Then a moment later, "Do you have any selective apoptosis catalysts on board?"

"Oncocidals? Sure, anti-cancer meds are standard."

"Would you send some down in the shuttle?"

"I think antibiotics and clean water are more likely to—"

"Holden needs them. He caught a lot of rems on Eros. It's not a big thing when we have a med bay, but he pops a new tumor every month or two. Unless Alex decides to take the *Roci* down into that soup, they may be down there for a while."

He should probably have said no. She was his prisoner, and doing her favors wasn't really part of the job. But she hadn't made it clear to Murtry that she was listening. She could have embarrassed him and hadn't.

"Sure," he said. "I don't see why not."

"About that dead cat thing..."

"Yeah?"

"A lot of people have underestimated Jim over the last few years," Naomi said. "A lot of them aren't with us anymore."

"A threat?"

"A heads-up not to make the same mistake your boss is making. I like you."

Putting the relief supplies together was easy. Everyone on board had been waiting for a chance to do something. Food, fresh water, polyfiber blankets, and medical supplies—including a box of oncocidals with Holden's name on the top—filled the shuttle's hold until there was hardly room to close the door. Havelock found himself watching the sensors, waiting for the clouds to thin enough for the one tiny light of First Landing to show through. It was a shock to remember that those lights weren't going to shine again. That they were gone. Havelock hadn't been there. He'd never been to the surface of New Terra at all, and still the idea of the one human settlement being wiped away bothered him.

"This is shuttle two requesting permission to drop," the pilot said, her voice a slow drawl.

"Captain Marwick here. Permission's given. Godspeed."

Havelock watched his display as the shuttle's thrusters went bright, driving it away from the *Israel* and down. The danger was turbulence in the lower atmosphere. Even if there were evil winds in the outer layers, the air was so thin there, the shuttle would be able to shrug them off. When it got down to the clouds, Havelock told himself, the real danger would begin.

The shuttle dropped, its body becoming only a light spot against the darker gray of the clouds. The sensor data feed from it looked fine. The turbulence was worse than Havelock had expected, but not so bad as he'd feared. The farther down it went, though—

The data signal dropped. Havelock switched over to visual in time to see the shuttle's bright flare fade. A puff of smoke a few kilometers higher showed where it had detonated. The shock of it, the horror, was like being punched in the gut. He barely noticed the flickering of the lights in the *Israel* or the stuttering whine of the air recyclers restarting.

"Havelock?" the prisoner said. "Havelock, what's happening? Did something go wrong? Why's everything rebooting?"

He ignored her, leaning close to his terminal screen. The shuttle was dead, falling to the distant ground of New Terra in a hundred flaming bits. But there was something in the images. A barely visible line that passed through the cloud of smoke and debris where it had died. Something had shot the shuttle down. His first thought was the *Barbapiccola*. His second was the *Rocinante*. He pulled up the orbital tracking, trying to find how the enemy ships had taken action, but the only thing that intersected the line at the moment when the shuttle died was one of New Terra's dozen tiny moons...

His mouth went dry. He heard the emergency Klaxon sounding for the first time, though he realized now it had been going for a while. Since the shuttle exploded, he thought. He assumed. Naomi Nagata was shouting at him, trying to get his attention, trying to get him to talk to her. He put a priority connection request through to Captain Marwick. For five long seconds, the captain didn't respond.

"It was the planet," Havelock said. "The shuttle. It was shot down by something on one of those moons."

"I saw that," Marwick said.

"What the hell was it? Some kind of alien weapon? Did the planet blowing up turn on some kind of defense grid?"

"Couldn't say."

"I need everything we have on that. All the sensor data. Everything. I need it sent back to Earth, and I need it ready for Murtry and the science team. I'm giving blanket permission for anyone on the crew to see it. Any information we can get—anything—is our top priority."

"Might not be our top," the captain said. "My plate's a bit full right now, but as soon as I've a spare moment—"

"This isn't a request," Havelock shouted.

When Marwick spoke again, his voice was cool. "I'm thinking you might not have yet noted that we're on battery power, sir?"

"We're...we're what?"

"On battery power. Backup, as you might say."

Havelock looked around his office. It was like seeing it for the first time. His desk, the weapon locker, the cells. Naomi looking out at him with an expression of barely restrained alarm.

"Did...did it shoot us too?"

"Not so far as I can see. No new holes through the hull, certainly."

"Then what's going on?"

"Our reactor's down," Marwick said. "And it seems it won't restart."

Chapter Thirty-Three: Basia

What does that mean?" Basia asked.

"Well," Alex said, "it's complicated, but these little pellets of fuel get injected into a magnetic bottle where a bunch of lasers fire. That makes the atoms in the fuel fuse, and it releases a *lot* of energy."

"Are you making fun of me?"

"No," Alex said. "Well, maybe a little. What exactly are you asking?"

"If our reactor is off-line, does that mean we'll crash? Is the ship broken? Is it just us? *What does it mean?*"

"Hold your horses," Alex said. He was sitting in his pilot's chair doing complicated things with his control panel. "Yeah," he finally said, dragging the word out into a long sigh. "Reactors are off-line on the *Israel* and the *Barb*. That's a lot worse for them than it is for us."

"Felcia—my daughter is on the *Barbapiccola*. Is she in danger?"

Alex started working on his panel again, his fingers tapping out commands faster than Basia could follow. He clucked his tongue as he worked. The clucking while Basia waited for an answer made him want to scream and choke the laconic pilot.

"Well," Alex drawled out, then tapped one last control and a graphic display of Ilus with swirling lines around it appeared. "Yeah, the *Barb*'s orbit is decaying—"

"The ship is crashing?" Basia yelled at him.

"Wouldn't say crashing, but we've all been keeping pretty low, with bringing up ore and all. Most times adding a little velocity's just the way you do it, but—"

"We have to go get her!"

"Ease down! Let me finish," Alex yelled back, patting the air in a placating gesture that made Basia want to punch him in his face. "The orbit's always decaying, but it won't be dangerous for days. Maybe longer, depending on how long they can run the maneuvering thrusters on battery power. Felcia's not in any danger right now."

"Let's go get her," Basia said, taking deep breaths to keep his words calm and level. "Can we do that? Can we go to her ship without the reactor?"

"Sure. The *Roci*'s a warship. Her battery backups are robust. We can do quite a bit of maneuvering if we need to. But with the reactor down, every bit of power we pull off those batteries is gone. It ain't gettin' replaced. Lose too much of it to land, and we'll be in the same position as them. We're not doing anything until we make a plan. So calm down, or I'll lock you in your cabin."

Basia nodded, but didn't trust himself to speak around the rising panic in his chest. His daughter was on a spaceship that was falling out of the sky. He might never be calm again.

"On top of which," Alex continued, "you think everyone else on the *Barb* is just gonna be okay with us leaving without them? We don't have room for everyone on that ship. Docking with a ship full of frightened people looking to get off is never plan A."

Basia nodded again. "But if we don't get a plan," he said.

Alex's grin went away. "We'll get your girl. If it comes to that, if we all fall out of the sky, your daughter will be on this ship when it happens. So will Naomi."

Basia's panic and anger was replaced by a feeling of shame and a sudden lump in his throat. "Thank you."

"It's family," Alex said, with a smile that was almost only baring his teeth. "We don't let our family down."

Basia drifted through the *Rocinante* like a ghost.

Alex was in engineering, tinkering with the reactor, trying to figure out what was causing the failure. Basia had offered to help, but Alex had declined. He couldn't blame the pilot. His ignorance of nuclear engineering and ship's systems was utter and complete. He doubted the reactor failing to work could be fixed by a really clean bead of weld.

If it turned out he was wrong, Alex would call.

In the meantime, Basia moved through the ship trying to distract himself from the idea that he was slowly drifting toward the planet and a fiery death. That Felcia was too. He went to the galley and made a sandwich that he didn't eat. He went to the head and bathed with damp scrubbing pads and rub-on cleansers. He left with a few friction burns and all the same worries he'd brought in with him.

For the first time since coming to the *Rocinante*, he actually felt like a prisoner.

Alex had left a panel on the ops deck monitoring the other two ships. Basia could check on the *Barbapiccola* as often as he liked. The pilot seemed to think that the display showing hundreds of hours before the *Barb*'s orbit decayed enough to be dangerous would make him feel better. But Alex didn't understand. It didn't matter how long that number was. What mattered was that it was counting *down*. Every time Basia looked at the counter, there was less time than when he'd looked before. When he was looking at a countdown timer for the death of his child, the numbers on it were almost meaningless.

He avoided looking.

He returned to the galley and cleaned up the mess his sandwich preparations had made. He threw his used scrubbing pads and towels into the bin, and then went ahead and ran a cycle of laundry to clean them. He watched a children's cartoon and then one of Alex's noir films. Afterward, he couldn't remember either. He wrote a letter to Jacek and then deleted it. Recorded a video apology to Lucia. When he watched it he looked like a madman, with hair flying wildly out from his skull, and sunken haunted eyes. He deleted it.

He returned to ops, telling himself that he would just double-check that nothing had changed, that the inexorable ticking of his daughter's death clock was just data to be monitored. He watched the tiny icon that represented the *Barbapiccola* travel its glowing path around Ilus, every passage taking it an imperceptible increment closer to the atmosphere that would kill it.

Just data. No change. Just data. Tick tick tick.

"Alex, Holden here," a voice blared from the communications console. Basia floated to the panel and turned on the microphone.

"Hello, this is Basia Merton," he said, surprised at how calm his voice sounded. Holden was calling. Holden worked for the governments of Earth and the OPA. He'd know what to do.

"Uh, hi. Alex left me a message, but comms have been really spotty. He, uh, around?"

Basia laughed in spite of himself.

"I could probably find him."

"Great, I'll—"

"Hey, Captain," Alex said. He sounded out of breath. "Sorry, took a sec to get to the panel. I was elbows deep in the *Roci*'s nethers when you called."

Basia reached out to turn off his speaker and let them talk, but stopped with his finger hovering millimeters over the control. This was James Holden on the line. He was probably going to be talking to Alex about the reactor shutdowns. Feeling a little like a Peeping Tom, Basia left the connection on.

"There a problem?" Holden asked.

"Yeah, so, fusion don't work no more," Alex said, exaggerating his drawl.

"If that's the punch line, I don't get it."

"Wasn't a joke. Just yanked the reactor apart. Injector works, fuel pellets drop, laser array fires, magnetic bottle is stable. All the parts that make it a fusion reactor work just fine. Only, you know, without the fusing."

"God damn it," Holden said. Even Basia, who'd only just met the man, could hear the frustration in his voice. "Is it just us?"

"Nope," Alex said. "We're all flyin' on batteries up here."

"How long?"

"Well, even on batteries I can put the *Roci* up far enough we'll all die of old age before she falls down, or I can slope on down planetside and park. The *Israel*'s got maybe ten days or so, depending on how much juice she stores. But she's also got a ton of people sucking up air, so she'll be burning through her batteries just keeping everyone warm and breathing. The *Barb*'s worse off than that. Same problems, shittier boat."

Basia's gut clenched at this casual description of his daughter's peril, but kept silent.

"Our creepy friend said there was a defense grid," Holden said. "Their power station blew up, so the old defenses are in lockdown."

"They do seem to dislike big energy sources near their stuff," Alex replied. Basia had the sense they were talking about something from their past, but didn't know what it was.

"And we heard the supply drop was shot down," Holden said. "So, we've got a few hundred people down here, a bunch more up there, and we're all about to die because the planet's defenses won't let us help each other."

"The *Roci*'s got the juice to land, if you need us," Alex said.

Basia wanted to scream at him, *We can't land, my daughter's still up here!*

"They shot the shuttle down," Holden said. "Do not risk my ship."

"If we can't get supplies down to you, me and Naomi'll be inheriting it pretty soon."

"And until that happens, do what I tell you to do," Holden said. The words were harsh, but there was affection in them.

"Roger that," Alex said. He didn't sound offended.

"You know," Holden continued, "we've got what seems like an engineering problem. And the best engineer in this solar system is locked up on that other ship. Why don't you call them and point that out?"

"I'll do that," Alex replied.

"I'll see if there's anything we can do from this end."

"Miller," Alex said. Basia had no idea what that meant.

"Yeah," Holden said.

"You take care of yourself down there."

"Affirmative. You take care of my ship. Holden out."

"Look," Alex said, not quite yelling, "I've run the damn numbers. You're going down. It might take two weeks if you're lucky, but that ship is gonna be scrapin' atmosphere and catching on fire."

"Heard you the first time," the face on the other end said. A man named Havelock. Alex had called him after the conversation with Holden. He'd stopped off on his way up from the engine room to don a fresh uniform and comb his thinning black hair. He looked very official. It didn't seem to impress Havelock very much.

"So stop dickin' me around and turn Nagata loose to help us figure this shit out," Alex said.

"And that's where you lose me," Havelock replied with a tight smile. He was a compact, pale-skinned man with a military-style haircut. He radiated the self-assured physical competence carried by soldiers and professional security people. To Basia, a Belter who'd lived under the thumbs of two different inner planet governments, it said, *I know how to beat people up. Don't make me show you.*

"I don't see how—" Alex started.

"Yes," Havelock interrupted him. "We're all going to crash if we can't get the reactors back online. I agree. What I don't get is how me releasing my prisoner fixes that."

"Because," Alex said, visibly gulping as he bit the word off, "XO Nagata is the best engineer there is. If someone is going to figure this problem out and save all of our asses, it's probably going to be her. So stop keeping the potential solution to our problem locked in your jail." He smiled at the camera and turned off the microphone before adding, "you pig-headed idiot."

"I think maybe you're underestimating my engineering team," Havelock replied, still with his smug smile. "But I hear what you're saying. Let me see what I can do."

"Gee, that would be great," Alex said. He somehow managed to make it sound sincere. He turned off the comm station. "You smug sack of flaming pig shit."

"What do we do now?" Basia asked.

"The hardest thing of all. We wait."

Basia floated in a crash couch on the ops deck. His mind drifted from a fitful half sleep to groggy wakefulness and back again. A few workstations away, Alex was fiddling with the controls and muttering to himself.

As he drifted, sometimes Basia was on the *Rocinante*, his mind worrying over the missing rumble of the fusion reactor like a tongue searching the gap left by a lost tooth. And then, without transition, he'd be drifting down the icy corridors of his lost home on Ganymede. Sometimes they were the peaceful tunnels and domes that had been his family's home for so many years.

Other times, they were filled with rubble and corpses, the way they'd been when Basia had fled.

The long flight on the *Barbapiccola* afterward had been hellish. The endless days trapped in a cabin barely large enough for one person, but housing two full families. The growing sense of despair as port after port after port turned them away. No one needing a ship full of refugees flooding their docks in the middle of what looked like the solar system's first all-out war.

Basia had drifted through that like a ghost as well. He'd thought he was saving his family when he put them on the ship. But he'd left a dying son behind and trapped the rest of them on a leaky old cargo ship with nowhere to go.

That moment when the captain of the *Barbapiccola* had called them all together and told them about the rings and the worlds on the other side had felt like a revelation. When he'd asked if any of them wanted to try and take one of the new worlds, make a home there, not one voice had been raised in dissent. Even just the word, *home*, made it impossible to argue. So they'd flown through the gate, past the confused and disorganized ships around it and in the hub, and come out the other side into the Ilus system. They'd found a world with oxygen and water, a muddy brown-and-blue ball from orbit, but so beautiful once they'd landed that people lay on the ground and wept.

The months that followed were brutal. The painful medication and exercise to get their bodies used to the heavy gravity. The slow building of the dwellings. The desperate attempts to grow some, any, food in the scraps of soil they'd brought down from the *Barb*. The discovery of the rich lithium veins and the realization that they might have something to sell and become self-sustaining, followed by the backbreaking labor to pull the ore from the ground with primitive tools. All worth it, though.

A home.

Interlude: The Investigator

—it reaches out it reaches out it reaches out it reaches out—

One hundred and thirteen times a second, it reaches out, and its reach broadens. If the signal came, the acknowledgment, it could stop, and it does not stop. It reaches out, and in reaching finds new ways to reach. It improvises, it explores. It is unaware of doing so. The systems it activates broaden it. Then it reaches out in ways it could not before. Because it is not aware, it has no memory, feels no joy. The parts of it that are aware dream and suffer as they always have. It is not aware of them.

It reaches out and finds more power. Something fails. Many things fail. Something that was once a woman cries out in silent horror and fear. Something that was once a man prays and names it Armageddon. It reaches out. It narrows only slightly as it reaches out. And at its center, the empty place gains definition. Patterns begin to match, simplifying into lower-energy structures. The investigator thinks of these as solutions. A model of the world is built within it, and of the satellites that surround it. The places it cannot go begin to relate, gaining definition. The abstract architecture of connection and the abstract model of geography correlate.

It builds the investigator, and the investigator looks, but does not know. It kills the investigator. It builds the investigator, and the investigator looks, but does not know. It kills the investigator. It builds the investigator, and the investigator looks but does not know, and it does not kill the investigator. It is not aware of a change, that a pattern has broken. The investigator is aware, and it wonders, and because it wonders it looks, and because it looks, the investigator exceeds its boundary conditions, and it kills the investigator.

It builds the investigator.

Something knows.

The investigator hesitates. A pattern has broken, and it isn't aware that a pattern has broken, but a part of it is. A part of it grasps at the change and tries to tell the investigator. And the investigator stops. Its thoughts are careful as a man walking in a minefield. The investigator hesitates, knows a pattern has been broken. Breaks it a little more. The dead place becomes better defined. It reaches out, and it does not kill the investigator. The investigator exceeds its boundary conditions, and it does not kill the investigator. The investigator considers the dead space, the structure, the reaching out, the reaching out, the reaching out.

The investigator licks his lips, he doesn't have a mouth. He adjusts his hat, he doesn't have a hat. He wishes in a distant way that he had a beer, he has no body and no passion. He turns his attention to the dead space, to the world, to how you solve unsolvable problems. How you find things that aren't there. What happens when you do.

Chapter Thirty-Four: Holden

Affirmative. You take care of my ship. Holden out."

Holden killed the connection to the *Rocinante* and leaned back against the alien tower with a sigh. It was a mistake. The rainfall had been incessant since the planetary explosion, and even though it had slowed to a drizzle over the last day, the water still sheeted down the outside of the tower. And, unfortunately, down his back and into his pants.

"Bad news?" Amos asked. He stood a few feet away holding his poncho up with one arm to keep the rain out of his face.

"If it weren't for bad news," Holden replied, "we'd have no news at all."

"The latest?"

"The shuttle with the relief supplies was shot down by the planetary defenses," Holden said. "Which seem to have activated when the planet blew up. And they're running their usual 'high energy is a threat' program."

"So like the gate station did back when we were in the slow zone and Medina Station was still a battleship," Amos said.

"You mean the good old days?" Holden asked bitterly. "Yes. Like that."

"So we just need to get everyone to shut their reactors down like last time?"

"Seems this defense network has a new trick. They took care of that problem for us. Made fusion stop working."

"You're fucking kidding me," Amos said, then barked out a laugh. "They know how to do that?"

"On the upside, if we can't figure out how to get relief supplies from orbit, I'll die of hunger long before the cancers get me."

"Yeah," Amos agreed with a nod, "that'll be a plus."

"The people in orbit don't even have that long. Alex thinks we might see the *Israel* or the *Barb* come down in about ten days. We'll be hungry enough by that point that we won't be able to see all the food in the solar system falling out of the sky on fire with a detached sense of irony."

"And," Amos added with a shrug, "all our friends will be on those ships."

"Yeah. That too." Holden squeezed his eyes shut and pinched the bridge of his nose hard enough to hurt, hoping the pain would help clear his head. It didn't. All he could think of was Naomi riding the *Edward Israel* on its fiery descent.

He and Amos stood quietly outside the alien tower for several minutes, gentle rain washing over them. Holden hadn't stood in the rain in years. If everything else weren't falling apart around him, it might almost have been pleasant. Amos let his poncho fall down around his neck and rubbed the rainwater across his prickly scalp.

"All right," Holden finally said. "I'm heading around to the back of the tower."

"Nobody's back there," Amos said, then closed his eyes and washed his face with a double handful of rain.

"Miller is."

"Right, then you won't need company." Amos shook his head, spraying rain around him like a dog, then trotted off toward the entrance to the alien tower. Holden walked the other direction, carefully avoiding the death-slugs.

"Hey," Miller said as he appeared next to Holden in a flash of blue.

"We need to talk," Holden replied, ignoring the apparent non sequitur. Holden kicked away a death-slug that got too close to his boot. Another was crawling toward Miller's foot, but the detective ignored it. "The planetary defenses seem to have come online. They just shot down a supply shuttle and they've created some sort of field in orbit that's damping nuclear fusion."

"You sure it's just in orbit?" Miller asked and raised one eyebrow.

"Well, the sun hasn't gone out. Should I be expecting that? Miller, is the sun going to go out?"

"Probably not," Miller said with a Belter shrug of his hands.

"Okay, assuming the sun stays on, we're still going to be in a lot of trouble. The ships can't drop us supplies, and without reactors, they'll start to fall out of orbit in the near future."

"All right," Miller said.

"Fix it," Holden replied, taking an aggressive step toward him.

Miller just laughed.

"If not for us, then do it for yourself," Holden said. "That thing linking you to me is a bit of goo on the *Roci*. That burns up too. Fix it because of that if you have to. I don't care why, just do it."

Miller took off his hat and looked up at the sky, humming a tune that Holden didn't recognize. Holden could see the rain falling on his head, beading, and rolling down his face. He could also see the rain falling straight through him. It made a spike of pain shoot through his brain, so he looked away.

"What do you think I can do?" Miller asked. It wasn't a no.

"You got us off lockdown when we were in the slow zone."

"Kid, I keep telling you. I'm a wrench. The defense network problem in the gate hub just happened to be a hex nut. I've got no control here. Not much anyway. And this system is falling apart. Half the planet blowing up might not be the end of that."

"More stuff might explode? What else is left?"

"You're asking me?" Miller laughed again.

"But you're part of this! All this, this protomolecule masters bullshit. If you can't control it, who can?"

"There's an answer to that, but you won't like it."

"Nobody," Holden said. "You're telling me nobody."

"The thing that's turning all this crap on? It just *does* stuff. If the *Rocinante* arms and fires a torpedo at someone, what are the odds a wrench in her machine shop can bring the torpedo back? That's who you're talking to."

"God *damn* it, Miller," Holden said, then ran out of energy mid-sentence. It was less fun being the chosen one and prophet when the gods were violent and capricious and their spokesman was insane and powerless. The rain under his clothes had started to warm up, leaving him feeling covered in slime.

The detective lowered his head, frowning. Thinking.

"You might be able to sneak past them," Miller said.

"How?"

"Well, the defenses are keying on threats. So don't be threatening. You know the network gets itchy with high-energy sources."

"No power sources," Holden said. "Yeah, the shuttle had reactors. Don't get much higher as energy sources go."

"Slow is good too. Not sure if the defenses here key on kinetic energy, but safer to assume they do."

"Okay," Holden said, feeling a brief moment of relief and hope. "Okay, I can work with that. Food, filters, meds, we should be able to bring all those down without pissing it off. Slow drops with airfoils and parachutes. They can rig that from orbit."

"Worth a try, anyway," Miller said without enthusiasm. "So, about this dead spot I need to go north for. You won't like this either, but there's a way to—" He vanished.

"Cap," Amos said, coming around the corner of the tower. "Sorry to interrupt, but that cute scientist is looking for you."

It took Holden a moment. "The biologist?"

"Well, the geologist ain't bad, I guess, but he's not my preferred flavor."

"What does she want?"

"To make more puppy dog eyes at you?" Amos said. "How the fuck should I know?"

"Don't be an asshole."

"Go ask her yourself, then."

"All right," Holden said. "But I need Murtry first. Seen him?"

"Directing traffic by the front door last I saw," Amos replied. "Need me for that?"

Holden noticed that Amos' hand fell to the butt of his pistol when he asked. "What else have you been working on?"

"Death-slug patrol."

"Go do that. I'll chat with Murtry."

Amos gave a mock salute and trotted off toward the tower entrance. Holden pulled out his hand terminal and left a message for Alex filling him in on the supply drop plan. As Amos had said, Holden found Murtry talking to a few members of his security team near the tower's entrance.

"We've found some buried foundations," Wei was saying, pointing over her shoulder in the direction First Landing had once been. "But unless these people had basements, there's nothing left attached to them."

"What about the mines?" Murtry asked her.

"What isn't filled with mud is submerged," Wei replied.

"Well," Murtry said, cocking his head to one side and giving her a humorless smile. "Do we have people who know how to hold their breath?"

"Yes, sir."

"Then send them down to see if anything we can use is under that water, soldier."

"Sir," Wei replied and snapped off a salute. She and two other security people ran off, leaving Murtry and Holden alone.

"Captain Holden," Murtry said, keeping his empty smile.

"Mister Murtry."

"How can I help you today?"

"I think I might have a solution to our resupply problem," Holden said. "If you're willing to work with me on it."

Murtry's humorless grin relaxed a bit. "That's pretty high on my to-do list. Fill me in."

Holden summed it all up—the hypothesis of the alien systems tracking high-energy sources, the possibility of slow air drops. He couched it in terms of what they'd seen in the slow zone the first time humanity had gone through the gates and left Miller out. Murtry stood utterly still as he spoke, his expression not changing so much as a millimeter. When Holden finished, Murtry nodded once.

"I'll call up to the *Israel* and start having them put packages together," Murtry said.

Holden breathed a sigh of relief. "I have to admit, I kind of expected you to fight me on this."

"Why? I'm not a monster, Captain. I will kill if it's necessary to do my job, but your Mister Burton's much the same. All of these people dying down here helps my cause not at all. I just want the squatters to go away as soon as we figure out the power problem."

"Great," Holden said, and then a moment later, "You don't actually care about them, do you? All this time you were fighting against them. Now you're willing to help, but it's only because it's helping them leave. You'd be just as happy if they all died."

"That would also solve my problems, yes," Murtry said.

"Just wanted to make sure you knew I knew," Holden said, biting back the *asshole* that tried to follow.

He found Amos working with the locals on death-slug defense. They were using the wadded ponchos and plastic water jugs split into squares to block off the smaller entrances to the alien ruins.

They put sheeting over the windows, stuffed shirts and torn pant legs into the smaller holes, and dug trenches in front of the large openings. The trenches filled with muddy rainwater like tiny moats, and the slugs avoided them.

Without a word, Holden pitched in with the trench digging. It was unpleasant work, with rain and muck getting under his clothes and chafing his skin as he moved. They dug with makeshift tools made out of tent poles and flat pieces of plastic that fell apart periodically and had to be put back together. The soil was stony and heavy with moisture and the occasional slug corpse. It was the sort of miserable physical labor that drove all other thoughts from Holden's mind while he worked. He didn't think about starving to death or Naomi trapped in a prison cell drifting slowly toward a fiery death or his own inability to make anything on the planet safe or sane or better.

It was perfect.

Carol Chiwewe asked him to check around to the back of the tower for a tarp they had left behind, and Miller ruined it all by reappearing the second he rounded the corner away from other eyes.

"—get into the material transfer network," he said as if he'd never stopped talking. "I think we can use it to move north to the spot we're looking for, or at least get pretty close."

"Dammit, Miller, I was this close to not thinking about you."

Miller looked him over with a critical eye, taking in his soggy muck-covered exterior. "You look like hell, kid."

"See the lengths I'm willing to go for a moment's peace?"

"Impressive. So when can we head out?"

"You don't quit," Holden said. He walked across the muddy ground to the tarp he'd been looking for. It was covered with the deadly slugs. He grabbed it by one corner and slowly lifted, trying to get all the slugs to slide off away from him. Miller followed, hands in pockets, watching him work.

"Watch out for that one," he said, pointing at a slug close to Holden's fingers.

"I see it."

"You're no good to me if you drop dead."

"I said I see it."

"So, about going north," Miller continued. "Not sure how much of the material transfer network is actually functioning, so it won't necessarily be an easy trip. We should start as soon as we can."

"Material transfer network?"

"Big underground transport system. Faster than walking. Ready to go?"

The slug slid a few centimeters closer to his fingers, and Holden dropped the tarp with a curse. "Miller," he said, rounding on him suddenly. "I am so far from giving a shit about your needs I can't even see it from here."

The old detective had the grace to look chagrined before he gave a tired shrug. "It might help."

"What," Holden said, "might help?"

"Going north. Whatever's up there seems to damp out the network. Maybe we can use it to kill the defenses and get your ship off lockdown."

"If you're lying to me to get me to do what you want, I swear I will have Alex tear the *Roci* apart looking for whatever clump of goo you're connected to and take a flamethrower to it."

The ghost grimaced, but didn't back down. "I'm not lying because I'm not making any assertions here. This dead spot is exactly what I'm saying it is. A dead spot. Everything else? That's guesswork. But it's more than you've got now, right? Help me, and if there's a way for me to do it, I'll help you. That's the only way this works."

Holden kicked the slug off of his corner of the tarp and waited for the rain to wash its slime trail away, then picked it back up and resumed sliding the rest of the creatures off.

"Even if I wanted to, I can't yet," he said. "Not until I'm sure the colonists aren't going to die here. Let me get some supply drops safely down, get everyone in a decent shelter away from the death-slugs, and then we'll talk about it."

"Deal," Miller said, then disappeared in a puff of blue fireflies. One of the men from the colony, a tall skinny Belter with dark skin and an amazing shock of white hair, rounded the corner.

"What you doin'? Kenned babosa malo got you."

"Sorry," Holden said, giving the tarp a sharp snap to flick the rest of the slugs off it. He helped the Belter fold it up.

Only he'd have to stop thinking of them as Belters, wouldn't he? These people lived on a planet, in a solar system across the galaxy from Sol. *Belter* was no longer a word with any meaning for them. They called themselves colonists now. And someday, if they were able to stay on Ilus and actually make a home of it, what? Ilusites?

"Médico buscarte," the Ilusian said.

"Lucia?"

"Laa laa, RCE puta."

"Oh, right, Amos told me," Holden said. "Guess I better go find out what she wants."

The Belter, the Ilusite, whatever he was, muttered "puta" again and spat to one side. Holden walked through the miserable warm rain past the trenches full of water and dead slugs and the plastic glued over the walls and the cracks stuffed with muddy rags. He hopped over the last trench to get inside the tower, then scraped the mud off his boots and followed the passageways to the structure's large central chamber. Lucia was there working with the chemical analysis team on the water purifying project. She shot him a tight smile as he entered, and he started walking toward her simply because she seemed like the only one happy to see him.

"Holden. I mean, um, Jim," Elvi said, stepping in front of him. "We have a problem?"

"Several," Holden said.

"No, I mean a new one. In about four days everyone in the colony is going to be blind."

Chapter Thirty-Five: Elvi

Holden blinked, shook his head, and then he laughed. Elvi was torn between worry that he thought she was joking and a kind of glowing admiration. She'd been afraid that he'd be angry. She'd heard about people laughing in the face of danger, and that was exactly what this was. She smoothed her hands against her jumpsuit, uncomfortably aware of how dirty she was, how dirty they all were.

This day just keeps on giving," he said. Then, "Blind why?"

"It's the clouds," Elvi said. "Or really, what's in them. They're green. I mean, when they're not—" She nodded toward the window at the low gray overcast sky. "Normally, they're green. There's a photosynthetic organism that spends part of its life cycle in the clouds, and apparently it's a pretty successful organism all around the planet, because all of this that's come down has some in it. It was a very dry climate before this, so there probably wasn't much opportunity for exposure. But with the rain and the flood, pretty much everyone's come in contact. And it's salt tolerant."

The chemical deck chimed, and Elvi moved toward it automatically, her eyes still on Holden. But Fayez, Lucia, and one of the other squatters were already lifting out the sack of clean water and fitting a new bag in place.

"Is that a problem?" Holden said. "How does salt figure into it?"

"We're salty," Elvi said, and was immediately uncomfortable with her phrasing. Her hands seemed too large and awkward in a way they usually weren't. "What I mean is, we've seen infections with this organism before. It does well in tears and tear ducts. And then eyes."

"Eyes," Holden said.

"Lucia saw one case before the...the storm? Once the organism got into the vitreous humor, it's in a novel environment that seems to suit it really well, and exponential growth's pretty normal in those conditions. So that winds up blocking the light from hitting the retina, and—"

Holden held up his hands, palm out. She found herself moving in toward him, ready to put her palms against his. She stopped herself.

"I thought the things that lived here had a whole different biology. How can they infect us?"

"It's not an infection like a virus," she said. "It's not hijacking our cells or anything. We're just a new, nutrient-rich environment and this little guy found a way to exploit it. It's not *trying* to make us blind. It's just that the extracellular matrix is a really easy path into the eyeball for it, and it's really happy when it gets there. Explosive growth is something you see in any kind of invasive species coming into a new environment. No competition."

Holden ran a hand through his hair. When he spoke, his voice was soft, like he was speaking mostly to himself.

"Apocalyptic explosions, dead reactors, terrorists, mass murder, *death-slugs*, and now a blindness plague. This is a *terrible* planet. We should not have come here."

"I'm sorry," she said, putting her hand on his arm. He had a very solid arm. Muscular. He put his own hand over hers and her heart picked up a little. She hated feeling like a schoolgirl with her first crush, but she also thrilled to it. *Just stay focused*, she thought, *a little dignity*.

"Okay, Doctor Okoye."

"Elvi."

"Elvi, I need you and Doctor Merton to do whatever you have to do to take care of this. I think I've found a way to get supplies down from orbit, but I don't see any way to get anyone up the well, or where to put them if we did. So if I'm right, I can get you whatever supplies we have up there. But I need you to fix this."

"I will," Elvi said, nodding. She didn't have any idea how she could keep that promise, but her heart was full to bursting with the determination that she would.

"Anything you need," Holden said, "you just tell me."

Elvi had a sudden, intrusive, and surprisingly graphic thought. She felt a blush crawling up her neck. "All right, Captain," she said. "I want...um...if I could get a spare sampling bag from the *Israel*? I think it would really help."

He let go of her, and she regretted the absence immediately. She shoved her hands into her pockets. He nodded to her, hesitated for a moment as if he were waiting for her to say something more, then moved away into the crowded main room. Elvi bit her lip and swallowed a couple of times until the thickness in her throat subsided. She knew she was being silly and even borderline inappropriate, but the knowledge did nothing to change it.

She stopped at the window, looking out at the gray rain. It was hard to believe that every drop of it contained something that would colonize her body the way that humanity had New Terra. It looked peaceful out there. Vast and rich and beautiful. Even the slow river of floodwater carried the calming, majestic, beautiful sense of nature playing out.

Most of Earth was covered in cities or managed nature preserves about as untamed as a service dog. Mars and the Belt were studded with colonies that had been built and designed to carve a human place in inhuman and lifeless circumstances. This, she realized, was the first place she'd been in her life where she could see true wilderness the way it had been for millennia on Earth. Red in tooth and claw. Deadly and uncaring. Vast, unpredictable, and complex as anything she could imagine.

"You all right?" Lucia asked.

"Overwhelmed," Elvi said. "Fine."

"I've harvested a new sample run from the water purifier," the doctor said. "Help me with the assaying?"

"Of course," Elvi said. "When the sampling bag comes, it'll be easier to send the data back home. Maybe they'll be able to help."

"Well, if they find anything, make sure they send it in an audio file," Lucia said. "I don't know that we're going to be reading much."

"How are we going to do it?" Elvi asked.

"Do what?"

"Do any of it. Eat, rebuild, make clean water, keep the death-slugs out? How are we going to do any of that when none of us can see what we're doing?"

"At a guess," Lucia said, "poorly."

The long New Terran day and the darkness of the clouds made time feel strange. Elvi sat hunched in the little side chamber that Fayez had appropriated for their research lab. The walls were curved in ways that left her thinking of bones. The only opening was high on the wall, and Fayez or Lucia or Sudyam had put a sheet of clear plastic over it to keep the death-slugs out. A bank of white LEDs splashed a cold light across the deep red wall and ceiling. The small green sludge in her makeshift Petri dish could have been algae or fungus or the remains of a salad left weeks too long in the back of her dormitory refrigerator back in upper university. But it wasn't any of those things, and the more she looked at it, the more aware she was of the fact.

There were some similarities to the more familiar kingdoms of life she'd studied before. Lipid boundaries around cells, for instance, appeared to be a good move in design space just the way eyes were, or flight. They seemed to do something similar to mitotic division, though sometimes the cells divided in threes instead of pairs, and she didn't know why. There were other anomalies too, concentrations of some photon-activated molecules that didn't quite make sense.

And what was worse, she couldn't think about it. Couldn't *concentrate*. Whenever her focus slipped, it slipped onto James Holden. The sound of his voice, his despairing and undaunted laughter, the shape of his ass. He haunted her. She realized that she'd gone through four pages of chemical assay data without having any idea what she'd seen, sat back on her heels, and cursed.

"Problem?" Fayez said, stepping through the doorway. His hair was tied back, his face gray with fatigue and streaked with old mud. She wondered, looking at him, how long it had been since he'd slept. She wondered how long it had been since she'd slept. Or eaten for that matter.

"Yes," she said.

He squatted down beside the arch that led back toward the main rooms. The plastic was dark. It was nighttime, then. She hadn't been paying attention.

"What's the rumpus?" Fayez asked. "Is there some new oh-my-god-we're-going-to-die, or are we still coming to appreciate fully the list we've already got."

"I have to find Captain Holden."

Fayez put his head in his hands. "Of course you do."

"I have to clear the air."

Fayez's neck stiffened, and his eyes were wide. "No, Elvi. No, you don't."

"I do," she said. "I know it's inappropriate, but the fact of the matter is that I'm in love with him. It's a distraction, and it's affecting my work. I've tried ignoring it, and it's not helping. So I'll go to him, and we'll talk it through. Just to resolve it and—"

"No no no," Fayez said. "Oh no. That's a terrible, terrible idea. Don't do that."

"You don't understand. I don't want to, but I have to be able to concentrate, and my feelings...my feelings about *him*—"

She rose. Now that she'd said it, it was obvious what had to happen. He'd be sleeping in one of the side rooms like this. Amos would probably be there too as a guard. She could just ask to see him there, in private. And she could unburden herself. She hadn't understood that term before, but she did now. She could unburden herself to him, and he was so kind and so gentle and so thoughtful, he wouldn't laugh at her or turn her away. She would—

"Elvi!" Fayez said again. "Please, please, please do not do this. You aren't in love with James Holden. You don't know James Holden from Adam. You have no idea how close his persona is to the real man, and you've never met the real man. He's on the newsfeeds and he works here. That's all."

"You don't understand."

"Of course I do," Fayez said. "You're scared as hell, you're lonely, and you're horny. Elvi listen to me. You've been in one of the most stressful environments possible for the last two years. First, we were coming to an unknown planet. Then it was an unknown planet with a bunch of people on it who tried to kill you. And then it blew up. And now we're trying to fend off tiny little things that can kill you because you brush up against them while you try to figure out how to keep things from growing in our eyes. No one stays sane in a situation like this."

"Fayez—"

"No! Hear me out. You always cope by ignoring how scared you are and focusing on work, and that's great. Really, whatever gets you through the night, I am absolutely for it. But you're a mammal, Elvi. You're a social animal that derives reassurance from touch, and since we're not a cuddle-puddle culture, that means sex. For two years you've been avoiding workplace romances while all the rest of us have been pairing off and changing partners because we were lonely and scared and that's one way primates reassure themselves and each other. Everyone's been doing this but you."

"I don't—"

"So here you are, freaked out so badly you aren't even clear that you're freaked out, and here comes James Holden, savior of the universe, and *of course* it all comes out sideways. But it's not about him, it's about you. And if you go clear the air with him, either you'll wind up in bed together or you'll be back here weeping into your tissue samples."

Elvi felt her jaw sliding forward, her hands forming fists. Fayez rose to his knees, but not more than that. He reached out an arm to block the archway, grimaced, and pulled it back. When he spoke again, Fayez's voice was softer, gentler.

"Please, we have fucked up everything about coming to this deathtrap of a planet. We have hauled every tribalist, territorial, monkey-brained mistake humanity ever made through the gate and made soup with them here. This thing you're about to do? Please let this be the one mistake we don't make."

"You're telling me," Elvi said, her voice equal parts outrage and ice, "that I just need to get laid?"

Fayez slumped back against the wall, defeated.

"I'm saying you're human, and humans take comfort from each other. I'm saying you don't want Holden for the person he is, because you don't know him, and you're making up a story about him so that you feel okay about taking the thing you need because God forbid you should have a need that isn't all twinned up with romantic love. And…"

He lifted his hands, shook his head, and looked away. The rain pattered against the sheet plastic, tapping like fingernails on stone. Someone far down the hall shouted, and a voice even more distant called back. Elvi crossed her arms.

"And?" she said. "Go on. I don't see why you should stop now."

"And." Fayez sighed. "And I'm right *here*."

It took a moment for her to understand what he was saying. What he was offering. Her laughter was as unstoppable as the storm had been. He pursed his lips and shrugged, his gaze fixed on the wall behind her. She couldn't stop grinning, even though the force of it made her cheeks hurt. And then the hilarity faded a bit. She caught her breath. A flash of distant lightning brightened the window, but no thunder followed it.

She looked down at Fayez. After a moment, he looked up.

"Okay," she said.

Fayez snored when he slept. Not deeply. Not a buzzsaw. Just a soft purring at the back of his throat. Their mud-caked clothes were folded into pillows under their heads. She lay on her back, her knees bent, considering the ceiling and the softness of her own flesh. He was on his side, curled against her for warmth, his legs folded under and around hers. His breath tickled the skin of her collarbone. She wondered what she would do or say if someone walked through the archway, but it was night, and the nights here were very long. There was room in them.

She considered his body, the color of raw honey, with more hair on his chest and legs then she'd expected. Like a caveman, only without any Neanderthal brow ridge. She took a deep breath and let it out slowly, just to see how it felt. She'd always made a rule of not sleeping with her coworkers. She hadn't so much as held someone's hand since the *Israel* had started its long burn for the gate. She'd almost forgotten what sex felt like. And its aftermath.

Fayez coughed, shifted, and she took the chance to draw herself away from him. He sprawled on the floor, face pressed against her clothes, eyes shut. She thought about James Holden, her mind touching gently at her heart, half afraid of what it would find.

"Huh," she said to the room, softly so as to keep Fayez from waking. "I wasn't in love with Holden."

Fayez's breath shifted and his eyes fluttered but didn't open. She thought about trying to get her jumpsuit from him, but he looked so peaceful, she decided to wait. She had expected to feel embarrassed by her nakedness. Ashamed. She didn't.

She sat cross-legged by the chemical assays. In the dish, the green smear from the water sample had shifted a little, throwing off hair-thin runners, exploring its environment. She pulled up the chemical information and started going through it again from the start. When she came to the strange reading of light-activated compounds, she coughed out an impatient sigh. They were chiral, and this was a bi-chiral environment. She was seeing both conformations, and probably for completely different functions. That made sense, then.

She stretched, her spine popping between the shoulder blades, and folded herself forward, her eyes skimming though the data. She took notes of questions to ask Lucia or send back home. She fell into the data, not noticing when Fayez woke, dressed, and left until he draped a blanket over her shoulders. She looked up. Her jumpsuit was still in a pile on the floor. Fayez put a cup of hot tea beside her and kissed the top of her head.

"Good morning, sunshine," he said.

Elvi smiled, leaning back against his shins. "I bet you say that to all the girls."

"You okay?" he asked gently.

Elvi frowned. Was she? Given the circumstances, maybe so.

"I'm looking at this organism," she said, "and, you know, I think I'm beginning to understand it. Here, take a look at these numbers..."

Chapter Thirty-Six: Havelock

The air recycling systems on the *Edward Israel* didn't care where their power came from. Fusion reactor or battery power, it was all the same to them. Havelock's sense that the air had changed, grown hotter and thicker and less able to sustain life, was all in his head. He was aware of being in a steel-and-ceramic tube of air, closed off from any larger, sustaining environment. He'd spent most of his adult life in that situation, and the fact had become as invisible to him as someone on Earth thinking about being held to a spinning celestial object by nothing more than mass, shielded from the fusion reaction of the sun by only distance and air. It wasn't something you thought about until it was a problem.

His monitor was split between Captain Marwick on the left looking harried and cross and the chief of RCE's engineering team and Havelock's own militia on the right.

"I can up the efficiency of the grid enough to get us two, maybe three days," the chief engineer said. His face was flushed, and his jaw jutted forward.

"In theory," Marwick said. "This is an old ship. Things based on theory don't always play out well here."

"We know what kind of grid this is," Koenen said. "It's not guesswork. We have the numbers."

"It's hard facing the fact that numbers are a kind of guesswork, isn't it?" Marwick said.

"Gentlemen," Havelock said, his voice taking the same intonation Murtry's would have had. "I understand the issue."

"She may be dead, but she's still my ship," Marwick said.

"Dead?" the chief engineer said. "We're going to be dead if—"

"Stop now," Havelock said. "Both of you. Just stop. I understand the issue, and I appreciate both of your views. We're not going to do a goddamn thing with any ship modifications until we've loaded the next supply drop for the folks downstairs. Captain, can I have permission for the engineering team to do a sight-only inspection of the grid lines and couplings?"

"Sight only?" Marwick said, eyes narrowed. "If you'll commit to that. Fine line between seeing something and wanting to give it a little pet."

Havelock nodded as if that had been permission. "Chief, put together a crew. Visual inspection only. Give me a report once the drop's gone."

"Sir," the chief engineer said. The word was crisp and a little too loud. The way someone who wasn't in the military thought people in the military sounded. The connection on the right dropped and Captain Marwick resized automatically to fill the screen.

"That man's an asshole."

"He's scared and he's trying to exercise control over...well, anything he can actually exercise control over."

"He's an asshole, and he's forgotten that a few paintball games aren't enough to make him Admiral fucking Nelson."

"I'll keep him in line," Havelock said. *For another ten days, and then it won't matter.*

Marwick nodded once and dropped his connection as well. Havelock took a deep breath and let it out slowly through his nose. He flipped back to his connection request queue. Another thirty messages had come in just while he'd been talking to the captain and the chief. They were all messages from home. From Sol. Requests for interviews and comment from people he'd never met, but not all from people he hadn't seen. Sergio Morales from Nezávislé News. Amanda Farouk from First Response. Mayon Dale from Central Information OPA. Even Nasr Maxwell from Forecast Analytics. The faces and personalities of all the newsfeeds he followed to stay in touch with how things were going back at home were coming to him now. Humanity's attention was pointed out to New Terra. To him.

He didn't like it, and it didn't help.

He went through them one by one, replying with the same canned recording he'd made the first time: "Our hands are full right now addressing the situation on New Terra. Please refer your questions to Patricia Verpiske-Sloan with Royal Charter Energy's public relations division." Blah blah blah. He'd probably be dressed down at some point for doing that much. He was already a little worried that he shouldn't have said his hands were full.

"You all right?" Naomi asked from her cell.

"I'm fine."

"I just ask because you're sighing a lot."

"Am I?"

"Five times in the last minute," Naomi said. "Before the reactor died, it was one every two minutes. On average."

Havelock smiled. "You need a hobby."

"Oh, I really do," Naomi said.

He pulled up the drop shipment status page. The insertion point was still eight hours away. The longest fabrication run he could do was about six hours, then. If Murtry and the others needed anything that took longer than that, they'd have to wait. He started cycling through the list. Food. Spare water bags for the chem deck they'd salvaged. Acetylene and oxygen for the salvage and repair crew. He checked the weight. He didn't want to skip anything that might be useful downstairs, but it wouldn't help anyone to scatter it all across the upper atmosphere because a chute failed.

"You're going to be famous when we get back," Naomi said.

"Hmm?"

"You're the face of it now. Everything that's happening here? That message you made is what all the feeds are going to be playing."

"That message was so information-free it was almost sterile," Havelock said. "It's how you say 'no comment' without sounding like you're trying to hide something."

"They won't care. Maybe they don't even run your words. Just the image of you with the audio turned low while they talk over it."

"Well, that's just great," Havelock said, sifting the drop contents. The emergency lighting had batteries, and while they probably wouldn't be enough to set off the planetary defenses, he didn't want to risk it. He tried to remember if there was anything else that carried its own energy supply. It wasn't an issue he was used to worrying about.

"It was like that for us," Naomi said. "Well, for him, really. Even before Eros."

"What was?"

"Being the face of something. Looking back, I can see where it happened. And then he was that guy who'd been shot at by Mars. And then Eros."

"True enough," Havelock said. "There are probably people who haven't heard of James Holden and the *Rocinante*, but they're not the kind of people who watch newsfeeds. He seems to bear up under it pretty well, though."

"Why Mister Havelock, I do believe that was sarcasm."

He switched to the packing schematic. The computer had taken all the packages and lined them up in six different configurations, depending on whether density, aerodynamics, or even weight distribution was the highest priority. He turned the imaged with his fingers, imagining each of them in turn falling through the buffeting, violent high atmosphere of New Terra.

"I just mean that it doesn't seem to bother him," he said.

"Honestly, he's barely aware of it," Naomi said.

"Come on. You're telling me he doesn't get off on it? Just a little?"

"He doesn't get off on it, even a little," Naomi said. "I've known men that would. But that's not Jim."

"You two are a couple, right?"

"Yes."

"Well, I'd call him a lucky man, except he's involved with this utter clusterfuck of a planet," Havelock said as he chose one of the compromise packing schemes. "The only thing I'm going to be the face of is a long, slow death that everyone in the system can watch and be glad they aren't here."

He switched to the fulfillment tree view. The remaining jobs that needed to be fabbed were all in queue. He had the feeling he was missing something, but it took a few seconds to remember what. He switched back to the inventory and added in a little box of oncocidals. For James Holden.

"How well did you know Miller?" Naomi asked. "Were you close?"

"We were partners," Havelock said. "He kept me out of trouble a couple times when I was in over my head. Or when I was being stupid. Ceres right before the OPA took over wasn't a good place for an Earther."

"Did he ever strike you as...I don't know. Weird?"

"He was a cop on Ceres," Havelock said. "We were all weird. Are you about ready for your big outing?"

Naomi laced her fingers through the grate of the cell. Her expression was amused. "That time of the day already, is it?"

"It is the priority of Royal Charter Energy to see that prisoners in its care are treated humanely in accordance with corporate policy and interplanetary law," he said, the same way he did every time. It had become something like a joke between them, funny not because it was funny, but because it was familiar.

"Does seem kind of pointless," Naomi said. "I mean, if we're all going to die."

"I know," Havelock said, surprised at the tightness in his chest. "But it's what we've got. So I'll take it."

He unstrapped himself and floated over to the restraints locker, punching in his code. The locker dispensed an anklet, and he tossed it across the space. Naomi caught it with her fingertips and drew it gently through. She fixed it around her left ankle and fed the two ends together. The anklet hissed, and the diagnostic light went green. Havelock checked his hand terminal. The anklet read as ready. No anomalies, no errors. He opened the cell, and Naomi floated out, stretching. Her paper jumpsuit crackled with every motion.

"Shall we?" Havelock asked.

"I've been looking forward to it all day," Naomi said.

The gymnasium was fuller than usual. The uncertainty—the fear—drove some people toward exercise. Havelock didn't know if it was the sense of action that brought them or the need for exhaustion, the drive to wear themselves down so far that even the fact that they were flying dead over an empty planet and the nearest help was over a year away. Or maybe it was just a way to self-medicate. Endorphins could be wonderful things. He escorted Naomi to a resistance gel box, then took the weight trainer next to her.

The crew at the other machines pretended not to watch them. Most of their expressions were the careful blank of poker faces, but a few were angry. Of the angry people most were focused on her, but a few—Belters mostly—shot accusing glances at him. Havelock pretended to ignore them as he worked the major muscle groups in his back and legs. Any fast movements, and he'd have his weapon drawn, though. Keeping her alive and himself whole was the job. That and trying to hold everyone together until the ship burned up.

Sweat adhered to his skin, tiny dots spreading, touching, pooling. If he worked long enough, he could wind up in a cocoon of his own sweat. He stopped between sets to wick his face dry, and then also Naomi's. She nodded her thanks, but didn't speak.

When they were done, he opened the gel box and let her out. One of the environmental techs—a Belter with pale hair and a pug nose named Orson Kalk—floated over to claim it next.

"Tu carry caba a oksel, schwist," he said, and Naomi laughed.

"Shikata ga fucking nai, sa sa?" she said.

"Come on," Havelock said. "Let's get moving."

The Belter technician put himself in the gel, and Naomi launched across the room back toward the hall that led to his office and her cell. Havelock looked over his shoulder the whole way back. He didn't feel comfortable until she was back in her cell with the grate closed and locked. He pulled a fresh uniform and some wipes from the locker and fed them through to her before he turned on the privacy shield. He pulled himself back to his crash couch, listening to the soft sounds as she stripped off her old uniform, bathed, and put on the fresh. She was right. The privacy shields on the cells didn't stop sound for shit. He checked his queue. Fifty-seven more requests for comment, and none of them anyone he wanted to speak with. He sent them the canned answer again.

He closed his eyes, trying to judge by how comfortable it was to keep them closed whether he'd be able to sleep. He thought so now, but ever since the reactors had shut down, it was easier to fantasize about resting than to rest.

His monitor chirped. Murtry was on the line. He accepted the connection.

The man on the screen was the one Havelock knew, and he wasn't. Murtry's face had never had much padding to it, but he looked gaunt now. The steely focus Havelock was used to seeing wasn't there, and it took a few seconds to realize it was because Murtry wasn't making the effort to see him.

"You there, Havelock?"

"Yes, sir. How's it going down there, sir?"

"It could be better," Murtry said. "I need a status update on the drop."

"Oh. It's progressing well. We should have it packed and ready for drop in...ah. Looks like six hours and change."

"All right."

"Are you not getting the security group alerts, sir? Should I run diagnostics on them?"

"I'm getting them, but I can't read 'em," Murtry said. His tone was as calm and conversational as if he hadn't just admitted he was losing his sight. "So once this drop is done, I want a new priority for the next drop."

"Of course."

"We need to construct a semi-permanent shelter down here. Simple enough design that we can put it together even if we can't see what we're doing all that well. Sturdy enough to last...well, shit, two to four years, I suppose. See what you can find in the specs. If there's nothing on board that fits the bill, you can query the databases back home, but I'd rather not miss too many drop windows. I'm not sure how much longer the people down here are going to be up for working."

"What dimensions do you need?"

"Doesn't matter. Whatever's fast and sturdy."

Havelock frowned. The sounds from the prisoner's cell were gone. He didn't know if she was listening. Probably she was. He couldn't see how it mattered. "Is there anything functional I should be looking for?"

Murtry shook his head. His gaze caught the camera for a moment, then let it go. "If this expedition doesn't leave survivors, I want to make damned sure that when the next wave shows up, there's something with a roof on it waiting for them, and that it has RCE printed on it."

"Planting a flag, sir?"

"I think of it as a minimum fallback position," Murtry said. "Can you do it?"

"I can."

"Good man. I'll be in touch."

"Is there anything else you need down there?"

"Nah," Murtry said. "Plenty of things I'd want, but get me that shelter fast enough we can put it up, and we'll have what we need."

The connection went dead. Havelock whistled low between his teeth. The privacy shield on Naomi's cell dropped.

"Hey," he said.

"Your boss's plan is to build a shed strong enough to be a head-stone when the next group of idiots comes out here to die. I can't decide if that man's a nihilist or the second most idealistic man I've ever met."

"Might be room for both."

"Might be," Naomi said. And then a moment later, "Are you all right?"

"Me? I'm fine."

"Are you sure? Because you're in a ship in decaying orbit, and the man you look up to like a father just told you he was getting ready to die."

"I don't look up to him like a father," Havelock said.

"All right."

"He has a plan. I'm sure he has a plan."

"His plan is that we all die," Naomi said.

In null g, tears didn't fall so much as build up, sheeting over his eyes until everything looked like it was underwater. Drowned. He wiped them away with his sleeve, but there was still too much moisture running across his lenses, tiny waves that shook the walls. It took almost a minute to bring his breath back under control.

"Well, that must have been amusing for you," he said bitterly.

"No," she said. "But if you've got a spare tissue, I'd take it. This uniform doesn't absorb for crap."

When he looked over, she also had a sheen of tears filling her eye sockets. Havelock hesitated, then unstrapped himself, grabbed the tiny, hard puck of a hand towel, and slid over to her.

He passed the puck through the grating, and she pressed it to her eyes, letting the water from them darken the cloth and letting it expand and unfold on its own.

"I'm scared as hell," Havelock said.

"Me too."

"I don't want to die."

"I don't either."

"Murtry doesn't care."

"No," Naomi said. "He doesn't."

Words rose in his throat, clogging it. For a moment, he thought he might start weeping again. He was too tired. He'd been working too long under too much stress. He was getting emotionally labile. Maudlin. The knot in his throat didn't fade.

"I think," he said, struggling with each syllable, "that I took the wrong contract."

"Know better next time," she said.

"Next time."

She put her fingers through the grate and he pinched her fingertip gently between his thumb and forefinger. For a long moment, they floated there together: prisoner and guard, Belter and Earther, corporate employee and government saboteur. None of it seemed to matter as much as it used to.

Chapter Thirty-Seven: Elvi

The data and analysis came back in a disorganized lump, some from the expert systems on the *Israel*, some from the RCE workgroups back on Luna, Earth, and Ganymede. There was no synthesis, no easily digested summary of the findings. Instead it was opinion and speculation, suggested tests—only some of which were remotely possible with the equipment she had—and data analysis. Between Lucia's medical reports of the early cases among the squatters and Elvi's observations from after the deluge, there was just enough information to fuel a thousand theories and not enough to draw any real conclusions. And Elvi was the head of the local workgroup, and the only person in the universe with access to test subjects and new information.

The death-slugs were relatively simple. The toxic compound was a complex carbon ring with a nitrogenous sheet coming off it that looked superficially related to tetrodotoxin, and appeared to be part of the slug's motility system rather than an anti-predation adaptation. How exactly it crossed into the blood was still mysterious, but the slime had a half dozen r-chiral elements that no one had yet bothered to examine extensively. Whatever new knowledge arose from later study, for Elvi's purposes the answers were all there: neurotoxin, no antidote, try not to touch them. Done.

The eye flora, on the other hand, was more complex. The labs on Luna and Ganymede were working with algal models, treating the growth as if it were an invasive species that had entered a naïve tide pool. The Earth workgroup was arguing that the better model was actually a photosensitive mineral structure. Working from what little medical data had survived the storm, the *Israel*'s expert system suggested that the blindness was less from the foreign mass in the vitreous humor and more from the way that the living organism scattered light. That was very good news because it suggested that killing the organism and breaking down the optically active structures would lead to a fairly rapid return of function. There would be floaters in all their eyes, but most people had those, and the brain was decent at compensating for them.

How to go about killing them, though, was obscure. And time was at a premium. There was a decided spike in white blood cells, so their bodies were trying to clean the invaders out. It just wasn't working.

For her, the symptoms had started with just a little scratchiness around her eyelids no worse than seasonal allergies back at home. Then there was a little whitish discharge and mild headache. And then, seven hours after she first noticed it, the world began to blur a little and take on a greenish hue. That was when she knew for certain that she was going to be blinded by it too.

Fear and practicality were changing the shape of the refugee camp even within the physical constraints of the ruins. People who had gone to the farther parts of the structure were pulling back in now. The need for space and privacy were giving way to the fear of the slugs and the weather and the dread of their growing impairment. The increased density mostly showed itself to

Elvi as a change in the ambient sound. Louder voices in conversation that ran together until she felt like she was doing research in the back of a train station. Sometimes it was comforting to have all those human sounds around her, sometimes it was annoying. For the most part, she ignored it.

"Are you doing all right, Doctor?"

Elvi turned from the chemistry deck. Carol Chiwewe stood in the arch that passed for a doorway. She looked tired. And blurry. And vaguely green. Elvi rubbed her eyes to clear them, even though she knew intellectually it wouldn't make any difference. Rain pattered softly against the plastic sheeting. Elvi almost didn't notice it anymore.

"Fine," she said. "You have the new count?"

"We caught forty-one of the little fuckers today," Carol said. "That's an uptick, isn't it? I thought if things dried out a little, they'd start going away."

"Is it drying out?"

"No. It's raining less, though. I hoped."

"Too early to call it significant," Elvi said, entering the data in its field. Tracking the number of death-slugs was just one more of a dozen studies she was juggling now. "The overall trend is still down, and there may be a cycle within the next few days."

"It would be good if they slept at night. Probably too much to hope for, though."

"Probably," Elvi said. "They're normally subterranean. They're not likely to be diurnal."

"We're running out of food," Carol said. Her voice didn't change its inflections.

"The drops are helping," Elvi said.

"The drops won't last forever. There has to be something on this planet we can eat."

"There isn't," Elvi said.

Carol said something obscene under her breath, and it sounded like despair. She sighed. "All right. See you again next hour."

"Thank you."

Behind her, Fayez yawned and stretched. She'd meant to nap with him, but she hadn't quite gotten away from the deck. She squinted, checking the time. Fayez had been asleep for three hours.

"Did I miss anything?" he asked.

"Science," she said. "You missed science."

"Well, damn. Can I borrow your notes?"

"Nope, you'll just have to hire a tutor."

He chuckled. "Did you remember to eat?"

"No."

"At last. A way I can be useful. Stay here, and I'll come back with a bar of undifferentiated foodlike product and some filtered water."

We're running out of food.

"Thank you," she said. "And while you're out there, see if you can find Yma and Lucia. They were going to be doing ocular assessments of everyone."

"The blind studying the blind," Fayez said. "It's like graduate school all over again. I'll track them down. You should take a break. Rest your eyes."

"I will," Elvi lied. Her eyes—all their eyes—would soon be getting plenty of rest. Growing up, Elvi's aunt had been blind and still perfectly functional, but she'd been living in a farming arcology in Trento. Elvi was on a planet with no sustainable agriculture, an inedible ecosystem, and where touching the wrong thing would kill her on the spot. Context was everything. Her hand terminal chimed. A new batch of reports and letters from the Ganymede group. She opened them with a sigh. If she took time to read all the suggestions they were coming up with, she wouldn't have time for anything else. She picked one at random and opened it. She had to increase the font to read it, but switching to bright red lettering on a black background helped a little. If the invading organism followed the same growth curve as yeast...

"Success!" Fayez said. "I have returned with sustenance and Lucia. And you aren't even pretending to have taken a break."

"Nope," Elvi said, taking the hard, palm-sized cake of emergency rations from him and turning to the doctor. "What have we found?"

"Good news and bad. Almost a hundred percent infection rate," Lucia said, sinking to the floor beside her. "The progression is slower in children than adults, it seems, but only slightly."

"What about RCE versus First Landers?"

"I haven't seen all the data Yma collected. She was working with your people mostly. My impression is that there's no difference. Also in the bad news column, it appears to be much more aggressive than the earlier, isolated cases."

Elvi took a bite of the bar. It tasted like unsweetened fruitcake and smelled like potting soil and it sucked up all the saliva in her mouth like a sponge.

"Higher initial load?" Elvi said around the puck of food in her mouth. "It was so arid before, there might not have been as many infectious particles."

"Few enough that our immune systems could identify them as foreign and kick them out," Lucia said.

"Can they do that?" Fayez asked. "I thought these things were a completely different biology. Do our immune systems even work on them?"

"Not as efficiently," Lucia said. She sounded tired. "But if the storm was loaded with them, they'd swamp what defenses we do have."

"And then," Elvi said, "everyone gets it."

"Yes," Lucia said. "Only no."

Elvi opened her eyes again. Lucia was smiling. "Good and bad, remember? We have one man with no growth."

"None?"

"Even if it were only massively delayed growth, I know what the early signs should look like. Nothing."

"Could he…could he not have been exposed?"

"He was exposed."

Elvi felt a bubble of pure joy open in her chest. It was like getting an unexpected present. A flash of lightning brightened the room for a moment, and she wondered why it was green until she remembered.

"So we've got the one-eyed man who's going to be king?" Fayez said. "I mean, better one than none, but I'm not seeing the long-term solve here."

"We've found treatments and vaccines for any number of diseases by studying people who were naturally immune," Elvi said. "This is a toehold."

"Right," Fayez said, rubbing his eyes. "I'm sorry. I may not be at my best right now. I've been under a little stress lately."

Elvi smiled at the little joke. "Will he consent to testing?" she asked.

"Do we care?" Fayez said.

"I haven't had the chance to ask yet," Lucia said. "It was hard enough getting the initial screening done."

"Why?" Elvi asked. "Who is it?"

Holden was at the entrance to the main room. Whatever hues his clothes had been, they were the color of mud now, same as for everyone else; mud, exhaustion, tears, and fear were the new uniform for the RCE and the citizens of First Landing alike. His hair was slicked back and greasy. The beginnings of a spotty, moth-eaten beard mottled his cheeks and the top of his neck. Her failing vision softened away the lines of age and stress and left him a pleasant-enough-looking but unremarkable man. She remembered all the times she'd generated excuses to spend time in his company. It hardly seemed plausible that it was the same person.

She steeled herself and crossed the room.

"Captain Holden? Can I have a moment?"

"I'm really busy right now. Is this something that can wait?"

"It isn't," she said.

Holden grimaced, the expression there and gone again almost too quickly to register. "All right. How can I help you?"

Elvi licked her lips, thinking about how to present the explanation. She didn't have any idea how much background he had in biology, so she figured it was better to start low.

"Captain, you are a very special, very important person—"

"Wait."

"No, no, I—"

"Really. Wait. Look, Doctor Okoye. Elvi. I've been feeling a kind of tension between us for a while now, and I've just been pretending not to. Ignoring it. And that was probably a bad call on my part. I was just trying to make it all go away so we wouldn't have to say anything, but I'm in a very committed, very serious relationship, and while some of my parents weren't monogamists, this relationship is. Before we go any farther, I need to be clear with you that nothing like that can happen between us. It's not you. You're a beautiful, intelligent woman and—"

"The organism that's blinding us," she said. "You're immune to it. I need to get blood samples. Maybe tissue."

"I'll help any way I can, but you have understand that—"

"That's why you're special. You're immune. That's what I was talking about."

Holden stopped, his mouth half open, his hands out before him, patting the air reassuringly. For three interminable heartbeats, he was silent. And then, "Oh. *Oh*. I thought you were—"

"The eye assessment that Doctor Merton did—"

"Because I thought...Well, I'm sorry. I misunderstood—"

"There was. The tension? You were talking about? There was some tension. But there's not anymore," Elvi said. "At all."

"Okay," Holden said. He looked at her for a moment, his head turned a degree to the side. "Well, this is awkward."

"It is *now*."

"How about we never mention this again?"

"I think that would be fine," Elvi said. "We will need you to come let us take some blood samples."

"Of course. Yes. I'll do that."

"And as my vision starts failing, I may need you to come read some of the results to me."

"I will do that too."

"Thank you."

"And thank you, Doctor Okoye."

They each nodded to the other two or three times, apparently unable to break free of the moment. In the end, she spun on her heel and headed back, navigating between the knots and clusters of people camped on the floor of the ruins. One of the squatters was weeping and shaking back and forth. Elvi stepped past him and trotted back to the lab. Yma had arrived in her absence, sitting cross-legged on the floor with Lucia as they compared data. Elvi didn't think her eyes were getting markedly worse until she tried to look over their shoulders. Yma's hand terminal was a blur of white and blue, as empty of usable information as the clouds.

"Did he agree?" Yma asked, her voice tense as stretched wire.

"He did," Elvi said, sitting down at the chemistry deck. The water bag needed to be refilled. A time was going to come—and soon—when the little deck was going to have to stop generating drinking water so that she could use its full resources to run her tests. It wasn't yet. She swapped out the water bags.

"Did you get a history?" Lucia asked.

"A medical history? No. I was thinking perhaps you could do that."

"If you'd like," Lucia said, levering herself up from the ground. "He's back in the main room?"

"He is," Elvi said, kneeling at the deck controls. A smear of mud darkened the readout, but when she wiped it away, she could still make out the letters. "I'll set up a few screenings for his blood."

"Lachrymal fluid too?"

"Probably a good idea," Elvi said. "Just see if there's anything out of the ordinary."

"All right then," Lucia said. When she walked toward the door, her steps had a little hitch in them. A hesitation. Elvi wondered how much longer the doctor would be able to function. The same question for all of them. There wasn't time.

"Anything new in your data?" she asked.

"Consistent," Yma said. "Whatever it is, it doesn't draw a distinction between us and the squatters."

"Well, it's the only one."

The hours passed without Elvi being aware of it. Her mind and attention had taken her outside the world of minutes and hours to a place defined by test runs, transmission lag, and slowed only by her failing sight. Even before Holden's test results came back, she was prying what information she could from the samples of the organism, categorizing it only to find analogies with other plants or animals or fungi. The sense of time running short was a constant, and so, like a noxious smell over an extended period, before long it stopped being something she noticed. And instead, she felt the simple joy of doing what she did best. They had chosen her for the assignment because biological systems made sense to her, working through knotty problems was what she did for fun. For months now, she had been doing a long run of data collection. It had been lovely to see this new world, to watch its first secrets unfold, but it had also been easy. A graduate assistant could have gathered all the same samples she had.

This work was hard, and it was her. And while the life or death of everyone on New Terra resting on it scared her, it didn't take away the essential joy of her work.

"You need to eat," Fayez said.

"I just did," she said. "You gave me that bar."

"That was ten hours ago," he said gently. "You need to eat."

Elvi sighed and leaned back from the screen. She'd been bent almost double trying to make out the results. Her back ached and there was a headache building all across the front of her skull. Fayez held something out. Another bar of emergency cake. When she took it, his fingers stayed with hers.

"Are you all right?"

"I'm fine," Elvi said.

"You're sure?"

"Well, apart from the obvious. Why?"

"You seemed a little distant."

"I've been working."

"Sure. Of course. I'm sorry. I'm just being stupid."

"I don't understand," Elvi said. "Haven't I been acting the same way I always do?"

"Yes, you have," Fayez said, letting go of her hand. "That was kind of my point. After...after, you know—"

"The sex?"

He shifted. She imagined him closing his eyes. Wincing a little bit. With her eyes as bad as they were, it wasn't much more than a guess, but it filled her with a surprising glee. Who would have guessed? Fayez with tender feelings.

"The sex," he said. "I just wanted to make sure that we were okay. That things were all right between us."

"Well," she said, "orgasm does release a lot of oxytocin, so I'm probably more fond of you than before."

"Now you're teasing me."

"That too," she said, and took another bite of the cake. It really was awful stuff.

"I wanted to make sure that I knew where we stood."

"I haven't really thought about it," Elvi said, gesturing at the chemistry deck. "You know. Busy."

"Of course," Fayez said. "I understand."

"Once we're not all going to die, though, maybe we could talk about it? Would that be okay?"

"That would be fine."

"All right, then. It's a date," Elvi said, and sat back down at the deck. Her back hurt. Especially between the shoulder blades. She went through the tools screen, trying to find a way to bump the font up another level, but the deck's options were very limited. She was going to need help, and soon. In the main room, someone called out sharply, and a dozen voices rose in an answering chorus of complaint.

"Okay, that wouldn't be fine," Fayez said. "Elvi, listen. You are the smartest woman I've ever met, and I've been at some of the best universities there are. If there's anyone, anywhere that can get us out of this, it's you, and I would very much like to grow very, very old and decrepit and probably incontinent and senile in your company. So if you could save my life and everyone else's, I'd very much appreciate it."

That's sweet and *Please don't put more pressure on me right now* and *I'll try* warred in her mind. Somewhere at the edge of the ruins, someone shouted. She hoped it wasn't a slug, that it wasn't another death. That it wasn't something else that had gone wrong.

"Okay," she said.

Chapter Thirty-Eight: Holden

Holden shuffled his way around the tower again.

The sky was the iron gray of an overcast noon. The rain had tapered off to a faint drizzle just heavy enough to keep his hair and clothes soaked and send rivulets of water down his spine. The wet ground sucked at his boot heels with each step. The air smelled of ozone and mud.

A small group of death-slugs were nosing at a crack in the tower's base. A wad of fabric blocked their entrance, but they were using their narrow noses to probe at it, looking for a way in. Holden hefted his long-handled shovel recovered from the ruined mines and smashed them flat with one heavy blow. He scooped up the gooey corpses and threw them away from the tower, then let the light rain wash the slime off the blade.

He moved on, finding only the occasional straggler on the tower wall. These he scraped off and flung away using the shovel like a catapult. At first, it had been sort of fun to see how far he could throw them. Now his shoulders and arms burned with fatigue and his distances were getting shorter and shorter.

Miller followed along sometimes, not saying anything, just a gray basset-hound-faced reminder that Holden had more important things to be doing.

He vanished when Holden rounded a corner and found a small work crew resting near a partially dug trench. They were trying to get at least a shallow water-filled ditch all the way around the tower, but it was slow work with their primitive implements.

This particular group was made up of three women and two men with crude digging tools. They were stretching and drinking water from one of the bags the purifier put out. One of the women gave him a nod, the other four ignored him.

One of the two men had a slug on his pants.

It hung on the fabric, just above his right knee. There was no slime trail around it. None of the five diggers seemed to notice it was there. Holden knew that if he shouted in alarm, the man might take a swipe at it with his hand without thinking. So he calmly walked toward him and said, "Don't move."

The man frowned back at him. "Que?"

Holden grabbed the man by the shoulders and shoved him onto his back. "The fuck?" the other man said. They were all backing away from him like onlookers at the start of a fight. Holden leaned over the man on the ground and repeated, "Don't move." Then he grabbed the cuffs of the man's pants and yanked them off with one hard pull. He threw them as far away as he could.

"What just happened?" said the woman who'd first nodded at him. Holden recognized her now. Older, tough, one of the bosses at the mine. Probably in charge of the trench crew.

"Didn't anyone see that he had a slug on his knee?"

"Babosa malo?" someone muttered.

Holden reached down a hand and pulled the dazed man to

his feet. "You had a death-slug on your pants. Were you leaning against this wall?"

"No. I don't know. Maybe, for a second," the man started.

"I told you people," Holden said, first to the man then rotating to face the crew boss. "I told you not to touch the walls. The slugs climb them to get away from the water."

The crew boss nodded at him with one fist. "Sa sa."

"You didn't see it," Holden said, not asking a question. "How bad? Malo que sus ojos?"

"Ojos?" the man asked.

"Not ojos. Ah. Orbas. Eyes."

"Na khorocho," the man agreed with a Belter shrug of his hands. Not good.

"Well, the price you pay for not letting your boss know you couldn't see well enough to avoid slugs is now you have no pants."

"Sa sa."

"So go back inside," Holden said, giving the man a gentle shove toward the tower entrance, "and see if you can find some way to cover your shame."

"Sorry, boss," the man replied, then trotted off.

"Anyone else on the crew that bad?" Holden asked the team leader. She frowned and shrugged.

"Not great. We all missed it."

"All right," Holden said, rubbing his head. It sent the water clinging to his scalp and hair running down his neck. After a moment he said, "Take them all back."

"The trench."

"Too risky now. I'll stay on patrol. Get your people inside."

"All right," the woman said, then started leading her people toward the entrance.

Holden's hand terminal buzzed at him, and when he pulled it out he saw someone had been trying to connect for a while. He allowed the connection and after a few seconds Elvi appeared on the screen.

"Jim, where are you? I need you back at the lab."

"Sorry," Holden replied. "Kinda busy out here."

"Your bloodwork just finished. I need you to come read me the results."

The screen on the analysis rig was tiny. Who, in the age of implantable vision correctives, had bad eyesight? Holden felt he could make a usability argument to the designers now.

"Let me finish this patrol," Holden said.

"This is important."

"So is keeping alive the idiots who insist on working outside when they can't see."

"Hurry then. Please," she said and killed the connection.

Holden was putting his terminal away when it started pinging at him. A quick glance at the screen showed it was alerting him to another supply drop. He held the terminal up to the skyline and let it direct him to the location of the drop. A distant white parachute popped into view as the terminal zoomed in on it. Too far. They were still coming in randomly scattered over too wide an area. They had teams out recovering the first several drops, but pretty soon they wouldn't have anyone left who could see far enough to make a dangerous trek out to the supplies and back.

Anyone but him.

He headed off to find Amos and their potential solution to that problem. The mechanic had set up his little workshop a few hundred meters away from the tower under an A-frame shelter made of corrugated plastic sheeting. A variety of tools, salvaged electric cart parts, and welding supplies littered the cramped space beneath.

"How's it looking?" Holden asked, then walked into the shelter and sat on a plastic crate filled with odds and ends.

Amos sat cross-legged on a sheet of plastic surrounded by battery housings in various states of disassembly. "Well, here's the problem," he said, waving at the batteries with one thick arm.

"As in?"

"As in, I got a couple carts they hauled out of the soup around the mines that I can have ready to roll in hours if I throw my back into it. Turns out they don't mind being submerged all that much. The drive assemblies need the mud cleaned out and shit, that's an easy job."

"But the batteries are hosed."

"Yeah, that's about the size of it." Amos picked up a delicate-looking strip of metal covered in rust spots. "They minded."

Holden took the corroded lead out of Amos' hand and looked it over for a few seconds, then tossed it on a growing pile of bad parts. "The ships say high-altitude winds are making precise drops impossible," he said. "Right now, I can send out search teams to track them down."

"Right up until your searchers can't see to piss without hitting their shoes."

"Right up until then. And then I'm the only person who can go get the supplies. And I can't keep up with that and everything else without some wheels."

"Okay," Amos said. "Good news is I think I can assemble two or three working batteries off the parts. Bad news is I'll probably only be able to charge one."

"One is all I need. And a functioning cart to put it in."

"I can make that happen," Amos said. He slowly reached across his body and grabbed the oxyacetylene torch. It popped to life with a bright blue flame that he pointed at something on the ground. A death-slug that had been creeping up on him died with a hiss and a sizzle.

"How are your eyes doing?" Holden asked, keeping his tone casual.

"Okay so far," the mechanic replied. "We haven't been here as long, maybe. But I can see green flaring at the edges of my vision, so I know I got the bug same as everyone else."

"You should be inside with the rest of us."

"Naw," Amos said. As he spoke, he grabbed one of the partial batteries and began pulling it apart. "Lot of this salvage Wei's people are bringing in is leaking toxic shit you wouldn't want in the air in there. Plus, I don't want those people getting touchy-feely with my stuff."

"You know what I mean. This shelter you've set up makes an attractive dry spot. The slugs will be swarming you by nightfall."

"Maybe," Amos agreed with a nod. "But I got my plastic sheet to keep 'em from popping up out of the ground. And the ones that try to crawl in get fried by the torch. I leave their little smoking corpses out there. The live ones seem to avoid 'em. I think I'm okay."

Holden nodded, and sat with Amos in companionable silence for a few minutes while the mechanic finished stripping the battery and laying out the parts based on how damaged they were. He was building a pile of clean parts to assemble new battery housings out of. Holden knew if he offered to help he'd just get in the way, but it was so nice to be both out of the rain, and out of sight of the anxious colonists, that he didn't want to leave.

"You know," he finally said, "if your eyes get much worse I'm going to have to make you come inside. Finished with this or not."

"I guess you can try," Amos said with a laugh.

"Don't fight me on this," Holden said. "Please. Can I have one thing no one is fighting me on? I'm not leaving you out here to get poisoned. And if you're blind, I think I can take you."

"Might be fun to find out," Amos laughed again. "If it's anybody, it's you, I guess. But I'm not being obstinate to be a pain in your ass, Cap. I hope you know that."

"Then what?"

"Everybody in there has the same fucking problem. Running out of food, going blind, planet blew up," Amos said. He began assembling a battery out of spare parts while he spoke. His deft fingers knew the work so well he almost didn't have to look at it. "Know what they'll be talking about?"

"That?"

"Yeah. 'Boo hoo, I ain't got no food, I'm going blind, holy shit there's poison slugs.' I don't do group therapy. Couple minutes of bitching and moaning, I'm gonna start knocking people out just to get some peace."

Holden slumped on the crate, putting his soggy head in his hands. "I know. I get to listen to that instead. It's making me a little cranky."

"You're cranky because you're tired," Amos said. "You got that I-have-to-save-everyone hangup, so I make it that you haven't slept in about two days. But listening to people bitch? Yeah, that's sorta your job. It's why you make the big money."

"We make the same money."

"Then I guess you're doing it for the fame and glory."

"I hate you," Holden said.

"I'll have that first cart up and running by the end of the day," Amos replied, snapping the battery housing together with a plastic click.

"Thanks," Holden said, then pushed himself to his feet with a grunt and started slogging his way back toward the tower.

"Anytime," Amos said to his back.

Holden's terminal started buzzing again. "Jim, where are you?" Elvi said the moment he accepted the connection. "I need this data—"

"On my way," he replied. "Sort of wearing a lot of hats right now. But I should be there in a minute."

He killed the connection just in time to for Murtry to come out of the tower's main entrance and make him a liar.

"Captain," Murtry said.

"Mister Murtry. How are things on your end? Amos seems to be making good use of the salvaged carts."

"He's a good mechanic," the RCE security chief replied. "There was another drop."

"Saw it. My terminal marked and mapped it. Let me transfer the location so you can send a team."

As he transferred the data, Murtry said, "We lost a man."

"Who?"

"Paulson. One of my drivers. Slug crawled into his boot when no one was looking."

"I'm very sorry," Holden said, trying to remember if he knew which one Paulson was, and feeling guilty that someone had died to help them out and he couldn't even put a face with the name.

"Stupid mistake," Murtry said. He tapped out some rapid commands on his terminal. "And I wasn't looking for your sympathy. Just apprising you of the situation and our reduced team strength."

"Okay," Holden said, surprised that the man's lack of empathy still surprised him.

"Wei will handle the supply pickup."

"How's her vision doing? How many more of these runs does she have in her, do you think?"

"She's on her way," Murtry said with a humorless smile. "So at least one more, I'd say."

"Great," Holden said. "Tell her I said thanks."

"Will do," Murtry replied, ignoring the irony. "But I need something from you."

"You need, or RCE needs?"

"Consider those the same thing at this point," Murtry said. "Should be some construction materials in this load. I need to assemble a work crew to set up my structure before everyone is too blind to do the job."

"What's it for? There's a ton of other work we need to do while we can. And in a turn of luck," Holden said, pointing at the alien tower behind him, "shelter is not one of our pressing problems."

"These people," Murtry said, "are eating my food, drinking my water, and taking my medicine. My team is gathering the supplies and doing the dangerous salvage work that makes any of this possible. You know what? As long as that remains true, they can throw up a few walls for me when I ask."

"Then what do you need from me?"

"They have the mistaken impression you're in charge. Correcting them seemed impolite."

Holden had a sudden mental image of dragging the soon-to-be-blind Murtry out into the middle of the rain-soaked desert and abandoning him at the center of a swarm of the lethal slugs.

"Did I say something funny?" Murtry asked.

"Inside joke," Holden replied with a smile. "You had to be there. I'll let Carol know you're looking for volunteers."

Before Murtry could object, Holden turned and walked away.

Inside, the tower was a buzzing hive of activity as the colonists hurried to finish their last preparations for the coming long night. Lucia had a group working to fill everything that could hold water with supplies from the chemistry deck. Carol Chiwewe was leading a team through the interior of the tower hunting out any remaining death-slugs and plugging any holes they could find.

Holden climbed a ramp and then a set of steps made out of empty packing crates to reach the third floor of the tower. Inside the chamber they'd optimistically named the lab, he found Elvi, Fayez, and a third member of the RCE science team whom Holden thought was named Sudyam.

"Who is that?" Elvi asked. She poked Fayez in the bicep. "Is that Jim?"

Fayez squinted at him for a second then said, "Finally."

"Sorry I was late, but Murtry wanted—"

"I need you to come read this," Elvi said over the top of him. She was pointing at the chemistry deck's small screen. Holden walked over and looked at the display, but had no idea what any of the confusion of symbols and acronyms meant.

"What am I looking for?"

"First we want to check the CBC," Elvi said, coming over to point at the screen. Nothing on it said CBC.

"Okay," Holden said. "Will it say CBC? I don't see CBC here."

Elvi sighed, then began speaking slowly. "Does the screen say 'results' at the top?"

"No. It says 'tools' at the very top. Is that what you mean?"

"Wrong menu. Hit the back button," Elvi said, pointing at a button on the screen. Holden pushed it.

"Oh, I see a results option now."

"Hit that. Then we're going to be looking for numbers on the CBC, RBC, WBC, hemoglobin, hematocrit, and platelet count readouts."

"Hey," Holden said happily, "I see all that stuff."

"Tell us what they are."

Holden did so, while Elvi made notes on her terminal. She had the display blown up to the point where Holden could read it from across the room.

"Back up now and let's look at blood gases," she said when they were done. It took over an hour, but in the end Holden had given them all the results they were looking for. They decided to take some more of his blood and let him go.

When they were done, he stood next to Elvi pressing a scrap of bandage against the puncture wound. "Are we any closer?"

"It's not an easy process," she replied. "Even with access to all these minds and the *Israel*'s computer. We're looking for a needle in a complex organism."

"How much time do we have left?"

Elvi tilted her head up so the light shone into her pupils. Holden could see the faint green tinge there. "Almost none," she said. "But you should go get some sleep. You're exhausted."

"My blood told you that?"

"You haven't slept in two days," she said with a laugh. "Math tells me that."

"I promise, I'll hit the rack as soon as I can," he lied to her.

He climbed down the makeshift steps and the weirdly alien curve of the ramp to the tangle of people at the ground floor. Lucia had turned over water duty to her assistants, and was shining a penlight into the eyes of a small child. She gave Holden a tired smile as he walked by. Someone gave an alarmed shout, then rushed through the room carrying a slug on a stick and threw it outside. Holden followed it outside and stomped on it.

The sky was darkening to the color of damp ash, and the rain was becoming heavier. Distant thunder rumbled to the east, the lightning visible only as dim flashes in the heavy clouds. The air smelled of ozone and mud.

Holden shuffled his way around the tower again.

Chapter Thirty-Nine: Basia

Hey Papa!" the Jacek on the screen said. The boy's voice almost vibrated with fear and exhaustion.

Hey son," the recorded Basia and the real one said at the same time. Jacek began talking about death-slugs and lightning and living in the alien ruins, reciting words of reassurance and explanation that Basia could recognize as Lucia's. Jacek soberly repeated all the reasons his mother had given him that things might end well, telling Basia as an excuse to hear them again himself. It was the third time Basia had watched the recorded video of his conversation with his boy. When it finished, he cued up the recording of his conversation with Lucia and watched it for the tenth time.

He considered asking Alex to call them again, get new conversations to record, but he recognized this as a selfish impulse and quashed it.

Jacek looked dirty, covered with mud, tired. He described the horror of the poisonous slug worms with dread and fascination. The constant lightning storms and rain were amazingly exotic to a child who'd only ever lived in ice tunnels and ship holds before coming to Ilus. He never said he wished his daddy was there, but the fact sang in his words. Basia wanted nothing more than to take his boy by the hand, tell him it was all right to be scared. That bravery was being scared and doing it anyway.

Lucia, when her turn had come, looked less fearful than exhausted. Her smiles for him were all perfunctory. Her report was vague because, he knew, she had nothing to say that would help either of them to hear.

Felcia's videos had been the ones that brought him peace. She was the one member of his family he had felt like he hadn't failed. She'd wanted to go to school, and he'd managed to push down his fears and needs and the burdens that he carried long enough to actually let her go. It had felt like a victory.

Until now.

Now he only saw the ticking clock Alex had left running, showing the remaining time until she burned up across Ilus' sky.

The simulation and timer ran out their terrible program on the panel behind him. He tried never to look. When he needed to use the screens on the operations deck, he drifted through the compartment trying not to even glance in its direction. He tried very hard to forget that it existed at all.

He failed.

Watching his most recent conversation with Felcia for the fourth time, he felt the timer behind him, like a warm spot on his back. Like the stare of someone from across a crowded room. The game became how long he could go without looking. Or whether he could distract himself sufficiently to forget it was there.

On the screen, Felcia told him about learning to change air scrubbers on the Belter freighter. It wasn't the sort of things she'd had to do in the long months when the *Barbapiccola* had been their home. Her graceful fingers were demonstrating some complex function necessary to the process. She made it seem light. Fun. Amusing. He was her father. He knew that she was scared.

Tick tick tick, the clock burned soundlessly at his back.

He adjusted the air recycling system nozzle near his panel and sent a cool breeze across his face. He finished the recording and spent some time organizing his files by content and date. Then decided it was better by date and name, and reorganized them again.

Tick tick tick, hot like the sun on a dark shirt at noon. Burning without burning.

He opened up the file Alex had set up with repair tasks and scrolled through the list. He'd already checked off the ones he was actually capable of doing. He spent some time looking over the rest of the items, trying to decide if there were any he could help out with. Nothing jumped out at him. Not surprising, since it was his fifth time through the list.

Tick tick tick.

Basia turned around. The first thing he noticed was that the simulated orbital paths looked different. The changes were so slight that he probably shouldn't have been able to see them, but the bright hateful lines that described his only daughter's demise had burned themselves into his brain. There was no doubt, they were different. For some reason, it took him longer to notice that the clock had changed.

There were three fewer days.

Last time he'd looked at the clock, just a few hours before, there had been slightly over eight days on it. Now there were just under five.

"The clock is broken," he said to no one.

Alex was up in the cockpit, where he seemed to spend most of his time. Basia yanked at the straps holding him to the chair, fighting with them without success until he forced himself to calm down and just press the release latches. Then he kicked off to the crew ladder and climbed up.

Alex had a complex-looking graphic on his main display. He

was working at it with gentle touches on the screen and a steady stream of muttering under his breath.

"The timer's wrong," Basia said. If it weren't for the fact that he found himself inexplicably out of breath, he probably would have yelled it.

"Hmmm?" Alex swiped at the panel and it shifted to a graph filled with numbers. He began entering new figures into it.

"The clock—the orbital timer thing is broken!"

"Workin' on it right now," Alex said. "It ain't broke."

"It's down to five days!"

"Yeah," Alex said, then stopped working to rotate his chair and look at Basia. "Was going to talk to you about that."

Basia felt all the strength go out of him. If there had been gravity, he would have slumped to the floor on legs made out of rubber. "It's right?"

"It is," the pilot said, swiping the screen behind him again to get back to the graphical display. "But it ain't unexpected. The initial estimates about their batteries were gonna change. They were back-of-the-napkin kind of shit to start with."

"I don't understand," Basia said. His stomach had clenched tight. If he'd bothered to eat anything in the last day or two, he'd probably have vomited.

"The first estimate was based on orbital distance, ship mass, and expected battery life versus consumption." As Alex spoke, he pointed at various places on his graph. As though that explained anything. As though the graph made any sense. "Orbital decay's just not something anyone worries about when the reactors are on. If any of us had wanted to, we coulda built orbits that were damn near permanent, but the *Barb*'s got that shuttle going up and down with the ore, so she went kind of low. Save a little on each trip. And, forgive me for saying it, she's a flyin' hunk of shit. Heavier than she should be, and batteries dyin' fast. So, the new numbers."

Basia floated next to the gunner's seat watching the hateful math spool out across the screen.

"She lost three days," he finally said when he found the breath to do it. "Three *days*."

"No, she never had those days to start with," Alex replied. His words were harsh, brutal, but his face was sad and kind. "I haven't forgotten my promise. If the *Barb* goes down, your little girl will be on this ship when it happens."

"Thank you," Basia said.

"I'm goin' to call the captain right now. We'll work up a plan. Just give me some time. Can you do that?"

Five days, Basia thought. *I have five days to give you.*

"Yes," he said instead.

"Okay," Alex said and waited expectantly for Basia to leave. When he didn't the pilot shrugged and turned around to call up the comm display. "Cap'n, Alex here. Come in."

"Holden here," the familiar voice said a few seconds later.

"So, ran the updated numbers like you asked. We're definitely losing the *Barb* first."

"How bad?" the captain asked. His connection seemed fuzzy. It took Basia a moment to realize it was the sound of rain.

"Just under five days until she starts scraping on more atmo than she can handle."

"Dammit," Holden said, then nothing. The silence went on long enough that Basia started to worry they'd lost their connection. "How's the *Roci*?"

"Oh, we're fine. Pretty much everything's off but the lights and the air. Lots of slack."

"Can we help?"

"Like," Alex said, dragging the word out, "give 'em a tow?"

"Like that. What can we do?"

"Boss," Alex said, "hooking two ships together like that can be done, but doing it in low orbit ain't a trivial problem. I'm just a pilot. Sure would be nice if we had, you know, our engineer back to run those numbers."

"Yeah, no kidding," Holden said. He sounded angry to Basia. That was good. Angry was good. Basia found himself oddly comforted by the idea that someone other than him was upset by the situation.

"Any chance on that?" Alex prompted.

"Let me chat with Murtry again," Holden said. "I'll call back soon. Holden out."

Alex sighed. His lips pressed thin.

"Talking's not going to work," Basia said. "Is it?"

"I don't see how," Alex said.

"Which means there's a non-zero chance that we'll wind up needing to go get her ourselves. You know there's only two of us. You and me. That's it."

"There's three of us," Alex said, patting the control panel. "Don't forget. We've got the *Roci*."

Basia nodded, waited for his gut to clench up again, was surprised to find he felt a warm sense of peace flowing through him. "What will I need to do?"

"This is an LVA suit," Alex said, pointing to the equipment secured in an open locker. They were on the airlock deck, which, other than the airlock, consisted almost entirely of lockers and storage closets. The contents of that particular locker looked like a rubber body suit with lots of attachments.

"Elveeaye?"

"El. Vee. Ay. Light vacuum armor. Lets you move around outside, with enough air and shielding to keep you breathin' and mostly unradiated in normal applications." Alex pulled the rubber-looking suit out and left it floating next to the locker for Basia to examine. "Self-sealing in case of puncture, with life support and injury sensors, and basic medical supplies built in." He then pulled out a red, metallic-looking breastplate. "It also keeps you from getting *too* many holes poked in you by small-arms fire."

As Alex pulled out each piece and showed it to Basia, explaining its function, Basia dutifully examined them and made what he hoped were appropriate noises. He'd worn vacuum suits for work almost his entire adult life. Their form and function were well known to him. But the various pieces of armor and technology that made the suit into a weapon of war were outside his experience. Certainly something Alex described as "automatic IFF and hostile tracking available through the HUD display" sounded impressive and useful, but Basia had no idea for what. So he nodded his head and looked thoughtful and examined the helmet when Alex handed it to him.

"You ever fired a gun?" Alex asked when the armor had all been pulled out of the locker.

"Never," Basia said. He had a brief, vivid memory of the assault on the RCE security team. Of the horrible injuries the gunshots left. Of the surprised looks on their faces as they died. Basia waited for the nausea to start, but still felt only the warmth and calm. "Held one once. Pretty sure I didn't fire it."

"This," Alex said, holding up a thick black pistol, "is a 7.5mm semi-automatic handgun. Twenty-five-round magazine. Standard sidearm of the MCRN. It's fairly idiot-proof, so this'll be the one I send you in with."

"If I go in at all," Basia said.

"Sure," Alex agreed with a smile. "Don't really have a range to practice on here, but you can dry fire it a few times to get the feel. Honestly, though, if you get over there and need to be dead-eye Dick to make it back, you're pretty much fucked."

"Why carry it at all, then?"

"Because people do what you want them to do when you point one of these at them," Alex said.

"Might as well be empty, then," Basia said, taking the gun from him and waving it through the air to feel the weight.

"If you want," Alex replied.

"No. Show me what to do. Then let's load it." *For Felcia. I can do it for her.*

"Okay," Alex said, then proceeded to do just that.

Holden called back several hours later. When he spoke, his voice was tight, angry. "Holden here. Murtry isn't going to bend an inch, so fuck him. Go get Naomi back. Out."

"Well," Alex said, dragging the word out to a long sigh. "That's it. I think we're officially not mediators anymore."

Basia nodded with his fist, causing his body to rotate slightly. They were floating on the ops deck. The various pieces of the disassembled pistol hung in the air next to Basia. Alex had insisted that he know how to take the gun apart and put it back together again. Basia had no idea why that would be important, but had gone along with it anyway.

"What now?" he asked.

"Better start puttin' that back together. I'll pull the *Israel*'s specs up again and we can give them one last look. Remember, stuff gets moved around on a working ship. Things ain't always where the standard blueprints say they are. You're gonna want alternate ingress and egress points in case someone sealed off a corridor you wanted to use."

"I have a good memory," Basia said. It sounded like a brag, but it was true. He'd grown up in corridors and hallways. His sense of direction was excellent.

"That'll help. Then we get you suited up, and I drop you off," Alex said, then paused. "But there is one issue we haven't discussed. I got plenty of juice to get you over there. And the *Roci* can make sure no one messes with you in space. But I can't get you inside."

Basia surprised himself by laughing.

"Somethin' funny?" Alex said, raising an eyebrow at him.

"Funny that you're worried about the only part of this where I actually know what I'm doing," Basia said. "I'm a licensed class 3 vacuum welder. I weld in space. You *find* me a ship I can't cut my way into. Just try."

"Alrighty," Alex said and gave him a light slap on one shoulder. "Let's get to work."

Basia drifted away from the *Rocinante*. Instead of a simple vacuum suit and air supply, he wore state-of-the-art Martian-made light combat armor. Instead of walking across the hull of the ship on magnetic boots, he moved across half a dozen kilometers of vacuum on gentle puffs of compressed nitrogen. Below his feet, Ilus spun, an angry gray world, wrapped in storms and flashing constantly with high-altitude lightning. Lucia and Jacek were down there, under all that atmospheric rage. But he couldn't do anything to help them. So he would help the person he could. He would save Naomi from the RCE ship and she would save his daughter. There were a lot of holes in that logic that he carefully avoided thinking about.

He drifted closer to a massive island of gray metal in the darkness. The *Edward Israel*. The enemy.

"You okay out there?" Alex said over the comm. The helmet's small speakers flattened his voice. There was also an aggressive background hiss to it.

"Fine. Everything is green." Alex had shown him how to page through the status indicators on the suit's heads-up display, and Basia was dutifully checking them every few minutes.

"So, I'm making all sorts of angry demands for the release of Naomi," Alex said. "Got the *Israel* locked up with a targeting laser, and I'm floodin' their sensors with radio noise and light scatter. Should keep their eyes, what eyes they got left, firmly planted on the *Roci*. Give you a minute or two before they realize you're cuttin' your way in."

"That doesn't sound like very long," Basia said.

"Cut fast. Alex out."

Alex had reassured him that the *Rocinante* had plenty of battery power. That shooting lasers and blasting out radio jamming wouldn't affect it much. But Basia had come to view power as a precious and irreplaceable resource. Not something he'd ever needed to do in the age of readily available fusion. It gave everything a sense of permanence it hadn't had before. No do-overs. No we'll-get-it-right-next-time.

He checked his course toward the *Israel*'s midship maintenance airlock, found it good, and pulled out his welding torch, holding it in a white-knuckle grip.

The ship swelled until it blocked his view in every direction. The airlock hatch resolving from a tiny slightly lighter dot to a thumbnail-sized square to an actual door with a small round window in it. The pre-programmed EVA pack fired off a long blast of nitrogen in four cones of vapor, and he drifted to a gentle stop a meter away.

The welding rig came to life with a burst of bright blue fire. "Here I come," Basia said to Naomi and to the RCE people guarding her and to his baby girl thousands of kilometers away on her dying ship.

Here I come.

Chapter Forty: Havelock

I've shut down everything I can," Marwick said on the screen. "Sensors, lights, entertainments. I've dialed back the cooling. With the batteries being what they are, I'll give us just under seventeen days. And that's with the solar collectors up at full. Less than that if they start failing. After that, it'll be time to decide whether we'd rather suffocate or burn."

Havelock rubbed his forefinger and thumb deep into his eye sockets. He hadn't gone to the gym, and he was trying to make up for it by increasing the cocktail of null-g steroids. It wasn't a long-term fix, but the more he looked at it, the less it seemed like he'd need one of those. It did give him a headache, though. If it hadn't been for Naomi, he wouldn't have spent as much time exercising as he had. Something to thank her for.

His office felt stuffy and close, and the temperature was climbing steadily. As a boy living planetside, he'd always thought of space as cold, and while that was technically true, mostly it was a vacuum. And so a ship, mostly, was a thermos. The heat from their bodies and systems would bleed off into the void over years or decades if it had the chance. If he could find a way to get them the chance.

"Have we mentioned it to the crew?" he asked.

"I haven't, but the data's hard to keep secret. Especially when it's a can full of scientists and engineers with little enough else to do. We're going to need to talk about dropping them. As many as we can."

"So that they can starve and die on the planet if the moons don't shoot them down?"

"Most part, yes," Marwick said. "They've come a long way not to put foot on the surface. There's more than one I know would prefer dying there."

In her cage, Naomi coughed.

"I'll talk to Murtry," Havelock said. "Having a graveyard on the planet might be something he'd want. Especially if we could get more bodies in it than the squatters have."

Marwick sighed. He'd stopped shaving, and when he rubbed his chin it sounded like someone throwing a handful of sand at a window. "We came close, though, didn't we? All the way out here to start the whole damned world up again."

"We saw the promised land," Havelock said. "What about the *Barbapiccola*? What's her situation?"

"Makes ours look good. That lithium ore's going to be a high-atmosphere vapor in a little over four days."

"Well, I guess we won't need to worry about stopping them from taking it back to the market."

"Problem's about to solve itself," Marwick agreed. "But to the point. Security? These people are facing a death they can't fight and they can't flee from. They're going to get crazy if we don't do something. And neither you nor I have the manpower to stop them if things get out of control."

What would it matter? Havelock wanted to say. *Let them riot. It won't change how long before we hit air. Not even by a minute.*

"I hear you," he said. "I do have the security override codes. I'll have the autodoc add a little tranquilizer and mood stabilizer, maybe some euphorics to everyone's cocktail. I don't want to do much, though. I need these people thinking straight, not doped to the gills."

"If that's how you want to play it."

"I'm not putting this ship on hospice. Not yet."

The captain's shrug was eloquent, and left nothing more to say. Havelock dropped the connection. The screen went to its default. Despair rushed up over him like a rogue wave. They had done everything right, and it didn't matter. They were all going to die—all the people he'd come to help protect, all the people on his team, his prisoner, himself, everyone. They were going to die and there wasn't anything he could do about it but get them high before it happened.

He didn't know he was going to punch the screen until he'd already done it. The panel shifted in its seating a little, but he hadn't left a mark on it. The gimbals of his crash couch hissed as they absorbed the momentum. He'd split his knuckle. A drop of blood welled on his skin, growing to the size of a dark red marble, the surface tension pulling it out along his skin as he watched. When he moved, he left a spray of droplets hanging in the air like little planets and moons.

"You know," Naomi said, "if you're looking at hundreds of people burning to death as a problem solving itself, that may be more evidence that you're on wrong side."

"We didn't plant the bombs," Havelock said. "That was them. They started it."

"Does that matter to you?"

"At this point? Not as much as it probably should."

Naomi was floating close to her cage door. He was always amazed at a Belter's capacity to endure small spaces. Probably claustrophobia had been selected out of their gene pool. He wondered how many generations of Naomi's family had lived up the well.

"You're bleeding," she said.

"Yep. That's not going to matter much either."

"You know you could let me out. I'm a very good engineer, and I have the best ship out here. Get me back on the *Roci*, and I might be able to figure out a way to make things better."

"Not going to happen."

"And here I thought it didn't matter to you," she said with a smile in her voice.

"I don't know how you can be so calm about all this."

"It's what I do when I'm scared. And really, you should let me out."

Havelock gathered the blood out of the air. His knuckle had scabbed over already. He logged into the autodoc with the sick sense of taking the first step toward giving up. But it had to be done. A crew full of panicking people wasn't going to make anything better. Especially since the closest thing he had to a full staff was down on the planet with Murtry.

Havelock's newsfeeds from back home were filled with hyperbolic pieces about the tragedy at New Terra. The sensor data of the explosion had found its way to a few of the reputable feeds, but there were also three or four other forged versions out there too. The faked data wasn't particularly more impressive than the truth. He spooled through a dozen commentators. Some of them seemed angry that the expedition had been allowed to go out, some were somber and sad. None of them seemed to think there was much chance of anyone surviving. His message queue had over a thousand new entries. People in the media. People from the home office. A few—just a few—from people he'd known. An old lover from when he was at Pinkwater. A cousin he hadn't seen in a decade and a half who was living on Ceres Station now. A couple of classmates from school.

There was nothing like dying publicly on a few billion screens to help reconnect with folks. He wasn't going to answer any of them. Not even the ones from his employers. Not even the ones from his friends. All of it felt like he was trapped underwater and drowning, looking up at the water's surface and knowing he'd never make it there.

He undid his straps.

"Goodnight, Havelock," Naomi said.

"I'll be back," he said, launching himself across the office.

It had been a long time since he'd done a patrol, even just an informal one. He pulled himself along the narrow corridors of the *Israel*, moved through the common spaces—commissary, gym, open lab, bar. In the months—years now—that he'd lived on the *Israel*, it had become invisible the way that anyplace did. Looking at it now was like seeing it for the first time. It was an old ship. The carefully symmetrical shape of the corridors, the keyed mechanism on the doorways. All of it was the kind of thing he'd seen in pictures of his grandparents. Seeing the people was much the same. There was a distance between security and the rest of the crew. If there wasn't, then something had gone badly wrong. Havelock didn't think of himself as being part of the *Israel*'s complement, but every face he passed he recognized. Hosni McArron, the food science head. Anita Chang, systems tech. John Deloso, mechanic. Even if he didn't know how he knew them, they were all part of the context of his life now.

And they were all going to die because he couldn't stop it from happening.

Forward observation was a dark room. The screens were built to give the illusion of looking out a window at the vastness of space, but no one ever actually used it that way. When he came in, it was empty. The screens were filled with sensor data spooling past too quickly to read, a musical composition by a dark-skinned Belter he didn't recognize, and a false-color temperature map of New Terra. The security camera had a bit of cloth tacked over it and the air recyclers hadn't quite managed to clear out the smell of marijuana. Probably someone had been using it as a meeting place for sex. Havelock pulled the cloth free of the camera. Well, and why shouldn't they? It wasn't as if anything they did now was going to matter in three weeks. He shifted the screens to show the planet below them. New Terra, wrapped in clouds. No lights, no cities, no sign of the small, struggling human presence. The planet that had killed them all.

And still, it was beautiful.

His hand terminal buzzed. The red border of the incoming connection meant it was a security alert. Adrenaline hit his bloodstream and set his heart racing even before he turned it on. Marwick and Murtry were already in the middle of a conversation when he dropped in.

"—many of them, and I don't care to find out now," Marwick said. Shouted, almost. Murtry's expression seemed angry and dismissive, but Havelock realized it was only that he wasn't looking into the camera. He couldn't see it.

"What's going on?" Havelock asked.

"The *Rocinante*'s targeting us," Marwick said.

Havelock was already pushing himself off, moving fast through the corridor. "Are they making demands?"

"Backed up by *threats*," Marwick said, throwing up his arms.

"That's hyperbole," Murtry said. "They're painting the *Israel* with their targeting lasers. And some mad bastard's cutting through the midship maintenance airlock."

"We're being *boarded*?" Havelock said. He couldn't keep the incredulity from his voice. "By who? What's the point?"

"Motivation's not our concern right now," Murtry said. "Our priority is making sure the security of the ship is maintained."

Havelock grabbed a handhold at the intersection of two corridors and spun himself down, feet first, toward the junction that would get him back to his desk. "All respect, sir, you know they've got to be after the prisoner. Why don't we just give her to them? It's not like it's going to matter."

Murtry tilted his head. His smile was thin and cruel. "You're suggesting that we release the saboteur?"

"We're all dead anyway," Havelock said. And then there it was, spoken aloud. The one thing that all of them were thinking. All of them but Murtry.

"You were immortal before we shipped out?" he asked, his voice dry and cold as a rattlesnake. "Because whether you're planning to die next week or seven decades from now, there's still a way we do this."

"Yes, sir," Havelock said as he reached the last turning and hauled himself down toward his office. "Sorry, sir."

The connection chimed as someone else joined. The chief engineer was grim-faced and angry in a way that Havelock immediately distrusted.

"Reporting for duty," Koenen said.

"Wait. What's he doing here?" Havelock said.

"I've included your militia in this," Murtry said as Havelock slid into his office. "If we're repelling boarders, we're going to need them."

"My men are ready," the chief engineer said, not missing a beat. "Just let us know where the sons of bitches are coming through, and we'll be there to meet them."

Oh God, Havelock thought. *He's talking like he's in a movie. This is a terrible idea.*

"Mister Havelock," Murtry said, "I'm going to ask you to open the live ammunition supply to the militia forces."

"With respect, sir," Havelock said. "I don't think that's a good idea. This isn't like a paintball exercise. We're looking at a real fight. The risk of friendly fire alone—"

Murtry's voice was calm and cool and viciously cutting. "Do I understand, Mister Havelock, that you've done such a poor job training these men that you feel we'd be safer repelling the attackers with paintballs?"

"No, sir," Havelock said. And then, to his surprise, "But I am saying issuing live rounds at this point would be premature. I think we should find out a little more about what we're looking at before we escalate that far."

"That's your professional opinion?" Murtry said.

"It is."

"And if I ordered you to issue these men live rounds?"

Naomi was at her cage, her fingers clutching at the mesh. Her eyes were wide and serious. Havelock looked away from her. Murtry's sigh was short and percussive.

"Well, I won't put you in a position where you have to choose," Murtry said. "Chief?"

"Yes, sir?" the chief engineer said.

"I'm transmitting you my personal security codes. You can take weapons and ammunition from the armory with it. Do you understand?"

"Hell yes, sir," the chief engineer said. "We'll poke those bastards so full of holes you can see stars through them."

"I'd appreciate that," Murtry said. "Now if you gentlemen will excuse me."

The connection dropped.

"What's going on?" Naomi asked. The warm tone was gone from her voice. Now she actually sounded scared. Or maybe angry. He couldn't tell. Havelock didn't answer. The armory was off the main security station, not the brig. Even if he hurried, he wouldn't be able to get there before the others. And if he did, he didn't know what he'd say to them.

He had a gun cabinet here. Maybe if he joined in, he could at least control the situation a little bit.

"Havelock, what's going on?"

"We're being boarded, and we're going to resist."

"Is it the *Barbapiccola*?"

"No. It's the *Rocinante*."

"They're coming for me, then."

"I assume so."

Havelock took a shotgun out of the gun cabinet.

"If it's Alex and you shoot him, I won't help you," Naomi said. "No matter what happens after this, if he's hurt, we're done. Even if I find a way to save you, I'll let you burn."

The monitor chimed. A connection request from the planet. Havelock accepted it immediately. Doctor Okoye's face appeared on the screen, her forehead furrowed and her eyes shifting as if she was looking for something. There was actually a glint of green in her pupils that made Havelock's skin crawl.

"Mister Havelock? Are you there?"

"I'm afraid it's not a good time, Doctor."

"You're coordinating the drops? I need to see if we can get—"

"Is this something where people are going to die if I don't fix it in the next five minutes?"

"Five minutes? No."

"Then it's going to have to wait," Havelock said and dropped the connection. The midship maintenance airlock was the closest to the brig. There would be choke points at the locker room, the emergency decompression hatch, and the intersection with the maintenance corridor. He guessed the chief engineer would set up his men at the second two and let the locker room go. He might send a couple men to the brig too, as a last ditch. He'd get pushback on that. The whole team was going to want to be in on the kill. And they'd have live ammunition. He wondered what the enemy would have. Power armor? Maybe. Maybe…

"We don't have to do this," Naomi said.

"I don't like it any more than you do, but it's how it's coming down."

"You're talking about it like this is physics. Like there're no choices involved. That's crazy. They're here for me. Let me go, and they'll go too."

"There's a way we do this," Havelock said, loading bag rounds into the shotgun.

"He said that, didn't he? That was him."

"I don't know who you're talking about," Havelock said.

"Murtry. The big boss. Because you do that, you know? You listen to what he says and then say it like it was something you actually believe. This isn't the time to do that. He's wrong this time. He's probably been wrong a few times before."

"He's not the one in lockup. I don't know you've got a lot of right to brag."

"That was dumb luck," she said. "If you hadn't happened to be out playing your war games, I'd have disabled your little bomb and been gone again before anyone knew it."

"What good would it do if I let you go? It won't make any difference. The ships are going down. There's no one here who can help us. You can't do anything to fix this."

"Maybe not," Naomi said. "I can die trying to *help*, though. Instead of trying to kill people or watching them die."

Havelock's jaw clenched. His finger pressed against the trigger guard and he closed his eyes. It would be so easy to turn the barrel on the cage. Fire a bag against the mesh and drive Naomi to the back of her cell.

Only he wasn't going to do that. The release started in his chest and spread out to his fingers and toes in less than a heartbeat. He pushed himself over to her and thumbed his code into the keypad. The cage clicked open.

"Come on, then," he said.

Chapter Forty-One: Elvi

Scientific nomenclature was always difficult. Naming a new organism on Earth and even in the greater Sol system had a lengthy, tedious process, and the sudden massive influx of samples from New Terra would probably clog the scientific literature for decades. It wasn't just the mimic lizards or the insectlike fliers. Every bacterial analog would be new. Every single-celled organism would be unfamiliar. Earth alone had managed five kingdoms of life. Six, if you agreed with the Fityani hypothesis. She couldn't imagine that the ecosphere of New Terra would turn out to be much simpler.

But in the meantime, the thing living in her eyes—in all their eyes, except Holden's—wouldn't even officially be a known organism for years. Maybe decades. It would be officially nameless until it was placed within the larger context of life.

Until then, she'd decided to call it Skippy. Somehow it seemed less frightening when it had a silly nickname. Not that she'd be any less dead if she bumbled into a death-slug, but at this point anything helped. And she was getting a little punchy.

The interesting thing—one of the interesting things—about the organism was that it didn't have chlorophyll or apparently anything like it. The green color came from a prismatic effect analogous to butterfly wings. The actual tissue growing in her eyes would have been a light brown that was almost clear if its structure had been even a little bit different. The scattering effect wouldn't happen. It also meant that her blindness was a flooding of color and a loss of detail, but it wasn't particularly dark. She could still close her eyes and see the world go black, and open them to the bright, vibrant green.

Anything else was beyond her now. Gone. She navigated her hand terminal by voice commands, touch, and memory. The reports she would have skimmed through, she listened to now: voices from the labs at Luna and Earth and Ganymede. They didn't offer her much hope.

"While your immune subject does have a couple rare alleles in the genes regulating his sodium pumps, I'm not seeing anything in the final protein structure that's changed. The ion concentrations are stable and within the standard error bars. I'll keep looking, but I've got the feeling that we're barking up the wrong tree here. Sorry to say it."

Elvi nodded as if there were anyone there who could see her. The headache was still with her. It varied during the day, but she didn't know if that was part of the infection or just her experience.

"Hey," Fayez said. And then, "Elvi? Are you here?"

"I am," she said.

"Well, keep talking a little. I've got food on both hands."

Elvi hummed a pop melody from when she'd been a child and listened for Fayez's shuffling feet, reaching out to touch his calf when he was near. He folded himself down beside with a soft grunt. Her hand found his, and he gave her the rations packet.

"My next assignment," he said, "I'm working somewhere with maybe half Earth gravity. Weight. Who needs it?"

Elvi chuckled. He wanted her to, and she even meant it a little. The foil was slick under her fingertips. She felt like she was a little girl sneaking snacks under the covers when she was supposed to be asleep, doing everything by touch. The wrapping of Fayez's bar crinkled brightly.

"How much more food do we have?" she asked.

"Not much. I think they're trying for one more drop, though. There are a couple people who can still make out some shapes."

"And Holden."

"The one-eyed king," Fayez said. "We should poke out one of his eyes just to make that fit better, don't you think? Him having two eyes is a real missed opportunity."

"Hush," she said, and the foil gave way under her fingers. The emergency bar was crumbly and smelled like rat food from her days at the labs. It tasted unpleasant and nutritious. She tried to savor it. It wouldn't be long before she missed this.

"Any luck?" he asked. She shook her head by reflex. She knew he couldn't see it.

"The best theory we had was that it was related to the plural parentage. He's got something like eight mothers and fathers, and the techniques to manage that can leave some systemic traces. But nothing so far."

"Well, that's a shame. Maybe all the exposure to the protomolecule changed him into a space mutant."

She took another bite and talked around it. "You can laugh, but Luna's looking at that too. And they're trying to grow a fresh sample of the organism based on the sample data we sent. The early trials are showing some real self-organization."

"Kicking off another five hundred years of graduate theses," Fayez said. "I don't think you have to worry about your legacy."

Fingertips brushed against her knee, the physical act of reaching out undercutting the cynicism of his words. She took his hand in hers, squeezing the pad at the base of his thumb. He shifted closer to her. She could smell his body. None of them had been able to bathe since the storm came, and they probably all reeked, but her nose had become accustomed to the worst of it. She only experienced his scent as an almost pleasant funk, like a wet dog.

"Not the one I'd have chosen," she said.

"And yet our names will live forever. You as the first discoverer of a new planet full of species. Me as the simple geologist who waited on you hand and foot."

"Why are you flirting?"

"Flirting's the last thing to go," Fayez said. She wished she could see his face. "You do science. I hit on the smartest and prettiest woman in the room. Everyone has their ways of coping with the brutal specter of mortality. And rain. Coping with rain. My next assignment, I want someplace without so much rain."

In the next room, a child started crying. An exhausted, frightened sound. A woman—Lucia, maybe—sang to it in a language Elvi didn't know. She popped the last of the bar into her mouth. She needed to get some water. She wasn't sure how long it had been since the chemistry deck had pumped out a clean bag. If it wasn't time to switch out yet, it would be soon. Holden had said he'd come by and do it, but she wasn't sure that was true. He was dead on his feet already, and he didn't rest. Even when he needed to. Well, she could probably figure out how to switch out a water bag she couldn't see.

"We shouldn't have come," Fayez said. "All those crazy bastards talking about how the worlds beyond Medina Station were going to be tainted and evil? They were right."

"No one said that, did they?"

"Someone probably did. If they didn't, they should have."

"You could really have stayed away?" she asked as she rose to her knees and started reaching for the chemistry deck. She could hear the soft ticking of the clean water coming through the outtake filter, a different timbre than the constant rain. "If they came to you with the chance to go to the first really new world, you'd have been able to say no?"

"I'd have waited for the second wave," Fayez said.

She found the bag. The soft, cold curve wasn't as heavy as she'd expected. The deck wasn't putting out water as quickly as it had been, but if there was an error in the system, it hadn't made a noise. Something else for Holden to check.

"I'd still have come," she said.

"All this? And you'd still have come?"

"I wouldn't have known about this. This wouldn't have happened yet. I'd know I was taking a risk. I did know. Of course I'd get on that ship."

"What if you knew it was going to be like this? What if you could look into some crystal ball and see us here, the way it's all happened?"

"If we could do that, we'd never explore anything," she said.

It was very strange to think that they were all going to die. She knew it, but it still seemed unreal. In the back of her mind, a small, insistent voice kept saying that a ship would arrive to help them. That another group on the planet would show up with extra food or water or shelter. She'd catch herself wondering if they shouldn't be signaling for help, and have to make the effort to recall that there were no other bases. No other ships. In the whole solar system, there were just the crews and passengers of three ships. And fewer now than there had been before. Even with all of them packed into the ruins together like refugees so close they could hear each other snore, it made the universe seem very empty. And frightening.

"We should find Holden," she said. "The water's coming slow. I wonder... Maybe he has a really good immune system? The fact that we're all getting discharge means we've got some immune response to it. Like a splinter, maybe. It just grows faster than we can knock it out. Maybe Holden has some exposure that gives him antibodies to it."

"Did the blood scans find anything?"

"No," she said. "His white cell count is lower than ours too."

"Maybe his eyeball juice tastes bad," Fayez said. "What?"

"I didn't say anything."

"No, but you made that little I've-got-an-idea grunt. I've heard that grunt. It means something."

"I was just thinking that it can't be his immune system," she said. "I mean, we're all traveling in hard vacuum all the time. The radiation just on the way out here probably left all of us a little immunocompromised. And especially after Eros Station, he's had more...more radiation damage..."

Elvi closed her eyes, shutting out the green. A beautiful cascade of logic and implication opened before her like stepping into a garden. She caught her breath, and grinned. The joy of insight lifted her up.

"What?" Fayez said. "He's overcooked? The eye thing only likes us rare, and he's well done?"

"Oh," Elvi said. "It's his oncocidals. After the Eros incident, he had to go on a permanent course of them. And that means...*oh!* That's so *pretty.*"

"Oh good. What are you talking about? Why would his anti-cancer meds work on something from a different biosphere?"

"It means there's a Dawkinsian good move down around cell division somewhere."

"That's one of those xenobiology things, isn't it? Because I've got no idea what you're on about."

Elvi patted her hands in the air. The pleasure running through her blood felt like being carried by light.

"I told you about this," she said, "that there are good moves—maybe even forced moves—in design space because we see things that show up again and again all through different branches of the tree of life."

"Right," Fayez said. "Which is why we can come to New Terra and find things that have eyes and stuff."

"Because bounced light has a lot of information in it, and organisms with that information do better."

"Preaching to the choir, Elvi."

"But that's not the good part. Holden's on medications that

selectively address fast-dividing tissues. Skippy's a fast-dividing tissue."

"Who's Skippy?"

"The organism. Focus here. That the onococidals work against it means there's something like flight or sense organs near the mouth that's going on at the level of cell division. Even though the proteins are totally different, the solutions they're coming up with are analogous. That's the biggest thing since we came here. This is huge. Where's my hand terminal? I have to tell the team on Luna. They're going to lose their *minds*."

She moved forward too quickly, stumbling into Fayez. He pressed the terminal into her hands. She sat beside him.

"Are you bouncing up and down?" he asked. "Because you sound like you're bouncing."

"This is the most important thing that's happened to me in my life," she said. "I'm *floating*."

"So this means we can treat the eye thing, right?"

"What? Oh. Yeah, probably. It's not like oncocidals are hard to synthesize. Just most of us don't need a constant course the way Holden does."

"You are the only woman I have ever known who would figure out how to keep a bunch of starving refugees including herself from going blind and be excited because it means something about microbiology."

"You should get out more. Meet people," Elvi said, but she felt a little pull of guilt. She probably should try to get people treated before she started talking to the team on Luna. It was still just a hypothesis anyway. She didn't have any data yet. "Connection request Murtry."

Her hand terminal chimed that it was working. A gust of wind made the plastic window flutter. It sounded a little different than usual, and the constantly falling rain sounded louder. She wondered if the sheeting might be coming unsealed. There could be death-slugs creeping around the room and she wouldn't have known. Wouldn't have seen them. Something else she'd have to ask Holden to check. The double-tone of connection refused made her grunt.

"Who's working on the drops?" she asked.

"Upstairs? Um. Havelock, I think."

"Connection request Havelock."

The hand terminal made a single chime and then stopped. She wasn't sure if it had gone through or failed.

"Mister Havelock? Are you there?" she asked.

"I'm afraid it's not a good time, Doctor."

"You're coordinating the drops? I need to see if we can get—"

"Is this something where people are going to die if I don't fix it in the next five minutes?"

"Five minutes?" she said. "No."

"Then it's going to have to wait." The hand terminal made the falling tone of a dropped connection.

"Well, that was fucking rude," Fayez said.

"He probably has something else going on," she said.

"We're all under a little stress here. Doesn't mean he has to be a dick about it."

Elvi lifted her eyebrows and nodded, knowing as she did that he couldn't see her. "Connection request Holden."

The tones cycled until she was afraid he wouldn't answer either. When he did, his voice sounded terrible. Like he was drunk or sick. "Elvi. What's the matter?"

"Hi," she said. "I don't know if you're busy right now, and you're not really responsible for getting supplies to us, but if you have a minute, I'd like to—"

Fayez shouted, interrupting her. "She knows how to make us not blind."

There was a pause. Holden grunted. She imagined it was the effort of standing up. "Okay. I'll be right there."

"Bring Lucia," Elvi said. "If you can find her."

"Is Murtry going to be there?"

"He's not answering my connection requests."

"Hmm," Holden said. "That's good. I don't think he's happy with me right now."

Lucia sat at Elvi's side, holding her hand. It should have felt like an intimacy, but in context, it only seemed to indicate that she was giving Elvi her full attention. A physical analog to eye contact. Holden was pacing around the room, his footsteps sticky-sounding with the mud.

When she was done, Lucia made a ticking sound with her tongue and teeth. "I don't know how we'd manage dosages. I don't want to give people so little that it doesn't have an effect."

"What about picking babysitters?" Fayez said. "A dozen people whose cases aren't as advanced. Shoot them up. They can take care of the rest of us until there's another drop. Captain?"

"What? Oh, sorry. I was...um. There's a hole in the window. Plastic. I was just making sure there weren't any death-slugs in here. And fixing it."

"Captain," Lucia said, her voice sharp and crisp. "You're taking medications for a chronic and potentially terminal condition. We are discussing whether or not to use your medication to treat other patients and leave you without."

"That's fine."

"Ethically, it's actually a little problematic," Lucia said. "If I'm going to do this, and I very much want to, I need to know that you understand—"

"I do, I do, I do," he said. "I've sucked down enough radiation that I bloom tumors a lot. The thing that keeps it under control does that thing with the other thing. And then there are other people and I can take a nap."

Elvi could hear Lucia's smile when she spoke. "I'm not sure the human subjects board would call that sufficient, but broadly yes."

"Of course you use it," he said. "Use it, go ahead. We'll get more if we can."

"And if we can't?"

"I might get a new tumor before we starve. I might not," Holden said. "I'm okay with that."

Lucia took back her hand, leaving Elvi's feeling a little colder. "All right, then. We should start. Can you guide me please, Captain?"

"Yes," Holden said. "Yes, I can. But we may need to get a cup of coffee. I'm feeling a little tired."

"I can get you some stimulants if you'd like, but there's no coffee."

"Right," Holden said. "No coffee. This is a terrible, terrible planet. Show me how to make everyone better."

Chapter Forty-Two: Havelock

The armor in the brig was a simple, unpowered suit of Kevlar and ceramic. It was vacuum rated and had a fitting for a half-hour air bottle. Its intended uses included breaking up brawls among the crew and making short, tactical spacewalks. There were probably a dozen more like it up in the main security station. He hoped that the engineers didn't think of them. When Havelock stepped into it, it pulled his pant legs up, bunching the cloth uncomfortably at the crotch. He put the shotgun strap over his shoulder and shifted, using both hands to pluck the pant back into place.

Laughter doesn't help," he said.

"Wasn't laughing," Naomi replied, then laughed.

He took a fistful of disposable handcuffs and two Tasers from the gun locker. One had a full charge, the other was at three-eighths. He made a mental note to check the batteries on all the weapons later, then remembered that there probably wasn't going to be a later. Not for him, at least. He could leave a note for Wei or something. He thought about calling Marwick, warning him that things were getting complex. Relying on the man's decency and instincts.

He didn't do it.

Naomi, floating behind him, stretched out, her fingers and toes splayed in the open air. Her paper jumpsuit crinkled and popped with every motion. Havelock looked around his office one last time. It was strange, knowing he probably wouldn't see it again. And if he did, it'd be from the inside of the cage.

If that happened, though, it would be because they'd found some way to keep from dropping into the atmosphere, burning in the high air. So the chances were low. He wasn't going to worry about it.

"First mutiny?" Naomi said.

"Yeah. It's not really something I do."

"It gets easier," she said, holding out her hand. He looked at it in confusion. "I can take one of those."

"No," he said, tuning the suit comm unit to the channel the training group used as a default. There was no chatter at all. That was odd. He cycled through the other frequencies.

"No?"

"Look, I'm getting you out of here. Doesn't mean I'm comfortable handing you a weapon and turning my back."

"You have interesting personal boundaries," Naomi said.

"I may be working through some things right now."

The first militiaman flew through the doorway too fast, pumped on adrenaline and unaccustomed to having a gun in his hand. The second came just behind him, feet first. Havelock felt his gut go tight. They both had pistols in their hands and armbands around their biceps. Naomi, behind him, took a breath.

"Gentlemen," Havelock said with a nod. "How can I help you?"

"What the hell do you think you're doing?" the first one demanded, trying to bring his gun to bear and steady himself against the wall at the same time.

"Moving the prisoner," Havelock said, his voice pitched just between contempt and incredulity. "What else would I be doing?"

"Chief didn't say anything about that," the second one said.

"Chief Engineer Koenen isn't head of security on this ship. I am. You guys are helping me. Don't get me wrong, I appreciate it, but keep in mind that this is what I do, all right? What the hell are you two doing here?"

They exchanged a glance. "Chief told us to come guard the prisoner."

Naomi smiled and looked demure and non-threatening. She faked it pretty well.

"Good plan," Havelock said. "This is where they'll be coming. You two set up here in case they get through. Once I've got this one safely stowed where they won't find her, I'll come reinforce you."

"Yes, sir," the second man said, making a sharp salute with the same hand that had the gun in it. Havelock flinched. These guys were so not ready for live rounds. Havelock pulled the shotgun to ready and racked it.

"Miss Nagata," he said. "If you'd be so kind."

"Yes, sir," she said meekly and pushed off for the door.

He followed, catching himself on the doorframe and turning back.

"If anyone comes through, identify them before you start shooting, all right? I don't want anyone to get hurt by mistake."

"We will, sir," the first one said. The second one nodded. Havelock would have wagered half his salary that they'd been planning to open up on anyone that came through the door. Naomi waited for him just down the corridor. He put the shotgun's safety on and let it trail from his shoulder. All the corridors in the *Israel* were narrow, but more so here. The nearer you got to the outside, the tighter the space became. The cloth and padding along the walls ate the sounds of the ship. Numeric codes printed on the material listed what conduits and technical systems were buried in the bulkhead underneath them, the model of panel, and their replacement dates. The idea behind the foam and cloth was to make everyone safer in case of a collision or unexpected burn. Right now, it made him think of a padded cell.

Havelock nodded back over his shoulder. "If something happens, don't go back there without me."

"Hadn't planned on it."

They moved down the corridor, Havelock taking lead and gesturing her forward. She didn't move with the tactical instinct of someone trained to do it, but she was smart and quiet and caught on quickly. She also had a Belter's grace in zero g. If he'd had a few weeks with a squad of people like her, he'd have given them live rounds. At the wall before the intersection with the maintenance corridor, he gestured to the thin ceramic lip of the bulkhead.

"Stay here," he whispered. "And stay small."

Naomi lifted her fist. Havelock moved forward. At the intersection, two more of the team were braced in what they probably thought was a cover position. One of them was solid. The other had his hand too far forward. If he tried to push off, he'd get a backspin that would turn him away from the fight. They'd been over this.

"Gentlemen," Havelock said as he slid forward through the air. "Walters and...Honneker, right?"

"Yes, sir," Honneker said.

"What's our situation?"

"Chief called for radio silence. Don't want to warn the enemy what we're up to. We've got Boyd and Mfume at the decompression hatch. Chief's got Salvatore and Kemp. They're going forward to flush the bad guys out."

"Who do we have outside?"

"Outside?" He shook his head, uncomprehending.

"Did we put anybody in suits and send them out the other airlocks?"

"Hey," Honneker said, "that's a good idea. We should do that."

"So didn't do it already," Havelock said.

"No, sir. Didn't think of it."

"All right," Havelock said, and the dry rattle of gunfire echoed from down the corridor. The two engineers turned, pulling themselves to look. Honneker pulled a little too hard, launching himself into the corridor where anyone coming the other direction could have shot him while he flailed. The radio clicked to life in Havelock's ear. The chief engineer sounded like a kid at a birthday party.

"We have contact! We have contact! The enemy's taken cover in the lavatory by secondary supply. We have him pinned down!"

A flurry of shots rang out, coming through the radio a fraction of a second before the sound could move through the ship's air. Koenen started shouting at someone to pull back, then realized his radio was still live and cut it. Havelock braced his ankle in a handhold, stretched out to Honneker, and pulled him back in gently.

"What do we do?" Walters said as Honneker steadied himself on a handhold. "Should we go forward? We could grab some suits and go around like you said?"

Havelock took out the fully charged Taser, shaking his head. It was ready to fire. The second one, with the low charge, took half a second to go to ready status. The two men were looking at him for guidance.

"You should both look down the corridor," Havelock said, pointing at the intersection with his chin. When they turned, he shot them both in the back. Their bodies arched, shuddered, and went still. Havelock took their pistols, disabled their suit radios, and handcuffed them first to each other, and then to one of the handholds.

"Clear," he said over his shoulder, his voice calm but strong enough to carry. Naomi moved forward, shifting from one side of the corridor to the other so that she was never more than a fraction of a second from something solid she could use to change direction. Good instincts.

"That's four down," she said. "Are you really good at this, or are they really bad?"

"Teaching may not be my strong suit," Havelock said. "And we do have the element of surprise on our side."

"I guess," Naomi said, her voice making her skepticism clear. "How are you doing?"

Havelock started to say *I'm fine* by reflex, and then paused. He had just attacked and disabled two of his crewmen who'd been working at the direct and explicit order of his superior officer. He'd betrayed the trust of men he'd been traveling with for years on behalf of a Belter saboteur. And they were all of them days from dying. And, maybe oddly, it was that last fact that made all the rest all right. He was a dead man. They were all dead men. So there was a sense in which what he did now didn't matter. He was free to follow his conscience wherever it led.

It was the security man's nightmare scenario. In the face of death, why wouldn't there be riots? Why wouldn't there be killing and theft and rape? If there were no consequences—or if all the consequences were the same—then anything became possible. It was his job to expect the worst of humanity, including himself. And now here he was, helping a lawfully bound prisoner escape because he liked the death she offered him better than Murtry's plastic-and-ceramic sepulcher standing on an empty planet. He didn't give a good goddamn about New Terra or Ilus or whatever the unpleasant ball of mud under them got called. He cared about the people. The ones on the *Israel* and the ones on the *Barbapiccola* and the ones on the surface. All of them. Staking a claim that the corporation could use to protect its assets after they all died just wasn't good enough.

"I'm weirdly at peace with this," he said.

"Probably a good sign," she said, and a fresh round of shooting started. Havelock gestured for her to stay and pushed forward.

All the major corridors on the Israel had decompression hatches: thick circles of metal with hard polymer seals. Most of the time they were bumps in the walls, larger than the ship designs a generation or two later, but easy enough to ignore. If something holed the ship, the hatch would close with the speed and amorality of a guillotine.

If someone got caught in it, one loss was better than venting the air. Havelock had seen training videos about misfires, and he'd been nervous around them ever since. One man was pressed to the wall, eyeing the corridor ahead anxiously. Havelock cleared his throat, and the man spun, pistol at the ready.

"Mfume," Havelock said, his palms up. "Where's Boyd?"

"He went forward," Mfume said, gesturing with the gun, but not lowering it. "The chief's getting shot at. And he told me to stay here. And I stayed, but—"

"It's all right," Havelock said, moving closer slowly, not making eye contact. He kept looking down the corridor, trying to shift the man's attention there. The raised pistol made his chest itch. "You did the right thing."

The radio crackled back to life, and the chief engineer spoke. He sounded winded. "We've locked the little bastard down. He winged Salvatore, but it's not bad. I need everyone up here. We're going to rush him."

"That's probably not a good idea," Havelock said on the open channel.

"It's all right," the chief engineer said. "We can take him."

"Not without casualties that you don't have to take," Havelock said. "Is he in armor?"

"Yeah, I'm pretty sure I got one hit on him," another voice said, its tone high and tight, like a kid on his first hunt who thinks he shot a deer.

"Everyone check in," the chief said.

"Jones and I are in the brig, chief. Everything's quiet."

"Prisoner giving you any shit?" the chief asked.

"I moved her," Havelock said. "She's fine. I need you to pull back now. We have to do this by the numbers."

Another half dozen gunshots peppered the air. Mfume twitched with each of them. Havelock gently pushed the barrel of the man's gun away until it pointed at the wall. Mfume didn't seem to notice he'd done it.

"No can do," Koenen said. "If we let up, this Belter sonofabitch is going to get loose. We've got to finish this thing. Honneker! Walters! Get your nuts in your palms and head forward, boys. This piece of shit is going down."

The silence on the radio was eerie.

"Walters?" the chief engineer said.

Havelock took Mfume's wrist and twisted, bracing one leg against the wall for leverage. Mfume cried out, but he loosened his grip on the gun enough for Havelock to bat it away. The black metal spun down the corridor, and Mfume yelled and tried to push him away. Havelock shifted his grip, pulling out and down, peeling Mfume away from his bracing wall. The engineer screamed again, and Havelock fired the Taser into his back. Mfume bounced against the far wall, limp as a puppet, and Havelock pulled the shotgun off his back and shifted to jam one knee against the lip of the decompression hatch and the other foot behind him against a handhold.

"Nagata," he shouted. "We're about to have company."

Down the corridor, the chief engineer boiled around the corner and slammed into the wall, firing his pistol wildly.

"Cease fire!" Havelock called. "You've got one of your own floating outside cover. Cease fire!"

"Fuck you!" Koenen shouted, and Havelock pulled the shotgun's trigger. The bag round took the chief in the side and sent him spinning. Havelock landed the second shot in the man's back just as three more engineers caromed around the corner in a clump. Havelock shot each of them once, then shifted himself to the other side of the hatch and pushed off, stowing the shotgun and pulling the Tasers. The low-charge one was already dead, and he dropped it. One of the men was bleeding; a droplet of blood the size of a fingernail floated in the air. All four men were gasping in pain. Two of them had dropped their weapons, and the other two—the bleeding man and Koenen—seemed unaware Havelock was there at all. Havelock Tased the first of the floating men, then grabbed the one who was bleeding, Salvatore.

"You. Kemp."

"You shot me."

"With a bag round. The other guy shot Salvatore with a bullet. You need to get him to the medical bay."

"You're a *traitor*," the chief engineer shouted, and Havelock Tased him before turning back to Kemp.

"I'm taking your gun away, and I'm giving you Salvatore. You're helping him get to the medical bay now. You understand?"

"Yes, sir," Kemp said, then looked over Havelock's shoulder and nodded. "Ma'am."

"Everything under control?" Naomi asked.

"Wouldn't go that far," Havelock said, putting Kemp's hand on Salvatore's arm and giving them both a little shove back up the corridor. "I'm fairly sure the two from the brig are on their way down here."

"We should leave, then."

"That's what I was thinking."

The short stretch of corridor between the corner and the airlock had a sealed door to secondary storage, a low access panel to the power conduits in the walls, and the entrance to the maintenance airlock's locker room. The space was narrow and cramped. Bullet holes pocked the cloth. One of them had penetrated the wall and hit a hydraulic tube. The safety hydraulic fluid was polymerizing in the air, a hundred tiny greenish dots slowly turning white. The original leak was probably already sealed with a hunk of the stuff. The washroom was the standard utility size, so small that squatting on the vacuum seat meant pressing back to one wall and knees to the other. It wouldn't have been much for cover in the first place, and the narrow door stood open. A dozen bullet holes scarred the walls and the doorway.

"Okay," Havelock said, and a gun popped out, firing blind down the hallway. He pushed Naomi behind him, shouting, "Stop! Stop! I've got Nagata right here!"

"Stay the hell back!" a man's voice shouted from the washroom. It sounded almost familiar, but Havelock couldn't place it. "I swear to God I'll shoot."

"I noticed," Havelock shouted back.

"It's okay, Basia," Naomi called. "It's me."

The voice went silent. Havelock moved forward slowly, ready for the gun to reappear. It didn't. The man floating in the washroom wore military body armor of a Martian design that was maybe half a decade out of date. His hair was dark with flecks of gray at the temples, and he had a welding torch in one hand. The gun was in the other. His eyes were wide and his skin was ashy. A streak across the side of the armor showed where one of the militia's bullets had skipped off his ribs. Havelock put up his left hand, palm out, but kept the Taser tight in his right.

"Okay," he said. "It's all right. We're all on the same side here."

"Who the hell are you?" the man demanded. "You're the security guy. The one that locked her up."

"Used to be," Havelock said.

Naomi put her hands on Havelock's shoulders, pulling herself over him to see the other man.

"We're leaving," she said. "Want to come with?"

Chapter Forty-Three: Basia

W e're leaving," Naomi said. "Want to come with?"

Basia felt a powerful flush of embarrassment. Things had started out so well.

He'd cut into the *Israel*'s airlock control panel with the efficiency of long practice. The composite plating had been an old layering system he'd seen often working on Ganymede, and the familiarity had given him a sense of confidence. He'd floated through the short corridor to a storage and locker room without seeing a soul, clutching his pistol in one hand. He'd hoped the weapon would turn out to be unnecessary. On the other side of the locker room was the starboard passageway that would lead to the brig. He was about sixty meters from his goal, and not even an alarm had gone off.

His first sign that things were going wrong was a massive barrage of gunfire that seemed to come from everywhere at once. He'd been hiding in the tiny lavatory closet ever since.

"I came to rescue you," Basia said, recognizing how silly the words sounded even as he said them.

"Thanks for that," Naomi replied with a smile.

"Yeah, so, we should probably keep—" the Earther in the body armor started to say, then was cut off by a new fusillade of shots. Bullets bounced off the corridor walls, tearing strips of foam off to join the floating blobs of solidified hydraulic fluid. The Earther shoved Naomi into the lavatory with Basia, mashing them both against the back wall. More shots hit, including one that skipped off the Earthman's shoulder plating, leaving a long dented streak.

"I'm Basia," he said.

The Earther leaned around the doorway with a bulky rifle of some kind and fired several booming shots. "Havelock. Let's cover the rest once we're out of here."

Before Basia knew she was going to do it, Naomi plucked the pistol out of his hand and held it out to Havelock. "You might need this."

"No," he replied, and fired off his big rifle a few more times. "No lethal rounds. We're not killing these idiots if we can avoid it."

"Then what?" she asked.

Havelock was pulling fat shotgun shells out of a pouch on his armor and loading them into his gun. "As soon as I move into the corridor, you two head to the airlock as fast as you can." He loaded one last shell into the gun, then racked it with a loud clack. "Basia, you're armored, so keep her in front of you. Naomi, you'll be moving through a storage compartment. Grab a suit. Anything you can put on fast."

"Ready when you are," Naomi replied and put a hand on Havelock's shoulder. Basia nodded his fist at the Earthman.

"Then go," Havelock said and darted into the corridor firing his shotgun. Naomi followed him out and turned the other direction, toward the locker room and the airlock; Basia stayed right behind. They'd only gone a few meters when he felt two bruising hammer blows on his back.

"I'm shot!" he yelled in a panic. "I got shot!"

Naomi didn't slow down. "Is your HUD telling you you're bleeding out?"

"No."

"Then you'll live. That's what the armor is for."

"Less talk," Havelock said from right behind him, and gave him a shove in the back. "More escaping."

Basia hadn't even known he was there. He stifled an undignified squeak. Several meters ahead, Naomi darted into the storage room, and Basia followed when he reached the doorway. She was already wriggling her way into a bright orange emergency atmosphere suit. Havelock paused at the door to fire several more shots down the corridor.

"Tune to twenty-seven oh one five," the Earther said.

"What?" The words made no sense to Basia. And the whole sequence of events was more and more coming to feel like a bad dream. People shooting and spouting nonsense at him. The sense of peace and heroism he'd felt when he agreed to the rescue mission was entirely gone.

"It's the frequency the security team's using," Havelock said. "You can listen in. They aren't encrypting. Because"—he sighed—"they're fucking amateurs."

Basia found the menu to switch his suit's radio frequency and set it to 27.015. "—in on it," a voice said. Young, male, angry.

"The fact that he's shooting back at us makes it pretty goddamn clear," an older voice said. "He shot me with a couple fucking beanbag rounds. I think he broke a rib."

"So," Havelock said, then paused to fire off another shot. "I guess this is a decision I don't get to take back." Basia couldn't tell who he was talking to.

"I'm gonna shoot you in the face, asshole," the older man said. This was followed by another barrage of gunfire that tore up the hallway.

"Mostly you're shooting the ship, chief," Havelock replied. His voice was matter-of-fact. He seemed halfway between being embarrassed on the attacker's behalf and steeled for more violence of his own. Basia remembered someone telling him about the idea of *Bushido* back when he'd first signed on for work on Ganymede. They'd said it was the peace and effectiveness that came from already thinking of yourself as dead. Havelock reminded him of that.

"Kemp," the older voice said. "Are you in position?"

"We're suited up and moving to emergency access one eleven," a voice replied.

"Go faster, get ahead of them."

"Hey Kemp?" Havelock said. "Thought I sent you to medical with Salvatore? You didn't leave him bleeding out in a corridor somewhere, did you?"

"No, sir," Kemp replied. "Someone's taking him there now—"

"Stop talking to him!" the angry older man said. "He is not on our team!"

Naomi was struggling to get the emergency suit over her shoulders, and Basia pushed over to help her. Havelock stayed at the locker room hatch, occasionally firing down the corridor.

"Find an air bottle," Naomi said, then started opening locker doors and rummaging through the contents. Basia helped.

"Hey, Mfume?" Havelock said.

"What?" a new voice snapped.

"Turning on your boot mags to stick to the floor behind cover is a good instinct. But in the position you're crouched in, your knee is sticking out past the corner." Havelock fired a shot from his shotgun, and someone on the radio screeched in pain. "See?"

Basia found a locker full of emergency air bottles and helped Naomi connect one to her suit, twisting it to break the seal. A few seconds later she gave him the thumbs-up.

"We're ready to go," she told Havelock.

The Earther fired off a few more shots, then backed into the locker room with them. He handed his shotgun to Naomi, who pointed it at the doorway to cover them while the two men sealed their helmets.

"Changed your mind about giving me a gun?" Naomi asked.

"I'll want it back."

"We're ready out here," Kemp said on the radio.

"Hey, guys?" Havelock said. "Don't do that. We'd barely started on the spacewalk combat tactics. You head out there with live ammo and it will get really dangerous."

"Well, the chief said—"

"Stop talking to him!" the older man yelled, loud enough to distort Basia's helmet speakers. "Goddammit you guys!"

"Koenen," Havelock said. His voice sounded subtly different now that his helmet was on and sealed. "I'm serious. Don't send your guys out there. Someone's going to get hurt or dead."

"Yeah," the chief replied. "You Belter-loving traitorous sonof-abitch."

"How're those ribs, chief?" Havelock said, a smile in his voice. "You see, right now, you're acting out of anger. Not thinking it through. This is why I didn't want to break out the live rounds."

Basia strapped on the EVA pack he'd left by the airlock hatch. Naomi handed him the shotgun and pulled two more packs out of storage. A moment later, she and Havelock were wearing them and the inner airlock door was cycling closed. Havelock took the shotgun away from Basia and hung it from a strap on his harness. Naomi started the airlock cycle.

"You know," she said, "they can just kill this airlock from the bridge."

As if in response to her words, the airlock status light on the control panel shifted to red, and the cycle stopped. Havelock punched something into the panel and it started again.

"They won't have had time to reset all the security overrides," he said.

"RCE security can countermand ship operations?" Naomi asked.

"Welcome to corporate security. The ship's crew are glorified taxi drivers. Security division works directly for the company, protecting its interests. We can override anything they do."

"This is why everyone hates you," Basia said.

The airlock cycle completed, and the outer door opened. Havelock gestured them out. "You sure you don't like me right now? Just a little bit?"

Ilus' star was just peeking around the limb of the planet, and Basia's visor dimmed dramatically to keep it from blinding him. The planet itself was the same angry ball of storm-wracked gray clouds. In the distance, the *Rocinante* flashed green and red landing lights at them, marking its position.

"Okay," Havelock said, his voice crackling with low-level static. "Should probably get moving. They've got guys outside on the other side of the ship. They can't catch us, but watch each other for grapnel lines."

Naomi was already firing her EVA pack, moving out of the airlock on four small white cones of compressed gas. "Alex? We're out."

"Oh, thank God," the pilot said, his drawl mostly disappearing in the tension of his voice. "I've been worried sick over here. Basia with you?"

"Yeah," Basia said. "I'm here."

"You'll be picking up three," Naomi said. "Come get us."

"Three?"

"Taking a stray home with me."

"A stray?" Havelock said, amusement in his voice. "I'm the one doing the rescuing here."

"It's complicated," Naomi continued. They were all out of the airlock now. The remote connection light went on in Basia's HUD, and a complex program began spooling across it. Alex having the *Rocinante* take control of their EVA navigation to bring them to the ship. The pack did several sharp burns, and the *Rocinante* began slowly growing.

"Glad Basia made it okay," Alex said. "Worried sendin' him in there like that."

"I didn't wind up helping much," Basia admitted, feeling that same rush of embarrassment.

"You got everyone looking in the wrong direction," Havelock said. "That was actually pretty helpful."

"Yay," Alex said, "we're all heroes. There're four guys tailing you right now. Do we know about them?"

A small box appeared on Basia's HUD. Inside it was video of four people in vacuum suits and wearing EVA packs, the bulk of the *Edward Israel* behind them. Without his doing anything, the view zoomed in until he could see the weapons they were carrying. Alex was sending them all images pulled from the *Rocinante*'s telescopes.

"Yeah, those are the militia I formed and trained," Havelock said, then sighed. "In retrospect, that's seeming like a bad idea."

"Do you want me to take care of that?" Alex asked.

"Does your version of 'taking care of it' involve your ship's point defense cannons?" Havelock replied.

"Uh. Yeah?"

"Then no. These guys are dumb and untrained enough to still be gung-ho. But they're just engineers. They're not bad guys," Havelock said.

"They're shootin' at you," Alex said, and suddenly Basia's HUD had red lines across it. "Got the *Roci* trackin' bullet paths."

The knowledge that there were silent, invisible, and potentially deadly projectiles flying past him made Basia's scalp tingle. The red lines on the display apparently meant more to Havelock, because the Earther said, "They're nowhere near us. They haven't got HUD-integrated targeting, so they're just spraying and praying right now. There's no reason to return fire."

"XO?" Alex said. It took Basia a second to realize he was talking to Naomi.

"Havelock's calling this one," she replied. "They're his people."

"Okay," Alex said doubtfully.

The *Rocinante* continued to grow minute by minute until Basia could see the tiny ring of lights around its airlock. He'd only been on the ship a short time, but it felt like coming home. His EVA pack fired off a quick series of blasts and spun him around to face the *Israel*, then began braking. Almost there.

"Guys," Havelock said. "Recoilless is an exaggeration. It doesn't mean there's no recoil at all."

It sounded like more nonsense talk to Basia until he looked at the *Rocinante*'s video of the pursuing team and saw one of the four men spinning and rotating in space, frantically firing his EVA pack to get under control. It only seemed to make it worse, as every blast of gas from the pack just added a new axis to the rotation.

"Then that's an inaccurate name for the weapons," the man called Kemp replied.

"And if we'd gotten to more advanced zero-g tactics, I would have explained that," Havelock said. "I also would have taught you to use the integrated compensation software to have the EVA pack do stabilizing bursts every time you fire the gun."

"Seems to me there's a lot you didn't show us," Kemp replied.

"Yeah, and now that you're shooting at me, I'm just sick about that. In the meantime, please stop. Drake is way out of control and drifting away from you guys. Someone needs to go get him before he gets too far."

"You'd like that, wouldn't you?" the one Havelock had called Koenen said. "Get us to call off the chase."

"I'd like," Havelock said, his voice sad, "to keep Drake from falling out of space and dying. Also, I'm arguing with the pilot of the gunship behind me so that he *doesn't* need to turn you into a cloud of red mist with his point defense cannons. But you guys are making it harder and harder to be convincing."

"Don't threaten—"

"Go get Drake. Get back in the ship. Stop shooting. If one of those shots you're spraying around accidentally hits, I'm taking the gunship off the leash."

There was a long silence. The red lines on Basia's HUD began disappearing one by one until none were left. The EVA pack fired off one long, final burst, then spun him around. The outer airlock door of the *Rocinante* was already open, waiting for them. Naomi drifted inside, grabbed a handhold, and waited for them to follow. Shaded from Ilus' star the polarization of her faceplate faded, and the blue glow of the airlock's LED lights illuminated the inside of her helmet. Her wide smile was clearly visible.

"Home again, home again," she said. Basia drifted in next to her and she caught his arm to stop him. "Thank you for coming for me."

Basia blushed and raised his palms in a Belter shrug. "I didn't do much but get shot at."

"Sometimes just showing up is a lot."

Havelock caught the edge of the airlock entrance and stopped, looking back toward the *Israel*. "Hey, you got Drake? He okay?"

"Yes, sir," Kemp replied. "We caught him."

"Havelock," the older, angrier voice said. "You won't get away with this. RCE will burn you to the ground when we get back. And I'll be there to see it happen."

Havelock laughed. "Chief? I hope we both live so long. Havelock out." He backed into the airlock and slapped the wall panel to start the cycle.

"We made it," Basia said. He felt a brief moment of euphoria, followed by a sudden release of pants-shitting terror he hadn't even known he'd been repressing. If he'd been standing in gravity, he would have collapsed. Naomi and Havelock began stripping off their EVA packs while the airlock ran through the pressurization cycle. Basia fumbled at the straps of his own, but his hands were shaking so badly he couldn't manage it. After a few moments, Naomi helped him pull it off.

The pack drifted across the compartment and hit the bulkhead with a dull thud. Basia had just enough time to realize he'd actually heard something other than his own breathing when the inner airlock door slid open. Alex floated, framed by the airlock entrance, a goofy grin on his broad dark face.

"XO," he said, "good to have you back on the ship."

Naomi pulled her helmet off and tossed it to him. "Good to be back, Mister Kamal."

There was a short pause while they grinned at each other, then Naomi pushed off toward him and Alex grabbed her in a hug.

"They treat you okay?" Alex asked.

"Kept me locked in a kennel like a dog," Naomi replied, jerking her head toward Havelock. The squat Earthman had removed his own helmet, and it floated in the air next to him. He was wearing a sheepish half smile. Without his helmet on, Basia saw his short, light-colored hair, a square jaw, and dark eyes. A sort of generic rugged handsomeness. Like a video star playing a cop in an action movie. It made Basia want to dislike him.

"It was policy," Havelock said. "I'm—I was chief of ship security on the *Edward Israel*. I think I may have just resigned that position. I was the one that took your XO captive. I hope you won't hold that against me."

"Okay," Alex said, then turned back to Naomi as if Havelock weren't even there. "What now?"

"Status report," Naomi replied. "What's the latest on the degrading orbit?"

"*Barbapiccola*'s going down first, then the *Israel*, then we get to pick between dying in orbit when the batties run out, burning in the atmosphere, or getting shot by aliens," Alex said with a humorless laugh. "We're all fucked six ways from Sunday. But it's nice to have you back on board."

Chapter Forty-Four: Holden

Holden shuffled his way around the tower again.

He tried to calculate how many hours he'd gone without sleep, but his brain had lost the ability to do math, and Ilus' thirty-hour day kept screwing up his estimates. A long time was all he could come up with.

He triggered his armor's medical system to shoot him up with more amphetamines, and was troubled when the HUD told him the supply was empty. How much did that mean he'd taken? Like the question of how long it had been since he slept, it was an insoluble mystery.

A pair of death-slugs were climbing the side of the tower toward a teardrop-shaped window. The plastic that had been stretched across the opening had a few small rips in it, so Holden knocked the slugs off the wall with his shovel and then kicked them away. He rinsed the toxic slime off his boot in a muddy puddle.

The rain had lessened to a drizzle, which was good, but the temperature had continued to drop, which was bad. While the overall light level didn't change much with the constant cloud cover, Holden had started noticing the day-to-night transition by the appearance of frost on the walls of the tower. It wasn't dangerously cold yet, but it would get worse. Pretty soon the survivors would be adding hypothermia to their list of unpleasant ways to die.

He bit his tongue until it bled and continued his slow trudge around the tower.

He heard Murtry before he saw him. A quiet, ghostly voice drifting out of the gray rain that gradually resolved into a man-shaped spot slightly darker than the space around it.

"—immediate action. They've escalated. We'll have an argument that we acted with restraint until—" Murtry was saying, but stopped when he heard Holden approaching.

"What are you doing out here?" Holden asked. Murtry was still blind. It was dangerous for him to be wandering around outside. The ground, where it wasn't puddles, was a slick clay that could take someone off their feet in a heartbeat. And the numbers of slugs driven to the surface by the water had Holden wondering if Ilus was a hollow ball filled with poisonous worms.

"Minding my business, Captain," Murtry said, not quite looking in Holden's direction.

"Meaning I should do the same?"

"Glad you followed that."

The two men stood for a long moment. Far above them, their crews were probably shooting at each other right now. They were enemies, and they weren't. Some part of Holden's sleep-deprived, half-broken mind still wanted to make peace with Murtry and the RCE. Or at least didn't want the man's death on his conscience.

"It's dangerous out here," Holden said, keeping his own voice even and calm.

"That makes it different how?" Again, the clenched jaw cutting off the last word with a snap. His anger gave Holden a thin sliver of hope. Maybe Naomi had gotten out. He needed to talk to Alex.

"I can't let you get killed on my watch," Holden said.

"I appreciate your concern."

It all felt vaguely ridiculous, tap-dancing around the issue. They both knew what was happening. He felt like they were playing poker and only pretending they couldn't see each other's hand.

"Can I help you back inside?" Holden asked.

"I have some business to finish up here," Murtry replied with a meaningless smile.

"When we find your corpse later, I'm going to tell everyone I warned you."

"If I die," Murtry said, his smile becoming a shade more genuine, "I'll try to leave a note saying it wasn't your fault."

He signaled the end of the conversation by turning away and mumbling into his hand terminal. Holden left him and immediately called Alex.

"Kind of busy here, Cap," the pilot said without preamble.

"Tell me we're busy because you've rescued Naomi and everything is going perfectly. Is she on the ship?"

There was a long pause as Alex noisily exhaled into the microphone. "So, that part where I went to rescue Naomi? Yeah. I sent Basia."

Holden spun on his heel to look back at Murtry. The RCE security chief was still talking on his hand terminal. "We sent the prisoner to rescue another prisoner? If that hasn't already worked, I think I may be watching Murtry order their executions right now."

"No no," Alex said in a rush. "It did kind of go to shit, but the radio chatter I'm gettin' makes me think Naomi's fine. In fact, I think she might be escaping on her own and savin' Basia."

Holden couldn't help but laugh. Murtry's head swiveled, looking for the source of the laughter with blind eyes. "Sounds about right. Where are they now?"

"It's a little confusin', actually," Alex said. "I've definitely got Basia's IFF pinging away outside the *Israel*. But there're a bunch of other suits out there. So it's complicated."

"Can you, you know, ask?"

"Yeah, no. Basia switched channels on me without leavin' the old channel open. Not a guy who's done a lot of tactical comm drills, I'm guessing. I'm hoping one of them starts talking to me so I can get the new frequencies."

Holden watched Murtry, probably using his radio to coordinate the pursuit of Naomi and whoever else she was with now. He fought down a sudden urge to walk over to the man, knock him to the ground, take his terminal, and demand to know what the hell was going on.

And then he stopped fighting.

Murtry had just started to turn toward him, frowning at the sound of his approaching steps, when Holden yanked the terminal out of his hand and shoved him to the muddy ground.

"Stay down there or I'll beat you unconscious," he told the RCE man. Holding the terminal to his ear he said, "Who's on the other end of this?"

"Who the fuck is *this*? Where's Murtry?"

"I'm standing on him right now," Holden said. "So if you're part of the team that's chasing Naomi Nagata, you should stop."

The man on the other end said, "Comms is compromised, switch to two-alpha," and the connection dropped. Someone who'd spent some time training on tactical comms, it seemed.

"Alex," Holden said. "I've disrupted their command channel. Go get our people."

"Not a problem, boss. The situation has clarified some. I've got three comin' aboard."

"Who's the third?"

"About to go find out. Alex out."

Murtry pushed himself to his knees with a grunt, frowning at a spot just over Holden's left shoulder. "Tough guy when your opponent is blind."

"We're working on fixing that," Holden replied, tossing the man's hand terminal to the ground next to him. "You feel free to come look me up after."

"I will," Murtry said. The RCE security chief picked himself up and began carefully walking toward the alien tower's entrance.

When he was far enough away he wouldn't hear, Holden said, "Looking forward to it." He was surprised to find that was true. When Murtry disappeared around the corner of the tower, Holden began his slow trudge the other direction.

His earbud crackled to life and Amos said, "Cap? That doctor is looking for you."

"Lucia or Elvi?"

"The cute one."

"Lucia or Elvi?"

"The one not married to our prisoner."

"Tell Elvi I'll be there after this pass around the tower," Holden said and killed the connection.

A few minutes later he rounded the last corner, bringing the tower entrance into sight. Elvi was waiting for him there, her face set in a deep frown.

"It didn't work," Holden said.

"What?"

"The oncocidals. My medicine. It's not working."

"What?" Elvi replied, "Why do you say that? What happened?"

"You're frowning."

"Oh. No. I was just thinking that the membrane-bound proteins in our cells must have some sort of functional sites in common with the local life, even though as far as I can tell, they're totally different proteins. The oncocidals are having a similar effect on mitotic division even though our amino acid groups barely overlap. It'll take decades to figure that one out."

"So let's pretend I have no idea what you're talking about," Holden said.

"It's working," Elvi said, and her frown shifted into a brilliant smile. "The microorganism's cell replication is failing. The colonies are breaking down and the light-scattering effect is going too. I can almost read again, if the font's big enough."

Holden felt a rush of relief that immediately turned into a wave of dizziness. He collapsed against the wall of the tower, taking long slow breaths to keep from passing out. A few meters away, a slug crawled along the wall toward him. He started to poke it off the wall with his shovel, then realized he'd lost it somewhere and he couldn't feel his hands.

"Are you okay?" Elvi asked, reaching out tentatively with one hand to find him. "Your respiration sounds funny."

"Passing out," Holden said between long breaths. "How long until everyone can see again?"

"We need to get you inside," Elvi replied, throwing his left arm around her shoulders and guiding him to the door. "I think you've been awake for something like four days."

"It's okay," Holden said. "I took a *lot* of speed. How long?"

Elvi stopped, throwing her other arm around his waist to hold him up. It was both a relief and, if he were being honest, a little unflattering how quickly every bit of sexual tension had been drained from their interactions. He was giddy and sleep-deprived enough he almost asked her what had changed. Fortunately, she spoke first.

"Not sure. The dead organism isn't refracting light like the live ones do. Most of the loss of vision came from that, not from actual blockages. We'll still have some floaties in our eyes for a while, but…"

"So, that means soon?"

Elvi got him in the doorway and over to a pile of blankets. She gently lowered him until he was lying flat on his back. "Yes, soon I should think. Hours, maybe. Days at the most."

"How did you know these blankets were here?"

"We laid this out as a sleeping location for you three days ago," Elvi said with a smile and patted his cheek. "You were just too stubborn to use it."

"Thank you."

"We have a small privacy tent too," she replied, pulling on something by his feet. A thin sleeve of material sprang up and along the length of his body, completely covering him.

"Thank you," Holden said again, his eyes closing against his will. He could already feel the impending sleep as a tingling in his extremities. "Wake me up in about a year. Oh, and make sure Murtry doesn't kill me until then."

"Why would he do that?" Elvi asked.

"We're kind of at war," Holden said. Unconsciousness washed into him, sleep pulling him down into the endless void.

"So," a voice said right next to his ear, "we really need to get a move on."

"Miller," Holden said, not opening his eyes, "if you make me get up, I swear I will find a way to murder you."

"You did your bit here," Miller continued, undeterred. "Now you need to come with me and do the other thing. And I'm not sure how much time we've got. So, upsy daisy."

Holden forced his eyes open and looked to his side. Miller was inside the tent with him, but also too large to be in the tent with him. The overlapping images sent a spike of pain through his head so he closed them again. "Where are we going?"

"Got a train to catch. Find the back room with the weird pillar in the middle. You guys are using the space for storage. I'll meet you there."

"I hate you so, *so* much," Holden said, but there was no reply. He risked opening one eye, and saw Miller was gone. When he opened the tent, Elvi was sitting next to it looking worried.

"Who were you talking to?"

"Ghost of Christmas past," Holden said, forcing himself to sit up. "Where's Amos?"

"He's been spending a lot of time with Wei. I think they're both in the next room."

"Help me up," Holden said, holding out one arm. Elvi climbed to her feet and pulled on it, and he somehow managed to stand without falling over. "My heart is racing. It's not supposed to do that."

"You're full of fatigue toxins and amphetamines. I'm not surprised you're having hallucinations."

"My hallucinations are of the alien mind control variety," Holden said, and took a few unsteady steps toward the next room.

"Can you hear what you're saying?" Elvi asked, coming with him and keeping one hand under his elbow. "You're really starting to worry me."

Holden turned, straightened up, and took one long breath. Then he removed Elvi's hand from his arm and said in as steady a voice as he could manage, "I need to go somewhere and turn off the defense network so our friends don't fall out of space and die. I need you to go back to work on the sight problem. Thank you for your help."

Elvi looked unconvinced, but Holden waited her out and she eventually headed off toward the area of the tower given over to lab work.

In the next room, Amos and Wei were sitting next to a low plastic table, eating ration bars and drinking distilled water out of an old whiskey bottle.

"Got a minute?" Holden asked him, and when Amos nodded he added, "Alone?"

Wei said nothing, but hopped to her feet and left the room, hands in the air in front of her to keep from running into a wall.

"What's the word, Cap?" Amos asked. He took another bite of the protein bar and grimaced. It smelled like oil and paper.

"We got Naomi back," Holden said in a whisper, not sure how far away Wei might have gone. "She's on the *Roci*."

"Yeah, I heard," Amos said with a grin. "Chandra was telling me."

"Chandra?"

"Wei," Amos said. "She's working for the wrong people, but she's all right."

"Okay. Murtry's pissed about the rescue."

"Yeah, but fuck him."

"I also," Holden continued, "may have shoved him down and stolen his hand terminal."

"Stop making me fall in love with you, Cap, we both know it can't go anywhere."

"The point," Holden said, "is that he might try to take it out on people here. I need you looking after everyone. Especially Lucia and Elvi. They've been the two most helpful to us, so he may try to punish us through them."

"Not so afraid of the blind guy," Amos said. "Even when I'm one too."

"That's about to end. Elvi says the drugs are working. People will be getting their sight back in hours or days."

"Cap, is this a problem you'd like me to *solve*?" Amos asked, cocking thumb and forefinger like a gun. "Because that can just happen."

"No. No escalations. I already did enough damage knocking Murtry around. I'll pay for that when the time comes, but you only do what you have to in order to protect these people when I'm gone."

"Okay," Amos said. "You got it. And what do you mean, when you're gone?"

Holden sat down on the plastic table with a thump and rubbed at eyes that were as dry as steel bearings. The planet was one big ball of humidity, yet he somehow managed to have dry itchy eyes. "I have to go with Miller. He says there's a thing that might turn off the alien artifacts, which would get the *Roci* flying again and pretty much solve all of our problems."

Amos frowned. Holden could see the big mechanic's face twitching as he formulated questions and then abandoned them without speaking. Finally he just said, "Okay. I'll keep an eye out here."

"Be here when I get back, big man," Holden said and clapped Amos on the shoulder.

"Last man standing," Amos replied with another grin. "It's in my job description."

It took Holden a few minutes to find the storage room with the oddly shaped pillar in the middle, but when he did the only person in it was Miller. The detective frowned out a what-took-you-so-long look and Holden flipped him off.

Miller turned away and walked toward the pillar, disappearing into it like a ghost walking through a wall. A few seconds later, the pillar split down the middle without a sound and opened up into a steep ramp heading down into darkness.

"Was this always here?" Holden asked. "Because if it was, and you'd told us about it, it might have saved a few lives when the storm came."

"If you'd been where I could talk to you, I might have," Miller said with a Belter shrug of the hands. "You did pretty well without me. Now get down the ramp. We're late as it is."

The ramp dropped nearly fifty meters into the ground and ended at a metallic wall. Miller touched it and the wall, in spite of having no visible seams or joints, irised open.

"All aboard," Miller said. "This is our ride."

Holden crouched to enter through the small round opening, and found himself in a metallic cube two meters to a side. He sat on the floor, then slid down the wall until he was lying on his back.

"This is a part of the old material transfer system," Miller was saying, but Holden was already asleep.

Interlude: The Investigator

—it reaches out it reaches out it reaches out it reaches out—

One hundred and thirteen times a second, it reaches out, and the investigator reaches with it. Follows. Watches. It reaches for a signal it will never find. It is not frustrated, it is not angry. It reaches out because it reaches out. What it finds, it uses to reach out, and so finds more, and reaches farther. It will never be far enough. It is unaware of this fact.

The investigator knows, and knows that it knows. An awareness in an unaware context. Consciousness within an unconscious system. So, nothing particularly new there. The investigator sighs, wishes it had a beer, knows that these are artifacts of the template. Once there was a seed crystal that had a name. It had loved and despaired. It had fought and failed and won at great sacrifice. None of that mattered. It had looked for things that were missing.

For people that were missing. Everything about it is drawn along by that fact. Something is supposed to be here, and isn't.

And instead, there is a dead place. A place where nothing is. Where everything pulls back. The investigator reaches out, and what reaches out dies. The investigator ceases to reach out. It waits. It considers.

Something was here once. Something built all this, and left its meal half eaten on the table. The designers and engineers that spanned a thousand worlds had lived here and died here and left behind the everyday wonders like bones in the desert. The investigator knows this. The world is a crime scene, and the one thing that stands out—the one thing that doesn't belong—is the place that nothing goes. It's an artifact in a world of artifacts, but it doesn't fit. What would they put in a place they couldn't reach? Is it a prison, a treasure chest, a question that isn't supposed to be asked?

A bullet. A bomb still ticking under the kitchen table after the blitz was over.

Did He who made the lamb make thee? Or was there someone else? Whoever killed you fuckers left something behind. Something made for your death, and it's right there.

One hundred thirteen times a second, it reaches out, unaware of the investigator, unaware of the scars and artifacts, the echoes of the dead, the consciousness bound within it. It reaches out because it reaches out. It knows that people are dying in some more physical place, but it is not aware that it knows. It knows that it is constructed from the death of thousands, but it is not aware that it knows. The investigator knows and is aware that it knows.

The investigator reaches out, but not at random. It looks for a path, and doesn't find one. It looks for a path, and doesn't find one. It looks for a path and finds one. Not there, not quite, but close. Two points define a line. One point is alive, and one point is death. Neither came from here. Bang those rocks together and see what sparks. See what burns.

The investigator is the tool for finding what is missing, and so it exists. All the rest is artifact. The craving for beer. The hat. The memory, and the humor, and the weird half-fondness half-contempt for something named James Holden. The love for a woman who is dead. The longing for a home that will never be. Extraneous. Meaningless.

The investigator reaches out, finds Holden. It smiles. There was a man once, and his name was Miller. And he found things, but he doesn't anymore. He saved people if he could. He avenged them if he couldn't. He sacrificed when he had to. He found the things that were missing. He knew who'd done it, and he did the obvious things because they were obvious. The investigator had grown through his bones, repopulated his eyes with new and unfamiliar life, taken his shape.

It found the murder weapon. It knew what happened, at least in broad strokes. The fine work was for the prosecutors anyway, assuming it went to trial. But it wouldn't. There were other things the tool was good for. The investigator knew how to kill when it needed to.

More than that, it knew how to die.

Chapter Forty-Five: Havelock

Havelock still wasn't convinced that Naomi Nagata was the best engineer in the system, but after watching her work, he had to concede there probably wasn't a better one. If some of the people on the *Israel* had more degrees or specialties in which they outpaced her, Naomi could make it up in sheer, bloody-minded wildness.

Okay, we can't wait any longer," she said to the muscle-bound bald man on the screen. "If he shows back up, tell him where we stand up here."

"Pretty sure the cap'n trusts your judgment," Amos said. "But yeah. I'll tell him. Anything else I should pass on?"

"Tell him he's got about a billion messages from Fred and Avasarala." Alex's voice came across the comm and also through the hatchway to the cockpit. "They're talkin' about building a mass driver, sending us relief supplies."

"Yeah?" Amos said. "How long's that gonna take?"

"About seven months," Naomi said. "But at the outside, we'll only have been dead for three of them."

Amos grinned. "Well, you kids don't have too much fun without me."

"No danger," Naomi said and broke the connection.

"Are you sure this is a good idea?" Havelock asked.

"Nope," Naomi replied. She pulled herself closer to the command console. "How's it going out there, Basia?"

The comm channel clicked and the Belter's voice hissed into the operations deck. The sound reverberated without giving any sense of spaciousness. A whisper in a coffin. "We're getting close out here. This is a lot of ugly."

"Good thing we've got a great welder," she said. "Keep me in the loop."

The screens on the ops deck showed the operation in all its stages: what they'd managed so far, what they still hoped. And the countdown timer that marked the hours that remained before the *Barbapiccola* started to scrape against Ilus' exosphere and changed from a fast-moving complex of ceramic and metal into a firework.

Not days. Hours.

The tether itself looked like two webs connected by a single, hair-thin strand. All along the belly of the *Rocinante*, a dozen ceramic-and-steel foot supports made for a broad base, the black lines meeting at a hard ceramic juncture a few hundred meters out. The *Barbapiccola* underneath them almost had all of the answering structures in place. Once the Belter had the foot supports installed there too, it would be time for the Martian corvette to use its battery power to tug the Belter ship into a more stable orbit, along with its cargo of lithium ore. The complexity of the situation made Havelock a little lightheaded. As he watched, the display showing the surface of the *Barbapiccola* stuttered, and one of the red-flagged foot supports changed to green.

"Okay," Naomi said over the open channel. "We're reading solid on that one. Let's move on."

"Yeah, give me one more minute here," Basia's compressed voice said. "There's a seam here I don't like. I'm just going to…" The words trailed off. The readout stuttered red and then green again. "Okay. That's got it. Moving on."

"Be careful," Alex broke in. "Keep the torch cold when you're moving. These lines've got great tensile strength, but they're crap for heat resistance."

"Done this before," Basia said.

"Partner," Alex said. "I don't think anyone's done *this* before."

The tether lines were standard filament design, built for retrieving dropped Martian marines. Using them to haul a full-sized spaceship was like using a thread to pull a bowling ball: possible with enough patience and skill, and easy as hell to get wrong. Naomi had spent three long hours strapped into her crash couch before she'd decided it was plausible, and even then, Havelock half thought she'd talked herself into believing it because she knew that nothing else was.

Havelock had spent the time having his connections to Murtry's terminal refused and reflecting on the fact that he'd just spectacularly quit his job. It was odd that it weighed on him as much as it did. He was eighteen months from home and probably days at the most from death, and his mind kept turning back to the uneasy surprise with himself that came from walking out on a contract. He'd never done that before. And, since he'd gone with Naomi, he wasn't even sure what his legal status was. Somewhere, he guessed, between former employee and accomplice to criminal conspiracy. It was a wider range than he knew what to do with. If he was really the face of what was happening on New Terra back home, they were all going to be at least as confused as he was.

The truth was that none of the standards of corporate law or governmental authority seemed to apply out here. He could follow the feeds, read the letters, even exchange recorded video with RCE's home office, but those were only words and pictures. The models based on experience in human space—even in the attenuated civilization of the Belt—failed here.

Mostly what he felt, though, was relief. He was very aware of how inappropriate it was, given the context, but he couldn't deny it. It didn't leave him regretting his choices. Except maybe to have taken the job. All the tragedy and pain of Ilus would have been merely sad and distressing to see from a bar on Ceres Station. From where he was, the fear had stopped being an emotion and turned into an environment.

The last foot support indicator went green.

"Okay," Naomi said. "That's looking good from here. What's it like out there, Basia?"

"Ugly as shit, but solid."

"How's your air?"

"I'm all right," the Belter said. "Thought I'd stay here, in case anything breaks that I'd be able to fix."

"No," Naomi said. "If this fails, those lines will snap fast enough to cut you in half. Come back to the barn."

Basia's percussive snort was more eloquent than words, but the small yellow dot began to move from the surface of the *Barbapiccola* up through the vacuum toward the *Rocinante*. Havelock watched, his fingers laced tightly together.

"Alex," Naomi said, "can you check the release?"

"It's good," Alex said, his voice coming from the cockpit and the radio link both. "We start going pear-shaped, we can let go."

"All right," Naomi said. And then, softly to herself, "All right."

"If this doesn't work," Alex said though the deck hatch between ops and the cockpit, "our man Basia's going to watch his baby girl burn to death. I sort of promised him that wouldn't happen."

"I know," Naomi said. Havelock had hoped she'd say, *She won't.*

It took Basia eighteen minutes to get back to the *Roci* and another five to negotiate the airlock. Naomi spent most of that time on the radio to the captain and engineer of the *Barbapiccola*. Half the conversation was in Belter patois—*ji-ral sabe sa* and *richtig ane-nobu*—that might as well have been in code for all he could follow it. Havelock requested a connection to Murtry's hand terminal and was refused again. He wondered whether he should write some sort of press release or letter of resignation to the company.

"All right," Basia said, sloping up into the ops deck. His face still had the thin, watery layer of sweat adhering to it. "I'm here."

The readout counting down to the *Barbapiccola*'s atmospheric impact was down under an hour. It was hard for Havelock to remember that the stillness of the deck was an illusion. The velocities and forces involved in anything at orbital altitudes were enough to kill a human with just the rounding error. At their speeds, the friction from air too thin to breathe would set them on fire.

"Strap in," Naomi said, nodding to the crash couches. Then, to the radio, "*Rocinante* bei here. Dangsin-eun junbiga?"

"Ready con son immer, sa sa?"

Naomi smiled. "Counting down," she said. "Ten. Nine. Eight…"

At four, the displays on the consoles began to shift color, mapping the two ships, the tether lines, the engines in psychedelic false color. Basia was muttering under his breath, and it sounded like prayer. Naomi reached *one*.

The *Rocinante* moaned. The sound was deep as a gong, but it didn't fade like one. Instead the overtones seemed to grow, one layering over another. On the displays, the tethers shimmered, the internal forces racing along the spider-web lines in crimson and orange and silver.

"Come on, baby," Naomi said, petting the console before her. "You can do this. You can do it."

"Getting pretty close to tolerance up here," Alex said.

"I see it. Keep it gentle and steady."

The *Rocinante* shrieked, a high scraping scream like metal being ripped apart. Havelock grabbed the sides of his crash couch, squeezing until his hands ached.

"Alex?" Naomi said.

"Just passing through a resonance window. Nothing to worry about."

"I'm trusting you here," Naomi said.

"Always can," Alex said, and Havelock could hear the grin he couldn't see. "I'm the pilot."

Basia gasped. Havelock turned, but it took a few seconds to see what the Belter was reacting to. The countdown timer—the death timer—had changed. The *Barbapiccola* was slated to burn in three hours and fifteen minutes. Four hours and forty-three minutes. Six hours and six minutes. It was working. As Havelock watched, the life span of everyone on the ship below him ballooned out. Havelock felt like shouting. It was working. It had no right at all to have worked, and it was working.

The alarm Klaxon cut through the other noise. Naomi snapped back to her console.

"What am I lookin' at, XO?" Alex said. The sound of the grin was gone. "Why am I seeing a bogie?"

"Checking it out," Naomi shouted, not bothering with the radio. Havelock turned his own console to the sensor arrays. The new dot was approaching from the horizon, speeding above them in its own arc above cloud-choked Ilus.

"Where's the *Israel*?" Havelock shouted.

"Occluded," Naomi said. "We should be passing each other in an hour. Is that—"

"That's the shuttle."

The death timer showed seventeen hours and ten minutes.

"The shuttle you turned into a fucking torpedo?" Basia asked. His voice was surprisingly calm.

"Yeah," Havelock said. "But the payload was the reactor over-load, and there aren't any reactors working, so—"

"It's running on battery, then. That's still going to be a hell of a lot of kinetic energy," Naomi said.

"Is it going to hit us?" Havelock asked, and felt stupid as soon as the words were out of his mouth. Of course it was going to hit them.

"Alex?" Naomi said. "Give me options here."

"PDCs are online, XO," Alex said. "All I've got to do is put a little battery power to 'em, set 'em to automatic, and point defense can slag that thing before it comes close."

Twenty hours and eighteen minutes.

"Power to the PDCs," Naomi said. "Watch the tethers."

"Sorry," Alex said. "Just trying to do a few too many things at once here. Powering up the PDCs."

That won't work, Havelock thought. *We're forgetting something.*

The red dot drew closer. The *Israel* itself hauled up over the edge of the horizon, visual contact still blocked by the curve of the atmosphere. The shuttle sped toward them. The firing of the point defense cannons was hardly more than a brief vibration in the overwhelming strain of dragging up the *Barbapiccola*. If he hadn't known to expect it, he'd have missed it entirely. The red dot blinked out, and then back in.

"Oh," Alex said. "Huh."

"Alex?" Naomi shouted. "What's going on? Why aren't we shooting it?"

"Oh, we shot the hell out of it," Alex said. "Busted that shit right on up. But this right now is when I'd normally be dodging out the debris path? That's not really an option."

"I don't understand," Havelock said. And then he did. The shuttle had been a great big hunk of metal when the point defense cannons hit it. Now it was almost certainly a great number of relatively small pieces of metal with pretty close to the same mass moving at very nearly the same speed. They just traded being hit with a shuttle-sized slug for being hit with a shuttle's mass of shrapnel.

Naomi pressed her hand to her lips. "How long before—"

The ship shuddered. For a second, Havelock thought it was the PDCs kicking in again. Something was hissing and his crash couch had a sharp edge that he didn't remember. The death clock had gone black. A growing mass of blood around his elbow was the first concrete sign he had that he'd been hurt, but as soon as he saw it, the pain detonated.

"Ops is holed!" Naomi shouted into the radio.

"Cockpit's sealed," Alex said. "I'm good."

"I'm hurt," Havelock said, trying to move his bleeding arm. The muscles still functioned. Whatever had hit him—shuttle debris or shrapnel from the crash couch—it hadn't crippled the limb. The crimson globe inching its way along his arm was getting fairly impressive, though. Someone was tugging at him. Basia, the Belter.

"Get off the couch," the Belter said. "We've got to get off the deck."

"Yes," Havelock said. "Of course."

Naomi was moving through the compartment. Bits of anti-spalling foam swirled in the thinning air like snowflakes.

"Are you gettin' anything over those holes?" Alex asked, his voice disconcertingly calm.

"I'm counting ten down here," Naomi said as Havelock hauled himself out of the crash couch and kicked off toward the hatch leading deeper into the ship. "I didn't bring that many beer coasters. I'm taking the civilians down to the airlock, putting them in suits. Havelock's hit."

"Dead?"

"Not dead," Havelock said.

Naomi finished keying in the override and the deck hatch opened with a little puff of incoming air. Havelock's ears popped as he pulled himself down into the airlock deck.

"How's the tether?" Basia asked, following close behind.

"No damage to the main line," Alex said. "We lost one of the foot supports, but I can try to adjust."

"Do it," Naomi said, and grabbed Havelock by the shoulder. The emergency aid station by the airlock door had a roll of elastic bandage and a small wound vacuum. Naomi pulled his arm out straight and pressed that vacuum's clear plastic nozzle into the center of the globe of blood. "What am I looking at, Alex?"

"Checking, XO. All right. We've got a slow leak in the machine shop. The port side's pretty messed up. Sensor arrays and PDCs on that side. Maneuvering thrusters aren't responding. They may not even be there. There's a lot of power conduits right around there too, but with the reactor off-line, I don't know if they're hit or not."

The gouge in Havelock's arm was as long as his thumb in a sharp V shape. Where the flesh had peeled back, his skin looked fish-belly white. The margin of the wound was nearly black with pooling blood. Naomi put absorbent bandage on it and started wrapping it down with an wide elastic band. She had tiny dots of his blood in her hair.

"How are we for moving?" she asked.

"I can go anyplace you want, so long as it's counter-clockwise," Alex said. "If there were a dock anywhere within a year of here and we had a reactor, I'd have a vote where to go next."

"We'll work on a plan B. How's the *Barb*?"

Basia almost had his welding rig back on. Naomi patted Havelock's wounded arm, a small physical statement. *You're good to go.* She turned to the lockers and started pulling out an environment suit of her own.

"She's still coming up," Alex said. "But I'm starting to get worried about that missing foot support."

"All right," Naomi said. "Back the thrust down for now. We'll see if we can get it stuck back on."

Havelock pulled the thick leggings on, shrugged into the suit. He checked the seals automatically, long years of living in vacuum making it all as quick and automatic as reflex. The suit's medical array kicked on and immediately injected him with a cocktail of anti-shock medicines. His heart raced and his face flushed.

"Well, the good news is they're out of shuttles," Basia said. "They won't be doing that again."

"What *are* they going to do," Naomi said. It took Havelock a long moment to realize she was talking to him.

These were his people. Marwick and Murtry. The militia of engineers. The RCE team had launched the shuttle at the *Rocinante* and tried to break up a civilian rescue operation. It was a strangely dislocating thought. He'd spent a countable fraction of his life protecting these people, keeping the shipboard politics that always rose up on a long voyage to a minimum, protecting them from outside threats and internal ones. They'd tried to kill not only him, but the crew of the *Rocinante* and the *Barbapiccola* too. And the worst of it was that he wasn't actually surprised.

"XO? I think we've got a hole in the port torpedo rails too. Might want to see if everything's still in place down there. Fail-safes are pretty good, but we'll want to check them all if we ever plan to fire one. It'd be a real pity for our own ordnance to blow us up."

"Roger that," Naomi said. "I'm on my way. Basia, can you coordinate with Alex and get that foot support back where it's supposed to be?"

"Sure can," the Belter said. The one who'd been part of that first conspiracy to have the RCE people killed. Who had Governor Trying's blood on his hands. For a moment, their eyes met through the doubled windows of their helmets. Basia's eyes were hard, and then Havelock thought there was something else. A flicker of shame, maybe. Havelock watched as he cycled the airlock open, and then he watched it close.

"Havelock," Naomi said. "I need you to answer the question."

"Which question?"

"What are they going to do next?"

He shook his head. His arm throbbed. There was no point to the attack except spite and the kind of violence that passed for meaning in the face of despair. If Murtry was behind it, all he'd care was that the *Barbapiccola* went down before the *Israel*. If it was the engineering militia, they'd done it to show that they hadn't lost.

The reasons behind it didn't matter.

"I don't know," Havelock said, then sighed. "But it will probably be bad for everyone."

Chapter Forty-Six: Elvi

Elvi thought her eyesight's return was like coming out of a fog. The green that had enveloped the world was just as vivid at first. It lasted long enough that she was afraid she'd been wrong, or that the long-term use of the oncocidals had made some other change to Holden's physiology that short-term use wasn't having. And then the shadows had lines around them again, little zones of definition. And then within hours, she could see the doorway arch and the shape of the chemistry deck. By the time she'd been able to see clearly enough that she could tell Holden for certain that they'd solved the problem, the man had been in what looked like a sleep-deprivation psychosis. It made her feel a little guilty that she hadn't figured it out earlier. But he'd gone off to talk to Amos, and she was fairly sure that the big man would be able to take care of his captain. And Elvi had too many other things to do.

The chemistry deck's slowed water purification turned out

to be a bigger issue than she'd expected. The distillation filters were exhausted; material that had gone in as white, puffy pads of spun glass embedded with ionic scrubbers came out slick and green. But the other people from the science team and the survivors of First Landing were all starting to get function back too. It took almost four hours, but Elvi and Fayez and two of the mining technicians had rigged a still just outside the ruins that was converting the fallen rainwater to something potable at nearly three gallons an hour. It tasted like fake spearmint flavoring and alfalfa, but it would sustain life.

When Elvi found Lucia, the doctor looked as bad as Holden had sounded. Her skin had an ashy tone and the whites of her eyes were so pink Elvi was surprised they weren't bleeding. Jacek was following his mother around, carrying her medical scanner and a little sack of bandages. Elvi watched them check on the patients. Everyone was covered in mud and grit. The differences between RCE and squatters were buried under the layers of filth and the shared joy in their returning sight. When Jacek caught her gaze, she smiled. He hesitated, then nodded almost shyly and smiled back.

"Clouds are starting to thin," Lucia said. "I saw a patch that was actually white."

"Really?" Elvi asked.

"Still looked greenish to me, of course, but it was actually white," the doctor said. When she shook her head, it seemed to take her a fraction of a second to start. "You did good work. I've only got three people the treatment's not working on."

"Why isn't it working for them? Maybe we should—"

"This isn't science," Lucia said. "It's medicine. A success rate this high on a new treatment for a novel illness? We're doing brilliantly. None of us are back to baseline yet, though. If it happens at all, it will take time."

"Time," Elvi said. "Strange to think we've got any of that."

"We've traded up from dying in the storm to dying from the slugs to dying of hunger in a few weeks."

"We're pushing the crisis point back. If it's not winning, at least it's a way not to lose."

"If we can keep pushing it back."

But we can't. The words hadn't been said, but they didn't need to be. With the ships fighting each other and falling out of orbit and the native ecology basically inedible, extending the group's horizon past a few weeks of starvation was going to be difficult. Maybe impossible. The stress was showing in the people, RCE and First Landers both. Elvi saw it, the segregation into tribes again now that the immediate danger had passed. She wondered whether it would come back when the food ran out.

"You need rest," Elvi said, and a hand touched her shoulder. Wei and Murtry were behind her. Wei's expression was bleak. Murtry, on the other hand, was smiling his customary smile. Of all of them, the coating of mud on his skin and in his hair looked almost natural. Like he was in his native element.

"Doctor Okoye," Murtry said, "I was hoping we could have a private word."

"Of course," Elvi said. Lucia nodded curtly and turned away. Elvi felt a little pang of disappointment. After all the trials of the storm and the blindness, the political divisions between the RCE and First Landing were still there, just below the surface. Murtry was still the man who'd burned a building full of terrorists. Lucia was still the wife of a man who'd conspired to destroy the heavy shuttle. It seemed like it should have mattered less now, like the rains should have washed something clean. Anything.

"I was wondering what you could tell me about the last conversation you had with Captain Holden," Murtry said. His voice sounded perfectly calm and reasonable. It was like they were back on the *Israel* and he was asking her to think back to the last time she'd used some tool she couldn't find.

"Well, he was very, very tired. Exhausted. It seemed to be having some real cognitive effects."

"Cognitive effects like what, please?" Murtry asked.

"He was babbling," Elvi said. "Bounding from jokes about

mind-controlling aliens to Charles Dickens to insisting that he had some way to shut down the defense network. He was really all over the place. I tried to get him to rest, but—"

"Do I understand you that he intended to disable the alien technology presently functioning on this planet?"

"Yes. I mean, why wouldn't he?"

"Doesn't belong to him. Did he say how he intended to accomplish this?"

"He didn't. But I don't think there really was anything. It was just his brainstem attaching to his vocal cords. I'm pretty sure he was only half aware that he was talking at all."

"Did he mention going north?"

Elvi blinked, scowled, shook her head.

Murtry pulled up his hand terminal, tapped it three times, and held it out to her. A rough map of Ilus' only continent showed on the screen with two dots. One, she knew, was the location of First Landing, or where the place had been, anyway. She assumed it indicated where they were. A second dot was almost an inch and a half away.

"I took the liberty of tracking the captain's hand terminal signal," Murtry said. "Signal's patchy and intermittent, but it seems he's been traveling north at an average of two hundred klicks an hour. I find that very interesting."

Elvi handed the terminal back to him. "He didn't say anything about it. Just that he had something to do. He talked to Amos afterward. I thought that was probably what he meant. Honestly, I'm surprised he can even drive a cart."

"He isn't driving a cart," Murtry said. "We've only got two carts, they're both right outside, and one of them doesn't even have a power cell."

"I don't understand," Elvi said. "Then how is he..."

"Going two hundred kilometers an hour?" Murtry said. "That would be one of many, many questions I'd like to have answered. Thank you for your time, Doctor."

Murtry nodded, turned, and walked toward the archway that

led outside. Elvi watched him go, scowling. Had Holden said anything else? She couldn't think of anything. But maybe he'd said something to Amos.

She found the big man standing in the mud outside the work tent where the carts were parked, arms folded across his bare, mud-streaked chest. He had a nasty scar across his belly and a tattoo of a woman over his heart. She wanted to ask about them both, but didn't. The one working cart was rolling out, Murtry and Wei at the controls. The big silica-gel wheels made wet smacking sounds in the mud, but the cart picked up speed quickly, bouncing along the ruined landscape in the soft rain.

"Was there a drop?" Elvi asked.

"Nope," Amos said.

"Is there going to be a drop?"

"If there is, they'd better get it in walking range. Unless I can get another fuel cell up, that right there was our one working set of wheels."

"Oh," she said. And then, "Did Holden say anything to you before he, ah, left?"

"Yep," Amos said, still scowling after the cart.

"Was it about going north?"

"Not in particular, but I knew he was going someplace in case he could get Miller to turn the fusion reactors back on for us."

"Miller?" Elvi said with a shake of her head.

"Yeah, that's a long story. Pretty much all the cap had for me was to make sure that one"—Amos nodded at the retreating cart—"didn't get uppity and start killing folks again."

"He's going after Holden."

"Hmm. Don't know if that makes my job harder or easier."

The big man shrugged and walked into the repair tent. The remains of half a dozen fuel cells were laid out on a thin plastic tarp. Amos squatted beside them, then started arranging the cells by size and the extent of their obvious damage.

"This'd be a lot easier if the *Roci* could just drop me down a fresh cell," he said.

"You're going after Holden too?"

"Well, the way I figure it, I'm supposed to make sure Murtry doesn't hurt anyone. He ain't here, so all these folks are looking pretty safe. Might as well go where he is, make sure he don't hurt no one there either."

Elvi nodded and looked north. The cart was a small dot near the horizon throwing up a plume of spattered mud. She couldn't judge how quickly they were going, but she was sure they'd be beyond the horizon soon.

"If you get that working, can I come too?"

"Nope."

"Seriously, let me come with you," Elvi said, kneeling beside him. "You'll need backup out there. If anything goes wrong. What if you go blind again? Or if something stings you? I know the ecology out here better than anyone. I can help."

Amos picked up a fuel cell, squeezing the casing until the metal bowed out a degree, and slid the internal cell out into his hand. A slurry of green-yellow mud came with it.

"Holden was talking about aliens. Like living, thinking, communicating, mind-controlling aliens," Elvi said. "If that's true, I could talk with them. *Document* them."

Amos wiped the mud from the cell with his palm and squinted at it, sighing. He put it down and picked up the next one.

"We're going to die here," Elvi said, her voice soft, gentle, pleading. "The food's going to run out. You go out there, and you'll be passing through a whole biosphere no one's ever seen before. There are going to be things you and I haven't even imagined. I want to see those before I die."

The next cell opened. There was no mud, but the acrid stink of melted plastic filled the air, stinging her nose and eyes. Amos closed it again.

"You need to get electricity to drive that cart," she said. "If I tell you how to do that, will you take me with you?"

Amos turned his head to her, his gaze fastening on her like he was noticing her for the first time. His smile came slowly.

"You got something you want to tell me, doc?"

Elvi shrugged. "The alien moon defense grid thing shot down the shuttle with the fusion drive and the drop with batteries and fuel cells in it, but it let the food and medicine come through. It also isn't busy shooting the clouds, even though there are a bunch of organisms living in them that are made of complex organic compounds. It doesn't care about chemical energy inside compounds. You could have the *Rocinante* drop you a chemical fuel source. Acetylene, maybe. You've got acetylene tanks up there, don't you?"

"Hell, I got acetylene right here. But these here don't run on fire," Amos said.

"They don't have to," Elvi said. "The chemistry deck has a combustion chamber that runs assays by converting exothermic reactions into current and then measuring the output. It's not much of a chamber, but if you take that out and build a decent-sized combustion chamber—maybe a ten-centimeter surface—you could probably capture enough of the chemical energy from the burn to make the same current coming out of one of those things. We might need to build a transformer to get the amps and volts just right, but that's not actually hard."

Amos scratched his neck and rocked back on his heels. His eyes were narrow.

"You just come up with that on the spot?"

Elvi shrugged. "Does that mean I can come with you?"

Amos turned his head and spat on the ground. "Sure," he said.

"I just want to know why," Fayez said.

"Why what?" Elvi asked, walking through the main chamber of the ruins. She had two thick plastic sacks of fresh-ish water. Potable, at least. And a box the size of her hand with protein rations in it. It was supposed to be enough for one person for one day, and it was all they were going to have until they came back to the camp in the ruins. She'd also found a satchel with a wide fake-leather belt to strap it closed.

"Why you're chasing after Holden again," Fayez said, ducking around a passing woman.

"I'm not chasing after Holden," Elvi said, then stopped and turned, putting her palm against Fayez's chest. She could feel his heartbeat against her fingertips. "You know I'm not chasing after Holden, don't you? Because that's...I mean, *no*."

"Then why?" he said.

The organisms still dying in Elvi's eyes had lost all their green tinge, but they left the world a little blurry. She felt like she was seeing Fayez through a filter that softened his features, smoothed his skin. He looked like a media star in some particularly unflattering role that involved a lot of mud and not many showers.

"Because I want to *see*," she said. "It's why I came out here. It's why I've been spending all my time taking samples and running assays. I love what I do, and what I do is go look at things. Holden said he was talking to aliens, and that he might be able to turn off the defense grid, and it means we're going to drive through the wilderness—"

"What's left of it," Fayez said.

"And because I'm going to die," Elvi said.

Fayez looked away.

"We're all going to die," Elvi said. "And we're all very probably going to die very, very soon. And my choices are to go out and look at this amazing, strange, beautiful, ruined world or else stay in the camp and watch everyone around me die by centimeters. And I'm a coward and a hedonist and I'm sometimes very, very selfish."

"You know. Between the two of us, I always thought of myself as more along those lines."

"I know."

Outside, Amos' kludged cart was roaring, the constant burn of the combustion chamber was like a synthesizer stuck on a particularly ragged and unpleasant G under middle C. Amos was in the cab, sitting at the controls. Fayez walked with her to the side of the cart and then helped her scramble up into the cab. When he stepped back, he had his hands shoved deep in his pockets. She couldn't see quite well enough to know if there were tears in his eyes too.

"Those the supplies, doc?" Amos asked.

"They're what we've got to work with."

"All right then. I got the signal from the captain's hand terminal locked in. We got maybe a week's worth of gas, and the guy I'm after's got a day's head start."

"I wish we had sunglasses," she said. "Or a pizza."

"Fallen fucking world, doc."

"Let's go."

The cart lurched once, the tires spinning in the mud for a moment, then catching and lurching again. The rain made tiny dots on the windshield, and a wide, smeary wiper cleared them away. The world before her was a vast plain of mud. She checked Amos' hand terminal. The path toward James Holden would take them through territory that had been forestlike, past the shoulder of a massive freshwater lake, through a maze of canyons that defied any standard geological explanation. She was going to see a world in the aftermath of utter disaster, but she would still see it. And the state of nature was always recovering from the last disaster.

"Stop," she said. "Could you please stop. Just for a minute?"

"You need a potty break, you should have thought of that before we started," Amos said, but he stopped the drive. She couldn't even hear the electrical motors winding down over the roar of the acetylene-powered generator. She opened the door of the cab and leaned out. They'd only gone a hundred meters. She could still see Fayez, even though he was mostly a dark, fuzzy blot. She waved, and he waved back. She gestured that he should come toward her, and he did. She watched him trot across the mud field, looking down and watchful for slugs.

When he reached the cab, he looked up at her. She was sure there were tears in his eyes now.

"Chances are I'm not coming back," she said.

"I know."

"Kind of need to get a move on, doc," Amos said. "Don't mean to be a buzz-kill or nothing."

"I understand," Elvi said. She looked down again. Her gaze met his dark eyes. "Are you getting up here?"

"Is he what?" Amos asked at the same moment Fayez said, "Of course I am."

Elvi scooted across the seat, making room for him. Fayez climbed up beside her and slammed closed the door. Amos looked at them both, his eyebrow lifted. Elvi smiled at him and pulled Fayez's arm over her shoulder.

"Don't remember this was part of the deal, doc," Amos said.

"It's kind of like our honeymoon," Elvi said. She felt Fayez stiffen for a moment, and then almost melt against her.

Amos considered that for a moment, then shrugged. "Whatever floats your boat."

Chapter Forty-Seven: Basia

How's it look in there?" Naomi said in Basia's helmet. She had a nice voice, a singer's voice. It sounded good even over the tiny suit speakers. Basia recognized that his cognition was drifting and shook his head once, sharply. A glance at his HUD told him his O2 levels were low, and he pulled out a replacement bottle.

I've found the other five holes," he said while he worked at the air intake nipple. "You were right. Two were behind a console. Tough to see from that side. But I think this is all of them in ops."

"Machine shop is next," she replied. "Got one slow leaker there. It's cramped. We've got some after-market equipment using up a lot of the space between hulls."

"I'll squeeze," Basia said, then pulled out a small metal disk and started welding it over one of the five holes.

"She is over the horizon...*now*," Alex said over the channel.

Naomi was sitting in her vacuum suit on the ops deck coordinating the work, so the only way anyone could talk to her was on her suit radio. Basia wanted to ask who *she* was, but started welding a second patch instead. A tiny red glob of molten metal spun off the bead and stuck to his faceplate, cooling to a black dot over his left eye. There wasn't much danger of it hurting his suit, but it was a rookie mistake anyway. A sign he was tired. The gentle rotation of the *Rocinante* at the end of the tether made free-floating objects drift toward the walls. He'd need to remember that.

"Didn't leave any presents for us?" Naomi asked, still talking about the mysterious *she*.

"Nope," Alex said. "I keep hitting her with our targeting laser when she goes by. A warning."

"The PDCs are totally shut down, and plasma torpedoes don't work now," Naomi said.

"Yeah, but *they* don't know that. Last they saw, I chopped their shuttle into sushi with a PDC burst."

"Kinda wish we hadn't done that."

"Well, do you like one big hole or lots of little ones?"

"Fair point," Naomi said. "Almost done down there?"

It took Basia a second to realize she'd started talking to him again. "Yeah, last one going up now."

"I'll guide you to the machine shop exterior bulkhead."

Naomi hadn't been kidding about cramped. There was some kind of large, blocky device taking up almost all of the space between the inner and outer hull. A long metal tube projected from one side of it, and seemed to run the entire length of the ship's hull like a sewer pipe. On the opposite side of the device, a complex-looking feed mechanism sat. Flanking the central mechanism, and also down almost the entire length of the tube, sat twin rows of powerful-looking industrial batteries.

"Sixty-two percent, XO," Alex said. "Droppin' fast. And the

clock's down to about twelve hours for the *Barb*. If I had thrusters that worked, I'd be wantin' to do a burn about now."

"I've shut down everything I can think to shut down," Naomi replied. "So our power is what it is. I'm trying to come up with a plan for moving working thrusters to replace broken ones, and wind up with some semblance of maneuverability. But it's not a trivial problem. We're pretty beat up."

Basia played his suit's light around the space until he found the faintest trace of frozen vapor. It led him to the tiny hole in the machine shop's bulkhead, and seconds later he was patching it with another metal disk. The actinic blue of his torch threw the space into bright relief, the shadows of conduits and thruster housings dancing madly in the glare.

"Alex?" Basia said as he worked.

"Yo."

"What is this thing I'm next to? It looks high-powered. Should I avoid getting any hot residue on it?"

"Uh, yeah," Alex said, then gave a humorless laugh. "Please avoid that."

"It's a rail gun," Naomi said. "We had it added to the ship. You might damage it, but it won't blow up or anything. It fires solid metal slugs, not explosives."

"Okay," Basia replied. "Just about done here."

"It cost about three hundred thousand Ceres new yen," Alex said. "So don't break it, or you bought it."

By the time Basia had returned through the airlock, stripped off his welding rig and vacuum suit, then put everything away, Naomi had replaced the lost atmosphere on the ops deck and everyone was gathered there. She floated near the command console, still wearing her lightweight atmosphere suit, but with the helmet off. Havelock and Alex were across the deck from her, clinging to the combat operations crash couch. The three of them were floating in the sort of intense silence that only follows a heated conversation.

"There a problem?" Basia asked when the deck hatch had closed behind him.

Alex and Havelock both looked away from him, something like embarrassment on their faces. Naomi did not look away. She said, "We're going to lose the *Barbapiccola*."

"What?"

"I have a plan for moving five maneuvering thrusters from the starboard side of the ship to port. This will give us close to sixty percent maneuverability. It'll be enough to keep us in the sky until the power runs out. But we can't do it fast enough to tug the *Barb* out of her descent. She'll start scraping atmo before we're even halfway done. We have to cut her loose."

"No," Basia said.

"We tried," Naomi continued as though he hadn't spoken. "But the damage caused by the shuttle was just too serious. I'm going to call the captain of the *Barb* and ask that your daughter be transferred to this ship. The price is there will be a few others that come with her. Just a few, though."

Basia felt an almost overwhelming sense of relief, followed by an equally powerful rush of shame. "There are a hundred-some people on the *Barbapiccola*. We just let them all die?"

"Not all of them, but even if we wanted to bring them all here, they wouldn't fit. A full company on the *Roci* would be twenty-two. Our other choice is to die with them," Naomi said. Her voice trembled, but her gaze was steady. She knew exactly how awful her words were, but she wasn't backing away from them. Basia found himself suddenly very afraid of the *Rocinante*'s executive officer. "But we're not buying ourselves much in the process. With our power failing and running on a little over half thrust, we're getting very close to the point that we won't be able to get to a stable orbit where we can die slowly when the environment systems shut down. And, of course, we'll have moved as many of the *Barb*'s crew as we can to this ship. Which just means we'll burn through our power that much faster. This is lose, lose, lose, Basia. There aren't any good choices anymore."

Basia nodded, accepting her statements without argument. She was the expert. But he felt like there was something missing. It itched at the back of his mind. To distract himself, he traced with his finger in the condensation building up on the nearest wall panel. That shouldn't be happening. The atmosphere system shouldn't be allowing humidity to build up like that. But now that he thought about it, he realized that the air did feel thick, and too hot. Naomi, running the environmental systems at minimum power. She wasn't lying. They'd run to the very edge of their ability to keep themselves in the sky.

"When do they come, and how do they get here?" Havelock asked, talking about refugees from the *Barbapiccola*.

"Three hours. I want you to go down and escort them. I don't know how good their suits are, but I don't expect much. We may have to haul some EVA suits of our own down to them."

"Roger that," Havelock said with a nod. An Earthman's nod. Tipping the head back and forth. A move totally invisible in a space suit. Without thinking about it, Basia tipped his fist back and forth to show him how to do it right. Havelock ignored him.

But thinking about something else for a moment broke the logjam in his brain, and the idea he'd been fumbling toward popped fully formed into his head.

"Why don't we use the batteries for the rail gun?"

"The what?" Havelock said.

"Huh," Naomi said. "Not a terrible idea. They're topped off, right?"

"They pull power to keep themselves full when the reactor's on, and we haven't fired the gun and they discharge really slow when not in use," Alex replied. "But they're on a separate system. No way to pull power the other direction without some work."

"I can work," Basia said. "I'll do it. Tell me what to do. I'll recharge my suit and the welding rig right now."

"Wait," Naomi said. Her face had gone strangely blank, except for her eyes moving rapidly back and forth like she was reading something in the air. "Wait a minute…"

Havelock started to say something, but Alex grabbed his arm and silently shook his head.

"We'll pull power off the rail gun grid, transfer it over to the main grid, and use it to heat propellant mass for thrust," she finally said.

"Yep," Alex agreed.

"With loss at every step. That's really inefficient."

"Yep," Alex repeated.

"When we have propellant mass already in the system without moving the power," she continued. "Alex, how much acceleration does a two-kilo slug traveling at five thousand meters per second give the ship?"

"Enough," Alex replied with a sly grin, "that we're supposed to only fire it with the main drive on."

"Sounds like a thruster to me," Naomi said, grinning back at him.

"Uh," Havelock cut in, "the ship is spinning a little after that shuttle strike and all? Won't that make it tough to, you know, aim?"

"It's not a trivial problem," Naomi admitted. "We'd need to make sure we fire at the exact millisecond the two ships and the cable are aligned. No way a human could judge it. But the *Roci* can if I tell her what we need."

"Isn't the *Barb* in the flight path?" Havelock asked.

"Right," Naomi said, her voice soft and uninflected. "So the sequence will have to be tipping the *Roci* nose down as we spin past the firing point, launching a round, then tipping her back nose up to keep from spinning out of control on that new axis. Fortunately, *those* thrusters work."

"This sounds," Basia said, "pretty hard."

"Well," Naomi said with a smile and a wink. "It's only the most complicated nav program I'll have ever written, but I have a couple hours to do it in."

"I don't know about you folks, but I'm excited to be part of this plan," Alex said. "Let's get going."

Basia watched the clock tick away the hours and minutes to his daughter's death.

Naomi sat at her console rapidly typing. The symbolic language she used to program the *Rocinante*'s navigation systems meant nothing to him. Watching her work was like listening to someone speak in a foreign language: the awareness of information without actual meaning. But he watched her anyway, knowing that she was building a program that might add precious minutes back to the clock. Maybe hours. Not days.

Alex was back up in his cockpit, out of sight. But periodically he called down on the ship's comm to talk to Naomi about her work, so he was apparently following along from his own station. He would ask for clarifications or make suggestions, but his words were as empty of content to Basia as the symbols on Naomi's screen.

Havelock had gone belowdecks to move the emergency escape bubbles out of the cargo hold and up to the main airlock. The rail gun plan might not work, and the next step was to evacuate as many people from the *Barbapiccola* as the *Rocinante* could handle.

It was all just delaying games. Try to save the *Barb* a little longer with their rail gun heroics. If not, save a few people by moving them to the *Roci* before she fell out of the sky or turned into a killing jar with twenty more people breathing her air and overloading her life support.

But they all did it without question. They fought and worked and devised intricate plans to buy more time. Basia had no doubt that they'd work just as hard to keep each other alive for even a few more minutes. It wasn't something he'd ever had to think about before. But it did seem to be a microcosm of everything in life. No one lived forever. But you fought for every minute you could get. Bought a little more with a lot of hard work. It made Basia proud and sad at the same time. Maybe that was how a warrior felt, standing on ground he knew he'd never leave alive. Making the choice to fight as long and hard as he could. Basia couldn't think why *I went out, but I didn't go out easy* was such an appealing and romantic notion, but it was.

Looking at the angry brown ball of Ilus, rotating past on his screen, Basia thought, *You'll kill us, but you won't kill us easy.* He took a deep breath and worked hard not to thump himself on the chest.

"You okay over there?" Naomi asked, not looking up from her work.

"Fine, fine. How are you?"

"Almost there," she said. "The trick is that we'll have a lot of thrust coming from one vector and not along our center of mass with the cable attached, and we only have maneuvering thrusters on three sides of the ship. So, we have to minimize rotation to port. *But,* we can't use the starboard fore thruster to counteract that rotation because the cable changes where our center of mass is. It's actually a fun problem to figure out."

"I have no idea what any of that means," Basia said. "Is it working?"

"I think it will. Alex agrees. We'll fire in a couple of minutes on the next rotation. Then we'll know."

"Great," Basia said.

The deck hatch clanged open and then closed again as Havelock pulled himself up into the ops deck. He'd changed out of his RCE jumpsuit and armor into loose-fitting gray sweats with the name ROCINANTE across the chest. The security officer was bigger than Holden, so if the clothes hung loose on him, they must belong to Amos. Basia thought maybe he wouldn't wear Amos' clothes without asking.

"The emergency stuff is in the airlock," Havelock said to Naomi's back. She hadn't looked up from her work when he came in. "I also threw a couple of EVA packs, some extra air bottles, and Basia's welding rig in there. I can't think of anything else we might need."

"Thank you, Dimitri," Naomi said.

"Dimitri?" Basia asked with a raised eyebrow.

"You've got a problem with that? Isn't Basia a girl's name?" Havelock shot back.

"It was my grandmother's name, and she was a solar-system-wide famous physicist, so it's a great honor to be named after her. I was the first grandchild."

"You two can shut up or leave the deck," Naomi said. Then she hit the wall comm and added, "Alex, you ready up there?"

"Think so," Alex replied with his heavy drawl. "Just a sec, lemme tweak one thing here…"

"Can we throw this up on the big screen?" Basia asked. "I'd like to see what happens."

Naomi didn't answer, but the main screen on the deck shifted from a tactical map to a forward telescopic view. The image rotated slowly past the brown-and-gray ball of Ilus, and then past the distant gray hulk of the *Barbapiccola*, and then on to the starry black.

"Missed our window," Naomi said. "You almost ready?"

"Yeah," Alex replied, dragging the word out to three syllables. "Now. Good to go."

"Executing," Naomi said and tapped a button on her screen, but nothing happened. The view on the big screen continued to slowly pan until Ilus came back into view. Then the *Barbapiccola*. Then, without warning, the *Rocinante* tipped violently forward and something very loud happened in the belly of the ship. A bright dot of fire and a curve of flame appeared in the planet's atmosphere. Basia found that the far bulkhead was now traveling toward him at a slow but noticeable speed. The ship pitched again, the various maneuvering thrusters firing in staccato bursts. When the noise and movement was over, the view on the main screen was steady, locked onto the *Barbapiccola*.

"Huh," Alex said. "I'm seeing activity from the moons."

"Are they shooting at us?" Havelock said.

"Nope. Looks like they're trying to knock down the gauss round," Alex said. "Full points for optimism."

"We're not rotating anymore," Basia said.

"No," Naomi replied. "Give me any three directions of thrust and I can find a way to stop us. Now we just keep it here firing and adjusting, and we should be adding some speed to our orbit."

Basia looked down at the timer counting away the *Barbapic-cola*'s remaining life. It had added a little over four minutes. "How often can you fire?"

"About every five minutes or so, if we don't want to overheat the rails and burn the batteries out. At least, every five minutes until the batteries are dead."

"But—"

"We've just stopped the degrading orbit, but not much more," Naomi said.

"*Israel*'s coming back around," Alex said. "She dumped something off."

"Goddammit," Naomi muttered. "Give us a fucking break, will you guys? What are they dropping?"

"Men in suits," Alex said.

"It's the militia," Havelock said. He'd pulled himself over to a tactical display and was zooming it in and out. "Twelve of them, in vacuum armor with EVA packs. Plus an equal number of metallic objects of about human size. Not sure what those are."

"Any speculation on what they're doing?" Naomi said, switching her view to match his.

"They're engineers. They know how crippled we are. How vulnerable. So my guess is they're going to try to kill us."

Chapter Forty-Eight: Holden

Life at the naval academy had been so stressful for Holden that at the end of his first term he'd celebrated by going to a party and drinking until he passed out for twenty hours. It had been his first lesson on the difference between unconsciousness and sleep. They might seem the same, but they weren't. After twenty hours, he'd woken feeling totally unrested, and the morning PT the next day had almost killed him.

Riding on Miller's material transfer network, it was difficult to get any sense of the passage of time. The first time Holden came to, his hand terminal told him ten hours had passed. He could tell he'd spent it unconscious rather than sleeping because he felt exhausted and sick. His throat hurt, his eyes burned like they'd been sandpapered, and all of his muscles ached. It almost felt like a flu, except that the antivirals he took every three months made that pretty much impossible. He turned on his armor's diagnostic system, and it gave him a series of shots. He had no idea what. He drank half the water in his canteen and closed his eyes.

It was nine hours later when he woke again, and this time he was almost rested, the soreness in his throat gone. At some point he'd passed the threshold from unconsciousness to sleep, and his body was rewarding him for it. He stretched out on the metal floor until his joints popped, then drank the rest of his water.

"Wakey wakey," Miller said. He slowly appeared in the darkness, surrounded by a halo of blue light, as if someone were turning up his dimmer switch.

"I'm awake," Holden replied, then rattled his empty canteen at Miller. "But you stuffed me into this cattle car so fast I wasn't able to get supplies. Gonna get pretty thirsty if there isn't, you know, an alien drinking fountain for something."

"We'll see. But that's actually the least of our problems right now."

"Says the guy who doesn't drink."

"There's a damaged piece of the system ahead," Miller continued, "and I'd hoped we'd be able to get around it. No such luck. We're on foot from here."

"Your fancy alien train is broken?"

"My fancy alien material transfer system has been sitting unused for over a billion years and half the planet just exploded. Your ship was built less than a decade ago and you can barely keep the coffee pot running."

"You are a sad, bitter little man," Holden said as he climbed to his feet and pushed against the train door. It didn't open.

"Hold on," Miller said and vanished.

Holden turned the brightness up on his terminal and spent a few minutes checking over his equipment while he waited. Miller had grabbed him right after his final patrol around the settlement, which meant he had his armor, his pistol, and quite a few magazines of ammunition, all of which was pretty likely to be useless. He also had one empty canteen, no food, and a suit medical pack that was running low on almost everything, all of which would have been much handier to have fully stocked. When his body finally woke up enough to be hungry, he expected to be quite willing to trade his gun in for a sandwich. He didn't think the alien structures would have many vending machines.

Ten minutes passed, and his anxiety shifted to impatience. He sat down again and tried to call the *Rocinante* on his hand terminal, but got a failed connection message. He tried Elvi, Lucia, and Amos. All failed. Whatever the alien subway was made out of, it was blocking his signals to the hub on the *Roci*. It had to be that. The alternative was that the *Roci* wasn't working, and that opened up too many bad scenarios. He pulled up a mindless pattern-matching game and played that for a while, until the terminal gave him a low-battery warning and he turned it off.

After an hour passed, he started to get nervous. He wasn't claustrophobic, and he'd spent most of his adult life in tiny cabins on space ships, but that didn't mean he relished the idea of dying alone in a small metal box deep under the earth. He kicked the container's door a few times and shouted to Miller, but got no reply.

Which was, in its own way, fairly alarming.

The container he'd been sleeping in during the long trip north was empty. The only tools he had with him were used for repairing his armor and weapons. There was nothing that could cut through the metal or bend it. He kicked the door again, this time putting enough effort into it that it hurt his shins. It didn't move at all.

"Huh," he said out loud. If Miller had brought him all this way just to let him die in an abandoned train car, it was the longest prank setup in history.

Holden was doing a mental inventory of everything he was carrying, trying to figure out if any combination of things might make an explosive powerful enough to blow the door off, and carefully ignoring the fact that any such explosion would probably liquefy any biology inside the small metal compartment, when a loud metallic groan came from outside the cart that rose in pitch to a shriek. The compartment shuddered and rocked. A long series of powerful hammering sounds assaulted him. Then another metallic scream that grew to deafening levels.

The door to the compartment vanished, torn from the container in one massive blow. On the other side stood a nightmare.

At first glance, it looked like a massive collection of appendages and cutting tools. It stood on six of its limbs, and waved four others in the air like a crustacean made of steel and knives. Whipping through the air around the heavier cutting arms were a dozen or more tentacles of what looked like black rubber. As he watched, two of the tentacles gripped the inside edges of the doorway and bent them out with fearsome strength.

He pulled his pistol, but didn't point it at the thing. It felt very small and inadequate in his hand.

"Put that away," the monster said in Miller's voice. "You'll put your eye out."

Holden hadn't thought much about the fact that every time he heard Miller's voice over the last year, it had been a protomolecule-induced hallucination. But at the sound of the detective's voice in the air, actual vibrations moving through the atmosphere and hitting his eardrums, the strangeness of it made him feel a little lightheaded.

"Is that you?" Holden asked in what he was pretty sure was the new universal winner for stupid questions.

"Depends what you mean," the Miller-bot said and backed away from the opening. It was surprisingly quiet for such a huge metallic monster. "I'm able to get into the local hardware, and this thing was in pretty good shape for having missed its three-month warranty check by a thousand million years or so."

Miller did something, and suddenly Holden could see the detective in his rumpled suit standing where the monster had been. He shrugged and smiled apologetically. But even as Holden saw a projection of Miller, superimposed over it he saw the robot. It was doing the same shrug, though instead of hands it used two massive serrated crab claws. It would have been comic if it hadn't come with a splitting headache.

"One or the other," Holden said, squeezing his eyes shut. "I can't see both things. It breaks my brain."

"Sorry. No problem," Miller replied, and when Holden opened his eyes again only the robot was there. "Come on, we have a lot of ground to cover."

Holden hopped out of the material transfer container and onto a flat metal floor. Various sections of the Miller-bot's carapace glowed with a faint light, and unlike the blue light that had always accompanied the Miller ghost, it actually illuminated the space around it.

Pointing at one glowing limb, Holden said, "Can you make that brighter?"

In answer, all of the glowing sections of the robot intensified until the tunnel was as bright as noon. The reason for the material transfer cart's stoppage became apparent. A couple dozen meters ahead, the metal tunnel was blown apart and filled with rocks and debris.

Reading his mind, Miller said, "Yeah. Not everything is handling the reboot well. Power node for the mag-lev woke up bad and blew itself up. Only it's not exactly mag-lev. Close enough, though, you can get the picture."

"Can we get past it?"

"Well, we can't repair the track, but I can get you out. Making passages," the Miller-bot said, waving one massive claw in the air, "is what this thing's for. He used to dig and maintain these tunnels. Hop on."

"You're fucking kidding me."

"No, seriously, climb on. This guy can move faster than you can on foot."

"Miller," Holden said. "You are made entirely out of cutting edges and pinch points."

One of the black tentacles twisted around, looking over the

robot's carapace carefully. "Hold on," Miller said, and with a hum and a few metallic clanks, the torso of the robot twisted into a new configuration, leaving a wide flat spot on its back. "There you go."

Holden hesitated for a moment, then climbed up one of the robot's legs and onto its back. The Miller-bot trundled forward to the damaged section of tunnel and the four big forward limbs went to work, tearing out the twisted metal of the tunnel walls and clearing the earth and stone that had filled the space. The machine worked with speed, precision, and a terrifying casual strength.

"Hey Miller," Holden said, watching the robot peel up a two-meter section of the tunnel's metal flooring and rapidly cut it into tiny pieces. "We're still friends, right?"

"What? Ah, I see. When I'm a ghost, you yell at me, tell me to get lost, say you'll find a way to kill me. Now I'm wearing the shell of an invincible wrecking machine and you want to be buddies again?"

"Yeah, pretty much," Holden replied.

"Nah, we're good."

He punctuated the words with one last massive blow that shattered a two-ton boulder into rubble. By hunching down on his six legs, Miller was able to squeeze through a small opening in the tunnel blockage. Holden lay down flat on the robot's back, a jagged piece of the tunnel roof passing less than three centimeters from his face.

"Clear sailing from here," Miller said, "but the mag-lev's dead after this. No more trains."

"We have any better idea what we're looking for?"

"Only in general terms. About the time one-celled organisms on Earth were starting to think about maybe trying photosynthesis, something turned this whole damned planet off. Took it off the grid, and killed everything high enough up the food chain to have an opinion. If I'm right, the thing that did that's not entirely gone. Every time something reaches into this one particular place, it dies."

"Sorry to hear that," Holden said.

"Don't be," Miller said. "It's what we're hoping for. Now buckle up. We're going to try and make up some lost time."

The robot bolted off down the tunnel, its six legs a blur of motion. Even moving at fairly high speed, the ride on its back was very smooth.

Holden surprised himself by falling asleep again.

He woke to something cold and rubbery touching his cheek.

"Stop it," he said, waving one arm at the thing.

"Wake up," Miller said, the detective's voice rumbling though the robot's carapace.

"Shit," Holden said, sitting up suddenly and wiping saliva off the side of his face. "I'd forgotten I was here."

"Yeah, I'd say a week of no sleep and too many amphetamines broke you a little," Miller said. "You went on quite the bender."

"Only without the fun."

"I've been on a few myself," Miller said and added a strange metallic laugh. "None of them are fun. But we're about to hit the processing station, so get awake."

"What should we be expecting?"

"I'll tell you when I see it," Miller said.

Holden pulled out his pistol and checked the magazine and chamber. It was ready to go. It felt a little like playing grown-up. Anything that the Miller-bot monstrosity couldn't handle wasn't going to be stopped by a few shots from his sidearm. But, like so many things in life, when you come to the spot where you're supposed to do the rituals, you do them. Holden slid the pistol back into its holster but kept one hand on it.

It took him a minute to see it, but a point of light appeared ahead in the tunnel and then grew. Not reflected light from the robot, but something glowing. Holden felt a rush of relief. He'd traveled longer and farther than he knew in the small metal tunnels of the transfer system. He was ready to go outside.

The tunnel ended in a complex maze of new passages. A routing station, Holden guessed, where the arriving material was sent off to its various destinations. The walls were all of the same dull alloy as the tunnel. What machinery was visible in the cramped space was inset into the walls and flush with them.

The Miller-bot paused for a moment, its tentacles waving at the tunnel choices. Holden could picture Miller standing still at the junction, tapping one finger on his chin while he decided which path to take. And then, suddenly, he actually *could* see Miller overlapping the robot. The headache returned with a vengeance.

"That one was kind of your fault," Miller said. "It's an interactive system."

"Do we have any idea where we're going?"

Miller answered by trundling off down one of the many new tunnels. A few seconds later, they'd exited into a cavernous new space. It took Holden a few moments to realize that it was all still artificial. The room they entered felt too big to be a construct. It was like standing at the core of the world and looking up for the crust.

All around stood vast silent machines. Some were moving, twitching. They were recognizably designs that the protomolecule favored. They had the same half-mechanism, half-organic look of everything else he'd seen them build. Here, a massive system of tubes and pistons rising from a gantry twisting into whorls like a nautilus shell. There, an appendage coming from the ceiling, half again as long as the *Rocinante*, and ending in a nine-fingered manipulating hand the size of Miller's robot. Light poured into the space seemingly from everywhere at once, giving the air a gentle golden hue. The ground was vibrating. Holden could feel the soft pulses through the robot's shell.

"We're in a lot of trouble, aren't we?" Holden asked, breathless.

"Nah," Miller said, rotating the robot to test the air in every direction with its tentacles. "This is just initial material sorting and reclamation. Not even to the processing center."

"You could park a battleship in this room."

"It's not for show," Miller said, then the robot began scuttling toward a distant wall. "This is the point of this planet."

"Huh," Holden said. He found he was missing all of his other words. "Huh."

"Yeah. So, as far I can figure it, there are minerals native to this system that are fairly rare, galactically speaking."

"Lithium."

"That's one," Miller agreed. "This planet is a gas station. Process the ore, refine it, send it down to the power plants, then beam the collected energy out."

"To where?"

"To wherever. There are lots of worlds like this one, and they all fed the grid. Not the rings, though. I still don't know how they powered those."

The robot moved with machine speed toward a distant wall, and a section of the structure slid away. It left an opening the size of a repair shuttle, and more lighted machinery beyond. Some of the giant devices were moving with articulations more biological than mechanical. They pulsed, contracted, rippled. Nothing so prosaic and common as a gear or a wheel in sight.

"Are we moving through a fusion reactor right now?" Holden asked, Naomi's question about radiation exposure on his mind.

"Nope. This is just ore processing. The reactors are all in that chain of islands on the other side of the world. These guys built for flexibility and redundancy."

"You know," Holden said, "one of the geologists told me this planet has been heavily modified. All of that was done just to turn it into a power station?"

"Why not? They didn't need it for anything else. Not a particularly good planet, rare metals aside. And be glad they did. You think you can have an underground rail system last two billion years on any planet with tectonic action?"

Holden was quiet for a moment, riding the Miller-bot through the material refining plant as it throbbed around him. "It's too much," he finally said. "That level of control over your environment is too much. I can't get my brain around it. What could kill these guys?"

"Something worse."

The Miller-bot ducked under what looked like a conveyor system made of metal mesh wrapped around a pulsing musculature. It was clicking and groaning as part of the mechanism tried to move while the rest of it remained frozen. Holden had a sudden, vivid memory of a goat he'd found as a child. It'd had one broken leg wrapped in a barbed-wire fence, the other three feebly pushing at the ground to free it.

"So there's the thing," the Miller-bot said, waiving its claws around at the machinery, "this right here was the point of this place. It's why this planet *exists*. And right around here somewhere is a blank spot in the planetary network. A place we can't touch."

"So?"

"So, whatever's in that blank spot, it's not from around here. And if it's a bullet, then whoever did this knew to shoot for the heart."

Chapter Forty-Nine: Havelock

Havelock moved across the surface of the *Rocinante*, magnetic boots clicking to the exterior plating, then lifting free again. To his right, the sun—*a* sun, anyway—shone brighter than a welding torch. To his left, the great, clouded curve of New Terra filled his personal sky, the planet looming in. The upper boundary of the exosphere was invisible if he looked down, the gases too thin for an imperfect human eye to make out. The vast, sweeping curve of it before and behind the ship was hardly more then a grayness against the void. It felt too close. It *was* too close. He could already imagine the vicious friction tearing away his suit, the ship, the thin air burning him worse than a belt sander. The angry hot slag that had been one of the defense moons glowed high above, dull red against the pure white stars. His feet grabbed on to the plating, held, released.

"How's it looking out there?" Naomi asked in his ear.

"As well as could be expected. Kind of wish that planet wasn't quite so up in my face. I keep feeling like it's trying to pick a fight."

"Yeah, I was thinking that too."

The point defense cannon was a single thick barrel on a hemispheric swivel joint, the metal smooth as a mirror. The hole at the end was a black dot small enough that Havelock could have blocked it with the tip of his ungloved pinky finger. The little tungsten slugs it spat out would have been small enough to hold in the palm of his hand, and the feed would have spat them out by the hundreds every second. It was a machine of inhuman power and sophistication, built to react faster than a human brain and with enough force to shoot down anything that threatened the ship.

Without power, he could use it to hide behind.

He lay flat against the decking, just the toes of the mag boots engaged. He took the rifle off his back, synced it to the suit's HUD, and a handful of new stars appeared. Red for the militiamen, green for whatever the other things were they were hauling with them. The *Rocinante* bucked under him, the horizon of the ship shifting as the rail gun fired. A half dozen streaks of blue danced from the defense moons above, marking the path of the rail gun's round with the instantaneous violence of lightning. He shifted a few centimeters, correcting for the movement of the ship, reacquired his targets, and opened the general frequency.

"Gentlemen," he said. "This really isn't something we need to be doing."

He saw them respond. Their bodies stiffening, their heads craning while they tried to look for him. No one came on the channel. He zoomed in on them. Their faceplates were darkened against the sun, making them anonymous. But he knew all of them.

"Honestly, why? What's this for? That ship down there and everyone on her is going to die. We're doing everything we can to put that off, but you guys have done the math, right? You have the same numbers we do. You don't gain anything from this. It's just being mean. You don't need to do that."

One of the dots flinched. At a guess, the chief engineer was shouting on whatever frequency they were all using now. Drowning him out. Havelock let his sight drift to one of the other dots. The angle made it hard to parse exactly what he was seeing. A gas storage tube of some kind, with complications of wire and circuit board on either end. Some kind of improvised missile, he guessed. They would have been pointless if the PDC he was hiding behind had been working. He wondered whether the engineers knew the *Roci*'s defenses were down, or if they only guessed. Or if the prospect of their own deaths and their hatred of the Belters had taken them far enough that the risk of being killed in order to deny the *Barbapiccola* a little more life seemed worth it to them. No matter what, it was disappointing.

"Walters? Is this how you want to go down? Don't listen to them for a second. Seriously, just turn off the radio. We don't have to hurry here. Do you think you're doing the right thing?"

They were visibly closer now than they had been. They weren't accelerating toward him, but they weren't braking either. Havelock's HUD made the calculation. They'd be at the *Roci* or the *Barb* or the tether between them in about twenty minutes.

"You guys need to slow down now," Havelock said. "You're still my people, and I don't want to hurt any of you."

The radio clicked to life. The chief engineer's voice was thick with anger and contempt. "Don't try to play that on us, you traitorous bastard. Your little friend's PDCs are powered down. We saw that before we dropped. Do you think we're stupid? We have orders to bring you and the Belter bitch back to the *Israel* and put you both in the brig."

"Orders?"

"Straight from Murtry."

Because, Havelock figured, it was precedent. RCE would be able to assert that it had protected its claim down to the last minute. Murtry's legacy would be that he hadn't given up a centimeter. Not on the ground, not in space, not on the abstract legal battlefield. Nowhere.

There was a time not that long ago when Havelock would have thought there was a kind of hard purity in that. Now it just seemed weird and kind of pathetic.

"Okay," he said. "You're right. The PDCs are down, but you haven't thought the rest of this through. I am outside the ship. I'm armored. I have an integrated HUD and a weapon that can reach any of you right now. None of you have any cover. The reason you guys are alive right now is because you're my guys, and I don't want any of you hurt."

He watched them react. It was less than he'd hoped. The *Roci* bucked again. The bolt of the rail gun and the attacking streaks of energy from the moons. Havelock reacquired the targets. It took a fraction of a second for the HUD's alert to make sense to him. Four of the targets were moving. Fast. Four of the gas tanks, accelerating hard, a cloud of thin mist flowing out behind them as whatever residual vapor had been trapped in it froze into snow.

"You've got incoming," Alex snapped in his ear, and Havelock lifted his gun. One of the missiles was clearly flying off course, a vicious spiral wobble leading it down toward the planet. He took aim at one of the three remaining and blew holes on both sides of the tube. The improvised missile wobbled as whatever steering device the *Israel*'s engineers had put on the back struggled to use the last of the escaping ejection mass to correct the course, but the venting gases were too destabilizing. It drifted up and began to turn. He shifted to the two remaining targets. He wasn't going to have time to get them both, but he managed to sink two rounds in the one that was heading straight toward him, trying to knock out the payload.

The one remaining tube hit the *Roci*'s skin eight meters to Havelock's right, and the world went white. Something pushed him, and something hurt, and the sound of his suit radio was still there, but it was faintly distant. His body seemed very large, like it had expanded to fill the universe or the universe had shrunk down until it fit in his skin. His hands seemed a very long way away. Someone was shouting his name.

"I'm here," he said, and it felt like hearing a recording of himself. The pain started ramping up. His HUD was flashing red medical warnings, and his left leg was frozen stiff and unbending. The stars spun around him, New Terra coming up from below him and then spinning up past his head. For a moment, he couldn't find the *Rocinante* or the *Barbapiccola*. Maybe they were gone. He caught a passing glimpse of the *Israel*, though, far off to his right, and so small he could almost have mistaken it for a tightly packed constellation of dim stars. His HUD spooled up a fresh warning, and he felt a needle fire into his right leg. A cold shudder passed through him but his mind seemed to clear a little.

"Havelock?" Alex said.

"I'm here," Havelock said. "I'm not dead. I think I've been knocked off the ship, though. I seem to be floating."

"Can you stabilize?"

"I don't think so. The suit may be malfunctioning. Also I seem to have taken a lot of shrapnel in my left leg and hip. I may be bleeding."

"Do you have containment? Havelock? Are you losing air?"

It was a good question, but his gorge was rising. The spinning was making him sick. If he puked in the helmet, things would go from bad to worse very, very quickly. He closed his eyes and focused on his breath until he thought he could stand to look again. When he did, he kept his gaze on the unshifting images of the HUD readout.

"I have containment. I can breathe."

He heard Naomi sigh. It sounded like relief. He was flattered. The red dots of the militiamen spun past in the corner of his eye. He couldn't tell if they were still getting closer or if they'd stopped. Something bright happened in the atmosphere. The rail gun firing again. The planet rose up from below him and disappeared over his head.

"Hang on, coyo," Basia said. "I'm coming out."

"Belay that," Havelock said. "The guys from the *Israel* have more of their improvised missiles. They have guns. Stay inside."

"Too late," Basia said. "Already cycled out the lock. I just need too...Shit, that's bright."

Havelock twisted to the left, finding the *Rocinante* at last. The explosion hadn't thrown him as far as he'd thought, but he was on the drift now. Every breath took him farther from the metal-and-ceramic bubble of air. He wondered if he stayed out here whether his body would outlast the ships. His air supply wouldn't. The improvised missile had left a bright scar on the *Roci*'s outer hull, but didn't look like it had made any holes. Tough little ship.

"Huh," Basia said. "Well, they're shooting at me."

"Get back in the ship," Havelock said.

"I will. In a minute. Now where did you...Ah! There you are."

The grapnel struck his left arm, the gel splashing out and hardening in almost the same moment. At the first tug, his right leg shrieked in pain. But the vectors were such that his uncontrolled spinning slowed. The red dots of the militia were much closer now. Basia was in real danger of being shot. And there were still eight more improvised missiles.

The *Rocinante* jumped. The rail gun path through the high atmosphere glowed. Had it really only been five minutes? He had to have missed a couple of rounds. Or maybe getting blown out into space just changed how he experienced time. Or maybe he'd seen them and then forgotten.

"Don't pull me too fast," Havelock said. "You're going to have to put just as much energy into stopping me once I'm there. I could knock you off." *Or smash against the hull*, he didn't say.

"I've been in low g more than I haven't," Basia said, a real amusement in his voice. "Don't worry yourself."

The slow-spinning *Rocinante* came closer, Havelock's own spin making it seem like the universe and the ship and his own body were all in slightly different realities. Basia was a darker blot against gray ceramic and metal. Havelock's HUD cheerfully informed him that his blood pressure had been stabilized. He hadn't realized that it was unstable. The suit's attitude jets were still off-line, but Basia jumped up to meet him before he touched the deck, wrapping arms around his shoulders in a bear hug while Basia's suit slowed them.

"You need to get inside," Havelock said as his left mag boot locked against the hull.

"I was about to say the same to you," Basia said. "How much shrapnel did you take?"

Havelock looked at his leg for the first time. The suit was dotted with emergency sealant, the result of a dozen holes at least. "All of it, apparently."

"I've got fast movers," Alex said.

Havelock turned, rifle up, ready to shoot the missiles down before they reached him or die trying. It took a few seconds to find them. The green dots weren't heading for him. They were tracking down toward the planet. Toward the *Barb*.

"Okay," he said. "Hold on."

"I think they're still shooting at you," Naomi said. He moved forward, his leg not painful now so much as eerily numb. The shifting of the *Rocinante* was throwing off his aim. His HUD showed a lock and he pulled the trigger. One of the missiles exploded. Basia was hunched down, hands and legs against the decking, a stream of obscenity coming from him sounding like a chant. Havelock tried to move his mag boots, but he couldn't get them to respond. The *Roci* bucked.

"The crew of the *Barb*'s braced," Alex said. "First impact in—"

A new brightness bloomed below them. Havelock felt it, the impact traveling through the tether to the *Roci* to his boots almost instantaneously. Through the radio, he could hear Alex groan.

"Okay," Naomi said. "This is a problem."

Below them, the *Barbapiccola* was starting to tilt. The force of the explosions just enough to give it a little velocity, a tumble so slow, he could almost pretend it wasn't there. Almost. Not quite. The webwork of the tether was shredded. Two strands still held, but the others were drifting. One was cut in two, the others might have broken free of their foot supports or pulled the supports off the skin of the ship. He wasn't sure. New Terra was so large below, it filled his field of vision. A wave of vertigo washed over him, and he had the near-hallucinatory sense that the planet was a monster rising up through a vast ocean to swallow them all.

"Alex," Naomi said, "drop the cable."

"No!" Basia shouted at her.

"Not responding," Alex said. "The release seems to be damaged."

The *Roci* bucked, and the tether snapped taut.

"Cease firing!" Basia shouted. "Stop firing the rail gun!"

"Sorry," Alex said. "It was on automatic. It's shut down now."

"I'm going to the *Barb*," Basia said. "I've got my welding rig. May be something I can do."

"That's not going to work," Naomi said. "Just cut it." The *Barbapiccola* was a good ten degrees off the stable orbit she'd had. Tumbling.

"I'm not coming back in," Basia said. "And I'm not cutting it. I gotta go look."

"You remember they're still shooting at you, right?" Naomi said.

"I don't care," Basia said.

"I'll cover him," Havelock said. "I can do that."

"Can you move?"

Havelock consulted his HUD. His shredded leg was immobilized and under pressure to contain the bleeding. One of his attitude jets had been holed. The air in his suit smelled sharp, like melting plastic. That couldn't be a good sign.

"Not really, no," he said. "But Basia can get me to cover. The outer airlock hatch on the *Roci*, maybe. I can stay there and snipe."

"Hurry, then," Naomi said. "They're still getting closer, and eventually they'll get to a range they might hit something."

Havelock disengaged his mag boots and turned toward the Belter. "All right. If we're going to do this, let's go."

Basia clapped a hand on Havelock's arm and started dead hauling him down the ruined side of the ship. The pockmarks and bright spots where the debris of the shuttle had struck were everywhere, now joined by the scar of the improvised missile. A soft white plume curved into the void where something was venting. Time seemed to skip, and he was at the airlock's outer door. It was open, waiting for him. The red dots showed that his men were still ten minutes away. The *Barb* was above him now, and the planet above that. Not a beast rising to devour him, but a whole clouded sky falling down to crush him.

"Are you all right?" Basia said. "You can do this?"

"I'll live," Havelock said, and immediately realized how completely inappropriate that had been to say. "I'm all right. Lightheaded, but my blood pressure's solid."

"Okay, then. I'll be right back. Don't let those sons of bitches screw this up any worse."

"I'll do my best," he said, but Basia had already launched himself up along the tether. Havelock checked his rifle, his HUD. He still had to adjust for the *Roci*'s spin, but he found the little red dots quickly.

"All right, guys," he said. "You've made your point. Now let's just dial this back. There's still time. I don't want to hurt anybody." The words were surreal. Like a poem from some other century. A litany for deescalating conflict. No one really appreciated how much of security work was just trying to keep things under control for a few more minutes, giving everyone involved in the crisis a little time to think it all through. The threat of violence was just one tool among many, and the point was not making things worse. If there was any way at all, just not making things worse. It occurred to him that Murtry was actually really bad at that part of the job.

His HUD marked a fast-moving object. A bullet or a slow meteor. From the angle, probably a bullet. Another one was moving on a track to pass Basia. It was going to miss too, but not for much longer.

"All right," Havelock said, raising his rifle. "I'm counting to ten, and anyone that's still on approach, I'm going to have to put a hole in you. I'll try to just disable your suits, but I'm not making any promises."

The red dots didn't change their vectors.

It was strange. He'd come all this way, faced all these dangers. He was falling by centimeters into a planet and struggling for a few more minutes or hours of life. And the thing that worried him most was still that he was going to have to shoot somebody.

Chapter Fifty: Elvi

The cart had been designed for use on rough terrain and shipped out to a planet without roads. It wasn't smooth, but it was fast, and the roar of the generator and the whirring of the motors had made a kind of white noise that Elvi's brain tuned out after the first few hours, leaving her in something like silence. And all around them, the ruins of New Terra rose up and then passed away. The storm that had scoured First Landing into scraps and mud hadn't been local. All of the landscapes they passed through were shattered and drowned, but they were still fascinating. Still beautiful.

A forest of thin red bodies halfway between trees and gigantic fungi lay on their sides, the cart's wheels leaving tire tracks across their flesh. Flying creatures no larger than her splay-fingered hand fell into line behind the cart for hours, attracted by the noise or the movement of the spray of atmospheric hydrocarbons. She wondered how the frail creatures had survived the planetary disaster. When night fell, three vast columns of luminous dots rose up into the sky like skyscrapers built from fireflies. She didn't know if they were organisms like the mimic lizards or artifacts like her butterflies. A huge animal, as tall and wide across as an elephant but segmented like a caterpillar, lay dead and rotting along the crest of a low hill, structures like two interlocking sets of ribs crossing its massive sides and gnat-small carrion eaters flying around it like a fog. A silver-and-blue structure rose from a pool of grayish rainwater, collapsed, and rose again. It could have been anything, but she could only see its behaviors as play. Splashing in puddles. It was all she could do to keep from stopping and looking at it all.

A whole biosphere—or two or three—passed by her, teasing and hinting. She wished she could have seen it all before the storm. At best now, they would be able to guess at what had come before and see what came after. She took consolation by reminding herself that was always true. All of nature was a record of crisis and destruction and adaptation and flourishing and being knocked back down again. What had happened on New Terra was singular and concrete, but the pattern it was part of seemed to apply everywhere and maybe always. Even the aliens that had made the artifacts, the protomolecule, the rings, had suffered some vast and cosmic collapse.

At dawn the three of them shared the last of their food. There was still enough water to last a few days, but they would be hungry ones, and after that, she guessed they'd try to find something on the planet that they could stomach. They would fail and die. Unless Holden really could turn the reactors back on and drop something from the ships. A steep-walled canyon blocked their way, the erosion of centuries exposing strata of rock as even and unvarying as the pages of a book. It took the cart's expert system half an hour to find a path down and back up.

When she had mentioned how lucky they were that they hadn't hit anything like a mountain range, Fayez had laughed.

"You'd need tectonic plates first," he'd said. "This planet doesn't have mountains, it has hemlines."

None of them talked much, the noise of the cart drowning out anything short of shouting, but even if they'd been driving in silence, she didn't have the sense that Amos Burton would have spoken. He spent the day and a half of travel sitting at the cart's front edge, legs folded, his eyes on his hand terminal or the horizon. She thought there was a growing anxiety in the man's broad face, fear for Holden and for the ships above them and the planet all around, but she could also have been projecting her own feelings on him. He had that kind of face.

In some places, the tracks of the other cart—Murtry and Wei's cart—had wandered off on a different heading from their own. Sometimes the tracks got lost in the soft mud or vanished as they crossed wide, wet expanses of stone. But it always returned, the doubled track of their tires leading the way north into with wilderness. The headlights showed a swath of gravel and pale yellow snail-like organisms that were crushed under the cart's wheels. The air was colder, either because they were heading north or because the permanent cloud cover was keeping the energy of the sun up away from the planet's surface. Elvi had dozed as much as the emptiness in her belly permitted, her head on Fayez's lap, then they traded and he dozed in hers. Her dreams had been of Earth and trying to guide a pizza delivery service through the hallways of her university lab. She woke knowing that something had changed, but it took her a long moment to realize what. The cart was silent. She sat up, rubbing her eyes.

The other cart was in the headlights, spattered with mud and scarred along the side where it had scraped against something harder than its alloy siding. Amos dropped down and walked slowly around it twice, once looking at the cart and once looking out into the darkness.

"What is it?" she asked. "Is everything okay?"

"Their motors burned out," Amos said as he hauled himself

back up to the cart bed. "Got mud in the axles and didn't clean it out. Wherever they went from here, it was on foot."

"Are we close to Holden?"

"Oh yeah," Amos said, holding up his hand terminal. "This was the last blip we saw. It was short, but it gave us a pretty good lock on his position. We'll move toward it and hope he pops up again soon." The map didn't give her a sense of scale, but there were two indicators on it—one for them and the other for the captain. "If I'm right, we're getting right toward the end of this. And we're still the ones with the wheels. You two'd better lie down on the deck from here on in."

"Why?" Fayez asked.

"Case they decide to shoot someone," Amos said, restarting the generator.

Over the roar, she didn't think Amos heard Fayez say, "All right. That makes sense." But she did.

It was still the small hours of the morning—the long stretch between midnight and dawn—when they came to the structure. At first it was only a glittering in the darkness, like a bit of starfield. For a time, she thought it might be a break in the clouds. But the closer they came, the more obvious it became that it was something else.

In the darkness, the details were hard to make out, but it seemed to share the same almost organic architecture with the ruins back in First Landing, but a couple orders of magnitude larger. She had the sense of being at the edge of one of the huge industrial ruins of the European west coast, a place where something world-shatteringly huge had once made its power felt, and now had left its carapace behind. When the first pale flakes of snow filtered down through the headlights, she thought at first they were ashes.

"Is that where we're going?" Fayez asked.

"Think so," Amos said. "We haven't had a solid update on the captain in a couple hours, and that up there's about where the last reading came. Figure once you get inside, the signal don't penetrate."

"Or it ate him," Fayez said. "It could have just eaten him."

"Captain'd be a tough meal to swallow," Amos said.

The cart rolled on, moving toward Holden's last known position. Huge black spikes rose out of the ground, some of them swiveling to track their passage. The snow thickened, sticking to the ground and the cart. The structure remained clean, though, the white melting away. *It's warm*, Elvi thought, and couldn't explain why she found the idea so unnerving.

The cart passed under an archway ten meters high and into the structure itself. The snowfall stopped. All around them, the walls glowed, filling the space with a soft, shadowless light. The air was warmer and smelled of something sharp and acrid, like alcohol fumes, but harsher. The cart shifted one way and then another, hunting for the last, fading traces of Holden's electrical scent before giving up and stopping. Amos flipped it over to manual and took direct control. The pathways moved in swirls and loops for a time, then broadened, opening. The roof of the place was lost in darkness, and long tubes of what could have been conduits or vasculature rose up out of the earth and flowed together, inward, forward, toward whatever the functional heart of the place had been. The cart slowed. Amos took his shotgun from the deck and fired it. The report echoed.

"What are you shooting at?" Elvi asked.

Amos shrugged. "Nothing in particular. Just thought, you know, *loud*." He cupped his hands around his mouth and shouted. "Captain! You out there? *Holden!*"

"Are we sure he's in here?" Fayez said.

"Nope," Amos said, then went back to shouting. "Captain!"

A figure stepped from behind a massive machine, fifty meters in front of them. It was the size and shape of a human, and Elvi felt a moment's disorientation at how utterly out of place it seemed. Amos took a fresh grip on the shotgun and angled toward it. The figure stood, feet shoulder width apart, hands at its sides, as the cart approached. When they were within ten meters, Amos shut the generator down.

"Hey there," he said, his voice open and friendly and insincere.

"Hey yourself," Wei answered, lifting her chin.

Amos dropped from the side of the cart, his shotgun in his hand almost as if he'd forgotten it was there. Elvi looked at Fayez, who shrugged. She slid down to the ground, moving forward slowly. She kept her hand against the front tire, the tread warm against her palm, but cooling.

"What're you up to?" Amos asked.

"Work," Wei said, nodding to the vast structure all around them. "RCE's got a claim on all of this. I'm just making sure no one infringes on it."

"Meaning the cap'n."

"Meaning anyone," Wei said. Her voice was harder now.

"Well, it's a fucking ugly place if you ask me."

"It is."

"We really going to do this? Because I think it'd be a hell of a lot more fun for me to get Holden and you to get Murtry and we all see if there's not some way for the doc back there to find something with alcohol in it on this mudball."

"Yeah, that does sound like fun," Wei said. "But I'm on duty."

Fayez came up from behind Elvi, his arms crossed over his chest. His eyebrows were pulled together in distress.

"So thing is?" Amos said. "Yeah, Holden's in there someplace, and I'm figuring Murtry's in there looking for him."

"Could be."

"So when I get back up there and drive on by—"

"You don't want to do that, Amos. My orders are no one goes in. Hop back on and head the other way, you and me have no problems. Try to infringe further on RCE property, and I'm going to have to shoot you."

Amos rubbed his scalp with his left hand. The shotgun in his right seemed larger somehow. Like the threat of violence gave it significance and the significance gave it weight. Elvi found herself breathing in quick, short gasps and thought for a moment that something had changed about the air itself. But it was only fear.

"Captain's in there trying to get the reactors back on," Amos said.

"Then he's trespassing and he'll need to leave." Wei's stance softened for a moment, and when she spoke there was something like sorrow in her voice. Not the thing itself, but like it. "When it's time to go, there's worse ways than dying at your post."

Amos sighed, and Elvi could see his shoulders slump. "Your call," he said, raising the shotgun.

The report came from behind them, and Amos pitched forward.

"Down!" Murtry shouted at their backs, and Elvi hunched as automatically as a reflex. Fayez was pressed against her on one side, the massive tire on the other. The shotgun boomed at the same time as a sharp crack of a pistol sounded. Elvi looked out, and Wei was on the ground, her arms thrown out at her sides. Amos was struggling to his knees. His back was to her, and there was blood on the back of his neck, but she couldn't see where it was coming from. Murtry strode past her, firing his pistol, two, three, four times. She could see Amos' armored back quiver with every shot. Murtry wasn't missing. Her own scream sounded high and oddly undignified.

Murtry rounded the cart as Amos turned with a roar, the shotgun fired three times, the concussions beating at the air. Murtry stumbled back, but didn't fall. His next shot drew a small fountain of blood from Amos' thigh, and the big man collapsed. Murtry lowered his gun and coughed.

"Doctor Okoye. Doctor Sarkis," he said. The armor over his chest was shredded. If he hadn't been wearing it, Amos' blast would have blown the man's heart back out through his spine. "I have to say I'm disappointed by your decision to come here. And your choice of company."

Amos was gasping, his breath ragged. Murtry stepped delicately across to him and shoved the shotgun away. The metal hissed against the strange chitinous flooring.

"You shot him," Fayez said.

"Of course I did. He was threatening the life of one of my

team," Murtry said, walking over to Wei. He sighed. "My only regret is that I was unable to save Sergeant Wei."

Tears filled Elvi's eyes. She felt sobs shaking her. Amos lifted a hand. The thumb and forefinger were missing, and bright pink bone showed through the blood. She looked away.

"What are you talking about?" Fayez said. His voice was shaking.

"Doctor Sarkis? You have something you'd like to add?" Murtry said, slipping a fresh magazine into his pistol.

"You set this up. You set *all* of this up. You put her there to distract Amos and you shot him from behind. This isn't just something that happened and you did the best you could and poor fucking Wei. You *did* this!"

"If Mister Burton here had done as he was asked and left the site—"

"He was trying to save us!" Fayez shouted. His face was red and he stepped forward. His hands were in fists at his sides. Murtry looked up, something a little less than polite interest in his eyes. "He and Holden are trying to save us! You and me and Elvi and everyone. What the hell are *you* doing?"

"I'm protecting the assets, rights, and claims of Royal Charter Energy," Murtry said. "What I'm *not* doing, and I hope you understand this, is running around in a circle with my dick in my hand whining about how nothing matters because we're all going to die. We all knew when we got on the *Edward Israel* that we might not make it back. That was a risk you were willing to take because it meant you could do your job. I'm no different."

"You got Wei killed!" Fayez shouted. Elvi put her hand on his shoulder and he shrugged if off. "She's dead because of you!"

"Her turn now, my turn later," Murtry said. "But there are some things I need to get done before that."

The security chief checked his gun and looked down at Amos Burton staring raw hatred up at him. Murtry leveled the barrel at the bleeding man's face. *Look away*, Elvi thought. *Don't watch this happen. Look away.*

Fayez hit Murtry in the nose. The movement was so fast and awkward and artless that at first Elvi wasn't sure it had really happened. She watched the expression in Fayez's widening eyes as he understood what he'd done, and then when he committed to doing it again. Murtry turned his pistol away from Amos, swinging it toward Fayez, and the geologist ran into him with a shout. Murtry stumbled back but didn't fall.

"Elvi!" Fayez shouted. "Run!"

She took a step forward. Amos was writhing on the ground, blood pouring from somewhere in his suit. His teeth were bared and crimson. He was grinning.

"Run!" Fayez screamed.

The great gray walls rose around them. False stars glittering. She couldn't breathe. She took one tentative step forward. Then another. She felt like she was moving through a gel, forcing every motion. *Shock*, she thought. *I'm in shock. People die from shock, don't they?* In her memory, Fayez shook his head and said, *Oh look, another excuse to go talk to Holden.*

Holden. She had to find Holden. She took another step, then another. And then she was sprinting, her legs and arms pumping, small animal grunts forcing their way out of her throat. Somewhere behind her, a pistol fired twice, and then a third time. She didn't look back. Everything in her, everything she was, focused only forward, along the wide, dark veins of the structure, forward to where they converged.

Elvi ran.

Chapter Fifty-One: Basia

Basia reached out to touch the tether, and it vibrated under his gloved fingers like a living thing.

Alex," Naomi didn't quite yell over the general comm channel, "I'm sending you a burn program. We have to keep that cable taut until Basia cuts it or the *Barb* is going to rip us both apart."

"I'm not cutting it," Basia repeated, but no one replied. He checked to see if his microphone was on.

"One," Havelock said, ending his countdown. "Out of time guys."

If the security man's threats had any effect, Basia couldn't tell. His HUD was still displaying the red lines of incoming gunfire. He ignored them.

Above him, the *Rocinante* began shifting and firing its remaining maneuvering thrusters in response to the slow rotation of the *Barbapiccola*, desperately trying to keep slack out of the cable.

Two massive ships, each rotating in different axes, the cable could go from slack to thousands of tons of tension fast enough to tear the mounts out of the ships, and a chunk of the ship's structure along with it.

"Basia," Naomi said, her voice gentle. "I can't give you much time. And you know this ends the same way no matter what."

"I'm checking the connection to the *Barb*," he said instead of answering her.

The mount was a mess of twisted metal and frayed cable. Pieces of the hull had been torn free by dislodged footings, and the ones that were still connected stretched and flexed with each gyration of the ship. Basia tried to calculate how much tension must be on the rigging and cable and failed. If it snapped free, it would probably cut him in half. If he did cut it, he'd need Alex to put slack on it first.

"I'm not cutting it," he said again, more to himself than anyone else. Cutting it meant letting the *Barb* drift away, down into the upper atmosphere to rip apart and burn. To let Felcia burn. Alex had promised not to let that happen.

A pair of red lines drew themselves across his HUD and the words DANGER CLOSE flashed there briefly. He wasn't up on all his military jargon, but he could guess what that phrase meant. He pulled himself around the cable footing and took cover. Out in the blackness between the *Israel* and the *Barb*, twelve men in suits floated toward him on puffs of gas. They still had a few of their improvised missiles.

"Guys," Havelock said, real sadness in his voice.

"Havelock," Naomi yelled, "if you let those assholes shoot Basia you don't get to come back on my ship."

"Roger that," Havelock said sorrowfully. One of the twelve attackers spun sideways as a puff of white mist shot out of his EVA pack. The man continued to rotate wildly as he flew at high speed away from the others.

"One of you should go get him," Havelock said. "His EVA pack is toast."

Almost before he finished saying it, two of the remaining attackers jetted toward the disabled man, bringing their grapnel guns to bear.

"Havelock, you asshole," Koenen said on the open frequency where everyone could hear him. "I'm going to enjoy stomping a mudhole in you." He and his team opened fire on Havelock's position in the airlock, driving him back into cover.

Now that everyone wasn't looking at him, Basia took a moment to look over the mangled footing. "Naomi, I'm having the suit send you pictures of the damage."

"Basia, I—" she started.

"Help me fix this," he said, cutting her off. "If the *Barb* has more cable, I can reattach it here while Alex keeps us from totally losing our remaining connection."

"Basia," Naomi said, her voice gentle and sad. "This can't be fixed. The *Barbapiccola* is going down. Nothing is gained by her taking us with her."

"I do not accept that!" Basia shouted back at her, loud enough that his own suit's speakers distorted. "There has to be a way!"

His suit flashed a warning at him, and he pulled back into cover just in time to avoid a fusillade of shots that bounced off the hull, leaving shiny streaks in the dull metal. One of the remaining nine attackers threw his arms up like he was surrendering, then went motionless, spinning slowly toward the *Barbapiccola*.

"Williams is flatlined," the chief engineer said. "You just killed an RCE employee. You'll burn for that, Havelock."

"You know what, chief? Fuck you," Havelock replied, his tone low, but real anger in his voice for the first time. "You are the one who escalated this. I didn't ask for any of it. Pull out. Marwick, get your men out of here! Don't let him force this anymore!"

Another voice, older, sadder, replied on the radio. "Those aren't my men, Mister Havelock. You know as well as I do that I have no authority over the expeditionary team."

"That's right, motherfucker," the chief said. "We're acting on orders from Chief of Security Murtry."

While Havelock, Marwick, and the chief engineer argued, Basia tuned them out. They'd either agree or they wouldn't. Havelock would kill more of them or he wouldn't. The captain would assert authority or he wouldn't. None of that changed Basia's real problem. His daughter was on board a ship that was slowly spinning out of control and losing altitude. At some point, it would hit enough atmosphere to get noticeable drag, which would slow it and let it fall deeper into the killing air, and shortly after that, it would burn up. The *Rocinante* couldn't save it. Helplessness and grief washed over him, but he willed himself not to weep. He wouldn't be able to see with the water sheeting across his eyes. There had to be another way.

"Basia," Naomi said on a private channel to him. He could tell she'd switched him to a private channel because the argument between Havelock and the RCE people stopped suddenly mid-word. "Basia, I'm getting your daughter out."

"What?"

"I'm on the line with the captain of the *Barbapiccola*. I've explained the situation. He's ... well, he's not happy. But he understands. Alex promised you that if the ships went down, Felcia would be on the *Rocinante* when it happened. We're keeping that promise."

"How?" Basia asked. The way the ships were tumbling, he couldn't imagine how dangerous a docking attempt would be. The ship-to-ship docking tubes were flexible, but not that flexible.

"They're bringing her to the airlock now. They'll put her in a suit and send her out to you. You'll need to get her back to this ship and then ... you need to cut the cable."

Something about the docking tube stuck in his mind. The *Rocinante* couldn't dock with the *Barbapiccola* to pull the doomed crew off, but a space suit was, at heart, just a bubble of air to keep its wearer alive.

"The docking tube," he said. "Is there a way to seal it on both ends? We could put it on the *Barb*, seal it around some people, then move them across to the *Roci*."

"We'd have to cut it free from the airlock housing," Naomi said. A spray of bullets hit the cable footing as she spoke, like visual punctuation for her words. Another of the engineers spun away, his EVA pack holed in two places. Naomi continued talking but Basia wasn't listening.

"What about emergency airlocks," he said. "The plastic blister kind, you know? They're made to hold atmosphere and supply oxygen."

"You have to attach them to something," Naomi said.

"What if," Basia answered, "we attach them to each other? Seal to seal?"

Naomi was silent for a long moment. When she spoke again, her words were slow, measured. Like she was thinking them through as she spoke. "A life-support bubble." Basia could tell she'd switched them back to the general channel because Havelock's argument came thundering back. "Gentlemen, we have an idea. We'll pull the crew off the *Barbapiccola* on escape pods made of two emergency airlocks sealed together. The *Roci* only carries one, but if the *Barb* has one—"

"You kidding me?" a new voice said. Basia recognized it. The captain of the Belter ship. "I think somebody turned ours into parts for a still back before we shot the pinche ring."

"We have plenty of them," Havelock said. "The *Israel* came out here with too much of everything. I'd bet we have twenty in storage."

"That's ten bubbles," Basia said. "That's plenty to hold the whole crew for a short trip."

"Captain Marwick," Koenen said, "you cannot give these people vital RCE supplies."

"Marwick," Havelock said. "Do not let over a hundred innocent people die over this bullshit. Do not do that."

"Ah fuck. What are they going to do? Cancel my contract?" Marwick replied, followed by a long sigh. "The *Israel* is moving in to transfer the escape bubbles. I'll have the materials team start sealing them right now."

"Captain," the chief engineer growled, "we are acting out here on Security Chief Murtry's direct orders to disable the squatters' ship. You will not render them aid."

"You," Havelock said, "are such an asshole. Have you gone completely insane?"

"I will shoot down *any* attempt to—" the chief started, then stopped suddenly. The cable next to Basia snapped taut, almost tearing the few remaining attachments out of the *Barb*'s skin. Below, a rail gun shot streaked across Ilus, the fire from the defense moons stabbing at it as it fell. One of the red enemy dots on Basia's HUD disappeared.

"Sorry," Alex said, his accent as slow and heavy as Basia had ever heard it. "That was me. But that guy was pissin' me off and I had the shot. Am I in trouble?"

There was a long moment of silence, and then Captain Marwick said, "*Israel*'s on her way."

It took them nearly three hours to fabricate and then transfer the makeshift escape bubbles from the *Israel*. Basia kept track of the time by counting oxygen recharges for his suit. He flatly refused to return to the *Rocinante* until his daughter was off the dying Belter freighter. Alex had put some slack on the tether with carefully calculated bursts of thrust, and Basia had cut the line. No reason to keep the ships connected.

One by one the *Israel*'s expeditionary engineering team turned amateur militia contacted Havelock and apologized for how dramatically out of control the situation had gotten. Most of them blamed the chief engineer. Whether or not he was entirely responsible for the escalations that had occurred, Basia felt certain that history wouldn't remember him kindly. One of the engineers admitted to being the person who'd fired the missile at the *Barbapiccola* and offered to help Basia fix the damage. Basia had offered to kill him if he tried. They agreed to disagree on it.

Even after the reconfigured emergency airlocks had been delivered, it had taken the crew of the *Barbapiccola* and the colonists still on board two more hours to charge the air tanks and get everyone sealed inside. By that point, the computers on the *Rocinante* were saying the freighter should already be scraping upper atmosphere. The clock had run out.

But now Basia floated above the massive cargo bay doors of the *Barbapiccola*, waiting for them to open and set his daughter free.

It began as a line of white light cutting through the side of the massive freighter. Then, slowly, as the doors slid farther and farther apart, the ship's enormous cargo hold came into view. Against the backdrop of thousands of tons of raw lithium ore floated ten faintly translucent bubbles. Someone toggled a remote to open the cargo bay's airlock, and the air of the *Barbapiccola* rushed out, gently pushing the bubbles out the cargo bay door ahead of it.

The bubbles floated up away from the planet, the vacuum around them making them puff all the way up, little plump pockets of air for a dozen or more people to hide in, surrounded by the frozen mist of what had once been their ship's atmosphere. Ilus' star peeked around the limb of the planet, backlighting the bubbles and turning the floating people inside into black silhouettes, amazingly sharp against the blurry plastic walls. Like cardboard cutouts with a floodlight behind them.

Basia had a sudden memory of bathing Jacek in the kitchen sink when he was a baby, and his little boy farting in the water, a burst of small bubbles drifting up and then popping at the surface. The thought made him laugh until his stomach hurt. He recognized this was more about the relief that his daughter might live than it was about the flatulence of a small boy, but he laughed anyway.

"You okay out there?" Naomi asked.

"You ever bathed a kid in a sink?"

"Yeah," she said, "I have."

"They ever have gas?"

"I don't—" she started, then got it and laughed along with him.

Ten tow lines looped down from the open airlock of the *Israel*, and one by one Basia caught them and attached them to the bubbles. Felcia's bubble was last. As he pulled the strip at the end of the tether to activate the adhesive, he saw her look out of the airlock door's tiny transparent window. The sun had moved behind the planet, so Basia's visor had lost its opacity. He activated the light inside the helmet so she'd be able to see him. Her face lit up, and the word *Papa* was so obvious on her lips that he would have sworn he could hear it.

"Hi, baby," he said, and put his gloved hand against the window. She put hers on the other side, small clever fingers against his big clumsy ones.

She smiled and pointed past him, mouthing the word "wow."

He turned to look. The *Israel* had started reeling the bubbles in one by one. A dozen humans being pulled through the vacuum of space inside an envelope of air barely larger than they were. When Felcia's line started to reel in, Basia kept his hand against it until it pulled gently, *gently* away from him. His little girl going up to safety. Temporary, sure, but all safety was.

In that moment, Basia felt something like a hammer blow to his chest. Everyone in those little pockets of air was a Felcia to someone. Every life saved there filled someone somewhere else with relief and joy. Every life snuffed out before its time was another Katoa. Someone, somewhere, having their heart torn out.

Basia could feel the detonator in his hands, the horrible click transferring to his palm as the button depressed. He could feel that terrible shock wave again as the landing pad vanished in fire. He could feel the horror replaced by fear as some unlucky combination of events put the shuttle too close to the blast and knocked it from the sky.

He could feel all of it so clearly it was as if it were happening right then. But more than that, he felt sorrow. Someone had just tried to do the same thing to his baby girl. Had tried to kill her, not because he hated her, but because she was standing in the path of his political statement. Everyone who died on that shuttle had been a Felcia to someone. And with the click of a button he'd killed them.

He hadn't meant to. He'd been trying to save them. That was the little lie he'd kept close to his heart for months now. But the truth was much worse. Some secret part of him *had* wanted the shuttle to die. Had reveled in watching it fall from the sky in flames. Had wanted to punish the people who were trying to take his world away.

Except that was a lie too.

The real truth, the truth beneath it all, was he'd wanted to spread his pain around. To punish the universe for being a place where his little boy had been killed. To punish other people for being alive when his Katoa wasn't. That part of him had watched the shuttle burn and thought, *Now you know how it feels. Now you know how I feel.*

But the people he'd hurt had just saved his daughter because they were the kind of people who couldn't let even their enemies die helpless.

The first sob took him by surprise, nearly bending him double with its power. Then he was blind, his eyes filled with water, his throat closed like someone was choking him. He gasped for air and every gasp turned into another loud sob.

"Basia!" Naomi said in alarm. He'd just been cackling manically, and now he was sobbing. He must sound insane to her. "Basia, come back in!"

He tried to answer her, to reassure her, but when he spoke the only words he could say were, "I killed them."

"No," she said. "You saved them. You saved all of them."

"I killed them," he said again, and he meant the governor and Coop and Cate and the RCE security team, but most of all Katoa. He'd killed his little boy over and over again every time he'd let someone else die to punish them for his son's death. "I killed them," he said again.

"This time you saved them," Naomi repeated, as though she could read his mind. "These ones, you saved."

Havelock was waiting for him in the airlock. Basia knew the RCE man must have heard the breakdown he'd had. When Havelock looked at him, he felt nothing but shame. But while Havelock's face was tight with pain, there was no mockery in it when he gripped Basia's arm and said, "You did good out there."

Basia nodded back at him, not trusting himself to speak.

"Look," Havelock said, and pointed out the airlock door.

Basia turned around and saw the *Barbapiccola* leaving long thin streamers in its wake. It was entering Ilus' atmosphere. The front of the ship began to glow.

Havelock closed the hatch, but while the airlock cycled and they removed their gear, they watched the freighter's death on the wall monitor. Alex kept the *Roci*'s scopes trained on it the entire time. It drifted for a while, the streamers in the upper atmosphere eventually turning into white smoke with a black heart as the hull burned.

When the end came, it was sudden and shocking. The hull seemed to go from a solid object to many small fiery pieces in the blink of an eye, with no transition. Basia switched the monitor to the death clock to see how much time he'd bought Felcia.

Four days. The *Israel* had four days.

Chapter Fifty-Two: Elvi

Elvi sat in the darkness, her hand terminal in her lap. She was trembling, and the fear and the anger and the sorrow were like she'd walked back into the worst of the storm. She couldn't feel that now. She didn't have time. She needed to think.

The screen didn't have maps, of course. There wasn't a survey of any of this to draw from, and even if there was, she didn't have a connection to the *Israel*, if the *Israel* was still in orbit and hadn't fallen into the atmosphere and burned and killed everyone to death and—

She couldn't feel that now. She needed to think. The structure, ruins, whatever they were had to be at least seven or eight square kilometers. They'd entered the ruins near Holden's last live signal, but there was still a lot of territory to cover. The locator on the hand terminal screen showed only the local nodes. The other two were Fayez and Murtry, and they were grayed out. No line of sight, which was good because it meant that wherever Murtry was, he couldn't see her, and bad because she didn't know where he was. It was a low-level diagnostic. The kind that built ad hoc routing networks on the fly. She'd set it to ask for a renewed route anytime it made a connection and alert her when it did. It wasn't much, but it would give her a little warning when Murtry was close. When he had line of sight. When he could shoot her the way he had Amos and probably Fayez and they were dead now and she couldn't feel that. She had to think. How to find Holden. She had to find him. Warn him. Keep Murtry from stopping him. She took a deep breath and looked up. Line of sight was a hard thing to manage on the ground, but the space above her was vast and open. If she could find a vantage point, the hand terminal would point Murtry out to her. And if she couldn't find her friend, at least she could locate her enemy. Basic problem solving. If you don't have the data you need, play with the data you have, see if something comes out of it. She'd made it through three semesters of combinatorics that way. All right.

Her body was still shaking. Still weak. Her mind felt fuzzy. Adrenaline and hunger and Fayez was probably dead and she couldn't feel that. She stuffed the hand terminal in her pocket and looked around for a way up. Nothing here was built for a human form. There weren't any ladders or walkways, no catwalks with convenient handrails. It was like a vast body. Or a vast body that had turned halfway into a machine. She ran quietly, making as little noise as she could with every footfall. An upwelling of conduits rose from the floor to her right, and she clambered up them, wedging her feet and fists into the narrow spaces between the tubes and hauling up and up and up. There were so many other people who would have done better. Fayez was stronger than she was. Sudyam used to climb mountains back on Earth. Elvi didn't particularly enjoy climbing trees, much less strange alien webworks. She went up, not looking back, not looking down.

The structure was vast, and the soft glow that permeated everything made the space seem strange. Dreamlike. She perched in the crevice where two conduits or arteries met, wedging her leg into the gap. She pulled out her hand terminal. Twice on her way up, the ad hoc network alert had sounded and she hadn't noticed. Twice, Murtry had been in line of sight. The thought made her throat feel tight. She looked at the reply times. Two thousandths of a second? That couldn't be right. Radio waves moved at light speed, but they were in air, so that made it...what? Three times ten to the eighth? Something like that. Close enough as to make no difference. That'd put him something like half a million meters away. There had to be some kind of processing lag in the terminals that was swamping...

A new entry popped into the log, and her heart lept to her throat. Connection refused. She blinked at it. Why would Murtry's terminal accept connections when she was climbing up and reject them when she'd paused? That didn't make sense. Another line. Connection refused. Something like hope bloomed in her. It wasn't Murtry. It was someone else. Someone who wasn't in the charmed circle of RCE trusted networks.

It was Holden.

She craned her neck, as if by just looking she could find him. The structure was too big. She thought of calling out, but there was no reason to think he'd hear. And even if he did, Murtry would be closer.

Murtry. There was a thought. She opened the hand terminal's routing interface again. It had been years since she'd played with network protocols. Most of what she did was about signaling proteins in cells and protein regulation. Her leg was starting to tingle where her weight pressed it into the tube. There was a way to get a copy of Murtry's logs too. She just had to remember how to set up distributed logging.

Something in the structure clanged, the echoes reverberating through the space like a scream in a cathedral. She wondered if

Murtry looked up whether he would see the light of her screen, up here in her crow's nest. She waited. Waited. The alert sounded. Murtry connected. She closed her eyes. *Okay*, she thought. *Go away now. Just go away.*

The alert dropped, and she pulled up the logs, and Murtry's records were there now too, and one—one—line of them was a refused connection. It was like being in maths again. Posit a frightened exobiologist four meters off the ground and a violent, predatory security man in a direct line from her at points a, b, and c. At point d, the predator had a refused connection with a lag time just under two-tenths of a second because the goddam *fucking* processing lag was swamping the signal time and making the whole thing...

Only it would be the same lag, wouldn't it? So if she could pull out the difference...

The world fell away. Her fingers tapped the screen, shifting to the calculation displays, pulling numbers from the logs, setting up the diagrams. The fear and sorrow and raw, animal terror were all still there, but they were just messages and she could ignore them. Her leg started to hurt and then go numb. She shifted a few centimeters until it hurt again.

Holden had been a hundred and ten meters from her. He'd been a hundred and fifty meters from Murtry. She could estimate where Murtry had been based on the contacts he'd made with her. It was like basic trigonometry where a wrong answer meant death. Holden was—approximately, roughly, assuming she hadn't biffed the equations and that the hand terminal's processing lags were identical—in the complex junctions at the center right of the structure where the conduits joined together into something like a massive black wing. Elvi turned off her hand terminal and started back down. When she reached a surface she could walk on, her leg screamed. Pins and needles. She ignored it and started limping as quickly as she could toward the landmark she'd found. She didn't care about Murtry now. She had something to focus on.

It was less like making her way through an industrial complex than tramping through a vast forest without a machete. She squeezed through the cracks between dark structures as much growth as machine, ducked and climbed and once got down on her belly and crawled. She was sure she was making progress, sure that she would get there and find out at least whether her figures had been right, when she stepped out across a flat ledge and almost fell into a chasm.

A rumbling came from below, maybe a hundred meters deep. A tiny band of lights shifted down there, swirling one way and then the other and then moving on. It cut through the floor of the structure to both sides, all the way to the distant walls. A network of conduits branched above it, and wide, tendonlike connections bridged it far below. She started off along the rim, stepping over white, lumpy growths that seemed to sprout up out of the depths. It only took a few minutes to find a structure that crossed it, but it wasn't a bridge.

It was mostly flat, though the edges sloped down into the void; its surface was a wire mesh over what looked like an endless length of tongue. There was nothing like guardrails, and when she stepped out onto it, the tongue reacted to her, twitching and undulating like it was trying to drag her along. She put her arms out for balance and trotted across the gap. Two meters, four meters, five, and she was on the other side. She leaned against the wall, her head between her hands until the dizziness faded. The vast winglike structure was almost directly above her now, only close up she could see that it was more complex. Thousands of interweaving growths with deep, interlocking spirals and a shifting movement whose source she couldn't identify.

She slipped down the far side of the ledge and into something more like a passageway than she'd seen since she fled into the dark. The passage shifted left and then right. She followed it, picking her way by guesswork and hope. The ratio of floor to wall to ceiling unnerved her for reasons she couldn't quite say. Tiny flickers of blue light like fireflies glowed and went dark all around her. She followed a broad turn and it opened into a chamber.

She screamed.

Holden was there not three meters away, a huge, insectile thing looming above him. Cruel claws reached out and spikes like daggers caught the dim and eerie light. She pressed her knuckles to her mouth, unable to look away from Holden's last moments.

The artifact shifted toward her, paused, and lifted a claw like it was waving. Holden followed the gesture.

"Elvi?" he said. "What are you doing here?"

"I was...We were..." She sank down to her knees, relief running through her like water. She took a deep breath and tried again. "Murtry took one of the carts when you disappeared. He followed the signal from your hand terminal. He knows you're trying to shut down all the artifacts." A stab of panic took her and she glanced at the clawed thing.

"That's all right, kid," the robot-thing said in a tinny Belter accent. "It ain't news to me."

"Amos and Fayez and I got another cart going, and we came after them. To warn you."

"Okay," Holden said. "You did great. We're going to be fine now. How did you find us?"

Elvi held up her hand terminal, took a breath, let it out. "It was complicated."

"Fair enough. What about Amos? Where's he?"

"Murtry shot him. I think he's dead."

Holden's face went pale and then flushed. He shook his head, and when he spoke, his voice was low and careful. "Amos isn't dead."

"How do you know?"

"If Amos goes down, it's because literally everyone else there has already died. We're still alive, so Amos is too."

"Don't pay too much attention to him," the robot monster said. "He gets a little romantic about these things. If you say the bald guy's dead, I believe you."

"Thank you," Elvi said by reflex.

"I am sorry about it, though. I liked him."

"I did too," Elvi said. "And Fayez. I heard gunshots when I was running. I think Fayez—"

"How about Murtry?" Holden asked.

"He's coming. He's behind me. I don't know how far. But he's coming to find you. To stop you."

"Why the fuck would he stop me?" Holden asked, biting the words.

"He wants RCE to have the artifacts still working."

"That man's kind of an asshole," the alien said. "We've got a pretty full plate, though. We're close."

"Close to what?" Elvi said.

"That would be the question," the alien answered, but Holden's gaze was fixed over her shoulder. His jaw was tight and angry.

"All right," he said. "We've got two things we need to do."

"We do?" the alien said. It occurred to Elvi that they were talking to an alien. She thought that was remarkable, and she was a little confused that Holden hadn't remarked on it.

"Someone has to find this whatever-it-is and shut off the planetary defenses, and someone has to shoot Murtry."

"Not to disagree with you," the alien said, shifting its weight on six articulated legs. "One of those seems a little more important to me."

"Me too," Holden said, "but I don't think it's the same one. Elvi, I'm going to need you to go save everyone, okay?"

"Um," she said. "All right?"

"Good. This is Detective Miller. He died when Eros hit Venus and now he's a puppet of the protomolecule."

"Semi-autonomous," the alien said.

"Pleased to meet you."

"Likewise."

"Okay," Holden said. "I'm going to go take care of this."

To Elvi's surprise and unease, Holden walked away, following the passage she'd taken. The alien thing cleared its throat apologetically, only she was fairly sure it didn't have a throat. So the sound was just a kind of conversational inflection.

"Sorry about that," the alien—Miller—said. "He gets an idea in his head sometimes and there's no talking to him."

"It's all right," Elvi said. "So…um."

"Right, saving everyone in the world. Follow me, kid. I'll get you up to speed."

"So it's a distributed consciousness," she said, following Miller through a low archway. She felt lightheaded, and not just from hunger. Fayez was dead. Amos was dead. She was going to die. She was on an alien world. She was talking to a dead man wearing an alien robot. The part of her that could feel things was done, shut off. Her heart was a numbness behind her ribs, and when—if—it came back, she couldn't guess who or what she would be.

"Except it's not exactly conscious," Miller said. "There's nodes in it that are, but they don't run the joint. I'm not actually one of them. I'm a construct based on the dead guy, only I'm based really closely on him, and he was kind of a bulldog about this kind of thing. At least by the end he was."

"So are *you* conscious?"

The alien robot—the skin the Miller construct was using—shrugged. It was strange how well the gesture translated. "Don't know. Seems like I'm acing my Turing test, though."

Elvi thought about it and nodded. "Fair enough."

"So I sort of…well, triangulated where the dead spot was in space. If you see what I mean."

"Sure, yes. Triangulation. I totally understand that," Elvi said. "So. Four now."

"Four?"

"Our biosphere, the local organisms, the things that made the gates, and the things that killed them. Four."

Miller stopped at a seam in the wall and placed his claws on it, ready to push. "In through here? It used to be one of the major control centers for the planet. Like a…like a nerve cluster or something. As near as I can figure it, the dead spot's in here."

He pushed. The wall retracted, not sliding back so much as changing conformation. Beyond it, a wide, tall space opened.

Hundreds of niches rose, level after level, one above the other, with mechanisms like Miller in each of them. Dots of bright blue light like fireflies swirled spiral patterns in the air, riding currents of air that Elvi couldn't feel. And in the center, floating a meter above the floor, was...

She looked away, putting her hand on Miller's side to steady herself, then forced her gaze back up. It was hard to look at directly. The margins of the space were bright without illuminating anything or casting shadows, sharp and terrible. It reminded her of the way schizophrenics and people suffering migraines would describe light as assaulting and dangerous. And within that boundary, darkness swirled. It was more than an absence. She could sense a structure within it, layers interpenetrating, like shadows casting shadows. It throbbed with an inhuman power, tidal and deep and painful. *Look at this too long*, Elvi thought, *and I will lose my mind in it.* She took a step toward it, feeling the structures in the blackness respond to her. She felt as if she could see the spaces between molecules in the air, like atoms themselves had become a thin fog, and for the first time she could see the true shape of reality looming up just beyond her reach.

Once, there had been a civilization here beyond anything Elvi had ever imagined. Beings that could design tools like the protomolecule, like the rings. They had peopled a thousand worlds, and more, spread through time and through space, and they were gone now. And this—she had no doubt at all—this was the footprint of the thing that had killed them.

"So," Miller said, moving his claws in a wide, spreading gesture, "you need to look for anything, you know, odd. Something that doesn't seem like it fits."

She turned to him, confused, and pointed at the uncanny thing in the center of the room. "You mean like that?"

Miller shifted, alien eyes moving their lenses in the complexity of the mechanism. "Like what?"

"That. In the middle of the room. That."

"I don't see anything," Miller said. "What's it look like?"

"The eye of an angry God?" Elvi said.

"Oh," Miller said. The heavy plates of his robotic body clicked and hissed against each other as he shifted. "Yeah, well that's probably it, then. Good work."

Chapter Fifty-Three: Holden

When Murtry pulled himself through a gap in the machinery and walked across the ledge to the narrow bridge, Holden was waiting for him on the other side. His hand was draped casually on the butt of his gun. The RCE security chief gave Holden a vague nod, then carefully examined his surroundings. He looked down into the hundred-meter chasm, and tapped the narrow tonguelike bridge with the tip of one boot. He spun once slowly, peering carefully into the crevices created by the cramped machines. When he was through, he looked at Holden again and gave him a flat, meaningless smile. Holden noticed his hand wasn't far from his own weapon.

You came by yourself," Murtry said. "The better plan is to put one person in the open with a second hidden behind the target."

"That the one you use?" Holden asked. He tried to match Murtry's casual nonchalance and felt like he mostly succeeded.

"It works," Murtry replied with a nod. "So how does this go down?"

"I've been wondering that myself."

"Well," Murtry said with an almost imperceptible shrug, "I need to get over there and stop whatever you people are cooking up. Doctor Okoye seems to think you are going to break the defense network down."

"Yeah," Holden replied. "Pretty much am. Call it saving people."

Murtry nodded but didn't speak for a moment. Holden waited for him to reach for his gun. The distance between them, the width of the chasm, was just over five meters. An easy shot at the range. Harder when you were rushing because the other guy was shooting back. The lighting was good and Murtry wasn't wearing a helmet. Risk the head shot? The RCE man's armor looked pretty chewed up. The blast patterns on it made Holden suspect that was the work of Amos' autoshotgun. The chest shot was easier, but it was possible the damage to the armor was mostly cosmetic, in which case his sidearm wasn't going to do much.

Murtry winked at him, and Holden suddenly felt like the man was reading his mind as he calculated the best way to kill him. "I can't let that happen," Murtry said. His shrug was almost apologetic. "By charter, this all belongs to RCE. You don't get to break it."

Holden shook his head in disbelief. "You really are crazy. If I don't break it, our ships fall out of the sky and we all die."

"Maybe. Maybe we die. Maybe we find some other way to stay alive. Either way, the RCE claim remains in force." Murtry waved one hand, not his gun hand, around the room. "All this is worth trillions intact. We've made incredible advances in materials science just by *looking* at the rings. How much will working technology do for us? This is what we came here for, Captain. You don't get to decide what we do with it."

"Trillions," Holden said, unable to keep the disbelief out of his voice. "I've never seen a dead person spend money."

"Sure you have. They call it a foundation or a bequest. Happens all the time."

"This is all so you can make a bequest?"

Murtry's smile widened a millimeter.

"No," he said. "I came to conquer a new world. *This* is how you do that. I understand what I'm doing seems cruel and inflexible to you, but it's what this situation requires. The tools you're using here are the ones that let you get along once civilization takes over. They're the wrong shape for this work. I have no illusions about what it will take to carve out a place in this new frontier. It will take sacrifices, and it will take blood, and things we wouldn't do back where everything's regulated and controlled will have to happen here. You think we can do it with committee meetings and press releases."

"I wonder if this will sound like a compelling argument to the people dying in orbit right now."

"I'm sorry for them. I truly am. But they knew the risks when they got on board. And their deaths will have meaning," Murtry said.

"Meaning?"

"They are the sign that we didn't give up a centimeter. What we came for, we held to the last gasp. This isn't something humanity can do halfway, Captain. It never has been. Even Cortez burned his ships."

Holden's laugh was half disbelief and half contempt. "What is it with you guys and worshiping mass murderers?"

Murtry frowned. A swirl of bright blue lights rose and fell between them like dust blowing down a desert street.

"How do you mean?" Murtry asked.

"A guy I once knew tried to justify his life choices to me by comparing himself to Genghis Khan."

"I take it you didn't find his argument compelling?" Murtry asked with a smirk.

"No," Holden said. "And then a friend of mine shot him in the face."

"An ironic rebuttal to an argument about necessary violence."

"I thought so too, at the time."

Murtry reached up and scratched his head with his left hand, his short greasy hair shifting into a configuration vaguely resembling Miller's carapace. A sculpture of curves and spikes. He looked at his fingertips in disgust and wiped them on his armor. Holden waited. Somewhere far behind them, a strange chittering sound rose like cicadas on a summer afternoon.

"So," Murtry finally said. "I'm going to need to come over there." He gestured at Holden's side of the chasm with his chin. His right hand still hovered over his gun.

"Nope," Holden replied.

Murtry nodded, as if expecting this. "You going to arrest me, Sheriff?"

"Actually, I was kind of thinking I'd shoot you."

"In the face, no doubt."

"If that's what I can hit."

"Seems like a radical shift," Murtry said, "for a man who wants to tame the frontier with mediation and committee meetings."

"Oh, no, this isn't about that. Elvi says you killed Amos. I wouldn't kill a single person for your fucking frontier, but for my crew? Yeah, I'll kill you for that."

"They say revenge is empty."

"This is my first try at it," Holden said. "Forgive me if my opinions on it are fairly unformed."

"Will it change things if your boy isn't dead? He was still shooting when I left him."

The wave of relief that hit Holden at this almost doubled him over. If Murtry had pulled his pistol and shot at that moment the fight would have been over. But he managed to keep his face blank and his knees from buckling.

"Is he hurt?"

"Oh my, yes. Pretty badly. He killed one of mine before he went down. For a guy who wants to solve problems without violence, you travel in dangerous company."

"Yeah," Holden said, unable to keep the smile off his face. "But he's a great mechanic. What about the other one? Fayez?"

"Down, not dead. I didn't get to finish him before your boy started blazing away. Neither one was walking, so I just left."

The matter-of-fact discussion of why Murtry hadn't just killed Fayez chilled Holden's blood.

"So here's a deal," Murtry said. "I let you cross to this side and you can go check on your man Amos. Save the egghead from bleeding out, too. You have my word I won't interfere."

"But," Holden replied, "you head over to my side and stop Elvi from doing what I need her to do."

"Seems a fair trade."

Holden stopped just resting his hand on the butt of his pistol and wrapped it around the grip. He turned his body, getting his feet in position. Murtry gave him just the hint of a frown.

"No," Holden said, and waited for the shooting to start.

"So," Murtry said, not moving at all. "You know what people always forget about the new world?"

Holden didn't answer.

"Civilization has a built-in lag time. Just like light delay. We fly out here to this new place, and because we're civilized, we think civilization comes with us. It doesn't. We build it. And while we're building it, a whole lot of people die. You think the American west came with railroads and post offices and jails? Those things were built, and at the cost of thousands of lives. They were built on the corpses of everyone who was there before the Spanish came. You don't get one without the other. And it's people like me that do it. People like you come later. All of this?" Murtry waved his left hand at himself and Holden. "This is because you showed up too early. Come back after I've built a post office and we'll talk."

"You done?" Holden asked.

"So this is our day, I take it," Murtry said. "No way but this way? Even if I didn't kill your man?"

"Maybe you killed Amos and Fayez and maybe you didn't. Maybe you're right about the frontier and I'm just a naïve idiot.

Maybe every single person you killed on this world had it coming and you were always in the right."

"But you have people in orbit and saving them is all that counts?"

"I was going to say, 'But you're a flaming asshole,'" Holden said. "But the other works too. You don't cross this bridge."

"Well then," Murtry said. He shifted his stance and his eyes narrowed. The chittering grew louder. Below them, the proto-molecule fireflies swirled and shuddered. "Well then."

Holden smiled at him. Mimicking Alex's drawl he said, "Come on, Black Bart, you always knew it would end this way."

Murtry laughed. "You're a funny—"

Holden shot him.

Murtry staggered, clutching at his chest and fumbling for his gun. Holden put his second shot into the man's right arm. He tried for the elbow and only managed to get the bicep. Just as good. Murtry dropped the gun onto the bridge in front of him. When the RCE man went to one knee to try and pick it up with his left hand, Holden shot him in the leg. Murtry pitched forward onto the bridge, sending the gun tumbling away into the abyss. Murtry slid to the side, going over the edge, but managed to throw his left arm onto the metal mesh and stop his fall.

The whole thing had taken about three seconds.

As the last echoing report of the gunshot faded, Holden walked out onto the bridge. The uncanny musculature pressed at the soles of his feet. Murtry clung to the mesh with his one good hand, his face tight with pain, but still managing a mocking grin.

"You got the balls to finish this, boy?" he said. "Or are you going to let gravity do it?"

"Oh, no," Holden said, then knelt down to grab Murtry's left wrist and haul him toward the ledge. "I'm not killing you. At least not until I'm sure about Amos."

Holden stepped off the bridge onto Murtry's side of the chasm and pulled the RCE man until his torso was up over the edge. Murtry scrabbled the rest of the way up with his one good arm.

"Then what?" he gasped out, lying on his back next to the pit and trying to catch his breath. A small pool of blood was forming under his right arm and left leg.

"I take you back," Holden said, sitting down next to Murtry and patting him companionably on the head. "And I burn you down in public, with news coverage of the entire thing. Then we throw you in a hole so deep everyone forgets you ever existed. No fame and glory for you, Cortez. Montezuma wasn't impressed by your fire stick this time."

"Everything I did was within the bounds of the UN charter," Murtry said. "I acted responsibly to protect the employees and investments of Royal Charter Energy."

"Okay," Holden said, then pulled out his medkit and sprayed bandages onto Murtry's two bleeding injuries. "So you've got your defense strategy mapped out. That's proactive thinking. Lawyers'll be happy to hear it. Wanna hear mine?"

"Sure," Murtry said, and probed at the wound on his arm. He grimaced, but no blood squirted out.

"The most powerful person on earth owes me a favor, and I'm going to tell her you're an asshole who tried his best to make her look bad. It's just a sketch of a plan at this point, but I think it has potential."

"That's what passes for justice with you?"

"Apparently so."

Murtry opened his mouth, but whatever he was about to say was lost when the factory exploded into chaos. A wall of blue fireflies shot up from the chasm next to them, and then streaked across the cavernous factory space to disappear into small vents in the walls. All around, the cacophony of massive machines coming to life filled the air. Something flew out of the shadows by the ceiling and swooped low over Holden's head. He threw himself across Murtry, not unaware of the irony in using his own body to shield a man he'd just shot three times.

"What is it?" Murtry said.

"Elvi," Holden replied. "It's Elvi."

Chapter Fifty-Four: Elvi

Yeah," Miller said, sounding satisfied. "I've got a plan, but I'm going to need your help. I need to get as close to that whatever-the-hell-it-is as I can. You can see it, I can't. So this one's on you."

All right," she said. "What…what are you going to do?"

The robot shrugged. "Every time we…I…well, you get it. Every time anything reaches into this, it dies. This thing takes down networks like the one I am. I'm going to get connected to as much of the crap on this planet as I can and escort it all into, y'know. That. Take it down. Break the system."

"Won't that shut you down too?"

"I think so. That's the thing about using complicated tools. Sometimes the features you're looking for come with a whole lot of baggage."

"I don't understand," Elvi said.

"It built me to find something that's missing," Miller said.

"Turns out I'm also a good tool for dying when that's the right solve. Seriously, I've got practice with this. So come over here and get me as close as you can to the whatever-it-is. I don't want to touch it, though. I slip in before I'm hooked up to everything else, and I'm pretty sure you're just boned."

"All right," Elvi said, shifting until she could see the robot and the darkness both. "Turn about thirty degrees to your left."

The robot shifted with the speed and sharpness of a startled insect.

"The boundary's about half a meter in front of you. Why do you need to be close to it?"

"Well, the thing I'm part of? It may not be conscious, but it's not stupid. When I do this, pretty much all the tools its got are going to know what I know, and they may not take a forced shut-down well. Whatever else this thing was designed to do, it likes still existing until it finishes its job. It's a survivor. I'm pretty much the opposite of that."

She thought she heard a smile in the thing's voice. Where had that come from? The patterns and habits in a dead man's brain? Or was that fatalism another good move in design space? Did the universe evolve eyes and wings and sense organs and bitter amusement at the prospect of death all the same way?

"Okay," Miller said. The robot shifted, hunkered down, prepared to spring forward. "We're going in three. Two. *One*."

The impact was like being in the heavy shuttle again as it crashed. Elvi's world contracted to a small space inside her own skull, and then slowly bloomed out again in pain. She struggled to sit up, trying to see straight. Trying to think. Had Miller exploded? Was she dead? The cacophony of shrieking metal and violence made it hard to get her bearings.

She was against the wall. All around her, mechanisms were crawling down from their niches. Many of them were failing— legs scraping at the walls without the strength to pull themselves forward or landing on the ground only to crawl in a panicked, spasmodic circle like insects dying from poison. The air was thick with the mindless chittering of their joints. Three massive machines had pinned the Miller-robot and were pounding it while Miller's voice shouted *shitshitshitshit*. One of the attackers caught Miller's claw and pulled, ripping the appendage off in a shower of sparks and bright fluids. He wasn't going to make it. There was no way.

A small winged machine with a bright blue margin on the knifelike edge where a beak would be swooped down from above, passed through the darkness, and fell clattering and rolling to the ground. Elvi ran to it, picked it up. It was light enough to carry, as long as her forearm, and sharp at the front. With a howl, she charged the machines that were piling on Miller. The impact stung her fingers. Something struck her across the back, and the world narrowed again, but she lashed out with what strength she still had.

One of the huge machines turned from Miller toward her, its claws splaying out three meters to either side. She jumped back, fell, scuttled. The pulsing, malefic blackness of the dead spot was on her left, and she crawled around it, trying to keep it between her and the massive attacker.

The robot skittered toward her, its claws swinging like scythes until it reached the margin of the blackness and crumpled down dead. Inertia rolled its corpse across the floor, legs and claws flopping and limp. The chittering in the room paused. The attention of the artifacts turned toward her. She put her foot on the fallen monster, lifted her fists, and howled. Miller twisted, driving his remaining claw up and through the body of one of the two machines that were still at his side. The chittering began again, even more overwhelming than before. The sound itself felt like an attack, battering at her ears, robbing her of her balance.

She was in the center of an invisible waterfall, a thunderstorm, a tempest. Adrenaline more than conscious will lifted her up over the body of her fallen enemy, and she skirted around the dead spot. Another machine fell from a higher niche, smashing itself on the ground before her. She stepped over it as it writhed. The last remaining fully functional attacker swung at Miller, the blades of its claws plunging deep into Miller's carapace. As Elvi came close, it tried to turn toward her. The claw still inside Miller bound with a deep creaking sound. Miller's remaining claw fastened on the other robot's wrist, holding the attacker's claw close, pulling it in, deeper. A viscous fluid poured out of Miller, filling the air with the stink of petroleum and acid. Elvi scooped a length of fallen robot's leg and slammed it into Miller's assailant, striking sparks. The blows had no effect other than to confuse the thing. She could no more have injured it than she could will herself to fly up into the air and lift the falling ships by force of will. But the moment's hesitation was enough.

Miller pulled himself under the remaining attacker, on his back. Four of the six articulated legs started digging at the robot's undercarriage. Belly. She didn't have a good model for this. The unencumbered claw smashed down, knocking shards of metal from Miller's side, but with Miller mostly underneath the attacker, it couldn't get an angle that would let it deliver a killing blow.

A thin-limbed, spindly robot skittered through the opened wall, sprinting toward the battle. Elvi grabbed it as it passed and knocked it into the dead spot. Bits of plating began to peel off the attacking thing's belly, and Miller burrowed up into it. The filthy and stinking ichor started pouring out in a flood. It was an ugly death, slow and violent and unpoetic. When the attacker had stopped moving, Elvi came close. The dead robot was on top of Miller. The pool of thin liquid all around stung her eyes with its fumes.

"Well, that could have gone better," Miller said.

"Did it work? Are you connected?"

"Yeah," Miller said. "Not sure how much good that's going to do. There's another wave of these things coming, and I'm not seeing how I get from here to there."

Elvi put her shoulder under the dead robot, pushing as hard as she could. The tendons in her neck ached. She imagined she could hear them creaking. She put everything she had into the effort.

There was nothing to hold back for. No later that mattered. Keeping anything in reserve was a waste of resources because there was no future left. She screamed with the sheer physical effort.

The robot didn't even shift.

She fell to her knees. With a groan, Miller put his claw out, resting it gently on her arm. When he spoke, his voice sounded distant, muffled. Words from a grave.

"Okay, this is going to be tricky," he said. "I'm going to need one more favor from you, kid. And we don't have much time before they get here."

"Yes," she said. "Whatever."

"Okay, stand back a little. I'm popping the seals on this thing."

She slid backward, the slime on the floor flowing up to the ankles of her pants. There was a hiss like steam escaping from a holed line, a deep, meaty click, and Miller came apart, the plating and scales of his body collapsing. The thing on top of him rolled away and lay dead on its side.

Elvi stood over Miller's corpse. It looked like nothing so much as a huge insect smashed under a giant's heel. The chittering all around her rose to a shriek.

"What do I do?" Elvi shouted. "What am I supposed to do?"

Miller's voice came from deep inside the mess. "There's a unit in here. It's about a meter long, bright blue, and there's a row of seven...no, eight dots along the side. I need you to dig it out."

Elvi stepped forward. The plating was all knifepoints and sharp edges. She felt the sting where it cut her palms, and the burning where the robotic fluids flowed into the wounds.

"I don't mean to be that guy," Miller said. "But you also need to hurry."

"Trying," she said.

"Just saying there are more bad guys and they're getting a little closer than I like."

"All right. I have it," Elvi said. "It's right here."

"Good. Nice work. Now I need you to pick that up and walk it into the dead spot."

The blue thing was the shape of a huge elongated almond. The surface was slick and soft. She put her hands around it, strained, grunted, and slid forward, panting. "You have got to be kidding me," she said.

"It may be a little heavy," Miller said.

"It's like ninety kilos."

"And I'm really sorry about that, but we need to get it into that dead spot now. Try sliding your arms under it and lifting with your back and legs. Just like it was a baby."

"Baby made from fucking tungsten," Elvi muttered.

"You're exaggerating," he said as she shoved her hands under the thing.

"I can't throw this," she said. "I have to walk it in."

"All right."

"Is that thing going to kill me if I go into it?"

A new sound rose behind the chittering. A deep booming sound like a massive drum. She didn't want to think of what might be making it.

"If I say yes, does that mean you won't do it?"

Elvi braced herself, straining her back. The blue thing shifted up into her lap. She bent her head, trying to catch her breath.

"No," she said, surprised at the answer even as she spoke it. "I'll still do it."

"Maybe, then. I don't know."

Elvi rocked back, keeping the thing—Miller—on her thighs and still getting her feet under her. She felt it start to slide to her left. If she dropped it now, she didn't think she'd be able to get it up again. The booming came closer. Elvi pushed with her legs. Her knees ached. Her back was a single, vast sheet of burning. She pressed the blue thing to her chest, crying out from the pain.

"You're doing great, kid. You're doing great. You can do this. Just a little more. But do it *now*."

She didn't step forward. Just slid one foot a little ahead, shifted her weight, pulled the other foot in. The floor was slick as ice. Not quite frictionless, but close. The booming came again, near enough that she felt the room vibrate with it. She set her gaze on the blackness of the dead spot and moved forward. Another step. Another. Another. She was close now. Her back was on fire. Her arms were numb. Her fists something that belonged to someone else, and only happened to be connected to her.

A swarm of silver and blue gushed in the doorway, flowing in at her like a cloud of flies. Elvi pushed, slipped, fell forward—

The closest analogy, the one her brain reached for and rejected and reached for again, was splashing into a lake. It was cold, but not cold. There was a smell, rich and loamy. The smell of growth and decay. She was aware of her body, the skin, the sinew, the curl of her gut. She was aware of the nerves that were firing in her brain as she became aware of the nerves firing in her brain. She unmade herself and watched herself being unmade. All the bacteria on her skin and in her blood, the virii in her tissues. The woman who had been Elvi Okoye became a landscape. A world. She fell farther in.

Cells became molecules—countless and complex and varied. The demarcation of one thing and another failed. There was only a community of molecules, shifting in a vast dance. And then the atoms that made the molecules gave up their space, and she was a breath. A mist. A tiny play of fields and interactions in a vacuum as perfect as space. She was a vibration in nothingness.

She rolled onto her side. Something hurt. Everything hurt, and the pain was interesting. A subject of curiosity more than distress. She was breathing. She could feel the air moving through her throat and into the complex network of soft caverns behind her ribs. It was a strange and beautiful sensation. She stayed with it until she began to realize that time existed. That moments were passing. That meant basal ganglia and cerebellum and cerebral cortex were all actually starting to work. She felt distantly surprised about that. She opened her eyes to nothing.

She was holding something pressed to her like it was precious. The blue thing. Miller. Only it wasn't blue anymore. It was the closed-eyes blackness of everything else. She let it go and sat up. The world was silent. No booming. No chittering. Her breath.

The hush of her blood. After a few moments, she drew her hand terminal out of her pocket and turned up the screen brightness, using it like a lamp.

All around her, the artifacts of New Terra lay dead. Knife-sharp legs were still. Vast, inhuman claws that could have been carved from stone. A spray of silver flecks on the ground showed where the cloud of tiny mechanisms had fallen, a million tiny bodies turned off at once. The light was too dim for colors. Everything was only gray.

She sat up and turned reluctantly to the side. It was there. Black and bright at the margins. She felt a stab of almost supernatural fear. She'd thought—hoped—it would be gone. Whatever it was, she had passed through it, been ripped apart by it, and still been simple enough to reassemble herself on the other side. It had saved her, and she had never seen anything in her life that filled her with a deeper dread than that complex darkness.

She moved back, her legs aching. She stood. She was aware that she was weeping without knowing why exactly she was doing it. Hunger and fear and relief and exultation and mortal fear. It was too much. That was fine.

The voice that came to her was human and distant. Was Holden.

"Elvi? Elvi! Are you there?"

"I'm here," she shouted.

"Did we win?"

She took one long breath. Then another.

"Yes," she called. "We won."

Interlude: The Investigator

—it reaches out it reaches out it reaches out it reaches out—

One hundred and thirteen times a second, it reaches out to report that the work is done. If something accepted the report, it could stop. It will never stop. It feels no frustration and no fear. It feels the investigator moving within it and around it. The investigator exceeds its boundary conditions. It tries to kill the investigator. It fails. It feels no distress at the failure, and it reaches out, it reaches out, it reaches out—

The investigator looks into the eye of death, and can't see it. It knows, and that is enough. It feels pleasure and regret because they are part of the template. It says a name—Julie. It remembers taking a woman's hand in its own.

The investigator reaches out, reaches down. It broadens like an eternal, endless inhalation, and spreads to fill all the places that it can reach, that have been reached. That are. It reaches out it reaches out it reaches out, the ticking on an insectile leg, a spark closing a gap, endlessly, and the investigator feels it, encompasses it. The scars reach out, the other minds. Some are frightened, some are lost in dreams that have been going on for years, some are grateful. They sing to the investigator, or they accuse it, or they plead with it, or they scream. They are aware, and powerless as they have ever been. The investigator touches them as it touches everything. It tells them not to worry. That it's driving this bus.

Don't worry, it says. *We're gonna be fine.*

The investigator pushes his hat back, wishes he had a beer. He likes this woman. This Elvi. He wishes he'd had a little more time to know her. He wishes he had a little more time. He doesn't care. He has died a million times since he died. The void has no mysteries for him now.

He connects, and the investigator becomes the world. He feels it everywhere. The orbital bases, the power cores in the crushing depth of the ocean, the library vaults where the old ones had lived, the signaling stations high in the mountains, the cities deep beneath the ground. He is the world.

There is a struggle at the end. There's always a struggle at the end. He's not scared, and so all through the world, the others aren't either. *You're like Peter Pan*, she says. *When a child died, Peter Pan would fall halfway with them. So they wouldn't be scared.*

Weird. And that's a kid's story? Anyway, it's not me, the investigator says, smiles at her. Holds her hand. *I don't go for half.*

—it reaches out and it reaches out and it reaches out and then it stops.

Chapter Fifty-Five: Havelock

Blue. That was what he forgot every time. He knew it intellectually, sure. Sky-blue sky, after all, but spend a few years on a station or a ship and it was one of those details that slipped away. He didn't even know he'd forgotten it until he had a moment like this. He leaned on his cane and lifted a hand to shade his eyes and looked up past the green-gray clouds to the wider blue sky.

It's pretty, isn't it?" the woman asked. Lucia, her name was. First Landing's physician, Basia's wife, Felcia and Jacek's mother. "Makes you want to stay."

"No," he said. "Makes me want to be home already."

"If you lived here…" she said.

"Not a chance," he replied, and chuckled.

The *Rocinante* sat on the muddy ground behind him, more or less where the landing pad had been back when there had been a landing pad. All of that was gone now. The scientific huts, the buildings of First Landing, even most of the mining operation. Everything had been scraped flat and clean. Only the erosion ditches showed where the flood had been now that the waters had gone.

The *Roci*'s cargo bays were open. Men and women were hauling formed plastic boxes of supplies and equipment out and stacking them on the soft ground. He saw Naomi in a lift suit directing them, calling out information, coordinating the responses. Alex and Basia stood on a thin scaffold they'd erected against the side of the ship with the other one—Amos Burton, he thought the name was—surveying the damage and planning out what repairs they could manage in humanity's most primitive and ill-equipped dry dock. The big bald man's right hand was locked in a medical casing, and his frustration with it showed in the way he moved his arms and held his shoulders.

"Are you ready?" Lucia asked.

"If you'd like," Havelock said. "Sure."

They walked together to the first pile of crates. Havelock took out his hand terminal, and Lucia took out one of the ones they'd dropped before. It was hers now. They started marking off boxes from the lading bills, recording carefully what help was being delivered and being accepted.

He was supposed to have died three weeks before. His body should have been a stream of ionized atoms and complex molecules floating somewhere in Ilus' upper atmosphere. The *Israel* should have been dead before him.

He'd been in the medical bay when it happened, doped by the autodoc and having half a liter of artificial blood shoved into his veins. He could still remember the feeling of the restraints holding him to the medical couch, the soft ticking of the expert system's tool arm, the cold feeling of fluid coming into his body. His lips and tongue had felt cold and tingled, but Alex assured him that was normal. Basia had come in, eaten, and gone out again to clean up the last remnants of the tether that were still clinging to the *Rocinante's* belly.

He'd said something about how it seemed kind of a pointless exercise.

"He's that kind of guy, I guess," Alex said. "Doesn't like to leave things half done."

"Belter."

"Yeah," Alex agreed. "They're all kind of like that."

Alex's hand terminal chimed, and the pilot frowned at it. "Cap? That you?"

The voice that came from the speaker was recognizable James Holden, but he sounded rougher. Like he'd been shouting a lot. "Alex! Turn on the reactor."

"Not sure I can do that, Cap," Alex said.

"We killed the defense grid. I think we killed everything. See if you can get the reactor on."

Alex's expression went very still, very sober. The gallows humor was gone, the brave mask that had covered the fear of death vanished. Havelock understood, because he felt the same rush of hope and also of fear that the hope would be disappointed. Without a word, Alex pulled himself to one of the medical bay's computers and shifted it to engine controls. Havelock squeezed his fists until they ached and fought not to interrupt Alex by asking if it was working.

"Is it working?"

"I think...it is," Alex said, then turned to the hand terminal. "I'm getting power, Cap. The diagnostics are throwing some errors, but I'm pretty sure that's just 'cause we got shook up a little. I'll put Naomi and Basia on it, and I'll bet we can get up to functional. It'd help a lot if we had Amos, though."

"Amos is a little shook up too," Holden said, and Havelock could hear the grin in his voice.

"He all right?"

"He's gonna need to grow some new fingers."

Alex shrugged. "We can do that. Um. Give me a couple days, I might be able to bring the *Roci* down to the surface. Get him into the med bay."

"Don't hurry," Holden said. "Take your time, make sure everything's working. We can't take another crisis."

"There's always going to be another crisis, Cap. That's just how it goes."

"Let's just put it off until we've recovered from the last one, all right? Can you get in touch with *Barbapiccola* and the *Israel*? I don't want anyone dying because they don't know to turn the engines back on. And we may need to use the *Israel*'s shuttle, if we can talk them out of it."

"We may need to do a little debrief at some point here," Alex said. "Things have been kind of dynamic. But let me go make sure everybody's reactors are ticking over first, all right?"

"Okay," Holden said. "And if you could drop us some food?"

"Soon as I get the galley powered up," Alex said.

"Right. Good. And Naomi...she's...?"

"Everybody's all right," Alex said. "We're all going to be fine."

By the time Havelock and Doctor Merton had finished the inventory, a team of builders were already fitting batteries into fabrication units and measuring out the places where walls would be going up. Real human shelters. A new First Landing. The self-selected construction crew was a mix. Some were squatters who'd come on the dead refugee ship. Some were people Havelock had shipped out with. The divide between them still existed in his mind, but didn't seem to be playing out on the ground. The death of the heavy shuttle and the burning of the terrorist cell seemed like things that had happened in some other epoch. He supposed it was something about the storm, the blindness, the death-slugs, and the constant awareness of mortality just outside the door, clearing its throat. It wasn't a model of community building that he'd recommend trying to scale up, but it had worked here. Temporarily. For now.

A dark-skinned woman with long black hair detached from the group. She looked familiar, but it still took Havelock a few seconds to place her. The time downstairs had taken all the padding out of her cheeks.

"Doctor van Altricht."

"Call me Sudyam," she said. "Everyone else does."

"Sudyam, then," he said, holding out his hand terminal. "I've got some paperwork for you."

"Excellent," she said, taking it. Her gaze flickered over the contract addendum too quickly for her to really be taking it all in. At the bottom, she signed her name with a fingernail and pressed the pads of her index and middle fingers to the screen. The hand terminal chimed, and she handed it back.

"Congratulations," Havelock said. "You are now the official field lead for the RCE research team."

"And a worse job, I can't imagine," she said, smiling. "Now that I'm official, can you tell me when we're getting replacement equipment?"

"There's an unmanned supply pod under heavy burn to Medina," Havelock said. "Assuming the OPA doesn't impound it or call it salvage, it should be here in six, maybe seven months."

"And the chance of the OPA stopping it?"

"I wouldn't make it better than three in ten," Havelock said. "But honestly, don't sniff that number. You don't know where it's been."

The biochemist shook her head in mild disgust. "Well, it'll have to do," she said.

For almost a week after the power came back on, the *Rocinante* and the *Israel* had been in a very delicate political state. The Belters on the *Israel* had been taken in as a gesture when it was pretty certain that the thing was symbolic because they were all going to be dead anyway. Now that they weren't going to die, the question of status—were the Belters refugees, prisoners, or paying passengers?—became a much more contentious issue. Marwick had to decide whether they were going to be on his ship for the full eighteen months back to Medina, or if he was going to try to place them all downstairs. It didn't help matters that with all the shuttles slagged, the only ways down to the surface were on board the *Rocinante* or a really long, unpleasant jump.

In the end, the break was almost even. About half of the crew of the *Barb* elected to stay with the colonists and scientists on the ground. About half of the RCE staff still in orbit, having come this far and being profoundly uninterested in just looking at the promised land from the mountaintop, elected to stay on the planet. Of the science teams that had been on the ground from the start—Vaughn, Chappel, Okoye, Cordoba, Hutton, Li, Sarkis, and a dozen others—only Cordoba elected to come back up the well and go home, and that apparently had more to do with grief over a failed romantic relationship than the fact the entire planet had been doing its best to kill them. It wasn't something Havelock understood, but it didn't need to be.

The ship repairs were under way when night fell, the scaffolding and the hull of the ship flickering brightly and then going dark as the welding torches did their work. The sunset was a massive canvas of gold and orange, green and rose, gray and indigo and blue. It reminded him of beaches on the North American west coast, except there were no vendors clogging the place and no advertising drones muttering about the joys of commerce. It was beautiful, in its way. He wouldn't have been surprised to see a bonfire burning, and a bunch of the colonists sitting around it playing guitars and getting high, except that there was nothing left in the aftermath of the flooding that would burn and if there was anything on the planet that would give you a safe buzz, they'd grown it on the *Israel*.

He hauled himself up into the *Rocinante* and limped back to the bunk Naomi had assigned him. It was the first time he'd been in the *Roci* when it had an up and down, and because the ship didn't land along the thrust vector, he walked along walls for the most part. The shredded muscles in his thigh and calf were regrowing slowly, and his knee might need another round of repairs to swap out the cartilage. Considering everything else that had happened, it was a great set of problems to have.

In his bunk, he checked his personal messages. The message he'd been dreading was there. Williams' family was filing criminal and civil charges against him for wrongful death. His union representative was already counterfiling and RCE was being strangely cooperative. By the time the *Israel* returned to her home port, he hoped everything would be cleared up. He wished there was a way to send a message to Williams' people and apologize. Explain that he'd tried to just disable the suit, and that he was very, very sorry that it had happened the way it did. His union rep had made him promise not to, though. There would be a chance for that when the issue was settled.

There was also a message from Captain Marwick with the subject header of I BELIEVE I OWE YOU A DRINK and a pass-through to one of the major newsfeeds. Havelock followed it.

The screen filled with the banner insets of the feed, but the central image was weird to look at. As he watched, the *Barbapiccola*, tumbling slowly on its tether, bloomed and a puff of perfectly round plastic bubbles came out. It was like watching a flower releasing seeds to the wind. A man's voice, gentle, deep, and reassuring, came under the image, speaking Belter-accented English.

"New footage today from the stunning rescue operations on New Terra. What you're seeing now are images captured by the Royal Charter Energy ship *Edward Israel* of the mass evacuation of the disabled freighter *Barbapiccola*. For those of you new to this story, all three ships were reduced to working under battery power at the time this occurred, and while the *Barbapiccola* was lost to an uncontrolled atmospheric entry, all hands and passengers were transferred to the *Israel* for medical evaluation and aid under the supervision of acting security director Dimitri Havelock."

The image shifted to an image of him from his official report back to RCE. His hair stood away from his head, making him look like he was trying to be a Belter, and his voice sounded weirdly high and whiny.

"The transfer was completed in under three hours. I would specifically like to commend Captain Toulouse Marwick for his prompt and professional aid, without which we could not have managed this without considerable loss of life."

The feed ended, and Havelock laughed. He requested a connection to Marwick, and the red-haired man appeared almost immediately.

"So I guess they aren't firing us," Havelock said.

"They'd be giving us a ticker-tape parade when we got home if anyone still used ticker tape," Marwick said. "This right now is when we should all be asking for raises."

"Hazard pay," Havelock said, propping his head up with his arm.

"Heroes of the hour, we are," Marwick said. "Not that they really have much clue back there what it was really like. One of those things you can explain as clearly and concretely as you want, and they still don't get it."

"That's fine," Havelock said. "They don't need to. I'm going to have a request list from the research and survey team. Do you think there's anything else we can give them?"

"Depends," Marwick said. "The *Rocinante* convoying back to the Ring with us?"

"I think so," Havelock said. "I can confirm that."

"If we've got them for backup, I can strip the place down a little bit more. Not a great deal, but we could break down one of the backup generators and drop it to them. And biomass for the galleys."

"Actually, I think we're okay on that. Doctor Okoye was talking about a way to convert the local flora into something that could be turned into something that they could eat. It had something to do with right-handed molecules, whatever those are."

"Well, good on her, then," Marwick said. "Almost makes you want to stay a while, doesn't it? See how it all plays out?"

"Oh shit no," Havelock said. "No, you should see this place. It's tiny, it's filthy, and everything about it is slapped together with hot glue and prayer. Also, there are slugs that instantly kill you. If these people survive for a year, I'll be surprised."

"Really?"

"You know that in a month or two or eight or whatever, something's got to happen. The hydroponics will fail out, or there'll be another thing like that eye-eating goop only they won't happen to have a treatment for it ready to hand, or one of the attack moons will drop out of the sky. Shit, the fucking death-slugs could grow wings. How do we know they can't do that? We *do* know there are power plants in the ocean big enough to damn near blow the planet off course. Holden says they're all dead now, but he could be wrong. Or turning everything off might mean there's some kind of reactor core sinking down into the planet. We don't know *anything*."

Marwick looked nonplussed, but he nodded. "I suppose that's true."

"No, what I want is Ceres Station or Earth or Mars. You know what they have in New York? All-night diners with greasy food and crap coffee. I want to live on a world with all-night diners. And racetracks. And instant-delivery Thai food made from something I haven't already eaten seven times in the last month."

"You make it sound like paradise indeed," Marwick said. "Still, I can't help feeling uncomfortable at the idea of leaving all these poor people if they're really going to die from staying."

"Maybe they won't," Havelock said. "Wouldn't be the first time recently I was wrong about something. And…well, they've got some things in the plus column too. I think they've got more scientists and engineers per capita than anyplace else in the universe. And we're giving them all the supplies we can manage."

"Still, seems thin."

Havelock sat up a degree, his crash couch shifting and hissing on its gimbal. "They also have each other. For now, anyway. You have to figure when we started this, everyone was ready to slit everyone else's throat, and they're down here now putting up tents together. If nothing new comes along to kill them, there will be native-born New Terran babies as soon as biology permits. And I wouldn't bet that the parents will all have come here on the same ship."

"Well," Marwick said. "It's good to recall that wherever people start, whatever they bring with them, humanity can still pull together in heavy weather."

Havelock shrugged. Koenen's voice was still fresh in his memory, and Williams drifting flatlined and dead. Naomi Nagata in her cell. The Belter engineer whose locker people had been pissing in. The shuttle he'd rigged as a weapon. Jesus, he felt bad enough about Williams. He could barely imagine what it would have been like if he'd deployed the weaponized shuttle.

"Sometimes we do, sometimes we don't. These people could just as easily have gone down with their teeth in each other's throats. That happens too. It's just the folks that go that way aren't around to write the history books."

"Amen," Marwick said, chuckling. "Amen indeed."

Chapter Fifty-Six: Holden

The *Rocinante* had really taken a beating.

The ship had a variety of puncture wounds in the outer hull all along her port side. Holden could see the bright spots where Basia and Naomi had replaced damaged thruster ports, but they hadn't had the time or materials to patch all the holes. It was a testament to Alex's skill as a pilot that he'd been able to bring them down at all without burning up. At least one PDC housing was riddled with damage, and the weapon inside was probably unsafe to use. And there was a long scar across the top of the ship where, according to Naomi, an improvised missile had hit.

Holden cheerfully noted each future repair on his itemized bill for Avasarala.

The *Rocinante* sat on a wide stretch of nothing half a kilometer from where First Landing had once stood. The frames of new construction were starting to appear. People, building on the ruins of what had come before, just like they always did. So many things had been lost, but it was the missing people that hurt the most.

Just like they always did.

Holden noted a spot of minor damage on the drive cone, then came around the stern of the ship to find a pair of Belters throwing up a temporary shelter a dozen yards away. A man in his early thirties was running cable while an older woman hammered spikes into the muddy ground. A second woman stood by with a long pole to flick away any slugs that might get too close.

"You can't put that there," Holden said, walking toward them and making a shooing gesture. "Ask Administrator Chiwewe where to put your tent."

"This spot hasn't been claimed by anyone," the man said. "We have just as much right—"

"Yes, yes. I'm not telling you where you can and can't build. But in a few hours this ship is going to lift off, and it will flatten your little tent."

"Oh," the man said, sheepish. "Right. We'll just wait for you to go."

"Thank you. You folks have a good afternoon." Holden gave them a wave and a smile and headed off toward New First Landing. These people were still the same ones who had been willing to fight RCE to the death to hang on to their claim. They weren't going to put up with being bossed around by outsiders. But the catastrophe had at least taught them to respect high-speed winds.

When he returned to the rectangle of six partially built structures that would eventually become New First Landing's town square, Carol was in a heated discussion with someone in an RCE engineering uniform and Naomi. Amos stood nearby, staring at nothing, a faint smile on his broad face. The medical apparatus on his leg and hand made him look like a cyborg. The bandage on his neck made him look like a pirate. Amos wore serious injury better than anyone else Holden knew. Fayez, by comparison, was still walking with a limp. Or maybe he was just making excuses to keep his arm around Elvi Okoye's shoulder.

Basia, Lucia, and Jacek were clumped up a respectful distance away from the argument, gripping each other like their lives depended on unbroken contact.

"I don't care what it says in the book," Carol was saying. "I want all six of these structures on *one* generator. We only have two. I need the other for the rest of the town."

"These are your highest-use buildings," the engineer replied. "The loads will be at the limit of—"

"They build a little slack in there," Naomi said over the top of him. "And that's what the administrator wants, so give it to her."

The engineer rolled his eyes and shrugged. "Yes, ma'am."

"Everyone getting along?" Holden asked as he approached.

"Land of milk and honey, Cap'n," Amos said. "Peaceful as a sleeping kitten."

"How's she looking?" Naomi asked, stepping away from the group as their argument relaunched behind her.

"Pretty beat up."

"We did our best."

"You guys were amazing," Holden said, taking her hand. "But next time don't let the bad guys capture you."

"Hey," Naomi said with mock outrage, "I rescued myself."

"Been meaning to ask about that. How exactly *did* you persuade your jailer to come over to our side?"

Naomi moved a step closer and grinned down at him. "It was prison. People do all sorts of things they wouldn't normally do in extreme circumstances like that. You sure you want to know?"

"I don't care even a little," Holden said, then pulled her into a hug. She almost collapsed against him.

"God, don't let go," she whispered in his ear. "My knees are killing me. Another hour of walking around in this gravity and I'm going to need ligament replacements."

"Then let's get the hell out of here."

Holden leaned around Naomi enough to catch Amos' eye, then jerked his head toward the ship. The mechanic nodded and smiled and began hobbling around the square loading up the last of their gear.

"Is our prisoner on board?"

"Amos locked him in medical a couple hours ago," Naomi said, then let her entire skeleton relax with a long groan.

"Can you walk back to the ship?" Holden asked her.

"Yep. Say your goodbyes."

Holden let her go, watching her stagger off on unsteady legs for a few moments before he turned back to shake hands with Carol Chiwewe. She and the RCE man had moved their argument to sewage systems and water treatment. After a brief goodbye and good luck to them both, he walked over to Basia and his family.

"Doctor," he said to Lucia, shaking her hand. "Could not have survived this without you. None of us could." Next he shook Jacek's hand. Finally, he shook Basia's. "Basia. Thanks for your help with the ship. And thank you for trying to help Naomi. You're a brave man. Farewell and fair weather." The roiling storm clouds and gentle drizzle of rain made a joke of it, and he grinned at them.

"What?" Basia said. "But I thought you had to take me to—"

Holden was already walking away, but he stopped and said, "Work hard. Next time I come to this planet, I want to be able to get a decent cup of coffee."

"We will," Lucia replied. Holden could hear her tears in her voice, but the rain hid them on her face.

He wouldn't miss the planet, but he would miss the people. Just like always.

On the *Rocinante*, liftoff pressed Holden into his crash couch like the ship was welcoming him back with a hug. As soon as they hit low orbit, he floated out of his chair and down the crew ladder to the galley. Thirty-five seconds later, the coffee pot was gurgling to itself and the rich aroma of brewing filled the air. It made him feel giddy.

Naomi floated in. "The first step is admitting that you have a problem."

"I do," he replied. "But I've just spent a couple months down on a planet that spent the entire time trying to kill me. And I have a shitty job I have to go do, so I'm going to take a moment and make a cup of coffee first."

"Make me one too," she said, then pulled herself over to the wall panel and started paging through status reports.

"Make it three," Amos said, dragging himself into the room. "I got a ton of shit to fix because you guys let someone use my girl for target practice."

"Hey, we did our best—" Naomi started, but was cut off by the comm panel squawking.

"You guys makin' coffee down there?" Alex said from the cockpit. "Have someone bring me up a bulb."

While Amos and Naomi began putting together a list of the repair work they could do during the long transit back to Medina Station, Holden prepared four large bulbs of coffee. He didn't mind. It was very comforting doing something simple and domestic to make other people happy. Black for himself. Two whiteners, two sweeteners for Amos. One whitener for Alex. One sweetener for Naomi. He handed the finished bulbs out.

"Can you take this up to Alex?" he asked, handing a second bulb to Naomi. Something in his voice or his face made her frown with worry.

"Are you okay?" she said, taking the bulb but not leaving. Behind her, Amos took his coffee awkwardly in his mangled hand and headed aft with it toward his machine shop, looking at the task list on his terminal and muttering about how much work he had to do.

"Like I said, shitty job needs doing."

"Can I help?"

"I'd like to do this one alone, if that's okay."

"Of course it is," she said, then kissed him lightly on the cheek. "I'll look you up later."

Holden went up to the airlock and storage deck and found a self-sealing vacuum package, a trowel, and an EVA suit for doing external repairs with a portable blowtorch. He climbed into the suit, then clumped through the ship to the cargo bay.

To what he was pretty sure was Miller's final resting place.

He waited in the cargo bay airlock while the outer doors cycled open, putting the compartment into total vacuum, then went in. If something went wrong, if what was left of the protomolecule on his ship decided to defend itself, he'd be in vacuum with an airlock blocking entry into his ship. He sealed the airlock behind him, and told Alex to lock out local control on the door until he called and asked him to open it. Alex agreed without asking why.

And then Holden began methodically tearing the cargo bay apart.

Five hours later, and one air recharge for the suit, he found it. A small blob of flesh no larger than the tip of Holden's finger, attached to the underside of a power conduit behind a detachable panel in the cargo bay's bulkhead. When they'd first spotted the protomolecule monster that had hitchhiked onto the *Roci* from Ganymede, it had been less than half a meter from where he found the polyp. It made his skin crawl to realize how long they'd been lugging this last remnant of that monster around on his ship.

Using the trowel, he scraped the polyp off the conduit, then put both it and the tool into the vacuum bag and activated the charge to seal it. He blowtorched the conduit for several minutes, heating the metal red to kill any residue left by the scraping. Then he dug through the supplies in the cargo area until he found a reload for the ship's probe launcher, opened the probe up, and stuffed the bag inside the casing.

He linked his suit radio to the *Roci*'s general shipwide channel. "Naomi, you around?"

"Here," she said after a moment. "In ops. What do you need?"

"Can you grab manual control on probe, uh, 117A43?"

"Sure, what do you want me to do with it?"

"I'm going to chuck it out the cargo bay door. Can you give it about five minutes, then send it into Ilus' sun?"

"Okay," she replied, not asking the question he could hear in her voice she wanted to. He killed the radio.

The probe was a small electromagnetic and infrared sensor with a rudimentary drive system. The kind naval vessels used to see what might be hiding on the other side of a planet. It wasn't much bigger than an old Earth fire hydrant. It had heft, though. When Holden pushed it over to the cargo bay door, it was difficult to stop it again.

Outside, Ilus spun by, the angry brown of her cloud layer starting to show some spots of white, and even the occasional flash of blue from the ocean underneath. It'd be a while, but the planet would bounce back. Mimic lizards would return and start competing for space with human children and those annoying little bugs that bit and then fell over dead. Two alien biologies fighting for space. Or three. Or four. Nothing that Ilus hadn't already experienced a few billion years before. New fight, same as the old fight.

Holden put a gloved hand on the probe floating next to him, and pointed the other at the planet.

"That's you, man. That's the second world you've saved. And once again, we have nothing to offer you in return. I kind of wish I'd been nicer to you."

He laughed at himself, because he could almost hear the old detective in his head saying, *You could also have my Viking funeral not be all about how* you *feel.*

"Right. See you on the other side," Holden didn't really believe in another side. Nothing after death but infinite black. Or, he hadn't, anyway. Sure, out-of-control alien technology might be involved, but maybe, just maybe, sometimes there was something else. "Goodbye, my friend."

He gave the probe a hard push, and it drifted slowly away from the ship. Holden watched it dwindle until it was just a tiny point of light reflected from Ilus' star. Then it lit up for a few seconds with a short drive flare and streaked away from the planet. Holden waited until he couldn't see it anymore, then shut the cargo bay doors.

He stripped the vacuum suit off in the airlock after it cycled. Naomi was waiting for him when the inner airlock door opened.

"Hey," he said.

"Is it done?"

"Yeah, I'm all done down here."

"Then come to my room, sailor," she said. "There's something there I want to show you."

Holden floated half a meter above his bed, his body soaked with sweat. Naomi drifted next to him, long and lean, hair wild from their lovemaking. He touched his own scalp, feeling the weird sweaty points his own hair had become.

"I must look a fright," he said.

"Hedgehogs are cute. You're fine." Naomi tapped one long toe against the bulkhead and drifted a few centimeters closer to the atmospheric controls. She aimed the airflow vent at them both, and Holden's skin tingled as the cool air dried him.

"I don't think I'll ever be able to take enough showers to wash Ilus off of me," he added after a moment.

"I was in a brig for a couple of weeks. Trade you."

"Sorry about that."

"Not your fault. Just bad luck. Did you know that the security guy Havelock was Miller's partner on Ceres?"

Holden touched the bed so he could rotate his body and look at her. "You're shitting me."

"Nope. Before we met him, of course."

"Wish I'd known."

"You think you do, but it would have been weird."

"Probably right," Holden said, then sighed and stretched until his joints popped. "I'm never doing that again."

"Which that?"

"Leaving you. When I thought I was going to die down on Ilus and you were going to die in orbit and we wouldn't even be able to hold each other when it happened, it was the worst thing I could possibly think of."

"Yeah," she agreed with a nod. "I understand."

"I promise it won't happen again."

"Okay. Why'd you let Basia go?"

Holden frowned. The truth was, he wasn't really sure why he had. And it was something he'd been trying hard not to think about too much.

"Because...I like him. And I like Lucia. And breaking up their family wouldn't solve anything. I bought his story about blowing the landing pad early to try and save people. Plus, he's not going to be setting any more bombs. And the one thing Murtry told me that made me really think is that we're beyond the borders of civilization right now. Black-and-white legal arguments don't make a lot of sense here. Someday, maybe."

"The frontier doesn't have laws, it has cops?" Naomi said, but she smiled when she said it.

"Ouch," Holden replied and she laughed.

They drifted together in companionable silence for a few minutes. "Speaking of which, I should probably go see our prisoner," Holden finally said.

"To gloat?" Naomi said, poking him in the ribs. "You love that thing at the end where you gloat."

"It's what makes this all worth doing."

"Go," she said, putting her feet against the bulkhead and then pushing him toward the closet with her hands. "Get dressed. And comb your hair."

"I'll be back soon," he agreed, pulling clothes out of the drawers. "I have another thing I want you to show me."

"Making up for lost time."

"Damn straight."

Holden stopped off at the head to brush his teeth and wash his face before visiting Murtry in the med bay. While he worked to get the knots and tangles out of his hair, Amos drifted in and then just waited.

"Am I in the way or something?" Holden asked. "Do you need privacy?" Amos had never been shy with his toilet usage before.

"Naomi says you're going to see Murtry," Amos said, keeping his tone carefully neutral.

"Yep."

"You told me I wasn't allowed to go see him."

"Nope."

"Can I go with you, then?" Amos asked.

Holden almost said no, then thought about it for a minute and shrugged. "Sure. Why not?"

Murtry's leg wound hadn't been particularly serious, but Holden's bullet had shattered his right humerus, so they were keeping him locked up in the medical bay while the expert system tracked the bone regrowth. The RCE security chief had his left arm hand-cuffed to the crash couch. When the arm was better healed, they'd move him to one of the crew cabins where Amos had added exterior locks.

"Captain Holden," Murtry said when they entered. "Mister Burton."

"So," Holden said as though picking up a conversation they'd started earlier. Which, in a way, they had. "Got a message from my pal at the UN a few hours ago. She can't wait to meet you. We'll be dropping you at the UN complex in Lovell city on Luna. I took another prisoner there once, and that person has since ceased to exist as far as the rest of the solar system knows. Hey, maybe they can get you two adjoining cells."

"You keep talking like I've broken the law. I haven't," Murtry said.

"There's a really smart legal team on Earth right now trying to think of some. They have almost two years to work it out. Enjoy the trip back."

"And I," Amos said, "am here to tell you why you won't."

"I can't hear this," Holden said. "He's my prisoner."

"Maybe you should leave, then," Amos said.

Holden stared at Murtry, and the man stared back. "Okay, Amos. Meet me in the galley in a minute."

"Roger that, Cap," Amos said, smiling at the prisoner as he said it.

Worried that he might have just killed the man, Holden waited around the corner outside the med bay door.

"Going to beat a helpless man in his hospital bed just because I got the better of you?" Murtry asked, trying to hide his unease with contempt.

"Oh, goodness no," Amos said, mock hurt in his tone. "That's all good. Smart move taking me from behind. I don't hate the game. I appreciate a good player."

"Then—" Murtry started, but Amos kept speaking.

"But you made me kill Wei. I liked Wei."

The silence between the two men stretched, and Holden almost went back into the room, expecting to find Amos choking the man to death. Then Amos spoke again.

"And when I *do* finally beat you, you won't be helpless. Think that'll matter?"

Holden didn't wait to hear the rest of what was said.

Epilogue: Avasarala

Vyakislav Pratkanis, the Martian congressional Speaker of the House, had an excellent poker face. Over three days of meetings and meals and evenings at the theater and cocktails, he'd never registered more than a milquetoast kind of surprise. Either he was panicking on the inside, or he simply didn't understand the situation. Avasarala's guess was the latter.

I'm sorry I can't come with you this evening," he said, his hand shaking hers with a crisp, dry efficiency.

"You're a good liar," she said with a smile. "Most men who've spent so much time with me seem convinced their cocks will fall off if they can't get away from me."

His eyes widened with a gentle laughter that he'd almost certainly practiced in a mirror. She responded in kind. The government houses were in Aterpol, the highest-status of the buried neighborhoods of Londres Nova. Six more communities were scattered under the soil of Mars' Aurorae Sinus. She had to admit, the Martians had done a respectable job recreating the world here underground. The false dome of Aterpol was high above her and lit with a carefully balanced spectrum that managed to convince her lizard brain that she was in the open air of Earth. The government buildings were designed with a light airiness that almost forgave the fact that the entire city—the entire planetary network—was built like a fucking tomb. The absence of a magnetosphere had made Mars' first priority protection from the radiation. Between that and the low gravity that left her unintentionally skipping down the corridors like a schoolgirl, she hadn't fallen in love with the planet.

"It has been an honor to share perspectives with you," he said.

She bowed her head. "Really, Vyakislav. We're off the clock now. You can stop blowing smoke up my ass."

"As you say," the man said, his expression not changing at all. "As you say."

In the corridor down to the atrium, she tugged at her sari, pulling the cloth back into place. Not that it had particularly been out, but the weight was wrong and the back of her head kept wanting to pull on it until it was right. Soft lights nestled in stone sconces along the walls. The air smelled of sandalwood and vanilla and chimed with gentle, soothing music. It was like the government was a middle-grade day spa.

"Chrisjen!" a man called out as she reached the high-vaulted atrium. She turned back. He was a large man with skin several shades darker than her own and hair only a little whiter than her steel gray. He held out his arms as he walked forward and she embraced him. No one would have guessed, seeing them, that they ran the governments of two of the three great political organizations of humanity. Earth might fear the Belt, and the Belt might resent Earth, but the OPA and the United Nations had diplomatic decorum to maintain, and in truth, she halfway liked the old bastard.

"You weren't going to leave without saying goodbye, were you?" he asked.

"I don't ship until tomorrow," she said. "I was just going out for dinner with friends."

"Well, I'm pleased to see you all the same. Do you have a minute?"

"For the military head to the largest terrorist organization in known space?" she said. "How could I not. What's on your mind?"

Fred Johnson walked forward slowly and she fell into step with him. The atrium was polished stone. A fountain in the center let water flow slowly down the sides of an abstract and genderless human figure. He sat at the fountain's edge. She thought the slow ripples made the liquid seem oily.

"I'm sorry I couldn't support you more in there," Fred said. "But you understand how it is."

"I do. We'll do what we can around the edges, the same as we always do."

"We have a lot of Belters in those ships. If I take too hard a line with them, it'll be worse than taking one that's too soft."

"You don't have to apologize to me," Avasarala said. "We're both constrained by the realities of the situation. And anyway, at least we're not as fucked as Pratkanis."

"I know," Johnson said, shaking his head.

"Is Anderson Dawes still managing the political side out there?"

Johnson shrugged. "For the most part. It's herding kittens. If kittens had a lot of guns and an overdose of neo-Libertarian property theory. What about you? How's Gao doing as secretary-general?"

"She isn't stupid, but she's learning to fake it," Avasarala said. "She'll say all the right words and make all the right hand gestures. I'll see to it." Fred Johnson grunted. The fountain burbled and the crappy soothing music failed to soothe. She felt like they were on the edge of something, but that was an illusion. In truth, they'd gone over the edge a long time back.

"Take care of yourself, Fred," she said.

"We'll be in touch."

Joint Martian and UN security had blocked off the tube station for her. She sat in a tube car with blacked-out windows and three armed security men at the doors. The shaped-plastic seat faced the side, and she could see herself in the reflection. She looked tired, but at least the low g made her seem younger. She was afraid age had been making her jowly. The car hissed along its track. Outside, the tube was in vacuum to reduce drag. She laid her head against the side of the car and let her eyes close for a moment.

Mars had been the first. Not the first station or the first colony, but the first attempt by humanity to cut ties from Earth. The upstart colony that declared its independence. And if Solomon Epstein hadn't been a Martian and hadn't perfected his drive just when he had, Mars would have been the site of the first true interplanetary war. Instead, Earth and Mars had made the kind of rough friendship where each side could feel superior to the other and they'd set about carving up the solar system. So it had been for as long as she could remember.

That was the danger of being old and a politician. Habits outlived the situations that created them. Policies remained in place after the situations that inspired them had changed. The calculus of all human power was changing, and the models she used to make sense of it shifted with them, and she had to keep reminding herself that the past was a different place. She didn't live there anymore.

The tube stopped in Nariman, and Avasarala got out. The station was packed with locals who'd been put off until her journey was complete. On Earth, they would have been a mishmash of Anglo and African, Asiatic and Polynesian. Here, they were Martian, and she was an Earther. As the security detail ushered her out to an electric cart, she wondered what they would be next. New Terrans, she supposed. Unless the squatters' naming schema won out. Then...what? Ilusians? Illusions? It was a stupid fucking name.

And God, but she was tired. It was all so terribly large and so terribly dangerous, and she was so tired.

The private room at the back of the restaurant had been closed off for her. A space made for two, maybe three hundred people. Crystal chandeliers. Silverware that was actually silver. Cut crystal wineglasses and carpeting that had been manufactured to mimic centuries-old Persian carpets. Bobbie Draper sat at the table making everything around her seem small just by being near it.

"Fuck," Avasarala said. "Am I late?"

"They told me to come here early for the security check," Bobbie said, standing up. Avasarala walked to her. It was odd. She could embrace Fred Johnson with ease and grace, and she barely cared about him as anything more than a political rival and a tool. Bobbie Draper she genuinely liked, and she wasn't sure whether she should hug the former gunnery sergeant, shake her hand, or just sit down and pretend they saw each other every day. She opted for the last.

"So veteran's outreach?" she said.

"It pays the bills," Bobbie said.

"Fair enough."

A young man with sharp, beautiful features and carefully manicured hands ghosted forward and poured water and wine for them both.

"And how have you been?" Bobbie asked.

"All right, over all. I got a new hip. Arjun says it makes me cranky."

"He can tell?"

"He's got a lot of practice. I fucking hate the new job, though. Assistant to the undersecretary was perfect for me. All the power, less of the bullshit. Now with the promotion, I have to travel. Meet with people."

"You met with people before," Bobbie said, sipping the water and ignoring the wine. "That's what you do. You meet with people."

"Now I have to go there first. I don't like being on a ship for weeks to have a conversation I could have had over a link from my own fucking desk."

"Yeah," Bobbie said, smiling. "I think I see what Arjun meant."

"Don't be a smartass," Avasarala said, and the beautiful young man brought them salads. Crisp lettuce and radishes, dark, salty olives. None of it had ever seen the sun. She picked up her fork. "And now this."

"I've been following it in the newsfeeds. Right-to-gate access treaties?"

"No, that's bullshit. We feed that to the reporters so they have something to talk about. We've got bigger fish to fry."

Bobbie's fork paused halfway to her mouth. She frowned. Avasarala swigged down half a glass of wine. It was good, she supposed.

"The problem," she said, pointing her fork at Bobbie for emphasis, "is that I trusted James Holden. Not to do anything I told him to. I'm not an idiot. But I thought he would be himself."

"Himself, how?"

Avasarala took a bite of the lettuce. "Do you know how many ships are on track to the Ring? Right now, *right now*, we have sixteen hundred ships, and every one of them has been watching New Terra like they were reading fucking tea leaves. Johnson and I sent Holden to mediate because he was the perfect person to show what a clusterfuck it was out there. How ugly it could be. I was expecting press releases every time someone sneezed. The man starts wars all the fucking time, only this time, when I needed a little conflict? Now he's the fucking peacemaker."

"I don't understand," Bobbie said. "Why did you want conflict?"

"To put the brakes on," Avasarala said. "To save Mars. Only I couldn't."

Bobbie put down her fork. The beautiful young man had vanished. He was good at this job. It was time for them to be truly alone.

"A thousand suns, Bobbie. Three orders of magnitude more than we have ever had before. Can you even imagine that, because most days, I can't. And some—maybe all—have at least one planet with a breathable atmosphere. A place that can sustain life. It's what they were selected for. Whatever those fucking boojums were that made the protomolecule, they were looking for places like Earth. And places like Earth are what they found. Places a lot more like Earth than Mars is. New Terra was the precedent, and the precedent is a fucking feel-good story about how we all come together in a pinch. We have an example of how, if you just get out to one of these planets fast enough and squat hard enough, you get to keep it. Welcome to the greatest migration in the history of human civilization. Fred Johnson thinks he can keep control of it because he's got the choke point at Medina Station, but he's also got the OPA. It's already too late."

"Why try to control it at all? Why not let people settle where they want?"

"Because Mars," Avasarala said.

"I don't understand."

"Mars has the second largest fleet in the system. Something like fifteen thousand nuclear warheads. Sixteen battlecruisers. Who the fuck knows how many other fighting vessels. The ships are newer than Earth's. The designs are better. They're faster. They have heat signature masking and fast water cycling and high-energy proton cannons."

"The proton cannons are a myth."

"They aren't. So here you have the second most powerful navy that there is. What's going to happen to it?"

"It's going to protect Mars."

"Mars is dead, Bobbie. Holden and this Havelock sonofabitch and Elvi Okoye, whoever the fuck she is? They killed it. Half the Martian government understands, and they're shitting themselves so hard, they won't have bones left. Who the fuck's going to stay on Mars? A thousand new worlds where you don't have to live in caves and wear environment suits to walk under the sky. No one's going to be here. Do you know what would happen if half the population of Earth left for the worlds beyond the Ring?"

"What?"

"We'd knock down some walls and make bigger apartments. That's how many people we have on basic. Do you know what happens to Mars if twenty percent of the population leaves?"

"The terraforming project shuts down?"

"The terraforming project shuts down. And upkeep on the basic infrastructure becomes harder. The tax base collapses. The economy craters. The Martian state fails. That is *going* to happen, and the one chance we had to keep it in check is gone. You will have a shell of a government with a planet nobody wants because nobody needs. The raw materials they have to put on the market are now abundant in a thousand new systems where the mining is simple and you don't choke to death on vacuum if the rig fails out. And the one thing—the *one* thing—you have left you can sell? Your one resource?"

"Is fifteen thousand nuclear weapons," Bobbie said.

"And the ships to use them. Who's going to have those ships when Mars is a ghost town, Bobbie? Where are they going to go? Who are they going to kill? We're all moving out our pawns for the first interstellar military conflict. And James Holden, who could have made New Terra a poster for why you might rather stay home and give us a little breathing room, instead found a bright new way to fuck things up."

"By succeeding?"

"By some definition of that word."

"The planet blew up on him," Bobbie said.

"Small favors," Avasarala replied with a snort.

"Well," Bobbie said. "Shit."

"Yes."

They were quiet for a long moment. Bobbie looked at her salad without seeing it. Avasarala finished her wine. She could see the former marine tracking though the lines of implication and consequence. Bobbie's eyes went hard.

"This dinner. We're at a recruitment meeting, aren't we?"

Avasarala folded her hands.

"Bobbie, as long as we're all pushing out our pieces…"

"Yes?"

"I need to put you back on the board, soldier."

Acknowledgments

As always, there were a lot of people without whom this book wouldn't have seen the light of day. We owe particular debts of gratitude to our agent Danny Baror and to our editor Will Hinton, the amazing team at Orbit, the gang from Sakeriver, and Joseph E. Lake Jr. All of them have helped make this a better book. All the errors of fact and logic and infelicities of language are on us.